THE
HARVESTER
CHRONICLES
JP KNIGHTS

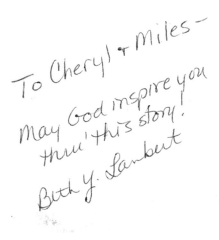

THE HARVESTER CHRONICLES

JP KNIGHTS

BETH Y. LAMBERT

REDEMPTION
PRESS

Published by Redemption Press, PO Box 427, Enumclaw, WA 98022 Toll Free (844) 2REDEEM (273-3336)

Redemption Press is honored to present this title in partnership with the author. The views expressed or implied in this work are those of the author. Redemption Press provides our imprint seal representing design excellence, creative content and high quality production.

Unless otherwise noted, all scriptures are taken from the *New King James Version,* © 1979, 1980, 1982 by Thomas Nelson, Inc., Publishers. Used by permission.

ISBN 13: 978-1-63232-417-7 (Print)
   978-1-63232-419-1 (ePub)
   978-1-63232-420-7 (Mobi)

Library of Congress Catalog Card Number: 2015943911

PRELUDE

The Beings were gathered in a large place. There were many of them, stretching as far as the eye could see. They stood quietly, their wings vibrating ever so slightly, creating a wave like a breeze over a field of grain. Excitement, as had not been felt for over two thousand years, emanated from the place, and the wings of the Beings shimmered such that the excitement was seen as well as felt. There was no sound at first, yet anticipation of the great event served as a prelude.

Suddenly, a horn sounded—a loud, clear note which held within it a decisive tone, yet a hint of sadness. The Beings caught the sound—the monumental mixed with the tragic, and the shimmering of their wings diminished minutely.

A voice rang out, "The time of Joel's prophecy has arrived! We will go out and labor as the Lamb That Was Slain has called us to do. Prepare your sickles, because the hour to reap has come! Harvesters, away!"

The old man awoke trembling. This dream had seemed so real! His dreams of late had all been magnificent with beautiful mansions and gardens. The night before, he had wandered alongside a crystal clear river with his wife. He sighed and held his head. The dreams were wonderful, but waking up to reality was torture. His love, his beautiful wife, had been gone for two years. He always had thought he would be the first to die, but the heart attack had taken her swiftly and unexpectedly, and he was left to mourn and try to live without her. Part of him wanted to stop the dreams because they reminded him of what he no longer had, but he looked forward to sleep each night when he would "see" her and stroll in those beautiful gardens.

But, tonight was different. What had the voice said?

"The prophecy of Joel," he whispered to the first signs of dawn coming through the curtains. He turned on the lamp beside his bed and reached for a well-worn Bible.

Funny, he thought, as he stared at the nightstand. The Bible lay open. *I'm sure I closed my Bible after I read last night.* He wearily dismissed this as he put his glasses on and pulled the Bible onto his lap. Then his eyes opened wide in disbelief as he looked into the open book.

"Joel?" His voice choked as he read the illuminated verse out loud. "*And it will come about after this that I will pour out My Spirit on all mankind; and your sons and daughters will prophesy, your old men will dream dreams, your young men will see visions.*"

The Being moved its hand away from the Holy Book and the light faded.

"It has begun!" it whispered to the frightened old man who heard nothing. "Do not fear, but prepare yourself to labor!"

The old man looked down at the verse again. A look of peace came over his face, followed by a new, determined excitement as he sat up in bed and eagerly reread the passage.

The Being smiled at the old man, and then turned and walked through the wall.

Black clouds raced upon the city and its surroundings. People hurried to get inside, but the deluge caught many by surprise. Torrents of water flooded the streets quickly, and motorists pulled off to wait out the storm.

A group of Beings watched the storm approach near the edge of the city.

"He must know," one whispered.

Another shook its head. "The times are well-guarded. He is just upset about the recent work done and the Lamb's success. He does not know that the Joel prophecy will begin here."

The Beings lingered for a few moments, and then they moved off toward the darkness. Thunder shook the ground and lightning lit up the sky. A few of the Beings headed toward a church parking lot where a few cars had pulled off. An older woman and a young girl sat in one car.

"Gramma, I'm scared," a little voice called from the back seat.

The woman looked at the girl in her rearview mirror and said, "Why don't we pray?"

The little girl nodded, and the woman spoke out loud, "Lord, please protect us during this terrible storm, even as we sit in the car in this parking lot. Keep us in Your Hands and give us Your peace. Amen."

Smiling, the little girl sat back in her booster seat and told her grandma about her day as the storm raged outside.

The Beings approached the car. They seemed to be brighter and bigger than when they had first appeared near the city. One Being stretched out over the car and serenely closed its eyes. Two other Beings seemed to hover near a utility pole.

Suddenly, lightning struck the utility pole! It exploded with a shower of sparks. The two Beings held out their hands and absorbed the shock, catching pieces of wood that would have hit the car, and deflecting the debris to an empty part of the parking lot. Inside the car, the woman and little girl jumped.

"Wow! Gramma, that was close!" the little girl cried.

"Oh, it was honey, wasn't it? But see, the pieces didn't come anywhere near us. Remember, we prayed for God to protect us, and He did!" the woman replied reassuringly. "Thank You, Lord!"

The three Beings gathered outside the car and smiled, then they looked up and quickly were gone.

"Gramma, did the sun just peek out? Is the storm over?" the little girl asked. "I just saw something really bright."

"Hmm . . . no, I don't think the sun came out, but the rain is slowing down and I think we can go meet Mommy now."

The woman started the car and headed out of the parking lot, thankful for their safety. The little girl smiled and looked up in the sky following three bright figures going up into the clouds, thinking some sun had shone through the storm.

CHAPTER 1

The park was quiet that morning. A group of Beings slowly came together by a playground. One Being sat on a swing and pushed into the air.

"There is a bit of thrill in this contraption. What do you call it?"

"A swing, He," spoke another Being with a twinkle in his eyes.

"Are we prepared?" a Being interjected, seemingly annoyed with the playfulness of the other.

We are, Ayin," the twinkle-eyed Being replied. "He will see me today to begin fulfilling the prophecy of Joel."

"Have we been noticed? You know *he* is the prince of the air!"

Twinkle-Eyes turned to the Being that had just spoken and was about to answer when another Being spoke up, "I have placed the necessary shields around us, Qoph. I will alert you if they fail."

Qoph gave a barely perceptible nod, then edged to the outer ring of Beings, held a palm up to block the rising sun, and peered away from the group.

"It is time," Twinkle-Eyes spoke quietly. "You all know your jobs. The Joel prophecy must be fulfilled before we can begin the reaping. We need their help. So it is written . . ."

His voice drifted off as each of the other Beings echoed, "So it is written."

The sun peeked through the curtains of the bedroom. Birds chirped their greetings to one another at feeders in the yard. A car slowed to put the Sunday paper in a box at the end of the driveway. The neighborhood was quiet except for a barking dog in the distance.

A phone rang in the house a few times before being answered. Shortly afterwards, a knock came on the bedroom door, followed by a voice calling, "Joel! It's Kyle on the phone. Joel?"

The door opened, and a woman peered into the room. She walked over to the bed and nudged a mass covered in sheets. "Joel! Wake up! Kyle is on the phone."

Something moved under the sheets and groaned. "OK, Mom." A hand emerged from somewhere and grasped the phone his mom positioned into his hand. His mom retreated, stepping over pillows strewn around on the floor, and closed the door.

"Hey, Kyle . . ." a sleepy voice murmured into the phone.

"Joel! Aren't you up yet? Remember, we're singing at church and they wanted us there to practice before? You gotta get up! We'll be by to pick you up in fifteen minutes, OK?" Kyle urged his friend.

A body rose up from the rumpled sheets and yawned into the phone, "Ahh . . . I'm up, I'm up. OK. I'll be ready, Kyle. See ya." Joel yawned again and stretched.

The fifteen-year-old sat up on the side of the bed, rubbing his brown, short hair and then his eyes. He stretched again and stood up, kicking pillows out of the way, and headed out the bedroom door. His mom, Kathy Stevens, was making coffee in the kitchen and looked up when Joel entered.

"Why's Kyle calling so early?" she asked while grabbing a box of cereal out of a cupboard and setting it on the table in front of Joel.

He sat down, opened the box and grabbed a handful. "I forgot that the youth are singing for church today and we're supposed to practice early. His family is picking me up in fifteen minutes."

Mrs. Stevens nodded, "Oh, that's right. I hadn't remembered either. You know, Pastor Art is away and Pastor George has the sermon today."

Joel groaned, "Not him! He's so boring, and he never smiles. Pastor Art always has cool stories and we sing neat songs. Pastor George makes us sing those old songs."

"They're called hymns, and it wouldn't hurt you to learn a few of them, you know," Kathy Stevens admonished her son, but then sighed. "Pastor George sure hasn't been the same since Mabel died two years ago. That was quite a shock to him even though he knows she's in heaven. Do you remember Mabel?"

Joel smiled, "Of course I do, Mom. She babysat me and always told me neat stories from the Bible. We'd pretend I was David and she was Goliath, and I'd get to throw Nerf balls at her until I hit her in the head and she'd fall to the ground." He paused. "She made the Bible and all this God stuff seem real and exciting."

His mom gave him a concerned look, "What do you mean, God stuff? Is something going on, Joel David?"

Joel hated when his mom used his full name. He always felt like he was in trouble. "I don't know, Mom. Sometimes, I just don't feel like God is real. You know, I can't see Him. I do all the things I'm supposed to do, but I'm not sure sometimes what it all means."

Kathy Stevens reached over and put an arm around her son. "That's why it's called faith—believing when you can't see, remembering the day you decided you wanted to believe what Christ did for you and just accepting that He did it."

"I guess so," Joel shrugged. "I'd better go get ready. Kyle will be here soon."

Joel left the kitchen and his mom mouthed a prayer for the Lord to strengthen his faith and to help him not give in to doubt. Outside the window, a Being smiled. Things were going as planned.

In his bedroom, Joel quickly dressed and thought about what his mom had said. He just wished he was like his best friend, Kyle. Kyle was sure of himself and threw himself totally into everything he did. Neither boy was into most sports, but they both did karate. Kyle was great at that and had even done some tournaments, winning one recently. Joel had been there to cheer him on. Joel did sometimes wonder about Kyle, though. Kyle loved to be in the spotlight and would do anything to get there. Every once in a while,

Joel had noticed Kyle doing a move in karate that wasn't allowed. Kyle would make sure none of the instructors were looking and then hit his opponent. No one had noticed that the moves were illegal. When Joel had questioned Kyle, he had responded that it didn't matter, because he had won!

A car horn blew, shaking Joel out of his thoughts. He ran out of the house and called out, "I'm leaving!" before racing to get in the car with Kyle.

Kathy Stevens stood outside the door with another prayer on her lips, "Lord, he's Yours, I know, but help him to make good choices in this world and show Yourself to him today so that his faith in You somehow is made stronger."

The Being standing beside her seemed to glow with each word. "Your prayer will be answered today in a way you would never have dreamed," he whispered. "God has favored you and blessed you through your son this day. The road will be hard, but we will be with him, helping him. And he will have others who have been chosen, who will also walk the road with him."

Kathy Stevens gave a quizzical look around her. The neighborhood was beginning to come alive with people coming out for the Sunday paper and others walking dogs. But she had heard something different . . . and she felt glorious, like someone had given her a big hug.

The Being smiled as he finished hugging Kathy. He loved this part of the Lord's work. He watched Kathy walk to the end of the driveway and grab the newspaper—she was still smiling. He could sense her wonder with what had just happened and knew she was in for a surprise very soon.

Kyle Thompson and Joel chatted on the way to the church about the new song their youth group leader had written for them to sing that day.

"Pastor Eric sure is awesome!" Kyle exclaimed. "He writes the best songs!"

Joel nodded his head in agreement, "But, you know he'd hate you saying he was awesome, because 'Only . . .'"

Kyle interrupted him, "'Only God is awesome.' Yeah, I know. He tells us that enough times, doesn't he?"

Joel barely had time to respond, "Yeah," when Kyle nudged him.

"Here we are. Thanks, Dad!" Kyle called as he opened the car door.

"See you boys at the service, OK?" Mr. Thompson waved as he spoke and drove off.

Joel and Kyle joined a few other teens making their way into the church on that bright, sunny morning. They all headed noisily to the youth room in a corner of the building, some talking about their school teams and others remarking about national sports events. A few guys called to Joel and Kyle to join them sitting near the back of the room. As they started toward them, a voice called out, "Everybody in their places, please!"

Joel turned to see a smiling young man in his twenties motioning to the group. Joel smiled himself. He liked Pastor Eric a lot. The youth group had really picked up in attendance since Eric had come to their church four months ago. Pastor Eric seemed to be comfortable with everyone, and his wife, Jenny, was fun, too. They were expecting their first baby soon, and Joel could tell that Eric was so excited about being a father. He was excited about God, too, and Joel felt better about things when he was around Eric. They had had some good talks lately, and Eric had answered some questions that had been bothering Joel about his faith. Joel automatically turned to head toward the youth pastor, but Kyle grabbed his arm.

"Brad and Dylan got a new app; let's go check it out!" Kyle urged.

Joel hesitated. Normally, he went right along with Kyle, but today he felt different. "Naw," he shook his head. "Let's get going with the practice. Pastor Eric is waiting for us."

Kyle looked a little surprised, but actually turned with Joel and motioned for the two guys to come along to the front of the room with the rest of the youth who were forming into lines.

Pastor Eric strummed his guitar and tuned a few strings while the kids quieted down. "We've sung this enough times in youth group, so I know you all know it. Let's just work on a little harmony, OK?" He nodded to a couple of girls in front. "Everyone sing like we've practiced before. When we get to the chorus at the end, I've asked Stacey and Rachel to do a little something special, so don't be surprised!" He continued to strum and the youth recognized the introduction. On cue, he nodded for them to begin:

Wonderful are Your works, and my soul knows it very well;
Wonderful are Your works, and my soul knows it very well.

My frame was not hidden from You,
When I was made in secret,
And skillfully wrought
In the depths of the earth.

Wonderful are Your works, and my soul knows it very well;
Wonderful are Your works, and my soul knows it very well.

Your eyes saw my unformed substance
And in Your Book they were all written—
The days that were ordained for me
When as yet, there was not one of them.

Wonderful are Your works, and my soul knows it very well;
Wonderful are Your works, and my soul knows it very well.

For You did form my inward parts,
You did weave me in my mother's womb.
I will give thanks to You
For I am fearfully and wonderfully made!

Wonderful are Your works, and my soul knows it very well;
Wonderful are Your works, and my soul knows it very well;

Wonderful are Your works, and my soul knows it very well;
Wonderful are Your works, and my soul knows it very well.

The youth sang and held the last note as the two girls finished the high descant that had been the harmonious surprise. Pastor Eric brought their voices down and then ended the song by pinching his thumb and forefinger together. He had stopped playing his guitar during the last chorus and the kids were pleased with the sound of their a cappella voices.

There was no noise for a second or two as the beauty of the song registered with the group, and then they broke out into spontaneous clapping and cheers.

Pastor Eric grinned and held up his hands. "I guess we're ready. Let's say a prayer, asking the Father to bless the message of this song and those who will hear it." He bowed his head and led the group in an inspired prayer.

Joel felt weird. Something was definitely different today. He felt good but a different type of good. It was deeper inside him. The song had actually meant something to him this morning. He had sung it many times before—he knew it by heart, but today he understood it! He had a sense of how incredible the human body was, and God knew him before he was even born! Pastor Eric had said this song was from Psalm 139. It told that God knew each day of his life long before his birth! Why hadn't this hit him before? This said that he was special to God! Joel remembered his mom telling him about faith that morning. Now, maybe he was starting to understand.

The prayer had ended, but Joel was still standing with his head bowed, thinking and basking in that warm feeling. He wondered if this was what it was like in heaven, with singing and praising God, when a nudge from Kyle brought him back to reality, and he lifted his head, smiling at his friend.

"Wasn't that incredible, Kyle?" Joel could barely contain his excitement.

"Huh?" Kyle raised his eyebrows in mock disbelief.

Joel was undeterred. "That was great, wasn't it?" he repeated to Kyle. "I mean, it sounded like we could have been angels praising God in heaven, didn't it?"

At this, Kyle laughed and flapped his arms like wings. "Oh, look, we're the Heavenly Heralds!" He poked at Joel's arm, "Come on, flap your wings, too, brother, and we'll fly right up to heaven!" Kyle bent over double laughing. Dylan and Brad burst out laughing as well, and a few other kids who were standing around joined them.

Joel's face fell and he felt foolish. He began to think of a comeback remark to get him out of the stupid situation he had gotten himself into when he felt a hand on his shoulder and heard a calm voice steadily at his side.

"I agree wholeheartedly with Joel. That sounded great and I do believe that's what it will be like in heaven when all we'll want to do is praise God for salvation and His goodness to us," Pastor Eric remarked. "Thanks, Joel, for encouraging us! OK, everyone, it's time to go out to the sanctuary and sit in our spot. Let's go."

Pastor Eric herded them all out of the youth room, and no one had a chance to say anything more about Joel's enthusiasm. Joel had to admit that he did still feel great about the song and its message. He couldn't explain why, either. Normally, he would just blend into the woodwork and go along with Kyle. He certainly would not speak up like that and look crazy to the other kids. It was OK to like Pastor Eric and all, but saying it was like singing in heaven? What was he thinking?

As Joel followed the rest of the group down the hall to the sanctuary, a Being hovered close by with his hands on Joel's back and shoulders.

Joel slowly took a deep breath. What was with him today? It was strange; he had never felt or acted like this before, yet he wasn't that bothered about it. He liked how he felt, though. He stood up straighter as he walked. Kyle looked over at him curiously, and then smiled. Joel smiled back. He would talk with Kyle after the church service and tell him about his new-found confidence, or was it the faith his mom had talked about? Joel didn't know, but he decided it was worth keeping the feeling he had right now. God was incredible, and he, Joel, was special!

The Being continued with Joel until the group had sat down in the front rows of the church, awaiting the start of the service. Many worshippers had already filled the sanctuary. Joel turned around and saw his parents sitting in their usual spot. Kyle's family was behind them. Kathy Stevens looked up and caught Joel's eye then she smiled. Joel smiled back and gave a little nod. Kathy motioned with her right index finger a little sign she had used for years to tell Joel she loved him and God did, too. Joel grinned broadly and signed back to her the same, and then he turned around as the worship leader greeted the congregation.

"Good morning, everyone! Isn't it a blessed day in the Lord? While folks are still coming in, why don't we stand and sing praises to our God," a middle-aged man called out from the platform at the front of the church.

The youth group stood together as musicians played an intro, and then they all joined in singing. Joel listened to the voices around him and had a sense of joy fill him as he contemplated this very thing happening in heaven. He smiled to himself and put more effort into the song.

Kyle nudged him and whispered, "Hey! Why the choral push today? You're acting weird!"

Joel shrugged his shoulders and just smiled at his best friend. He wasn't going to let Kyle spoil this for him.

The service proceeded as usual, and soon it was time for the youth to sing. Pastor Eric led the kids up to the platform and then spoke to the congregation.

"The song we are going to sing has special meaning to me. It was one of the first songs the Lord gave to me when I asked Him to help me learn more Scripture. I'm not very good at memorizing, but I found I could learn verses if they were put to music. So, the Lord gave me this tune, and the next thing I knew, I had learned the verses of Psalm 139:13–16. May this song bless you as it has blessed me and the youth group." Pastor Eric then strummed the intro as he moved to the side of the platform.

The youth group burst into song, "*Wonderful are Your works . . .*"

Joel sang with all his heart, and for the first time the song had meaning to him. The group blended perfectly, and Joel closed his eyes for a moment, taking in the harmony. He opened his eyes and gazed out at the congregation.

Suddenly, Joel's eyes caught something bright in the back of the sanctuary. He turned his head to look more directly at the brightness. It seemed to be a person, yet bigger. A face looked right at him and smiled. Joel's heart skipped a beat! He stopped singing, and his eyes widened in fear.

What, or who is that thing? he thought. He looked over to Pastor Eric, who still strummed his guitar, oblivious to the congregation.

Joel turned slightly to look at Kyle beside him. Kyle was singing with his head facing toward the bright thing, but he had no surprise or concern on his face.

By now, Joel's heart was pounding and his throat felt like he was being strangled. He looked again to the back of the sanctuary. It was gone! Joel moved his head around to see if it had moved to another part of the church, but he saw nothing. There was no sign of the bright person anywhere!

CHAPTER 2

Joel continued staring at the spot in the back of the sanctuary, oblivious to the song the youth group was still singing. An elbow in his side made him turn his head.

Kyle looked at his friend with a wrinkled forehead and mouthed, "What's wrong?"

Joel shook his head, still stunned.

Kyle shrugged and continued singing, looking out to his parents and smiling as they nodded their heads in time to the music.

The beautiful sounds of the descant echoed for a moment as the group finished the song. The teens stood, silent, waiting for the congregation's response, hoping the song had been enjoyed.

The sanctuary burst into clapping and calls of "Praise the Lord." The youth, as a group, seemed to heave a sigh of relief. Pastor Eric smiled from ear to ear and bowed slightly at the applause, gesturing to the young people from the side. The kids nudged each other and grinned as they stepped from the platform and moved to join their families.

Joel hurried to whisper to Kyle, "Did you see it, too?" He looked anxiously at his friend.

"See what?" Kyle whispered back.

"That bright thing at the back of the church while we were singing," Joel quickly answered.

Kyle glanced at him with his eyebrows wrinkled in curiosity and shook his head no. He moved into the pew with his parents and looked curiously at Joel.

Joel was shaking as he stepped over his parents to sit down. He took one more look at the back of the sanctuary, but nothing was there.

Kathy Stevens leaned toward Joel and whispered, "Joel that was wonderful! I could really feel the Lord was here while you guys sang!" She stretched her arm around him and hugged his shoulders briefly. Then she pulled back and came forward to look at his face. "You're trembling! Are you OK? Are you sick? You look pale!"

Joel felt embarrassed. "Naw, I'm OK. Just got nervous I guess." He smiled weakly. "Really, Mom, I'm fine."

She stared at him for a moment with her eyebrows furrowed, then sat back, nodding.

An elder now came to the podium. "We are blessed to have Pastor George minister to us today while Pastor Art is away. He tells me that he has a special message to share with us. Let us pray for the Lord to speak through His messenger."

Joel bowed his head as the prayer started, and then he peeked behind him to see if the bright thing had returned. Kyle caught his eye and smiled, giving him a thumbs-up sign. Joel turned around quickly. The prayer ended and Joel looked up to see an old man walk to the pulpit. He had gray hair and was balding a little bit. A gray suit hung loosely from his shoulders, indicating that previously he had weighed a bit more. A cane he normally held in his hand was left back by a platform chair. Instead, he hugged an old Bible close to his chest as he approached the pulpit. The church grew quiet in anticipation of his first words.

Pastor George looked out at the congregation and seemed to be lost deep in thought. He said nothing but stared mindlessly ahead. The few who sat in the front row, however, could see his lips moving all so minutely. An elder sitting behind him on the platform finally cleared his throat, trying to awaken the old man from his thoughts.

"Ah . . . yes . . ." Pastor George mumbled, laying the Bible down on the pulpit and bracing his hands along the edge. "Forgive an old man for contemplating his words today. I believe I have a most unusual message to deliver, and some of you may think I have lost my mind, but I assure you that the Spirit leads in places man may not necessarily understand at times." He paused, gazing at the faces in the sanctuary. "Will you please turn in your Bible to Joel 2:28–32? Let us stand for the reading of His Word."

The people looked at each other in amazement. This was something new and unexpected. Many people shuffled papers and purses off onto the pew, and soon everyone was standing.

"And it shall come to pass afterward that I will pour out My Spirit on all flesh; your sons and your daughters shall prophesy, your old men shall dream dreams, your young men shall see visions. And also on My menservants and on My maidservants I will pour out My Spirit in those days. And I will show wonders in the heavens and in the earth: blood and fire and pillars of smoke. The sun shall be turned into darkness, and the moon into blood, before the coming of the great and awesome day of the Lord. And it shall come to pass that whoever calls on the name of the Lord shall be saved. For in Mount Zion and in Jerusalem there shall be deliverance, as the Lord has said, among the remnant whom the Lord calls."

Pastor George paused, and then said, "So reads the Scripture according to the prophet Joel. Amen."

A few people responded with a weak, "Amen."

"You may be seated," Pastor George instructed. He stared intently out into the congregation. "I know we have not in the past done much with the Minor Prophets, but I believe there is relevance for today in this passage, and I am excited to share what the Lord has shown to me!" His voice rose in a crescendo and he smiled automatically. "We are living in wonderful times, and the Lord is preparing to use every one of us in anticipation of His second coming!"

A murmur seemed to build throughout the room. Joel had forgotten that Pastor George could really get people moving. Before Mabel had died, the couple had been eager to help with the youth, and they had come to like Mabel and George a lot. He had changed so much after Mabel's death, and soon the youth group forgot about him. But now, Pastor George had people's attention again.

Joel looked down at his mom's Bible and reread the passage, *"your young men shall see visions."* Maybe that was what happened before—some kind of vision? He looked back up to focus on what Pastor George was saying.

"I think we'd all agree that many things are happening in the world today that would point to the soon-coming of our Lord. Many think that the passage I just read already was fulfilled long ago. That may be true, but I believe that it is a message for us *now*. The Spirit has shown me that this prophecy has relevance for our present lives. God is preparing to accomplish a remarkable revival through us! We need to get ready, study the Scriptures, look for ways to speak to others about the Lord, and pray for His help. I have a pneumonic I'd like to use to help us—actually the word *Joel*."

"First, J stands for Join. We need to join together in fellowship. We need to join together in prayer. We need to join together in Bible study. We need to join together in worship. As Satan prepares to battle for the world, we have to prepare to fight him. Many of you have heard the old adage, 'United we stand, divided we fall.' Satan would prefer that we be divided. Catholics against Protestants, Jews against Christians . . . even Lutherans against Baptists. The list could go on and on. As we focus on our similarities in Christ, the walls will go down and we will better arm ourselves with the armor of God. The Lord wants us to be involved in what He is doing in the last days. By *us*, I do mean Christians in general, but I also mean *us* of our congregation right here. There may be those among us who will receive gifts such as those Joel prophesied about—if we are blessed in this way, those who the Lord chooses need the support of fellow Christians right here!" Pastor George tapped the pulpit with his index finger for emphasis.

"O stands for Offering. We need to bring ourselves as an offering to the Lord for Him to use us. This could be sacrificially for some," he added, looking at the congregation with raised eyebrows. "Many of us have become complacent in our service. I would admonish you with the words of David in 2 Samuel 24:24, *'I will not offer . . . to the Lord my God with that which costs me nothing.'* It may be money, or it could be time. It could be that parents must offer up a child for His service or even that children let their parents go do something different for the Lord."

Joel glanced over at his mom, envisioning her somewhere in Africa, or maybe an inner city. . . . He smiled, thinking that she would be at home wherever God wanted her to be, that's just the way she was. But would he be able to let go of her and let her do that? Now, that was turning things around a bit. He wasn't sure he could do that!

"E stands for Evangelize. Now I know this is a hard one for most of us. You all tell me that you are not preachers, and you couldn't do what I have done for most of my life. That may be so," then he chuckled, "at least many can't do it with *my* flare!" The congregation laughed along with him, and some focused even more to hear the words of the fervent pastor they knew from a few years back. He smiled at them and said, "Evangelizing is *not* ramming the Word and gospel down someone's throat! The apostles spoke with conviction, and Jesus Himself was gentle. Remember how He was with the woman being stoned? His quiet, gentle response brought her to salvation. The Bible says that the Spirit will give us the words to speak if we just trust our Lord to help us. There are many times that words are not appropriate. Our actions speak very loud. Be yourselves, but be open to the Spirit giving you opportunities to evangelize.

"And, finally, L stands for Light. Jesus is the Light of the world according to John 8:12. There are times of darkness ahead, but He will never leave us without guidance."

Joel had borrowed his mom's Bible and turned to the passage in John. This light thing interested him for some odd reason. He read it again, *I am the light of the world. He who follows Me shall not walk in darkness, but have the light of life.*

Cool, thought Joel.

He glanced up at the platform and gasped. The bright thing was there again, and it was standing right behind Pastor George!

Joel's mom leaned close and whispered, "What's wrong, Joel?"

Joel stared and his heart pounded, "Don't you see it, Mom? Up there behind Pastor George?"

She peeked up between the heads in front of her and shook her head, "No, I don't see anything. What do you see?"

Joel rubbed his eyes in disbelief and then looked up again. There it was, still there, and now it looked like it had its hands on Pastor George's back! He stared at the figure. The brightness seemed to mesmerize him. The figure then turned and looked right at Joel! Joel started to tremble but then he heard something, not out loud, but in his mind.

"Do not fear and don't be afraid, for the Lord has blessed you, Joel, with a wonderful task. Trust and feel the peace of God. I will meet you later today. Look for me!"

The voice stopped. The Being smiled and then disappeared.

Joel's heart had pounded for ten straight minutes after seeing the bright figure and hearing the voice in his head. Only after leaving the service to get a drink could he get himself calmed down. He procrastinated about going back into the sanctuary and was just ready to open the door to go in when Kyle pushed the door open and stepped into the hall.

"Hey! What happened to you, Joel?" whispered Kyle. His eyes opened wide, and he exclaimed, "Oi! You look like you've seen a ghost! What's going on? Are you sick? Do you want me to get your mom?"

Joel shook his head and replied, "Naw. I'm OK, I think." He paused for a moment. Should he tell Kyle about what he had seen? He didn't want to seem crazy, but Kyle was his best friend. Something in him hesitated and he made a split-second decision not to say anything.

"Let's go back in, Kyle. I'm alright," Joel added.

Kyle gave him a questioning look and then opened the door and they both headed back to their seats.

The Being hung back in the hallway after touching Joel's back during his conversation with Kyle.

Hmm . . . that was close! He mustn't say anything to anyone until we meet. Lord, help him! he prayed silently.

Joel was lost in thought as his family drove home after church. His mom babbled away about how good Pastor George's sermon was, and his dad interjected his opinions from time to time. His dad, Doug, was a quiet man, an accountant who was more at home with numbers than with most people. Joel took after his dad in most respects, but he always seemed to feel closer to his mom. She was a high school principal in a different school district close by. She loved working with kids and was well-liked by the students and teachers. When she attended a karate competition, she was always surrounded by her students and had a hard time being able to concentrate on Joel's event because of the many who also wanted her attention. Joel used to resent the fact that his mom "belonged" to a lot of other kids, but lately he had come to terms with how important her job was and how great she was at it. She never let her job come between her and her family, and she had become quite good at shuffling responsibilities so that Joel could count on her to be there for him.

The drive home was short, and Joel was glad that nothing had been said about his strange behavior during church. As they walked into the house, however, Joel's mom touched his arm.

"Joel, can we talk?" Kathy Stevens sounded concerned.

"Ah, sure, Mom," Joel answered cautiously. "What's up?"

Kathy hesitated and then asked, "What did you see during Pastor George's sermon?"

Joel bristled a bit. He didn't want his mom to know that he was seeing things, yet he didn't want to lie. "Um . . . I don't know, just something bright. Maybe something like before a migraine?" He offered, hoping his mom would be satisfied.

"Oh, yeah," she replied thoughtfully. She knew the visual aura from her own migraines could be very distracting. They didn't happen often, but they were nasty when they did. Joel had had a handful of migraines, although she didn't remember any auras with them. "Did getting a drink help?" she asked.

"Yeah. I mean, I think," Joel said. "Maybe lunch will help?" He knew his mom would jump at the chance to feed him.

"Got it. I'll have food on the table in about twenty minutes. Do you think you can make it until then?" She tilted her head and smiled. "By the way, that song you and the youth group sang was incredible. I wanted to sing along. It made me feel like," she hesitated, "well, like what singing in heaven could be like." She sighed and turned to go into the kitchen.

Joel's eyes were wide with surprise. That was how he had felt! That was so weird! He and his mom agreed about a lot of things, but this was too much of a coincidence. It was turning into a strange day!

CHAPTER 3

Lunch tasted good to Joel. His senses were particularly alert, and the simple fare could have been a gourmet banquet! Joel finished with a satisfied groan and patted his stomach.

"That was great, Mom!" he exclaimed.

Kathy raised her eyebrows in mock surprise. "I spent hours and hours slaving over the hot stove to prepare this feast. Your appreciation humbles me!" She bowed as she spoke in a fake accent. She stood and laughed, "Though, I have to agree, these leftovers certainly seemed to taste quite good to me, too! The flavor improved overnight, somehow." She shrugged her shoulders and picked up some plates to clean off the table.

Joel stood and grabbed some items and followed her to the kitchen. A Being folded his arms in a corner of the room as Doug Stevens licked his lips after taking one last bite from his plate.

"Hmm . . . It does taste better than last night. She must have used a new recipe or herb that needed more time to sink into the food," he murmured in a calculating tone so typical for his accounting nature.

The Being chuckled to himself and then moved through the wall into the kitchen, where Kathy and Joel were putting dishes into the dishwasher.

"What are you up to this afternoon, Joel? You and Kyle getting together?" Mrs. Stevens asked.

Joel shook his head and said, "No. He has some family birthday party to go to. I haven't decided what to do. I'm done with my homework," he added, knowing his mom would ask that next.

Kathy smiled, acknowledging Joel's dig on her habit of making sure homework was done. Oh, well . . . that was largely what she did with high school students, and that part of her job overflowed into her home life.

"You know, I was thinking. . . . It's such a nice day. Would you want to go with me over to the park? We haven't been there for a long time. You and I used to go for a walk every Sunday when you were younger," Kathy reminded him.

Joel pondered the request. Normally he hung out with Kyle or a few others of the guys, but for some reason, his mom's suggestion seemed like fun. He remembered those walks from years ago with fondness.

"OK," he remarked nonchalantly.

His mom looked amazed and then smiled. "Alright then! I'll get my walking shoes on, and we can go."

"Go where?" Doug's voice interjected behind them.

"Oh," Kathy paused and turned to face Doug. "Joel and I are going over to the park. We haven't gone for a long time and couldn't waste a beautiful day like this inside. Do you want to go?"

The Being moved over to Doug with a concerned look. It closed its eyes and concentrated, as if in prayer.

"Hmm. . . . That sounds really nice, but I think I'd like to just sit on the back patio and read the paper, if that's OK with you two," Doug added apologetically.

Joel smiled, "That's OK, Dad. We know you're not into nature that much." Then he teased, "We also know that you'll most likely end up in the hammock, taking a nap!"

Doug began to protest but noticed the look of amusement on Joel and Kathy's faces, then shrugged his shoulders and chuckled, "Am I that transparent?" He left the room, grabbed the paper, and headed out to the hammock, calling, "I may as well start here, since I usually end up here!"

A few minutes later, Joel and his mom were walking down the neighborhood sidewalk. They took more of a casual approach to the walk, noticing changes in homes and yards which had gone unnoticed in the busyness of their lives the past year or two. Usually, they drove past in a hurry, getting to youth group or karate with Kathy's meetings in-between. Now, they took in a beautiful garden, recently transformed from an unsightly corner by their green-thumbed neighbor, Mrs. Wright.

"Wow! Look at that garden, Mom," Joel exclaimed. "There must be every color of the rainbow in all the different flowers!"

Kathy nodded, "Eileen sure has made that ugly corner into a pretty picture."

Both stopped, gazing at the beauty. Kathy stooped down and gently cradled a bloom before leaning over and whiffing the air.

"Ooh . . . I just love these miniature roses! They smell so . . . good!" She closed her eyes and breathed deeply.

"Hello, Kathy and Joseph," a squeaky, but gentle voice called.

Kathy looked up to see Eileen Wright coming across her lawn with a spring in her step and a sparkle in her eyes.

Joel rolled his eyes and whispered, "Will she ever get my name right?"

His mom turned to him and smiled. She whispered back, "She has always called you that, no matter what we told her!"

Kathy stood and greeted her neighbor, "Eileen, what a beautiful garden you have put in here! This is amazing!"

Eileen's petite face lit up with a smile. "Thank you, Kathy! I just put the finishing touches on yesterday, adding in some salvia for an up-and-down splash of color and these pansies for something close to the ground."

Joel noticed some figurines and craned his neck to see what they were. "What are those statues, Mrs. Wright?" he asked.

She came alongside him and took his arm, pulling him closer to the figures. "Don't you know what they are, Joseph?"

Joel cringed at the name again but tried to decide what the little statues could be. "Are those fairies?" he guessed, knowing that a number of his girl classmates talked about such things being in their own gardens as decorations.

29

"Oh, no, Joseph! No fairies here," Mrs. Wright spoke sadly, obviously disappointed that he had guessed wrongly.

Kathy tilted her head and gazed at the small figures then motioned for Joel. "Come here, Joel, and look at this one. I think you'll know what they are."

Joel moved to join his mom and followed her pointing index finger to a foot-high figurine. It was made of a painted ceramic and glistened even in the mid-afternoon sun. The serene face looked upward, and delicate wings projected from its back. It was clothed in a flowing robe which draped over the arms, ending in gentle folds near hands clasped in prayer. Joel nodded, wondering why he would have thought this was a fairy when it was so apparently an angel. He glanced back at the placid face and was struck by a feeling that the face of the angel looked familiar! He stared at the features for a moment before Mrs. Wright cleared her throat in anticipation of his second guess.

Joel rolled back on his heels and turned sideways to look up at Mrs. Wright. "It's an angel," he declared firmly and watched her face crinkle up in a smile.

"Yes, dear," she squeaked happily and then added to Kathy, "I've been collecting various angels suitable for garden life for about ten years. There are all kinds if you know where to look for them—metal, ceramic, wood, plastic. I put my favorite ones out here for everyone to enjoy. That ceramic one was made by a dear friend from your church, I believe. Mabel Boyd?"

Kathy nodded and said, "Yes, we knew her well. She even watched Joel for us quite a bit." Kathy thought it coincidental that she and Joel had just spoken of Mabel that morning.

Joel looked curiously at his mom, also struck by the coincidence.

Eileen continued discussing the ceramic angel. "I do like this one by Mabel best. The wings seem to be real, and they glisten no matter what time of day it is. It must have been a special type of glaze that she used."

The three of them looked back at the angel. The wings did shine and looked like they were fluttering ever so slightly in the sunlight.

"So, where are you two headed on this lovely day?" Eileen questioned.

"We're going for a stroll in the park, like we used to," Kathy informed her.

"Well, isn't that nice!" Eileen exclaimed as Joel stood and Kathy patted his back. "Have a good time, and stop by anytime to see my garden!"

Kathy and Joel waved and continued on their way toward the park. They enjoyed watching a squirrel run ahead of them and scamper up a tree. A few birds pecked at dandelions in some lawns. Soon they reached the bordered edge of the park, noticing nicely manicured bushes, freshly mulched gardens with begonias and marigolds, and playground areas surrounded by natural wood benches.

"Wow!" Joel murmured, gazing around at the transformations.

Kathy, likewise, was astonished. "It sure looks like our tax dollars have done some good. I knew that some in the community had pushed for improvements at this park, but I had no idea that all this had been done." She glanced at Joel and remarked, "All I remember are some walking paths with a set of old swings over there." She pointed to an area that now contained a plethora of playground equipment, including some new swings bordered in the back by a stretch of woods.

"Makes me want to be a little kid again," Joel commented ruefully. "And look at the walking path—it's paved with markings to allow bikes *and* walkers or runners."

"You and Kyle could come over here and bike while I walk in the evenings," Kathy suggested hopefully.

"Yeah, I guess so," Joel paused and added somewhat gloomily, "but Kyle isn't into biking anymore. He says that's for little kids."

Kathy stared at her son a moment before carefully choosing her words. "You know, Joel, you don't always have to do what Kyle tells you to do. You have a mind of your own, and I happen to think you've got a good head on your shoulders. Follow what the Lord wants you to do, OK?" Then she added, "And I'm not saying that just because I'm your mom. I'm saying that because I see great qualities in you that have sort of been hidden 'cause you follow Kyle around."

Joel hung his head for a moment. He knew his mom was right, and there were times he really didn't want to go along with Kyle, but Kyle was a leader and a very persuasive one at that. It was just easier to follow him than to make waves.

A hand touched him on his shoulder. Joel looked up to see his mom smiling at him, and he couldn't help but to smile back. She raised her eyebrows in a silent question of whether he understood her. He nodded his head and said, "I've been thinking about that, Mom. I'm just not a very *natural* leader," he admitted.

"Hmm . . ." she mused, "It is more what you *choose* to do with what God has given you than just having the gift. Jonah had the gift of prophecy, yet he kept running away from it, and look at the mess he got himself into! Plus, he wasn't happy at all. Paul and Silas were in prison for choosing to use God's gifts, and they were joyful and singing! It goes back to your choices. Remember that, Joel!"

Kathy smiled and tussled Joel's hair with her hand. "It looks like they've measured the path and marked a mile. Are you up for it?"

"Absolutely!" Joel said with enthusiasm. His mom had a way of knowing what he needed to hear, and already he felt some resolve to be what God wanted him to be, even if Kyle made fun of him. It wasn't that Kyle was a bad friend; Joel knew his mom liked Kyle and was glad that Joel had a best friend. It's just that Kyle could influence him to do things that sometimes he didn't want to do.

They started off at an easy pace but soon were walking quickly, admiring the new gardens and some ponds. The renovations to the walking path included some bridges over a bubbling stream and pleasant curves around a rock garden leading to a diversion of the stream which cascaded over some artistically placed waterfalls. Neither spoke much, hesitant to spoil the beauty around them, but had they spoken, mother and son would have discovered the same thoughts flowing through their minds. Bible verses telling of God's grandeur were recalled along with Scripture admonishing man to praise the creator or even the rocks would cry out. It was a walk filled with wonder, such as they had not experienced for a time. As they returned to the playground and slowed, a twinge of pain made Joel stop in his tracks.

"What's wrong?" his mom asked.

"I think I have a blister. I forgot that these aren't good shoes for walking in," Joel moaned.

"Hmm . . ." Kathy did her characteristic sound as she thought. "I'd like to go around again, but I noticed a path near the waterfall which would get me back to the house more quickly. Why don't you stay here, and I'll walk home and get the car to pick you up? No sense in you hobbling around, making that worse."

"OK," Joel agreed. "I'll sit over here on the swings and watch for you to pull in to that parking lot." He nodded toward a lot at the entrance to the park.

Kathy Stevens nodded back and gave Joel a quick kiss on his cheek, and then she headed off along the path.

Joel limped over to the playground area and plopped down into a swing. He found himself pushing the swing into the air and soon was soaring high, a big smile on his face.

"Ah . . ." he sighed, closing his eyes and letting the air rush over him as he leaned back into the cadence of pumping the swing. Briefly, the thought came to him that Kyle would certainly tease him if he saw him swinging, but he pushed it out of his mind and relaxed in the freedom the swinging sensation gave him. The chorus the youth had sung that day came to him, and he began humming the tune. Soon, however, he couldn't help but sing out loud, praising God with all his might!

Joel became aware of another sound. A strange feeling came over him as he realized that someone else was nearby singing with him. Quickly, he stopped singing. He opened his eyes and was relieved to see no one on the walking path, yet the singing continued. Joel stopped pumping the swing and slowed, detecting the musical notes coming from somewhere behind him. He placed his feet and dragged them, bringing the swing to a stop, and stood up. Turning around, he expected to see someone from the youth group ready to pummel him with pebbles or mulch, but what he saw stopped him dead in his tracks and made him gasp.

CHAPTER 4

Standing at the edge of the woods was the bright person he had seen twice at church that day! The facial features were neither male nor female, but it bore a strange resemblance to the ceramic angel in Eileen Wright's corner garden. It was tall, perhaps six and a half to seven feet, with a stature and physique hidden by flowing robes such that arms, hands, legs and feet were not immediately seen. Its skin and robes seemed to glow with an ethereal light.

Joel froze with fear. His mouth went dry as his heart pounded, and his whole body trembled. He tried to scream, but, as in a dream, no voice emanated from him. Time stood still or moved ever so slowly, as Joel attempted to turn and run. But, in that split second that lasted an eternity, Joel saw something that kept him from bolting: the bright person smiled. It wasn't a usual smile that strangers give each other; it was closer to the smile his mom gave him when she was reassuring him about something. In an instant, Joel felt emotions of love, peace, and trust fill him.

They stared at each other for a moment, then it spoke. The voice was masculine and had a rich, musical quality to it.

"Hello, Joel," he said, the smile crinkling his eyes and making them seem to twinkle.

Joel found his voice again but was barely able to whisper, "Who are you? How do you know my name?"

"I am a servant of the Most High God, and His Son, the Lamb That Was Slain. I know you because you are known of God," Twinkle-Eyes remarked.

Joel furrowed his eyebrows in puzzlement, but a moment later, fear filled him. "Are . . . are . . ." he stuttered, "are you an angel?"

Once again, Twinkle-Eyes smiled that strange, wonderful smile that made Joel stop trembling. "That is a term that has been used for us, yes," he declared.

Joel's thoughts seemed to clear, and he remembered the bright person he had thought he had seen earlier in church.

"Was it you I saw in church this morning?" he questioned.

"Yes," Twinkle-Eyes responded.

Well, that explains some things, Joel thought. "Why couldn't anyone else see you?" Joel asked.

Twinkle-Eyes hesitated and then said, "It is only for those who are fulfilling the prophecy of Joel."

"What?" Joel shook his head as he tried to understand.

"Come, let us sit down," Twinkle-Eyes motioned to a bench near the playground.

Now, Joel could see feet move out from under the robe and walk to the bench. He also saw hands and arms appear, hanging relaxed at the angel's side. But one thing was not there that he had expected—wings!

Joel followed the angel to the bench and sat down at one end. They sat in silence for a while as Joel took in the whole bizarre situation. He must be dreaming, was his conclusion.

"You may touch me. I am real," Twinkle-Eyes said, in seeming response to Joel's thoughts, "although, there are protections in place to keep others from seeing me. You may notice that I have no shadow."

Indeed, Joel looked around and saw there was no shadow, even though the sun was now shining down on the angel. One would have thought the glow itself would have caused a shadow, but none was there!

Joel hesitated then reached over and carefully touched the angel. His hand jerked back as he came in contact with an energy force that sent static-like tingles through his skin!

"Oh . . .!" he breathed in surprise. "What's that?"

"That," Twinkle-Eyes paused, "is some of our Lord's power that He has given us to do His will. Every part of our being is dedicated to Him, and we reflect His power this way."

"Is that what makes you glow?" Joel asked.

Twinkle-Eyes nodded and said, "Yes, but there is more to it than that. In time, you will understand what else is sorely needed, and you will be a part of giving it to us."

For the first time, Joel noticed that the angel rarely used *I* and usually spoke in plurals. "What do you mean, 'us'?" he questioned.

"Ah . . . yes." Twinkle-Eyes bowed his head and then looked directly at Joel. "I am not the only one sent by the Most High God for this work. There are many of us, some of whom you will meet at the right time. For now, I am to be the one to introduce you to the Joel prophecy and the work ahead of us. We don't want to be too bold and attract the attention of the evil one, so I am to work quietly with you, training you in the role you are to play in this most noble and significant quest. There will be others who will be a part of this, and it is important for you to learn how to make use of the gifts they have been given, as well as your own gift."

"My own gift? What are you talking about?" Joel huffed a sigh. "I'm not good at anything."

"Oh, you have gifts, Joel; you just haven't chosen to use them yet!" Twinkle-Eyes exclaimed, sounding so similar to what Kathy Stevens had said a short time previously. "Now, I need to instruct you in a few things before your mother returns."

Joel sat back in awe. This angel person did seem to know a bit of what was happening, but this all was *so* weird!

"OK," Joel managed to say.

"Good," Twinkle-Eyes responded. "First of all, you need to realize that you have been chosen for this long before you were born. You and your family have been specially protected, hoping that the right choices would be made so that you could fulfill the prophecy. Second," the angel stopped as Joel interrupted him.

"Whoa! Chosen? What choices? What are you talking about?" Joel sputtered out in a torrent.

Twinkle-Eyes seemed undisturbed by the questions. "Well, of course you were chosen. You sang about it this morning—the song from Psalm 139. The lives that came together through the ages to result in your birth were prayed for. They all chose to serve the Lord Most High, and you have also chosen Him. So, now the time of the fulfillment of the prophecy of Joel has come. The host of heaven has been waiting for this moment, and all worship the Lord Most High in anticipation of this grand event leading to the final battle with the evil one."

Joel's hair stood on end at the sound of this news. He was to be involved somehow in the last battle with Satan?

"Uh . . . look, I think you have the wrong kid!" Joel stuttered. "I'm only fifteen, and I don't want to be like David slaying Goliath!"

Twinkle-Eyes reached out and touched Joel. The initial static feeling gave way to a warmth that spread quickly through his body. His heart stopped pounding, and he gazed at the Being beside him.

Comfort . . . peace . . . trust. The angel's lips were not moving, yet Joel clearly heard him say those words.

"I am sorry, Joel. My excitement has overwhelmed you. Do not dwell on the future. For right now, know that the Lamb That Was Slain has given you His peace," Twinkle-Eyes spoke aloud.

"You must not tell anyone of our meeting. It is crucial that I train you for a time in secret. Your parents and Kyle must not know anything about me or what I have told you. Your mother will receive a special comfort regarding these happenings, but that is our affair, not yours. You will know what you need to do. You will not see me all the time just yet. It would be too distracting. But, call me anytime you need me."

Twinkle-Eyes withdrew his hand from Joel's arm, and suddenly, the angel was gone!

Joel sat there a while, his body still tingling from the angel's touch, his brain reeling from what the angel had said. He glanced down at the ground, where something shiny caught his eye. A ray of the sun had reflected off of a stone lying in the grass. He absent-mindedly picked it up, rolling it around in his fingers. It was a brilliant blue, and was very smooth and polished.

All of a sudden he realized that he didn't know the angel's name, and he murmured aloud, "What's your name?"

A voice spoke near his ear, "Anytime you need me, just call for the servant of the Lord, and I will come."

CHAPTER 5

Joel didn't know how long he had been sitting alone on the bench before a beep from a car horn stirred him. He still felt the warmth from the angel's touch, and his mind reeled from the news the angel had given him. He looked up to see his mom jogging toward him, their car in the lot behind her.

"OK, Joel, your chariot awaits you!" she joked as she reached him. "How does your foot feel now?"

Joel breathed deeply. The angel had said he couldn't even tell his mom. His thoughts suddenly cleared, and he stood with a new-found resolve to do just as the angel had instructed him. He took a step and realized his foot felt fine.

Kathy Stevens showed Joel something in her hand. "Here's a Band-Aid I grabbed for you."

"Oh, uh, thanks, Mom," Joel sputtered. "I think I'm OK without it for now." He stepped toward her. "Thanks for coming to get me. I'll be fine if I don't walk so fast," he reassured her.

"Well, your dad was asleep in the hammock, as we predicted," she commented, turning to meet Joel. "He didn't even hear me leave with the car!" They walked a few strides together and she continued, "How would you like to go for some ice cream from our favorite place?" she questioned, raising her eyebrows, her eyes twinkling.

"Sounds great, Mom," Joel remarked nonchalantly, "we haven't gone there for a while."

"Good!" Kathy said as they reached the car and got in. "I wonder what flavors they'll have today," she added, grinning.

She started the car and backed out of the parking space. Joel glanced back at the playground, wondering when he'd see the angel again. He wasn't sure, but it seemed as if the playground had a sort of glow around it. As the car pulled away, he thought he saw the angel, sitting on the bench just as it had been before.

An hour later, Joel and Kathy Stevens were back at home, having enjoyed a treat of homemade ice cream. Kathy stifled a yawn, put her arms up, and stretched.

"I think I may go lie down, Joel. Thanks," she paused and hugged her son, "I really enjoyed spending that time with you!"

Joel lately had felt awkward returning his mom's hugs, but today, he squeezed her tight and planted a quick kiss on her cheek.

"I liked it, too, Mom," Joel replied, smiling.

Kathy smiled back and then turned to go into her bedroom.

Joel thought of something and called to his mom, "Hey, Mom, are we going to church tonight?"

"Hmm . . ." Kathy said as she looked over her shoulder at Joel. "I have some curriculum to work on, and I was going to lie down for a while, but I should be able to go. It's usually a short service. Your father has a meeting with one of his clients who insists on doing the books on Sunday evening, so he can't go." She looked curiously at Joel and asked, "You know Pastor George is speaking again tonight, don't you?"

That's exactly what Joel was wondering. He had seen the angel standing behind Pastor George this morning, so maybe the angel would be there again tonight! Plus, there was something in the message that had piqued Joel's interest, though he'd have to think of what it had been.

"Yeah, Mom, uh, that's OK; he seemed different this morning, like . . . he was happier or something," Joel offered.

"I think you . . . are . . . right," Kathy emphasized the words, pondering while she spoke. "Well, get me up in time to grab a bite before we go, OK?"

"Sure, Mom," Joel answered, watching his mom again turn to go to her bedroom.

Joel hurried to his bedroom and found his Bible. He flopped down on his bed and tried to remember some of the things Pastor George had said that morning. Joel had been so preoccupied with seeing the angel that he hadn't paid close attention to what the message was, yet he did remember clearly something that would be hard to forget—the Scripture had been taken from the book of the Bible that was the same as his name!

In the past, Joel was always disappointed that the Bible book of Joel was so hard to understand. He initially was thrilled that a book was "named after him," but he lost the enthusiasm when his mom explained that the Bible was written many years before he was born. Then, when he was old enough to try to read the Bible himself, he had found the book confusing and pretty useless for a kid of eight years old. A "minor prophet" is all he remembered hearing about the book of Joel, and he hadn't looked at the book again.

Now, though, he had met an angel! Something told him that Pastor George using a passage from the book of Joel was not a coincidence, and he wanted to find out what was so important in that tiny little minor prophet book of the Bible. And, the angel had mentioned being involved in the prophecy of Joel.

Joel paged through the Bible. He was fairly unfamiliar with those prophetic books that came after Psalms and were at the end of the Old Testament. He tried to remember where the book of Joel was but reverted to reciting the books mechanically as he had done in children's church years before. Surprisingly, the old chant came back to him: ". . . Ezekiel, Daniel, Hosea . . . *Joel!*–Got it!" he exclaimed.

He tried to scan the little book quickly, but didn't see anything that he remembered from the sermon.

"Mom's notes!" he murmured, recalling that his mom usually took notes during the sermons and kept them in her Bible . . . and she usually put her Bible on a stand in the living room because she did her reading there at night.

He sprang off his bed and headed straight to the living room. The end table was empty! Where would he find her Bible? Joel closed his eyes and tried to think. Yes! She could have dropped everything on the stool in the kitchen when they came home that day. He retraced his steps and peeked into the kitchen. There it was! He sighed in relief and grabbed the Bible. Sitting at the kitchen table, he opened the book and flipped through the pages. Numerous notes from messages would easily have fallen out if the book had not been laid flat. Joel slowed down and carefully turned to the book of Joel, hoping to find a characteristic note referring to the sermon's Scripture. Unfortunately, the book of Joel was empty! Joel's heart sank, and a heavy sigh left his chest. Closing the Bible, he was about to return to his room when he saw a paper sticking out from the front of the book. He opened the cover, revealing a small piece of paper with today's date on it, and there he saw it—a reference to Joel 2:28–32! Grabbing the note, he ran to his room and shut the door. Eagerly he found the passage and read it out loud:

"And it shall come to pass afterward that I will pour out My Spirit on all flesh; Your sons and your daughters shall prophesy, your old men shall dream dreams, your young men shall see visions."

Yes, that was the part he remembered before seeing the angel behind Pastor George. Strange, he felt pretty calm about the whole thing now. Had it really happened? He was certain it had, but it was very hard to believe! So, what actually was a vision? He pulled a dictionary off of a shelf by his desk and turned to the definition.

Hmm . . . there were at least four possibilities. He read the first one: it involved something seen in a dream. Well, he knew he hadn't been dreaming! The second definition talked about imagination. No, he didn't think he had imagined the angel. But, wait! Joel read on: "direct mystical awareness of the supernatural, usually in visible form." Yes! That fit! He quickly scanned the other definitions, but they weren't helpful.

Joel wasn't sure about the mystical part of things, but he knew people would think he was crazy if they knew he had seen an angel.

He lay back on his bed and went over and over the conversation he and the angel had had. All of a sudden, he had an idea—he needed to write everything down. Now . . . before he forgot anything!

He jumped off his bed, searched for a pen and notebook, then sat down at his desk. How should he start? Breathing deeply, he put a date at the top of the page and then wrote the heading:

I met an angel today.

Joel paused, furrowed his eyebrows, and then leaned over the page. He wrote furiously, detailing the day's events, even inserting the Scripture from the book of Joel. At the end, he put an asterisk and printed the definition of vision. Done. He looked at his clock and realized it was almost time to leave for church. The notebook needed to be hidden. He searched the room with his eyes until he found the perfect place—between some large atlases he had on the shelf. His parents wouldn't find it there. Satisfied with the placement of the notebook, he grabbed his Bible and headed out to the kitchen. His mom wasn't out there yet, so Joel carefully replaced the sermon note with the Scripture on it in the front of her Bible and returned the Bible to the stool. He jumped slightly when he heard his mom's voice.

"Hey, Joel! I was coming to get you. We have enough time for a quick sandwich before church. Can you grab some paper plates for me?" Kathy asked, coming into the kitchen and opening the refrigerator.

"Uh, sure, Mom," Joel said, trying to sound normal. He headed over to the microwave and took some paper plates off the top of it. "Uh, how was your nap?" he questioned.

Kathy breathed deeply and replied, "Good. I guess that walk in the park really helped to calm me. I think I fell asleep as soon as I lay down!" She paused and then said, "Though, I had a strange dream. . . . I can't remember it right this moment, but it made me feel good."

Joel's ears perked up at that, wondering if that was what the angel meant in saying his mom would have special comfort.

Pastor George left the church after the morning service feeling strangely invigorated. It seemed that the congregation had responded well to the message, judging by the many comments said to him as he greeted worshippers leaving the sanctuary. The completeness in his spirit had returned after such a long time!

"Lord, thank you for using a stubborn old man again," he prayed silently as he drove home.

Entering the small house he and Mabel had moved to after their children had grown, he spied Mabel's picture on the TV stand. Walking over and picking the picture up, he spoke softly to Mabel's likeness, "I miss you so much, my dear, but the Lord still has work for me to do, and I'm excited about doing it. Do you mind if I stay here a little while to complete His will? I'm not sure what really is going on, but I know that the Lord is using me for something right now . . . and it seems to be pretty important." He paused, and then chuckled, "It's not like some things the Lord does aren't important, they all are . . . but *you* know what I mean." He bowed his head, tears coming to his eyes and continued, "It makes me feel useful again, like you always made me feel. I depended on your strength so much and maybe . . . too much. The Lord is to be my strength." George raised his head and peered into his wife's eyes in the picture. "Could it be that I used you as a crutch instead of totally trusting the Lord, Mabel? I . . . I . . . I didn't mean to," he stammered. "Well, the Lord has given me another chance, and I know you would want me to trust Him completely and step out in faith and do whatever He is leading me to do, right?"

The picture glowed and an almost imperceptible nod from Mabel's head, accompanied by a gentle smile on her face, appeared within the frame. George stifled a gasp of surprise, blinked his eyes hard, and then looked again. He stared at the photograph, moving it so that he could see Mabel from different angles, but the picture was flat and still.

"Hmm . . ." he murmured and then placed the picture back on top of the TV. Cocking his head to one side, he smiled and said to himself, "It looks as if life is going to get *very* interesting!"

George turned and walked to the kitchen. A Being left the TV area and followed him, watching him carefully. George prepared a simple lunch, sat at a corner bench table, and bowed his head.

"Thank you, Lord, for this food," he said mechanically and then stopped. Repositioning in his chair, he breathed deeply and started over. "Lord, I thank You for all You have provided for me. Thank you for not giving up on me when I let myself wallow in self-pity after Mabel's death. Your grace is now sufficient for me, and I humbly submit to Your will. I don't understand what part I am to play, but whatever it is, I will trust You. Help me to accomplish the work You have for me to do. I excitedly await Your guidance. Thank you for the food You have given to me. Amen."

He took a bite of his lunch and smacked his lips. "I don't know how a tomato sandwich could taste so good, but this one sure does!" he murmured. He chuckled to himself and said, "Somehow, I think *everything* is going to seem better now, Lord!"

The Being smiled with satisfaction and looked heavenward with a wistful sigh. How he wished to be back in heaven with the worshippers of the Lord. The assignment was difficult in that he had to remain on earth for a while. At least he was with this one, the near-saint who was so willing to obey the Lord. It hadn't been hard to rescue him from the sadness that had enveloped him for so long. The demons had done their job well but now had moved on to discourage others, thinking that George was finished and no longer useful. Funny how Satan had miscalculated again. It really was no surprise to the Being.

George quickly ate and pushed his plate aside. He picked up his cup of coffee and pulled his Bible in front of him. Opening to the book of Joel, he read over the Scripture he had used that morning, searching for what the Lord might want to say that evening. His mind seemed blank. He paged through the worn Bible, wondering why the Joel passage seemed without inspiration now. Pausing to take a sip of coffee again, he let the pages fall through his fingers. He looked out the window, taking in the sunshine as it beamed in on him. Glancing down at his Bible, he noticed a ray of light illuminating a paragraph. He leaned forward to see better, reading the title, "Take Heed to Your Ministry."

"Oh, what do we have here?" he rhetorically questioned. George fingered the verses as he read them silently. A wide grin spread across his face and he nodded his head. "Got it, Lord!" he exclaimed out loud. He pulled a tablet and pen from the shelf nearby and began scribbling notes.

Standing behind George, the Being smiled and continued resting his palms on George's shoulders. "This adopted child of God at least makes my work easy and pleasurable while I must remain on earth," the Being thought.

A small group of the congregation gathered outside the church in the parking lot after the morning service. Their routine was to grab some lunch together and then go to one of the homes to discuss the sermon and to pray. They all seemed bubblier today and chatted excitedly, deciding on a restaurant. After eating, they met together in a widow's house and spent a half hour going over the Scripture Pastor George had used, along with notes most of them had taken, highlighting the main points. Soon, they knelt and prayed, thanking God for answering their prayers. For several years, this same band of dedicated Christians had been meeting like this. They had all felt led to pray regarding God's work in their community and found their common interest had bonded them together as prayer warriors. None of them would describe themselves this way, but the Beings who gathered in the room with them knew this was so. The Beings gathered strength from the prayers voiced to the Lord Most High, knowing that these very prayers were enabling them to do His work in the community.

The prayer meeting went on for an hour. The Beings in the room appeared to glow and stand taller as the prayers were offered. As the final amen was uttered, all the Beings placed hands on the kneeling individuals. Although the praying was over, none of the group felt inclined to get up. They did not know exactly what happened at the end of each Sunday prayer time, but they all felt wondrously renewed and energized as they lingered after the prayers. It had started perhaps six months ago. They all had noticed a special sensation after the prayer time. At first no one said anything, but when it happened each time, they soon began to quietly question each other and realized all of them were being blessed the same way. Wisely, they humbly thanked the Lord for what was happening and chose not to dwell on the Blessing itself. In fact, each of them privately prayed for the Blessing not to interfere with their prayer meeting. Today, they all agreed that Pastor George's sermon could be the start of the Lord's special work in their own community—the answer to the years of prayers! They had all felt the change within the church as Pastor George spoke, and they all were excited to be a part of God's work. Little did they know what huge role they were playing in the fulfillment of the Joel prophecy!

CHAPTER 6

The church service was definitely more crowded than usual for a Sunday night. Joel and Kathy Stevens greeted a number of people and then made their way to their seats. Joel anxiously looked around, hoping to see the angel, but no glowing figure came into view.

The worship leader asked them all to stand for prayer as the service began, and an elder came to the pulpit to pray. The prayer was earnest yet short, and soon the congregation joined together in singing.

Pastor George peered out at the worshippers, noting only a few young folks in attendance. He started to question the content of his sermon for the evening, but quickly scolded himself for presuming to know better than the Lord. He bowed his head and prayed silently to yield to the Spirit.

After the singing ended and offering was taken, Pastor George was introduced by the elder who had initially prayed.

"We were certainly stirred by your message this morning, Pastor George, and we look forward to what the Spirit has laid on your heart for us this evening," the man exclaimed, turning to face George and motioning him to come to the pulpit.

Pastor George smiled and moved forward, again clutching the worn Bible in his hand.

"Thank you, Ray," Pastor George said warmly. "Will you all stand for the reading of the Word?" he directed to the congregation.

They were ready for him this time and rose to their feet in unison, many holding Bibles in anticipation of the sermon.

"Let us turn to 1Timothy 4:12–16," he instructed and paused while many paged away from Joel, where they had thought he would continue from the morning message.

Pastor George read heartily, "'*Let no one despise your youth, but be an example to the believers in word, in conduct, in love, in spirit, in faith, in purity. Till I come, give attention to reading, to exhortation, to doctrine. Do not neglect the gift that is in you, which was given to you by prophecy with the laying on of hands of the eldership. Meditate on these things; give yourself entirely to them, that your progress may be evident to all. Take heed to yourself and to the doctrine. Continue in them, for in doing this you will save both yourself and those who hear you.*' May the Lord bless the reading of His Word."

Joel's eyes were riveted to the verses in Timothy. He didn't even hear Pastor George invite them to be seated, and Kathy had to pull him down to the pew seat. He reread the passage, and he was drawn to the same sentence: "*Do not neglect the gift that is in you, which was given to you by prophecy.*" This was what the angel had said to him and even his mom had told him that afternoon at the park. It sure seemed like God was trying to tell him something! Joel looked up and concentrated on what Pastor George was saying.

"When we consider what the Lord told us this morning, we must realize that *all* of us will be needed to accomplish the final harvesting of souls before Christ returns. Remember what the Scripture in Joel spoke of: '*your sons and daughters shall prophesy... your young men shall see visions.*' Our young people sang to us this morning and ministered to us. It is very possible that God will raise up our youth *right here* in our church. So we need to make sure we are doing all we can to help our young people. Let's look at the passage in Timothy in more detail.

"Verse 12 says: '*Let no one despise your youth.*' What does that mean? I believe it has a two-fold message, one for our youth and one for the adults in the church. For our young people, each one should not only believe that he or she can be used of God but also be looking to use the talents God has given. Remember, Jesus taught in the temple when he was only twelve. David killed Goliath when he was a young man. Miriam spied out what was happening to her little brother, Moses, when she was but a girl. I'm not sure myself how the prophecy in Joel will play out with our youth, but I am positive that God is planning to use them." Smiling, he added, "Perhaps some will work with angels, others could prophesy in ways that direct us to act, I don't know, but our youth need to embrace their godly roles in such a way that God can use their talents.

"Many of you remember the comic book heroes of yesterday. The 'good' guys seemed to all go through a stage of denial, then awkward acceptance of their powers, and then true development of their powers in ways that benefited man. The 'bad' guys skipped all steps but went straight to the development of their powers. They didn't learn that with great power comes great responsibility to use that power correctly. So it could also be with God-given talents and gifts—those given these things must be patient and," he paused, shrugging his shoulders, 'go into training,' you might say."

Joel was listening intently, sitting forward with his elbows on his knees. The moment Pastor George referred to working with angels, he sat up straight and his mouth dropped open. *How did he know?* he thought. Then when Pastor George mentioned training, Joel sat back in amazement. *That's what the angel had said,* he mused. But then he realized that he had clearly seen the angel behind Pastor George during the sermon that morning. *Maybe, Pastor George has seen it, too,* he wondered.

Pastor George was continuing on regarding adults. "Now, we, as adults have a special duty regarding *our* role in the Joel prophecy. God will use our knowledge and foundation in the faith to equip our youth to act. Tell me, what would *you* do if your son or daughter was given a gift of prophecy during these end times? We must be careful not to be jealous of the gift. You may think that would not happen, but consider a thirteen-year-old actually telling us of a future event or mission. I hazard a guess that a few parents would feel it their place to interpret or handle the message, because who will believe a kid! I think if you are honest with yourself, you will see how we will need the grace of God to accept our youth's involvement without sticking our noses into it all and messing up what God has given them to do.

"Then, what if someone's child does not receive a gift? Jealousy could ruin relationships and hinder the Lord's work. We must dedicate ourselves and submit not only our lives, but also the lives of any youth who the Lord chooses. Remember, only one set of parents were chosen to have Moses, or Samuel, or David, or Deborah, or Mary. I believe God will give a special grace to those whose children are to take part in this exciting time, and everyone should support the work.

"Moving on in the Scripture is an exhortation for young Timothy that our youth can take to heart: *'Be an example to the believers in word, in conduct, in love, in spirit, in faith, in purity.'*

"Wow—young people are to be examples to other Believers! Isn't that backwards from what we normally think? Usually, we talk about being good examples for our kids, and rightly so, but our youth should also show us what the touch of the Lord can do in any life. I don't know about you, but that humbles me! God wants us 'wise, old adults' to be encouraged by our youth to be better Christians.

"The writer of this letter, Paul, then explains some of what it takes to be a good example: *'Give attention to reading, to exhortation, to doctrine.'* It takes studying, fellowship, and knowledge of the Bible to develop the gifts God has given. Yes, doctrine is important for all of us. How can we tell a lost world that Jesus is the only way if we don't really understand that and believe it? Most of us love to hear that God loves us. We feel all warm inside. But, our God is also holy and cannot tolerate sin. No matter how good you are, your sin keeps you from God and only the blood of Jesus can restore a right relationship with our holy God. We *have* to understand these key truths, and our youth need to wholly embrace these truths in order to be used of God.

"Verse 14 is so important for all of us: *'Do not neglect the gift that is in you, which was given to you by prophecy with the laying on of the hands of the eldership.'*

"This would indicate that some may be given gifts and refuse to use them for some reason. Oh, people," he paused, "a gift from God is a precious thing and must be honored, accepted with grace . . . *and used!*

"In this church, we dedicate infants to the Lord. Some of you have been here when, occasionally, someone has been stirred by the Spirit to say a word regarding a particular infant during the dedication. I had not really thought of this for a long time, but some of our children have had the laying on of hands in dedication along with a word of prophecy. I don't believe we thought anything of it at the time, just something nice that was said about a little baby, but the Lord has reminded me that His word does not return to Him void. It is possible that, unknowingly, we, ourselves participated in 'giving' the Lord's gift to some of our children!"

Joel was intrigued and wondered if he had been one of the ones that had some prophecy about him at his dedication. He'd have to ask his mom.

"Verse 15 stresses that those who are given these special gifts are to '*meditate on these things; give yourself entirely to them, that your progress may be evident to all.*' It certainly seems that the gifts are life-changing, life-encompassing, and should be life-apparent, meaning that others should be able to monitor the growth in use of the gift.

"Finally, the last verse gives a caution with a wonderful promise: '*Take heed to yourself and to the doctrine. Continue in them, for in doing this you will save both yourself and those who hear you.*' What does this mean? I think it warns again that the truth of the gospel must be presented and painstakingly guarded to stay accurate. No element of falsehood can be tolerated because we're down to the last opportunity for others to come to the Lord before the great battle with Satan begins. Satan uses half-truths to pull people away from the Lord, so we have to work extra hard to stay true to the Word of the Lord. It is interesting that the caution does not give a negative consequence, but rather talks of what the hard work accomplishes: '*You will save both yourself and those who hear you.*' What an encouragement! Taking the gifts that are given and using them for the Lord's work actually results in people coming to salvation through the blood of the Lamb! That is awesome! We need to prepare for a great revival that involves the gifts that have been given. I don't know what gifts, although it was pretty clear that one was for prophecy. I don't know who will have the gifts, but I am fairly certain that the time is *now*! Are you ready? Do you want to be included? I know I do!

"As I close, I would like to invite anyone who wants to be included actively in what the Joel prophecy could do in our community to come to the front and participate in a prayer. Could we all stand while Brother John leads us in a song? Those of you who would like to pray, please come forward."

Pastor George backed away from the pulpit as the organ began to play, and the worship leader started to sing. Joel felt weird; his heart was pounding and his palms were sweaty. He looked up and noticed a number of people walking to the front of the sanctuary. Quickly he made a decision and moved to step in front of his mom to go forward, but his mom was also moving out of the pew. She headed to the front, and Joel followed her. He had never gone forward before, but he immediately knew it had been the right thing to do. He stood beside his mom, who glanced at him, smiled, and then reached for his hand to clasp. She bowed her head, so Joel did, too.

The singing ended, and Pastor George began to pray, "Oh, Lord, we come before You to ask that we can be involved actively in what You plan to do. You have made it clear to me and others that the end time is near, and You want to bring as many to salvation as will choose to accept it, but they need to hear the Word first. Help us to be totally open to the gifts You may give to those in our community, especially the youth. Bless our young people. Bless Pastor Eric as he guides them. Bless our pastors and elders. Help us to be Your servants, oh Lamb of God. Amen."

Joel and the others stood quietly for a minute. He peeked to see what was happening and noticed that the pews were empty and everyone was up front!

A woman's voice lifted up and cried out, "The Lord is pleased with His people! He wants you to know that your prayers are being answered. He bestows on those here a special blessing. He is pleased to give His gifts to open hearts that are willing to use them. The time is now for the prophecy of Joel! Prepare! The Lamb of God is coming soon and there are souls to be harvested before that great day of the Lord. Awake! Take hold of your gifts, arise to your calling. Wonderful and awesome things await you. Don't hesitate. Do not fear, for the Lord your God goes before you now as He did with Moses and Joshua. Look to Him for guidance. Call to Him when you need help. He is pleased with you! He loves you!" Her voice seemed to echo through the sanctuary as she finished.

A warmth filled Joel, beginning deep inside and spreading outward. His heart was thumping so much that he thought it would come out of his chest. He had never experienced anything like this at his church before! It was exciting and very different, yet Joel felt unusually calm instead of scared. He noticed that Pastor George was praying again, but it was quite soft, and Joel couldn't tell what he was saying. The next thing he knew, Pastor George was standing in front of him and touching his forehead.

"Father, anoint us with Your Spirit to do Your will," Pastor George quietly prayed.

Joel looked up at him and their eyes locked. A strange sensation came over Joel, and Pastor George's eyes widened as if seeing something glorious. Pastor George gently placed his hands on Joel's shoulders and whispered, "Lord, anoint this young man and help him to do the work You have chosen for him to do. Make him strong in Your might and protect him from the evil one. Help us here in his church to support him and his family. Thank you for letting me participate now in what I have only dreamed about. Amen."

Pastor George hugged Joel and then moved next to Kathy Stevens, keeping one hand on Joel's shoulder. Kathy's eyes were still closed as Pastor George placed his other hand on her shoulder, closed his eyes, and whispered yet another prayer, "Father, bless this mother and strengthen her for the journey ahead. Anoint her with Your Spirit just as You gave grace to Mary, Elizabeth, and

Hannah. Protect her from the enemy. Amen." Pastor George hugged her and smiled warmly as she lifted her head, acknowledging his prayer with her eyes. He moved on to the next person, praying simply and quietly.

They stood patiently while Pastor George went to each person and prayed for them until he returned to the platform and dismissed them. Holding both arms up in a blessing, he quoted, "*The Lord bless you and keep you; the Lord make His face shine upon you, and be gracious to you; the Lord lift up His countenance upon you, and give you peace.*" Pastor George smiled and added, "We have witnessed a wonderful thing tonight, and we are now participants in what the Lord is planning. Continue to pray for the Lord to guide us, be alert to what the Lord wants each of us to do, and come back again Wednesday night to see what the Lord has to say to us. Thank you and good night!" As he stepped down from the platform, he turned toward Joel and Kathy, giving them a knowing smile and nod, and then turned back to greet those around him.

Joel stood frozen to the spot for a moment until his mom nudged him and said, "You OK, Joel?"

Joel continued looking at Pastor George for a second and then nodded, saying a bit hesitantly, "Yeah . . . yeah, I'm OK." He looked down at the floor, trying to grasp what had just happened and then peered at his mom, hoping for some reassurance.

Kathy sighed deeply and then walked with Joel back to their pew. It seemed like she wanted to say something, but she ended up picking up her purse and Bible and walking to the back of the church. Joel grabbed his Bible and followed her. They went to the car in silence and got in. Kathy placed the key in the ignition but didn't turn it. She breathed heavily and then turned to face Joel.

"Joel, I want you to know that I am very proud of you for choosing to follow the Lord. Your dad and I have tried to do our best in giving you the foundation spiritually to make good decisions, but you are of an age now that *you* need to be choosing whether or not to do the Lord's work. I want you to know that your dad and I are ready to help you in your spiritual journey. We can't make your choices for you, but if you need guidance, please come to us,

OK?" She placed her hand on Joel's arm, and Joel was certain there were tears in her eyes.

Joel was astounded. Did she know what had happened today? The angel had said not to say anything to his parents, but his mom somehow seemed to know. Joel wasn't sure what to say, but tried to choose his words carefully. "Mom, I think God may want me to be involved maybe like Pastor George was talking about. I don't quite understand it all, but I have decided to do whatever He may ask me to do."

Kathy bit her lip and let the tears flow. She reached over to Joel, her voice cracking with emotion, and cried, "Your dad . . . and I . . . will be here . . . for you, Joel." She couldn't say a word more, but hugged Joel tightly. Letting go of him, she smiled through her tears with a look of love and then started the car and pulled out of the parking lot.

Pastor George said good night to the last of the congregation and waved to the man locking the doors. He went to his car and got in. Only then did the impact of the evening hit him, and he sobbed with tears of joy. Speaking out loud, he thanked God, "Lord, You have done what You promised to do many years ago. You have been faithful even though we forgot. I feel like Simeon must have felt when he held the newborn baby Jesus in the temple! My eyes have seen the hope that You showed me long ago, and I praise You. Thank you, Father! You have given me a new life, and I look forward to the work You have for me!" Laughing boisterously, he yelled out, *"I love you, Lord!"*

The Sunday afternoon prayer group gathered briefly in the foyer after the service. No words were said. They shook hands or hugged and gave each other a quick sign with one hand. They dispersed, leaving the church with praise on their lips.

Anyone passing the church that evening noticed a faint glow surrounding the building while Pastor George was speaking. They thought the church had just installed some outside illumination, but it was a supernatural light, usually not visible to human eyes, bathing the church. It was apparent only because of the power of God emanating from the Beings who enclosed the area in a protective spiritual shield so that the enemy could not disturb those inside.

CHAPTER 7

Joel awoke Monday morning to his alarm and lay quietly in bed after turning the buzzer off. He had come home from church last night and written more in his journal, trying to describe the events that had happened as well as summarizing Pastor George's sermon from 1 Timothy. It all seemed like a dream, and it was hard to know if everything that had occurred was real. He sighed and rolled out of bed. As he went to leave his room, he felt a strong urge to pray. Kneeling down beside his bed he spoke out loud.

"Lord, was I just dreaming that I met an angel, or did that really happen? Now it seems like it didn't really happen. I want to be a part of Your work, but I'm no one special. If all that did happen, why would You want to use me?" Joel prayed. He looked up and around his room, half expecting the angel to appear, but nothing happened. He closed his eyes again and finished, "Help me. Amen." He got up, looked around the room one more time, and then went out into the hall.

His parents were in the kitchen eating breakfast. His dad greeted him, "Morning, Joel! Did you sleep OK?"

"Yeah, fine, Dad," Joel smiled, and then headed to get showered.

Kathy sighed, watching Joel disappear down the hall and turned to her husband, "Do you think we should see if he wants to pray? He's going to need our support."

Doug reached out and took Kathy's hand. "He needs to find his way, Kath. I think it may be best to wait and see what happens. We shouldn't interfere with the Lord's work. I know it took us by surprise a bit, but we promised to let him go. You know God will take care of him, don't you?"

"Yes . . . I know. I think it's just hard as a mother, not only to let him grow up, but to let him grow up this early and in this way," Kathy tried to explain.

"I wish I had been there last night," Doug mused; "you described something incredible, but apparently it was not in the Lord's plans for me to be there. My client was very specific about when he needed to meet with me, and yet he actually complained about getting together on a Sunday night, like *I* had been the one to set up the meeting."

Kathy and Doug finished eating and spent a few moments reading a devotional and praying, as they normally did, before Joel made it into the kitchen to eat. Soon, they were each heading out, with Doug going to his office, Kathy driving to her school, and Joel catching the bus to his school. But, before going in separate directions, Joel turned and grabbed his mom and dad in a group hug—something they hadn't done since he was in elementary school.

"Love you!" he murmured into their ears, and then, seeming somewhat embarrassed, rushed down the driveway to meet others waiting for the bus.

Doug and Kathy hugged each other a little more before getting into their cars and backing out. Behind some shrubs at the side of the house, a Being smiled and nodded.

Joel went straight to his locker when he got to the public school and deposited some books for later classes while retrieving others for the morning.

"Hey, Joel!" a voice called from the other side of the hall.

Turning, Joel saw Kyle trying to maneuver through the crowded area toward him. Joel shut the locker and moved to meet his friend. Kyle smiled widely and shouldered Joel as they met in the middle.

"So. . . you didn't call last night. Busy with your folks?" Kyle rambled on. "I was stuck at my aunt's birthday party. Nothing to do except terrorize my little cousins," he snickered. "The food was good, though." He continued with bits and pieces of what he had done until the two friends had to go different directions for first period. "See ya later!" he called and headed into a classroom.

"Whew!" Joel thought, being glad that he didn't have to tell Kyle anything about the day before. He didn't know why, however. They normally shared everything with each other. Somehow, Joel figured what had happened with him and the angel the day before would only make Kyle howl with laughter. He knew his friend pretty well and wasn't sure how to talk about the day without spilling the beans to Kyle. As he made his way into class and sat down, he decided to silently pray that he'd be able to interact with Kyle normally and avoid anything that would compromise his agreement with the angel to not tell anybody.

The angel stood behind Joel and glowed ever so slightly as he prayed. Closing its eyes, it raised its hands, entreating God to do this request.

On the other side of the room, a quiet girl named Jill thought she noticed some sparkles in the air by Joel. She squinted her eyes trying to make out what she saw, but decided it was just the sun reflecting off the blinds into the room. The sparkles disappeared, and she returned to getting her work for the class out.

The angel watched her and whispered to itself, "Not yet, my friend, but soon, very soon, you will see."

Late in the day Joel and Kyle finally had some time to talk. Joel tried to be nonchalant and soon found himself caught up in a typical conversation with Kyle. Before running to get his bus, Kyle called out, "I'll call you tonight after I finish my homework."

Joel waved back to him while nodding in agreement. He jumped onto his bus and found a seat, sighing as he collapsed onto the cushion. He felt relieved that Kyle had not questioned him about Sunday, and he silently thanked God. Someone nudged him, and he absentmindedly moved close to the window as the person sat down. He felt peculiar for a moment, and, glancing at his new seatmate, he gasped.

"Hello, Joel," said a familiar voice.

Joel peered into the face of the angel he had met the day before! The features were the same, yet the body was that of a youth dressed in a T-shirt and jeans. There was still a faint glow surrounding him, but no one else on the bus seemed to notice or care.

"How . . . I mean . . . what . . . " Joel stuttered, trying to formulate a million questions into one. He shook his head to clear his thoughts and then spurted out, "How did you get here?"

"Why, I walked onto the bus with everyone else, Joel," the angel explained matter-of-factly.

"Do they see you, too?" Joel asked.

"Yes," the angel replied, "but not as you see me. To them, we are both sitting here, looking out the window, not speaking."

"You can do that?" Joel asked in amazement. "Wow!"

The angel looked intently at Joel and spoke softly, "It is not my power, but the power of the mighty God and of His Son, the Lamb."

Joel immediately recognized the reverence with which the angel spoke. "I think I understand," he uttered and then paused. "I was hoping that I'd see you today. I wondered if it all had been real or just a dream."

Nodding, the angel said, "Remember, God hears all your prayers."

Tilting his head, Joel thought of the various prayers he had said during the day, from the first prayer for help that morning to the prayer to talk normally with Kyle. The angel was right: his prayers had not only been heard, but answered.

The angel spoke again, "We will study and talk tonight. There is much you need to learn."

"What about my homework?" Joel asked.

"You will have the ability to finish it quickly," the angel replied. "Part of your work includes staying involved in your school and other activities, at least for a while."

Joel raised his eyebrows in amazement, "Cool!"

The angel looked seriously at Joel and remarked, "The work you have to do is difficult. You may think that some of what happens is advantageous, but you will find it to be the least of your thoughts as you choose to do the Lord's bidding."

Feeling somewhat rebuked, Joel's shoulders fell, and he slumped back in his seat. "I still don't think I'm the person for this job you keep talking about," he sighed.

Smiling, the angel chuckled and said, "Oh, you certainly are. You just have to believe it and not let discouragement take over."

The angel touched him on his arm, and Joel felt the tingle of God's power surge through his body, pushing away any doubts.

Joel straightened up and, with determination, said, "I'm ready when you are!"

The angel nodded and said, "It is time for us to get off the bus."

Looking out the window, Joel was surprised to see familiar homes of his neighborhood. The bus slowed and stopped. The angel stood and walked up the aisle ahead of Joel, hopping off the bus steps like any of the other passengers. Joel followed, and then the two walked up the drive to Joel's house together. Joel reached for a hidden key to open the door, but the angel merely turned the doorknob, and then pushed the door open.

Joel watched with surprise and blurted out, "How'd you do that?"

"You will soon learn that 'with God, all things are possible'" the angel explained. "Jesus *did* say 'I am the door,' you know," he added, winking at Joel, his eyes twinkling.

Joel laughed. "I didn't know angels could be funny!" he exclaimed as they both entered the house.

The angel nodded and said, "If you think about it, Joel, God is the inventor of humor and laughter. Look at the creation he made—it is certainly beautiful, but can you also see the humor in the making of a giraffe's long neck or the antics of monkeys? He is the originator of the comical; it was all in His mind and He spoke it into being."

Joel had never thought about that. It was sort of neat to imagine God laughing, and in that moment, something like an anteater being created purely out of God's humorous thoughts. He remembered one night at a family gathering, how his uncle had them all in stitches doing a funny game with hilarious animal motions and they had laughed until their cheeks hurt. God had given that humor to them through his uncle. Joel envisioned some weird animals that would have been created through their game and could picture that happening at creation. He smiled at the images going through his mind and for a moment or two, totally forgot the angel at his side.

"You would have loved seeing creation, Joel," the angel spoke softly, bringing Joel out of his musings. "Making the heavens and the earth were truly spectacular, but my favorite was the sixth day when He created the different animals. His voice roared, and the mighty lion sprang out of nowhere. His tone changed a bit, and a gorilla growled, leaping out of the trees. It was incredible! At one point, his voice barked, and a red fox ran into the meadow, but next a slightly different bark was heard, and a Great Dane stood proudly before Him. The animals all gathered in anticipation of His next work. Then, finally, a great silence occurred. We wondered what was wrong, or was He finished? At first we heard nothing, but then a soft, beautiful sound began slowly and seemed to flow like a current through the air; we were mesmerized by the song that developed into a symphony. The music built to a great crescendo, and then . . ." the angel stopped, with a look of complete wonder on his face.

"Then what?" Joel asked excitedly. "What happened?"

The angel looked at Joel, his countenance barely containing his own excitement. "And, then . . . then . . ." he paused again, "God created man."

Joel's body tingled with the thrill of the angel's description of the creation of man. He could not speak but held the image in his mind for what seemed like hours. His surroundings disappeared and in his mind's eye he witnessed the grand event. He remembered the song the youth group had sung and how special he felt afterwards. This was immensely more inspiring as he heard the song that man's life had produced. He, too, was part of that beautiful music that God had sung in creating mankind. He knew it! He had heard the music that his own life had contributed, and he felt so small and yet so important. His life had been needed to complete the song. The angel had not said this, but Joel knew it to be true!

Allowing the vision to fade was difficult, but Joel willed himself to look once again at the angel. Sometime during the experience Joel had grabbed hold of the angel's arms, and now was held up by them. He felt very strange. At first the angel's report was like listening to a story, but then Joel could see it as it was happening, and the song—he heard the music God had used to create man. Joel knew he was trembling. He wasn't scared; rather, he felt excited and somehow honored to have witnessed the event as he did.

The angel held him securely without speaking, and then gently set him down on a chair in the kitchen. He filled a glass with water and handed it to Joel.

Joel sipped the water while gazing at the angel.

"What happened? It seemed like I was really there," he whispered.

"You had a vision. You did see it," the angel quietly explained.

Joel sat back, contemplating the enormity of not only the vision, but that he had been permitted to see it.

The angel tilted his head and looked deep into Joel's eyes. "It is part of the gift you have been given. You are needed to communicate God's purest thoughts to the world around you. You will see things that have been, are happening, or will happen. You must use the gift to bring the lost to Him."

Joel was tempted to deny what the angel was telling him, but he knew it was true. He knew that he had been given a great and terrible gift. He didn't know how it all was to work together, but he could not refuse this work that he was being asked to do, no matter how terrified he felt about the responsibility. The vision had sealed that. Without him, the song was not complete.

After a few moments of silence, Joel questioned, "How . . . how will something like that bring people to Jesus?"

"The Word of God is very powerful on its own, Joel. You will bring it to life. John 1:14 says, '*And the Word became flesh and dwelt among us.*' Do you know who that is talking about?" the angel asked.

Joel thought for a second and then answered, "That's about Jesus, isn't it?"

"Yes," the angel said. "So when you speak the Word of God, you are telling others about Jesus and His wonderful salvation. We will help you to understand your visions and to know how to relay their messages to others properly. It helps if you know certain Scriptures well. The enemy knows the Word also and can use it falsely to turn individuals away from the Most Holy God. You must never use the Word for personal gain or boast regarding your abilities. Those things will bring you dangerously close to the enemy. Remember, if you feel threatened or tempted to misuse your gift, 'call upon the name of the Lord.'"

Nodding, Joel suddenly felt very small. The angel immediately placed his hand on Joel's arm and with a look of alertness, peered at the kitchen ceiling. Joel sensed the electricity as soon as the angel touched him. His feelings of inadequacy were drowned in a powerful warmth of love.

Curious, yet cautious, Joel asked, "What's wrong? I felt awful for just a moment, and then your touch took it away."

The angel removed his hand and placed a finger at his lips to quiet Joel. He held his other hand out as if stopping someone from continuing. He kept this position for nearly a minute. Finally, the angel relaxed and gazed at Joel intently.

"That was the enemy, Joel," he pronounced with some gravity.

"The enemy!" Joel exclaimed, although somewhat in a whisper. "Who . . . who . . . exactly is the enemy? I know Satan is the enemy. Is he here?"

"No," the Angel said. "You are currently not known to him, but his demons are always out, doing his evil work. We must be careful not to attract their attention before the time of training has been completed. Otherwise you would be a target for their attack, and your gift may be recognized. Then our work and your work could be jeopardized. The Lord Most High protects you, Joel. But you always have a choice. Choose the wrong path and much could be lost." The angel waved a palm to the outside. "A demon of inadequacy passed by and tried to cast its negative feelings onto the inhabitants of these few homes. Your house is protected, but now that you have used your gift, you are more easily affected by their powers. You must learn to cast off any negative thoughts, Joel, or the demons will return. Most are minimally intelligent and can't figure much out, but others are captains and leaders who may discern that you are working against them purposely and look for ways to stop you."

Joel tried to take in what the angel was saying and thought of something. "Can I see demons like I can see you?"

The angel breathed a sigh and nodded, "You may start seeing them as you develop your gift. I must warn you, Joel. Demons are ugly, vile creatures, but they have cunning. Many servants of God have been turned away from Him by the persuasiveness of the demons in their masked attire, but had they only been able to see those terrible creatures, they would have run to the *strong tower* of the Lord and been saved."

The two sat quietly for a while before Joel spoke up, "Should we start my training?"

"Yes," the angel said with a smile, impressed with Joel's courage to continue, "but first," he pointed to Joel's backpack, "you have some homework to complete, I believe."

Joel laughed and reached for the backpack, unzipped the top and pulled out some books and papers. "Are you sure you can't snap your fingers or something and my homework would be done?"

"No shortcuts are allowed," the angel declared, smiling. With that, he walked to the side of the kitchen.

"Are you leaving?" Joel asked. "We didn't do any *training* yet," he emphasized.

"I will be back this evening. Look for me. Remember not to say anything to your parents," the angel instructed. He then walked through the wall and was gone.

CHAPTER 8

Joel shook his head in amazement. His homework was done! His parents should be home any time now, and he had completed his homework in half the time! He decided to set the table for dinner—that way he could be ready for the angel as soon as he was done eating. His chores were such that he could either set the table or clean off afterwards. He normally wasn't done with homework in time to set the table, so he got stuck with cleaning it off. It was much better to set the table, he quickly decided, as he put the last utensils down. He heard the garage door go up and went to see who was home first. To his surprise, both parents were home. He grabbed some bags from his mom and greeted her.

"Hi, Mom!" Joel said pleasantly and then turned and said, "Hi, Dad!"

"Hi, Joel," they both responded with smiles.

"How was your day?" Kathy asked, as they walked into the house.

Joel shrugged nonchalantly, "It was fine. How 'bout you guys?"

Kathy spoke first, "My day was amazingly good for a Monday."

Doug agreed, "I had a good day, too!"

"I picked up some things for chicken stir-fry, so dinner shouldn't take too long," Kathy informed them. "Joel, could you take a break from homework and help me some?"

"I'm done," Joel told her.

Kathy looked playfully shocked and smiled, "That's unusual, Joel! Are the teachers slacking off for some reason?"

"Nah," he replied, "it just went faster today. Anyhow, sure, I can help you. The table is set already."

Now his mom looked genuinely surprised, and, glancing at Doug, said, "Hmm . . . OK. Well, let's wash up these veggies, and you can cut them while I turn on the wok and prepare the chicken."

Doug jumped in to help as well, and before long they were sitting at the dining room table, enjoying a healthy meal. Kathy told some amusing stories from her day, and Doug added in some funny comments about his. Their laughter was interrupted by the phone ringing. Joel jumped up and grabbed it.

"Hello . . . oh, hi, Kyle. Tonight? Uh . . ." Joel paused with his eyebrows furrowed, "Um . . . I've got somethin' I have to do tonight. . . . Nah, I'm done with my homework. . . . It's somethin' else. . . . Well, I gotta go. See ya tomorrow? OK. Bye." Joel put the phone back, sat down again at the dining room table, and resumed eating.

Kathy and Doug looked curiously at each other and then at Joel.

"Uh . . . not that we're nosing into your personal stuff, Joel, but what *somethin' else* is going on tonight? Your mom and I don't have anything on the calendar. Did we miss an item?" Doug inquired.

"Oh, no, Dad," Joel replied. "It's just that I decided to do some things myself tonight." Seeing his parents' concerned look, he added, "Some church stuff, you know?"

Kathy slowly nodded her head, glanced at Doug, and said, "OK. Sure, we understand. Let us know if you need any help," she paused and looked intently at Joel, "or if we can do *anything*." She smiled at him weakly.

Joel didn't know what to say. He couldn't talk to his parents about what was going on, yet sometimes it seemed like they *knew* something already. "Uh . . . OK, Mom. I'll remember that," he offered. Changing the subject, he chirped, "Is there any dessert?"

Picking up on the not-so-smooth transition, Kathy rolled right along with it and quipped, "Lemon meringue pie! I'll go get it." And with that, she got up, glanced at Doug, and went into the kitchen, leaving Doug and Joel at the table.

Doug took the cue as his opportunity to talk to Joel about church the previous night. "So, your mom told me that church was a bit different last night. What did you think?"

Joel perked up, "Yeah. It was really cool, Dad. Pastor George talked about helping the young people who may be asked by God," he paused, and added, "*somehow*, to do something to bring others to salvation before Christ returns. Then he asked anyone who wanted to be a part of that to go to the front to get prayed for. It turned out that the whole congregation went up!" he exclaimed. "Then Pastor George prayed for each person." Joel got quieter, "Even for me and Mom. He prayed sort of . . . special . . . for us. I don't know why. It was kinda weird. . . ." he looked directly at his dad, "but *good. It made me feel strange."* Joel decided at that moment to tell his dad what he had told his mom. "Dad, I think God may want *me* to be involved somehow with what Pastor George is talking about . . . you know?"

Doug nodded, encouraging Joel to go on.

"So . . . there may be things I have to do. I may not be able to talk to you and Mom about it, either," Joel commented hesitantly.

"Oh?" Doug wasn't expecting this. "Why is that? Your mom and I are here to help you. God gave us that responsibility when He made us your parents."

"Well," Joel began, searching for the right words, "that's true. But just like I can't be saved through you and Mom being Christians—I have to ask Jesus into my heart myself." He stopped, hoping he wouldn't spill the beans about the angel. "God may have certain things that He asks me to do alone, without you being directly involved." With sudden insight, he added, "I'm not talking about running away to be a missionary in Africa, or anything like that."

Doug was visibly relieved.

"Dad," Joel smiled, "I'm still a kid in school. There are certain things that I'm *not* going to do. You guys still get to take care of me, OK?"

"Right," Doug breathed out heavily, slightly embarrassed that he had misunderstood Joel and jumped to conclusions. At that moment, Kathy returned to the room with a tray of pie slices.

"Here we go. . . . Dig in, everyone!" she exclaimed, chancing a furtive look at Doug. Handing out the desserts, she almost commented on the conversation she had overheard, but on second thought, she kept quiet about that and merely said, "Bon appétit!"

The angel backed away again into a corner of the dining room behind Joel. That had gone better than expected. Joel was easily inspired by the Spirit, his own soul being sensitive to the things of the Lord. Kathy, too, paid close attention to the nudging of the Spirit. Doug, on the other hand, still used his head too much. His knowledge of Scripture was solid, but sometimes the application was automatic and calculated. He needed prayer to soften his heart to hear the Spirit better. The angel moved through the wall to the back yard and headed toward an old swing set in the far corner with the rusty swings creaking in the breeze. He sat down on a swing and the creaking stopped, as though the chains had just been oiled. He would wait here for Joel.

A few minutes elapsed, when, sure enough, Joel appeared, clutching his Bible and a notebook.

Excitedly, he exclaimed, "I saw you out here when I got up from the table. Is this when we get to start? Won't my parents think I'm crazy if I'm talking to no one out here if they can't see you? But I guess they'd freak if they *did* see you!"

The angel smiled, his twinkling eyes lighting up, "They will see you studying your Bible and taking notes, but will not suspect that you are with anyone, nor hear you speak to me, just like today on the bus. Shall we get started?"

Joel nodded, his heart thrilled and pounding.

"First, we will pray," the angel reached to touch Joel on the arm and then proceeded. "Lamb of God, through Your Spirit, open the eyes of Your servant, Joel. Open his mind and heart to Your Word and Your teachings. Show him the way he is to take. Give him the strength to do Your will. Anoint him with Your power. In the name of the Lamb, amen."

The angel removed his hand from Joel's arm and then kicked the swing into motion. Joel was caught by surprise and stared, amazed at the antics of the angel. He wasn't sure whether he should swing also or wait for the angel. The answer was evident as the angel slowed to a stop.

"Ah . . . even a small swing is somewhat exhilarating!" the angel commented. "Now, let's begin. Open the Word to Genesis." And with that, the angel began in earnest to show Joel sections of Scripture that would help him.

Joel was fascinated. He had never thought the Bible could be so alive and pertinent. He scribbled furiously as the angel pointed out verse after verse. Before he knew it, the angel had stopped.

"Go on," Joel urged. "I'm keeping up."

"We are done for tonight, Joel," the angel said.

Joel's face fell. "But this is so cool," he implored. "Can't we do more? I never realized how everything fits together in the Bible."

The angel smiled, "Your enthusiasm is admirable, but it is already darkening and you must rest. We will meet again tomorrow. Goodnight, Joel." The angel touched him briefly and then disappeared.

"Joel, it's time to come in," Joel heard his mom call.

His arm still tingling, Joel gathered his things and got up from the swing. Walking toward the house, he realized it *had* gotten dark out without him noticing. He opened the door to go in the house and glanced out at the swing. The angel was sitting on the swing again, the area bathed in a golden glow. He waved to Joel, who waved back. There was a longing in Joel's heart to stay out with the angel, but reluctantly he stepped into the house.

The next day went much the same way. Joel was able to avoid any major conversation with Kyle at school again. Kyle had an extra karate practice to go to, so that took care of the evening. Joel met the angel on the swings and drank in the Scripture that night. The angel reminded Joel about the Wednesday evening service at church and told him they wouldn't be meeting that night. When Joel expressed disappointment at not studying with the angel, the angel remarked that he was not the only teacher Joel would have. Others, such as Pastor George, his parents or friends, may be used of the Lord to teach Joel certain items. All Joel had to do was keep an open heart and let the Spirit lead him.

Wednesday at school, Joel could not avoid Kyle any longer. Kyle approached him as soon as he got off the bus.

"What a week so far! I've hardly had time to talk with you with extra karate and all . . . I've had trouble even getting my homework done! Man!" Kyle exclaimed.

Joel nodded to his friend and said, "I forgot that you get busy with karate this time of year. How's it going?"

Kyle grinned, "Well, I got that one move I was working on, and I'm sparring pretty good. You know how we run and do a flying kick over the pillows?"

Joel nodded his head in affirmation.

"I can go over six of them now!" he boasted.

"Wow!" Joel was genuinely impressed. Kyle maybe did some questionable moves, but he was truly good at karate. "When's the next match?"

"Oh, not for another week. Can you come? It's next Tuesday," Kyle informed Joel.

"Probably," Joel said, happy to be talking naturally with his friend.

"Whatcha doin' tonight?" Kyle asked as they walked to their lockers.

Joel hesitated, but then spoke nonchalantly, "I think I'll go to the Wednesday night service at church."

Kyle nodded, "I hear Pastor George is speaking again."

Joel looked surprised at Kyle and answered, "Yeah, how'd you know?"

"Oh, I heard my mom and dad talking to some church person on the phone last night, and they said that," Kyle responded. "He sure was interesting on Sunday morning. It'd be fun to see what he comes up with next, but I still have my English book report to do. With all these karate practices, I haven't gotten it done. Let me know how it is, OK? I gotta go. See ya later!"

With that, Kyle hurried away. Joel breathed a sigh of relief, grabbed his books, and headed to his first class. He wondered how long he would have to keep his secret!

When Joel got home from school, he quickly did his homework and then pulled out his Bible. He heard his parents get home from work and went out to help with supper.

"Um . . . could one of you take me over to church for the service tonight? I'm done with my homework and thought maybe I'd go . . . that is, if someone could take me?" he ended in a question.

Not missing a beat, Kathy Stevens answered, "Your dad and I already discussed it, and he can go with you. I have an urgent school board meeting to attend."

Noticing Joel's surprised look, Doug Stevens remarked, "Since I missed Sunday night, and your mom told me that it was such a great service, I don't want to be out of touch with what's going on . . . so I had decided to go tonight and see if you wanted to go with me."

Joel smiled broadly, "That'd be great, Dad! Wait 'til you hear Pastor George! He really has some neat stuff he's talking about now!"

Doug nodded and clapped his son on the back, "Well, let's get supper and make sure we're not late!"

The family proceeded to eat. The Being hovered just outside the window with a peaceful smile on his face. Suddenly, an almost imperceptible shadow moved over the back yard. The smile faded from the Being's face, and he quickly raised his arms as if he held the house in his hands. Closing his eyes, but lifting his face upward, he concentrated. Something like blue sparkles of electricity seemed to emanate from his fingers. It spread in a close-knit pattern over the house until a woven blanket of sparks covered the structure.

Inside, the lively conversation suddenly stopped. The Stevenses looked at one another with curiosity and slight alarm.

"What is that? I felt chilled for a split second, and then I felt warm," Kathy said.

Doug shook his head, "I don't know. I just felt weird, almost panicky. I wonder if a thunderstorm is nearby. They say lightening can travel for miles, and you don't even hear the thunder."

Joel remained quiet for a moment. He could see a faint blue light outside the window, and he had not only felt cold, but scared. He wished he could call out loud for the angel. A thought quickly occurred to him and he said, "You know that song we sometimes sing"—Joel started singing: "*Call upon me, come and pray to me and I will listen to you.*"

Kathy and Doug nodded and joined in.

"*Seek and find me, when you search for me with all of your heart.
And I will be found by you, declares the Lord.
And give you future and a hope, declares the Lord.*"

As they sang, the Being outside grew in stature. The blue sparks shone brightly, although no one but Joel could see. The shadow seemed to pause in the middle of the back yard and then moved off in a different direction. The Being waited until he was sure the shadow had gone, and then he pulled his arms and hands in as if gathering a sheet off of a clothesline. The sparks disappeared into his fingers, turning his fingertips the faintest shade of blue before the entire envelope around the house was gone.

Joel noticed the blue light vanish. The chill in his soul had left as quickly as it had come. The family finished singing the chorus.

Doug spoke first, "That sure was strange! I didn't think our singing could chase a storm away, but things seem OK now."

"What made you think of that song, Joel?" Kathy asked curiously.

Joel shrugged, "I don't know. It just came to me when I thought of times when I was little and a storm would come and you guys would remind me that God is only a prayer away."

Kathy laughed, "You're right! Remember that one time when the lights went out and you got really scared?"

Joel finished the story, "And we sang every Bible school or Sunday school song you could think of! I think we were all hoarse by the end of the storm!"

They all laughed and Doug added, "I think we did s'mores in the fireplace that night, too!"

The conversation again went light-hearted as the family finished their meal and cleaned up the dishes. Kathy headed out to her meeting and waved to Doug and Joel as they, too, drove away.

The Being stood sentinel for a time, his eyes scanning the skies. Once satisfied that the shadow truly was gone, he disappeared.

CHAPTER 9

Pastor George ate his supper while in deep thought. He liked to keep things organized, understanding that different people came to certain services. There was a core group who came to all services, but usually there was that large group Sunday morning; a smaller, slightly different group came Sunday night, taking in those who worked daylight shift; and finally a small, dedicated bunch came Wednesday evening. He tried to separate his sermons so that the same group got a particular series. Now he was confused. He had spent the first part of the week in prayer, trying to sense what the Lord wanted him to speak about Wednesday evening. It was an hour until the service and he still hadn't a clue what to talk about. A number of times he had found himself pondering the Joel passage again, but his years of discipline had shaken him from going there, attempting to find something new for the Wednesday parishioners. What was he going to do?

Fingering his Bible with his left hand while he ate, he shook his head in dismay at himself for letting things get this far. He knew better than to go to the church unprepared! His disgust had nearly ruined his appetite. Letting his eyes wonder over to his Bible while he silently rebuked himself, he once again saw the pages open to Joel.

"Why do I keep coming back to Joel?" he murmured. "I need something different for tonight," he complained. Then, he straightened up, almost as if something bit him in his lower back. Shaking his head, he stared at the Bible pages. "You've been trying to tell me for days, haven't you, Lord?" Sighing, he muttered, "It may be hard to teach old dogs new tricks, but . . ." He pushed his plate away and pulled his Bible toward him. "Joel, it is, Lord!"

Grabbing some paper, he leaned over the Bible and began to pour over the words. A smile spread across his face as he read a particular section. Nodding his head, he started scribbling notes. The minutes passed and soon he glanced at the clock. There was just enough time to get to the church now.

The church was filling up. More people were there than usual. Joel and Doug went to their typical pew, but some new people were sitting there. Undeterred, Joel proceeded forward and chose a closer seat on the side section. He noticed immediately that of the group on the platform, Pastor George was not to be seen. Joel's heart sank since he was looking forward to what Pastor George would preach about this night. The song leader began by asking everyone to stand for prayer.

As they stood, Doug leaned over to his son and asked, "Wasn't Pastor George to talk tonight, too?"

Joel nodded affirmatively and then bowed his head in prayer. Soon after the prayer they were singing some praise songs and a few hymns. None of the people in charge seemed concerned that Pastor George was not present. But as the congregation sat down in preparation for the rest of the service, Pastor George came in from a side door, and with a glance, dismissed the leaders on the platform. He walked straight to the pulpit. Joel noticed that he didn't have his cane at all and that he seemed to stand taller with an air of confidence.

"I know you have just sat down," Pastor George began, "But would you please stand for a word of prayer and the reading of the Word."

Everyone stood. Pastor George prayed for guidance and that the words of his mouth would be what the Lord desired His people to hear. With the amen, Pastor George spoke, "Let us open the Bible to the book of Joel."

Joel grinned and his heart raced. He turned to the book quickly, having placed a bookmark there. He looked expectantly at Pastor George, awaiting the directions of what verse was to be read. To his surprise, Pastor George was looking straight at him, his eyes slightly narrowed as if trying to make out something on Joel's forehead and tilting his head at the same time, like he was listening to something. Joel felt himself getting warmer, with little tingles everywhere.

With a barely discernible shake to his voice, Pastor George asked, "Would you mind, young man, reading Joel 3:12–16," nodding to Joel. "You may stay there, but speak loudly, so that all may hear."

Joel's hands immediately began to sweat, but he nodded to Pastor George and cleared his throat quietly before reading:

"*Joel 3:12–16: Let the nations be wakened, and come up to the Valley of Jehoshaphat; for there I will sit to judge all the surrounding nations. Put in the sickle, for the harvest is ripe. Come, go down; for the winepress is full, the vats overflow—for their wickedness is great. Multitudes, multitudes in the valley of decision! For the day of the Lord is near in the valley of decision. The sun and moon will grow dark, and the stars will diminish their brightness. The Lord also will roar from Zion, and utter His voice from Jerusalem; the heavens and earth will shake; but the Lord will be a shelter for His people, and the strength of the children of Israel.*"

Although Joel had stumbled a bit while trying to say *Jehoshaphat*, his voice was clear and projected well in the sanctuary. He breathed deeply when he was done and then looked up at Pastor George.

Pastor George was still staring strangely at Joel, but then he smiled warmly, saying, "Thank you, young man. May the Lord bless the reading of His Word. You may be seated."

Joel felt his dad place a hand on his shoulder as they sat down.

"Good job, son!" Doug whispered to Joel.

Joel turned to his dad and gave him a quick grin before they both settled down to listen to Pastor George.

Outside, once again, the Beings were stationed around the church building. Periodically, a glow emanating from them would intensify. People driving past thought the nighttime luminosities were inviting and attractive. Many believed that solar-powered lights had been installed!

Joel sat, fascinated with Pastor George's reflections on the verses describing the coming judgment for the wicked and how they appear to be given opportunity to choose for the Lord prior to that final judgment. Pastor George had them turn to Matthew 9, tying together the harvesting imagery in verses 37–38: *"Then He said to His disciples, 'The harvest truly is plentiful, but the laborers are few. Therefore pray the Lord of the harvest to send out laborers into His harvest.'"*

The last statement hit Joel. *"Pray the Lord of the harvest to send out laborers into His harvest."* Was that what the angel was training him for—to help harvest souls for the Lord? The enormity of that thought made Joel turn cold. Fear gripped his heart as it had never done before.

The angels surrounding the church sensed the change immediately. A shadow was growing inside the sanctuary! Twinkle-Eyes motioned for two other Beings, and they quickly entered the building. From the back they saw the demon. It had its bony fingers encircling Joel's chest and had a wicked grin on its face. Twinkle-Eyes went straight toward the demon, while another angel proceeded to an older lady sitting in the back. The third angel looked around intently and then saw what it was looking for.

Twinkle-Eyes grabbed the demon by the shoulders and tried to tear it away from Joel. The demon shrieked but held firmly to Joel. The figures were moving and wrestling, yet Joel could only feel the chill.

The other angel knelt in front of the old woman. It looked intently at her and gently placed its hands on her arms. She looked up from her Bible and seemed to stare right at the angel, and anyone watching her saw her paying attention to Pastor George. Then her eyes closed, and her lips moved in a silent prayer. The angel looked around and spied another individual listening closely to the Pastor. It quickly moved to that man and the same thing occurred—after a moment with the angel holding the man's arms, the man closed his eyes and prayed. This happened again and again, while Twinkle-Eyes and the demon continued the battle.

The third angel, meanwhile, moved stealthily toward the Stevens' normal pew. Four people occupied the seats. Two adults were listening to the pastor, and a child looked at a book. Sitting by the aisle, however, was a well-dressed woman, who at first glance appeared no different from any other person in the sanctuary. The angel, however, saw the shadow and darkness that seemed to diffuse out of her like steam from a simmering pot. Her face, in the past, had been beautiful to behold, with kind eyes and a ready smile. Now, she looked cold and indifferent, her attention more on a broken fingernail at one time and some lint on her slacks at another. Years ago, she would have enjoyed this service, but a broken relationship had made her bitter. She shut her heart against any attempt at love for fear she would be hurt again. Her sister had made her come tonight; at least that's how she perceived it, since she had run out of excuses. For months her sister had asked her to come along, and for months she had come up with one reason or another to get out of it. But she had no excuse for tonight, and now she was stuck here.

The angel moved toward her. It could see the demonic mist coming from her more and more. The shadowy mist moved in a stream toward the wrestling demon, like an attached umbilical cord.

Approaching her slowly, the third angel did not want to disturb the battle going on around Joel. This was the woman's vulnerable time, and the angel had mere moments to act. It placed its palms over her upper back, but did not touch her. It began to pray. By this time the second angel had enlisted a half dozen of the worshippers in prayer. A soft glow of light seemed to cushion the air between the angel's hands and the back of the woman. The shadowy mist dissipated below the angel's palms, increasing in size and allowing the hands to fall onto her back ever so lightly.

She felt it. A tiny glint of hope made her feel warm. She had not let anything get through the wall she had put up for many years. She had forgotten how wonderful hope was. Fear had pushed it away. Hope now seemed to spread through her body and break through her sadness. Looking over at her sister, she wondered if the others sensed what she did. A smile crept over her lips as she looked at her niece. The little girl was getting sleepy and had crawled into her father's lap. So innocent and pure . . . so full of wonder and happiness . . . safe with her daddy. The woman remembered that she used to go to her father and receive comfort and love. Maybe it was time to crawl into her Father's arms and let Him take care of her. Tears started to flow down her face. Her sister noticed and took her hand.

The angel watched the darkness leave the woman like a sheet being removed from some furniture put in storage. Underneath was something new and brilliant. As the shadow finally left her body, the demon realized, too late, that its possession was gone. It had no place to return to. It released its grip on Joel—that had been just something to play with since it had become bored with the woman's lack of struggle against its lies. The angel wrestling it was stronger now. The demon had experienced this before, and it knew it was defeated. With a lurch, it freed itself from the angel and hurled upward, through the roof of the sanctuary, dragging the chains that had bound the woman and sounding a loud screech of dismay before disappearing into the darkness.

Twinkle-Eyes immediately placed his hands on Joel's shoulders. The chill from the demon's touch had penetrated nearly to Joel's soul, and that would have been a wound difficult to heal. The other two angels hurried over to Twinkle-Eyes and joined him in placing their hands on Joel. Initially, they each noticed the chill of fear, but their prayers of hope warmed Joel. The prayers of the warriors in the sanctuary strengthened the angels and they glowed radiantly.

Joel had sat unmoving for ten minutes while the battle raged around him, unaware of the reason why he had nearly crumbled with fear. But now, he relaxed and was reminded of some of the verses Twinkle-Eyes had shared with him: *"Trust in the Lord with all your heart, and lean not on your own understanding. . . . My peace I give to you, not as the world gives do I give to you."*

Then another verse came to him: *"I hope in Your word."*

Hmm . . . Joel thought, *I don't exactly remember that last verse. It must be in the Bible somewhere, though. I wonder where that came from.*

The third angel smiled and looked over at Twinkle-Eyes. It shrugged its shoulders and whispered, "I couldn't help it!"

Joel felt encouraged again as he listened to Pastor George speak of the work that needed to be done before Christ returned. He remembered what he was thinking about earlier: *Pray the Lord of the harvest to send out laborers into His harvest.* Somehow he knew that he was part of the harvesting Christ had spoken of. He wasn't sure how he was to help, but he knew he would. Silently he prayed, *Lord, help me to do what You need me to do in harvesting souls for Your kingdom. Help me not to be afraid. Don't let me allow fear to get in the way. I really want to do this for You. Amen.*

Around him, Twinkle-Eyes and three other angels had gathered and placed their hands on him. The angels glowed and their radiance enveloped Joel, bathing him in a warm light, and penetrating into his body until he shone just like the angels surrounding him.

Suddenly, Joel saw them! They were beautiful and majestic. He felt as if he was part of them. He recognized Twinkle-Eyes immediately and then gazed into the faces of the other Beings, turning his head slowly from one side to the other.

"You have received a blessing from the Lamb That Was Slain for your obedience, Joel. Although fear may try to attack you, you are now protected by the Lord's own power—the power that raised Him from death! *Always remember this moment.* Although His power may not always seem to be there, the memory of this time will stir up the same power again, any time you need it!"

Joel heard Twinkle-Eyes' voice yet saw no movement of his mouth. The two other angels nodded in agreement and solemnly removed their hands from Joel. Twinkle-Eyes was last to let go of Joel's hands, and smiling, he and the others disappeared.

The warmth of the angels' touch stayed with Joel for a long time. Opening his hands, he noticed a shiny yellow stone. Wondering where it came from, he absentmindedly put it in his pocket. When he finally became aware of his surroundings again, Joel realized that Pastor George was finishing up with his sermon and announcing that they would go into some prayer time. Minutes passed by quickly as different prayer requests were named, and then Pastor George did a strange thing. He came down from the platform and knelt at the front altar, leaning forward and covering his face with his hands.

The congregation stared at the strange sight. The altar had been more of a decoration for the sanctuary. Most had never seen anyone kneeling at it, even though altar calls were done occasionally. Finally, one of the elders rose and followed Pastor George's example, kneeling at the altar. Soon, the people within the church emptied the pews and headed toward the altar. Doug and Joel found spaces and knelt down with the others. The altar was filled on both sides now. A few stragglers at the back came slowly forward and sheepishly got down on their knees.

Pastor George seemed to know when all were in place and spoke in a loud, but humble voice, thanking God for His blessings and for salvation. He then quietly uttered, "Lord, forgive me for wallowing in self-pity after Mabel died. I'm sorry for not trusting You. Help me to rely on You now. I ask that You use me however You would like to. I offer myself as Your servant. Lead me to do Your work in this church and my community. Thank you . . . for . . . making me . . . alive again!" His voice stuttered and died away into sobs.

The elder beside him place a hand on Pastor George's shoulder and continued the prayer, "Father, thank You for bringing Pastor George to us and renewing his commitment to You and this flock. We offer ourselves to Your service and pray that You will use us to send out laborers into the harvest!"

As he ended, a woman next to him started praying, remembering some of the prayer requests that had been named. When she was done, the woman next to her prayed for the leadership of the church, and it went on like this around the altar, each person praying for someone or thanking the Lord for something.

The prayers had gone halfway around the altar when they reached the family who had been sitting in the Stevens' usual pew. The little girl listened intently as her father, who was on her right, prayed first. Her mother then opened her mouth to pray, but was interrupted by a little voice.

"Dear Jesus, thank you for my mommy and daddy and for Auntie Gail who came with us tonight and for my puppy, Rufus, and my kitty, Paws. Thank you for sending angels to keep me safe when the lightening hit the telephone pole. Amen."

At the mention of angels, Joel jerked his head up, wondering if the little girl had seen Twinkle-Eyes, but then sighed when she finished her sentence.

Others were so moved by the girl's honest prayer that many faces showed tears. Her mother's voice cracked with emotion as she thanked God for her family.

The well-dressed Auntie Gail shook when it was her turn to pray, but without the demon possessing her, she no longer felt fear. She took a deep breath and spoke, "Lord . . ." she hesitated. "Lord, I've shut You out of my life for a long time, but I would like to ask You to forgive me. I've been terrible and mean for too long. Help me to let Your love fill me again. I choose to hope in You and to believe in Your promises. Thank you that my sister, her husband, and little Adele never stopped loving me and praying for me. Tonight, You have answered their prayers, because I want You back in my life." Her voice faltered as she hung her head and sobbed.

By now, tears were flowing from nearly every eye in the sanctuary.

Little Adele, oblivious to the emotions everyone was feeling, leaned over to touch her aunt, and whispered loudly, "Auntie Gail, it's OK. Just remember that God sends His angels to keep us safe!"

Gail smiled at her little niece through her tears and whispered back, "I'll remember that, honey!"

Joel watched the family as they hugged each other. His heart felt full of happiness for the spiritual rebirth of Auntie Gail. He thought he detected a glow around her, but he wasn't sure. Still wondering if little Adele had really seen angels, he was startled by the person next to him saying, "Amen." It was his turn to pray!

He bowed his head again and stuttered, "Dear God . . ." Joel stopped and took a big breath. He began again, "Lamb That Was Slain for us, thank you for saving us. Help us to listen to You and to become laborers for Your harvest. Amen."

Joel felt his dad grip his shoulder for a second before starting to pray. "Lord, thank you for answering prayers and showing us Your promises from years ago. Help us, as parents, like Abraham and Sarah or Hannah, to give our children back to You so that You can work many wonders through them. Amen," Doug finished.

Doug gave Joel a shoulder squeeze. Joel looked at his dad. There were tears in his eyes, and his lower lip quivered slightly. Doug gave a heavy sigh followed by a weak smile, then bowed his head again as others prayed. Before bowing his head, Joel's eyes caught those of Pastor George. He was staring at Joel curiously like he had earlier. Joel felt a warmth fill his insides as if Twinkle-Eyes was touching him. He smiled at Pastor George, who returned the smile, albeit with a strange look. Then they both bowed their heads while others prayed.

The prayer service did not take long. Many came over to Gail afterwards and welcomed her. Adele had her share of attention as well—her simple faith had encouraged quite a few! Others went to Pastor George and thanked him for his message. Doug and Joel lingered, talking to some friends about the exciting events.

As Joel turned to leave, someone caught his arm, and said, "May I speak with you, young man?"

Pastor George stood there, with a kind smile on his face.

Joel smiled back at the old man and said, "Sure."

The pastor held onto Joel's arm and guided him to a side of the sanctuary. "May I ask you a question? You are Joel, aren't you? The little tyke my Mabel used to watch?" he asked.

Joel nodded.

"I think you've noticed some different things happening in church. I believe that God has also spoken to *you* somehow, am I right?" Pastor George inquired.

Joel hesitated. He wasn't to tell anyone about the angel, so he just nodded his head again and offered, "Uh . . . I think so."

Pastor George peered at Joel. "I see something when I look at you, and it makes me feel like I do when the Spirit nudges me," he confided. "It's almost like . . ." then his voice trailed off. He stared at Joel once more, shaking his head slightly. "Oh, never mind—I'm just an old man." He paused, and then finished with, "If you need anything, young man, please know that I'm available, and regardless, I'm praying for you and whatever the Lord wants you to do." With that, he shook Joel's hand and turned to go.

Joel didn't know what to make of that conversation. His dad motioned for them to leave, so Joel made his way to the exit, still pondering what Pastor George had said. Sometimes it seemed like Pastor George actually knew what was going on, even though he didn't come right out and say it.

Pastor George turned back to watch Joel leave. He was sure there was a glow around that young man. He had dismissed it Sunday evening, but tonight he was sure of it. There was something special going on with Joel, and he knew it. "Patience," he told himself. "Patience . . . and prayer," he murmured, but in his heart he knew God was using Joel, and he was eager and curious to know how. "Patience, my heart," he vowed.

The glow around the church lasted long into the night, long after even the angels had dispersed to their various assignments. A shadow passed not far away and paused ever so briefly, noting the radiance associated with the church, wondering if it was worth reporting. In the end, it decided it really was nothing to worry about. That church had, in times past, been quite a battleground, but it had been a while since anything happening there had truly shaken the dark ranks of the spiritual world. The shadow needed more to substantiate a report. It dismissed the finding and went on.

The Being looked up, satisfied. The defenses were holding rather well. The prayers of the Believers that night had strengthened the spiritual hedge around the church such that the enemy would not even suspect the work that was going on there until it was well-established. The presence of the demon had surprised them all, but the deliverance of the woman had been glorious. The Lord has His purpose in it, and the Being did not question that. Even so, the necessary protections were *his* assignment, and he did not want to be surprised again. One more search around the church should do it, and then he would stand sentry until the morning.

CHAPTER 10

Joel and Twinkle-Eyes continued meeting after school and on weekends for a number of weeks. Kyle was busy training for a special karate tournament. He frequently lamented the fact that he and Joel weren't able to spend time together like they had previously, but he blamed it on the extra karate he was doing. Joel was glad he didn't have to explain anything to Kyle at this point. Kathy and Doug Stevens also seemed to be busier than usual, so they didn't notice Joel's daily appointments with the swing set in the back yard.

"Swing time," as Joel referred to it (to himself) became a highlight in each day. He and Twinkle-Eyes pored over Scriptures. Joel was a quick learner and good student. The years of Sunday school had paid off, for most things made sense to him now, and he saw how wonderfully the Bible fit together with each point Twinkle-Eyes showed him.

There had been no further visions of other angels, and Joel often asked if he'd get a chance to meet any additional angels. Twinkle-Eyes just smiled and told him to be patient. Pastor Art returned and did the Sunday morning services, but he was pleased when Pastor George asked to be involved again and do Sunday evenings and Wednesdays. Pastor Eric had been away since the Sunday morning the youth sang, but now he was back and fully engaged in the youth activities on Sunday evenings before the regular church service. Joel made a point to be at each service and meeting. Pastor Eric noticed his increased participation and took great joy in answering any questions Joel had regarding his faith.

One Sunday evening during youth group, Pastor Eric spoke about the second coming and how they not only needed to be ready, but they should be actively involved in telling others about the Lord. Joel was quick to answer some questions Pastor Eric brought up, and soon the two were engaged in a somewhat animated discussion. A number of the kids stared at Joel in amazement and wondered how he became so knowledgeable about such things. Dylan elbowed Kyle and nodded at Joel. Kyle ignored the nudge but eyed his best friend curiously.

"Hey Joel!" Kyle called after youth group was over and the kids were filing out of the room.

Joel had been finishing another discussion with Pastor Eric about some element of the second coming he didn't understand when he heard Kyle.

"I'll talk to you again, Joel," Pastor Eric said, understanding the need to end the conversation.

Nodding, Joel turned and headed over to Kyle at the door. "Hey, Kyle. That was cool to hear about the second coming, wasn't it?" Joel spoke excitedly, unable to hide his interest.

"Yeah, right . . . if you, like, believe in fairies and demons and angels," he said with some disdain. "What's happenin' to you lately? You're, like, some Jesus freak or something. Aren't you takin' this whole church thing a little far?"

Joel had forgotten that he and Kyle had barely spoken in weeks. The time with Twinkle-Eyes had changed Joel. He was not the follower he had always been before. Now he had a passion for the Word and the things of the Lord. He saw Kyle somewhat differently now and knew that their friendship was on the line unless he could somehow encourage Kyle without letting him know about the angels. Actually, he had been praying about how to talk to Kyle, and so he breathed a prayer for the Lord to help him speak to his best friend.

Smiling, he walked out of the youth group's room, and Kyle followed him. Joel stood up straight and said matter-of-factly, "I've made a commitment to the Lord, Kyle. I decided to follow Him with all my heart and to try to serve Him. I know I'm just a kid, but He can still use me. I'm trying to learn as much as I can from Pastor Eric and the other pastors."

Kyle stared at him in disbelief.

Joel continued, "You know I haven't been very good in sports or much of anything, really. I'm not very good at karate, like you are."

At this, Kyle nodded his head in understanding.

"So . . ." Kyle began, "You think this church thing may be where you fit in?"

"Yeah," Joel admitted.

The two friends were silent for a moment. Joel patiently let the news sink in.

Kyle thought for a second and then smiled and clapped Joel on the back. "Hey, that's OK! You gotta find what works, you know?"

Joel breathed a sigh of relief and grinned back at his best friend. He realized that he had missed the relationship with Kyle over the past weeks, and he was glad to feel like things were back on track with Kyle.

Kyle motioned toward the sanctuary and said, "We'd better hurry or we won't get our seats, OK?"

"Oh . . . yeah!" Joel remembered.

The two boys rushed down the hall laughing together and entered the sanctuary just before the music began. They squeezed into a crowded row with other teens from the youth group as the worship leader asked everyone to stand for prayer.

Twinkle-Eyes gazed at the youth surrounding Joel.

"He needs partners in his quest," he spoke quietly to another angel at his side.

"Yes. He needs companions other than you," the other angel agreed. "The others are being prepared for service and will soon be ready to join him." Pausing, the angel then asked, "What of his friend, Kyle?"

Twinkle-Eyes sighed heavily. "I don't know. There is darkness in him that is hidden from most of those around him, but I believe Joel has seen it. It would be good for the prayer warriors to pray for Joel's protection from any dark influence Kyle may have on him."

The other angel nodded knowingly. "I will make them aware. Their prayers of late have given much strength to all of us. They will continue to be faithful to this task."

Turning to his friend, Twinkle-Eyes smiled, "You also have been faithful to the task, Kaph. Thank you."

Kaph blushed, if that is possible with angels.

They both looked back to Joel, who was obviously enjoying the service and appreciating the closeness of his friends, which had been lacking over the past weeks.

Kaph suddenly seemed overcome with emotion and actually leaned against Twinkle-Eyes for support.

Twinkle-Eyes quickly supported the angel and, with concern, asked, "What's wrong, Kaph? Do you sense darkness near?"

Shaking her head, she straightened up with his help. "No . . . it's just that Joel . . ." She paused, looking intently at the teen.

"What? Is he OK? What do you see? What do you hear?" Twinkle-Eyes asked calmly, yet with urgency.

Kaph smiled at Twinkle-Eyes and said, "He is praying . . ."

Twinkle-Eyes looked curiously at her and encouraged her to continue, "Yes?"

She went on, "He is praying . . . and thanking God for his friends, especially Kyle."

Twinkle-Eyes nodded, "Thanks is powerful, isn't it?"

Kaph smiled broadly and answered, "Oh, yes, it is!"

"Perhaps you need to go rest now, Kaph," Twinkle-Eyes admonished her.

"Yes. That is a good idea," she replied. "But it really does help me, little by little, to feel stronger."

Twinkle-Eyes tilted his head with acknowledgement and watched his friend leave the church.

Jill peered out her bedroom window at the rising sun. She loved being up early! She pulled her Bible off her nightstand and opened it again to Matthew 21:22. *"And whatever things you ask in prayer, believing, you will receive."*

Turning then to a page marked in the back of her Bible, she looked for the next reference to prayer in the concordance. Although she lately started her devotions with the verse in Matthew, she was gradually going through all the verses in the Bible which used any part of the word, *pray.* She spent some time reading the verse and the comment on it in her study Bible. Finally, Jill knelt at the side of her bed and prayed. She started praying for her family, then her friends, then her pastor and others in ministry, and finally for herself. Interspersed in the prayer were sentences of thanks and praise. Jill tried to apply what she was learning in her study about prayer as she prayed. She humbly asked God to guide her and show her His will for her life. Just as she was finishing, she heard her father calling for her to get ready for school. She smiled as she quietly said, "Amen," and then answered her father with an, "OK, Dad!"

Jill made her bed and quickly dressed. She stood by the window and opened the drapes completely, letting the light of the sun stream into her room. As she turned around, sparkles seemed to hover opposite the window, where the sunbeams landed on her wall. She closed her eyes and then opened them again, thinking she had gotten a sun flash from the rays. But, no—the sparkles continued and even seemed to grow!

Now, she was scared. She had been seeing the sparkles more and more recently. A show on TV that she had happened to see had talked about someone seeing weird things, and they ended up with a brain tumor! Her heart raced as she rubbed her eyes, willing the sparkles to go away. She opened her eyes again and stared at the aura before her. It was taking the shape of something—something awesome and grand! Chills ran up and down her spine, but were quickly replaced by a gentle warmth as she watched a figure appear with a kind face and beautiful, majestic wings.

"Hello, Jill," a voice spoke.

It was a light, clear voice, reminding Jill of a rippling brook.

Jill stared in awe for a moment, not able to say a word and trembling at the sight of the Being in front of her.

"Peace and love to you from your Father in heaven," Jill heard the voice say. It seemed to smile and then continued, "Your prayers have been answered. The Father will certainly guide you in His will. He is so pleased with your devotion to Him that He wants to use you now!"

The Being stretched its robed arms toward Jill in a graceful movement. Jill stood, cemented in place as the Being touched her. Static-like tingles coursed through her body, forcing her to jump back.

"Wow!" she murmured softly, as she sat down on her bed, still feeling the energy the Being had transferred to her. "What are you?" she asked quietly.

"I am what you are thinking I am—an angel of the almighty God. He has seen your obedience," it spoke reverently. "Are you surprised, Jill?"

Jill thought for a moment and then responded, "No, I think God has been preparing me to do something for Him." She breathed heavily and tentatively said, "This isn't the first time I saw an angel, is it? The sparkles . . . are they . . .?"

"Yes. You were not quite ready to fully see us, but it is time now," the angel said. "Look for us—now you are ready!" And with that, the angel disappeared through the bedroom wall.

Jill gasped and then looked down at her arms where the angel had touched her. Her skin seemed to glow. The warmth of the energy lingered as Jill pondered the visitation. She felt something in her hand; turning her hand palm up and extending her fingers, she gazed at a brilliant, smooth blue stone. Her thoughts were interrupted by a knock on her door.

"Hey, Jillie-Bear," her father called, using a pet name he had given her when she was a baby. "Are you ready? The bus will be here in ten minutes."

Jill blinked a few times, put the stone in her pocket, and looked up to where the angel had disappeared. Watching some sparkles that remained, she paused and then replied, "Uh, yeah, Dad. I'm coming." She grabbed her backpack and opened the door.

Her dad was standing there, waiting for her.

"Well, don't you look nice," he exclaimed. "You have a rosy glow about you!" he added, as he swept her into a bear hug.

Jill hugged her dad and clung to him a little longer than usual. "Thanks, Dad!" she sighed, happy and calm.

They walked arm in arm to the kitchen and sat down to a quick breakfast. Bowing their heads, her dad led them in a quick prayer, and then they ate. Before leaving the table, he picked up a Bible and read a verse along with a devotional reading.

Jill hugged her dad again and then ran out the door to catch the bus to school. She smiled as she recalled the Bible verse her dad had read.

Acts 10:30–31: *"So Cornelius said, 'Four days ago I was fasting until this hour; and at the ninth hour I prayed in my house, and behold, a man stood before me in bright clothing, and said, 'Cornelius, your prayer has been heard, and your alms are remembered in the sight of God.'"*

Jill didn't remember what the devotional was about, but she marveled that God would reaffirm what she had seen by providing the verses her dad had read. She was excited that her commitment to prayer had been rewarded with the visit from an angel. She also wondered what was meant by the angel saying she was ready now.

Ready for what? she thought.

Across town, a young lady stepped off her bus and walked into the Catholic school. The school was one of only a few left that actually had many nuns as teachers. Many of the graduates ended up taking vows and serving God in the Catholic Church. The priest who was the school administrator was devout and sincere. Father John loved his work, ably communicating to the students the incredible holiness of God along with the greatness of His love. His biblical studies had shown him that God would soon be gathering more followers before the end of the world. He hoped that God would be able to use him and the students he worked tirelessly to prepare for God's service.

Father John watched the students disembark the buses from his office window. Seeing the student he was waiting for, he turned and made his way to the school entry hall, nodding to the greetings each student offered.

"Hello, Elizabeth," he said, after making eye contact and motioning for one to come to his side.

"Hi, Father John!" Liz Morris exclaimed. Her eyes twinkled and her face broke into a huge, engaging smile. Her pale green eyes were in contrast to her jet-black hair, which hung straight to the middle of her back. Her face held a hint of some different ancestry, perhaps Asian or even American Indian. She was a beautiful girl.

"Are you ready for today's Advanced Biblical Studies debate? I have it on good authority that Our Lady's team has prepared *extra* hard for this match," he spoke with a bit of feigned irritation.

Liz raised her eyebrows in response to the challenge. "I do believe we have an edge over the Banners," she said confidently.

"Oh?" Father John inquired with some real interest. "What could that be?"

"Father John, don't you know that our world-renown instructor has taken special pains to make sure we are not only extremely well-prepared, but also the favorite of the head judge. Our instructor has been down this road himself and has taught us all the memory tricks he himself used to become the American champion a few years back," Liz said with pomp.

Father John responded with mock indignation, "This so-called favoritism is not acceptable at St. Luke's Catholic Academy, I'll have you know. Who is this instructor, how has he manipulated such things, and how could the head judge be so compromised?"

Liz did not hesitate one second in her reply, "Our instructor, I admit, has some questionable relationships, but . . ."

"Questionable relationships?" Father John exclaimed.

Liz continued with a mischievous grin. "But," she persisted, "he is *in* pretty good with the head honcho upstairs, so I'm not worried about the favoritism, since that's the very kind of personal relationship he wants us to have with, you know," she paused and pointed up, "the Big Guy!"

Liz and Father John both laughed out loud at their little inside jokes. Other students passing by looked with admiration at the pair. Everyone wanted to be friends with Father John. He fostered an image of a respected mentor amongst the students. No one ever felt that they were alone in the school. Father John had an uncanny way of knowing when a student needed someone to listen to them, a limit set, or fatherly advice. It was not unusual to see him with a student, sitting on one of the many benches placed throughout the school, praying with one hand on the student's shoulder and the other hand raised in supplication to His heavenly Father.

Father John smiled at Liz as she hurried off to her first class. He thought to himself, *She is special to You, too, isn't she Lord? Why do I sense that something fantastic, yet difficult, is in her future soon? Please be with her, Lord!*

The priest walked back to his office to prepare for morning mass. He sat down at his simple desk and gazed at the Holy Scriptures laid out before him. *Why these verses, Lord?* he wondered. He knew from years of subjection to God that the leading of the Spirit should not be ignored, so he pressed on with finishing his notes. Before long, his assistant knocked at the open door and cleared her voice, gently reminding him of the time for the mass.

The auditorium was filling with the student body, and soon the litany had progressed to the time for Father John's homily. He motioned for everyone to stand for the reading of the Holy Scriptures.

"*Joel 2:28–29: And it shall come to pass afterward that I will pour out My Spirit on all flesh; Your sons and your daughters shall prophesy, Your old men shall dream dreams, Your young men shall see visions. And also on My menservants and on My maidservants I will pour out My Spirit in those days.*"

Father John raised his head and nodded, signaling the students to sit down.

"You are the generation who will see this prophesy come to pass, and many of you will participate in the great outpouring of God's Spirit in the last days," he began. "I have worked to prepare many of you for this incredible mission, and it seems that soon our Lord will begin to show a number of you what you are to do in the harvesting of souls for the kingdom of God."

The humble priest of God explained to the captivated students what the verses in Joel meant. He ended the brief sermon with an encouragement: "Search your heart for how God may want to use you. Your instructors and I are available for any counsel if God shows you a particular gift is to be used for His service."

Father John stepped away from the podium and allowed the mass to finish as usual. But, instead of the students filing away to their classes, he noticed that most of them were engaged in lively discussions with their teachers, and many seemed to be coming toward him with earnestness.

"Father John, Father John!" a few called out, "Can we talk to you?"

"Of course, my children," he said calmly. "What is this about?"

The students looked at each other, some visibly hesitant to speak.

One young man finally spoke up, "It's just that we all feel called to do something for God, just like you talked about."

Father John stared at the young people in front of him and then looked out at the auditorium filled with students who had not gone back to class. A great chill seemed to start at the back of his neck, and his heart began pounding. For the first time in a long time, he was speechless. He reached for the arm of a chair nearby. Some students grabbed his arms and helped him to sit down.

He trembled and prayed, *Lord, what am I to do? Please help me!*

A warm sensation began in his shoulders as a calming peace spread through his spirit. He looked up at the students around him and stood up.

"God answered my prayers that He would use you," he began. "But, I didn't really believe that He'd do it," he confessed. "Please forgive me," he entreated them, hugging the students standing next to him. Looking out at the full auditorium, he shouted, "Everyone, everyone—please take your seats again!"

The teachers hustled the students back to their seats and soon all was quiet. Father John stood in the front with his head bowed. Finally, he raised his head and stretched his arms out as he often did for a blessing.

"*Great is the Lord!*" he began.

"*And greatly to be praised!*" the auditorium thundered as the students and teachers shouted.

Father John heaved a great sigh and then spoke, "Since I came to St. Luke's, many years ago, I have prayed for God to use those whose lives He allows me to touch here. And, even in a greater call, for God to use those lives to accomplish the grand harvesting of souls before the final battle when Satan is cast down forever. I have prayed for this until my energy is spent and my voice gone. Yet, when God showed that He heard my prayer and is answering it, I did not expect or believe it. Forgive me, please . . . all of you . . . for my lack of faith. But God has strengthened me now, and He *will* complete this endeavor in you!" He paused, gazing out past the seats to the back aisle.

Most assumed he was gathering his thoughts, but in truth he was staring at a figure in the back. For a few moments he allowed his gaze to linger, and then directed his comments again to the student body.

"If God, indeed, desires all of us to seek Him regarding our parts in His harvest, then we would do well to listen. In light of this, I ask all of you to return to your homerooms. There, your teachers and instructors will lead you in prayer and begin to search for what the Lord of the harvest would have each of you do." Father John dismissed them with, "God be with you!"

"And also with you!" the teachers and students responded.

Many jumped up with excitement, eager to get to class and discuss the strange mass. Others were more pensive, pondering what their part could be in this great event Father John spoke of. The auditorium cleared quickly, and the sounds echoing in the halls soon died down.

Father John spoke quietly to his assistant, "Please notify all teachers that I would like a moment of their time after students leave today."

She nodded her head and then hurried off to carry out her duties.

Father John looked out across the empty auditorium, praising God for this unexpected blessing. He also hoped to see the figure again, but doubted if the vision would persist. Alas, the back aisle was void of any sign of body or spirit.

"I saw it."

Father John spun around to find Liz standing at the side. She was pale, and her eyes showed her fright.

She now fumbled for words. "I . . . saw it in the back, too." She swallowed hard and asked, "What was it?"

The priest walked over to her and guided her to a chair. He gently helped her to sit, and then he pulled another chair close to sit beside her.

He breathed heavily and then said, "It was an angel, I believe."

She nodded, "That's what I thought."

"Once before, I think I saw it. It was very long ago when I was on a youth retreat with my church. I was trying to decide if I should pursue the priesthood. How I struggled with that decision . . . until one night. I went out into the woods, to a quiet spot I had found, and I prayed. I prayed for hours . . ." Father John's voice trailed off as he recalled the sacred moment.

Liz prompted him, "Then what happened?"

Father John continued, "I had been crying my eyes out. But it was like . . . like Jacob's struggle with the angel. I wasn't going to stop until I had my answer. And then I felt it." He stopped, as if Liz knew exactly what he meant.

"Felt what?" she pressed.

"The warmth . . . the peace" he sighed, "and finally, the answer." He faced her, and looked deep into her eyes. "I knew that I was to become a priest. There was no longer any doubt. The feelings were so tangible that I remember grabbing my arms to see if someone had put a blanket over me. When I looked around me, I saw it then. It was a lot closer. I could see its face. It was so kind and peaceful; I knew it had been there to help me. Before I could ask it anything, it moved off and was gone. I didn't know what I had seen. Was it real? Was it a vision? Was it a dream? I didn't know. I thought about it all the time. As I went through the monastery and took my vows, I often asked the older, wiser priests if they had ever seen an angel."

"Had they?" Liz asked.

Father John sighed, "No. And many of them would not even entertain the possibility. But I never lost hope." He reached inside his robes and then withdrew his closed hand. "This always reminded me that God meant for me to believe." He opened his hand. A brilliant blue stone lay in his palm.

Liz looked at the priest with questioning eyes, yet said nothing.

Father John placed the smooth stone in her hand.

She wasn't prepared for the little shock the stone seemed to give her. "Wha . . .?" she exclaimed.

Father John nodded and agreed, "I know. It's strange. I found it in my hand after the angel left back then. I know it wasn't there beforehand. I've gotten used to the energy, but it always is there. I carry it with me all the time. Not everyone can sense its energy, though. I've tested it with many 'religious' people, and quite a few of them see nothing unusual about it, even the incredible color. To me, it is quite vibrant. But to others, it just looks dull. But you . . ." he pointed at her and then took the stone from her hand, "I was pretty sure that you'd be able to feel it, especially after you saw the figure in the back. I was surprised when I felt it again, but the warmth was there, just when I had asked God for help . . . after all you students felt led to be involved . . . I looked in the back, and there it was."

Liz swallowed hard before speaking. "I saw it before that, Father John."

Father John couldn't believe his ears! "What? Where?" he gasped.

"It was standing behind you when you sat down before, you know . . . when all the kids were coming to ask you what they should do . . . and you got really pale and had to sit down? It was there. I saw it put its hands on your shoulders, and you got some color and got up to talk to us again."

Father John nodded. "So that *is* why I felt the warmth. I wondered about that. It was just like what happened years ago at the youth retreat." He then asked, "What did it do then? Did you see anything else?"

Liz nodded, "Yeah, uh, it went to a couple of kids and touched them." She stopped and thought, "Oh . . . and it went to a few of the nuns and teachers, too, before it went to the back." She looked down at her feet, and then added, "And it looked at me, too." She gazed up at Father John. "I sort of freaked out! It seemed like no one else could see it but me! That is, until I saw you looking at it—that made me feel better, you know . . . like I wasn't going crazy."

"It is something grand to behold!" Father John acknowledged.

Liz continued, "Then when you started talking again, it came over to me."

"What!" Father John exclaimed, his eyes opening wide.

Nodding, Liz added, "It talked to me, too."

"What? What did it say?" Father John urged.

"It told me that my work will be different than what is happening at St. Luke's," she confessed.

Father John leaned back, surprised by this, "Really? Did it tell you what you are to do?"

"Yes," she affirmed. "It told me that I am to work with Joel and use the gift of prophecy to further the kingdom."

"Who is Joel? A boy in Sister Kim's room?" he asked.

"No. It is someone I haven't met yet, but will soon. There are others like me, too, and we all are being prepared for a big thing," she finished.

"Hmm . . ." Father John pondered. "I had hoped that you would be a leader here in this revival of sorts, but you must do what God has set before you."

Liz gulped, but nodded, dropping her head.

Father John thought she was upset and reached toward her to touch her arm and pray, but stopped when he saw her withdraw her hand from her pocket.

As she opened her hand, he saw a brilliant green polished stone.

CHAPTER 11

Jill expected to see angels everywhere as she traveled to school in the bus. She looked up at the blue sky—nothing. She peered intently at the homes and trees on the bus route—nothing. The trip to school was disappointing—no angels seen. The bus stopped at school, and Jill grabbed her backpack. She stood, waiting for an opportunity to move into the aisle and get off the bus. A girl in the aisle from the next seat back paused long enough for Jill to quickly insert herself into the stream of kids shoving to exit the bus. Jill barely acknowledged her, moved ahead, and skipped down the steps to the sidewalk.

"Everyone sure is in a hurry today, aren't they? You'd think they all love school!" a girl's voice said as Jill headed toward the main school door.

Jill turned around to face the other student, and her mouth dropped open.

"It's you!" Jill exclaimed excitedly, recognizing the face of the angel in a teenage girl's body with sparkles emanating from her face and hands, like being illuminated from somewhere behind her.

"Hi, Jill!" the angel said with a lovely smile.

Jill could hardly contain herself. "Were you on the bus with me the whole time?"

"Yes," answered the angel-girl. "You seemed to be preoccupied by the things *outside* the bus—I didn't want to interrupt you."

Jill giggled, "I thought angels flew around in the sky or something; I didn't think you'd be on the bus with me!" She looked around at the students detouring around them. "Can everyone see you now?" she asked.

"Yes, they see me, too, but not quite as you do," the angel-girl replied.

Nodding, Jill offered, "They can't see your sparkles, right?"

The angel-girl laughed, holding up her hand before her in examination. "Sparkles? Is that what you call it? Hmm . . . I suppose that is a reasonable way to describe the Father's power in me." She looked back at Jill, and continued, "No, the others cannot see the sparkles. That is *your* gift!"

The two started walking together into the school.

"So . . ." Jill began, "are you going to hang out with me in school, or what . . . um . . . do the teachers think you're a new student?"

Angel-girl shook her head, "No. I merely wanted to encourage you, help you to believe that we are real, and show you that God has a plan for your life. His Spirit is within you, Jill." The angel leaned in slightly and said, "Look for us later. You will know what to do."

With that, the angel-girl smiled and moved off into the crowd of teens jamming the hall. In seconds, Jill could no longer see her.

A collision with someone behind her woke her from her reverie.

"Oh . . . hey, Jill. Sorry," a boy said.

Jill looked around and grinned at the guy, "That's OK! I stopped in the middle of this mess—a good way to get run down! See you later in English Lit!"

The boy nodded and smiled, then maneuvered his way through the crowd.

As he moved away, Jill gasped. She was fairly sure she could make out a figure made of faint sparkles that was in step behind the boy. Another jolt from someone running into her startled her into stepping aside, and with that she lost the sparkle figure from view.

She went straight away to her locker and grabbed her books for the next few classes, but all the while she was thinking, *Was that another angel?*

Jill would admit that she didn't really pay attention in her classes. Luckily, she was a good student and most subjects had reviews for midterms, so she allowed herself a little daydreaming until it was time to head to English Lit. Jill made sure she was the first one in the room. The other students filed in, chatting about this or that. Then she saw the boy from earlier come into class. Jill was disappointed to see that there were no sparkles following him.

I must have been wrong about there being an angel following him, she thought. *The excitement of meeting an angel this morning had me seeing sparkles everywhere, maybe?* she reasoned. *But the angel-girl told me to watch for them,* Jill's spirit countered.

The teacher began the lesson, and soon the class was discussing a new short story they had read the previous night in their homework. The piece was definitely secular, and Jill had been offended by some of the blatant attacks on Christianity in the story. She had even responded to one of the homework questions with that opinion and had pointed out that the story would not have been allowed if the same story line had been against Islam because of the public school's stance on tolerance.

But it's allowed if it's against Christianity, thought Jill with frustration.

Apparently, another in the class was thinking the same, because almost instantly Jill heard that comment from a classmate in response to the discussion.

"Don't you think it should be just as wrong to speak against Christianity as it is now to speak against other religions?" asked the student.

Jill looked to see who had asked the question. Her heart started to race and her eyes opened wide.

Standing behind the student was an angel! Its hands were placed on the student's shoulders, and it had a concentrated look on its face. This angel had different features than the angel-girl Jill had spoken to. The sparkles were definitely there. Jill remembered that the other angel had referred to it as the Father's power. She stared at the angel, mesmerized by its splendor. In a moment, she found herself gazing into its eyes. It was looking at her!

Instantly, Jill knew somehow that it wanted her to pray. She blinked a few times, wondering if the angel had telepathically told her this, or if something else had done it. She looked at the boy the angel was touching. It was Joel, the one who had run into her that morning who she thought had the sparkles trailing behind him!

Jill looked back to the angel and gave an almost imperceptible nod. She then stared at Joel and prayed for him: prayed that he would have the courage to continue speaking up for Christ; prayed that he would have the right words to say; prayed that God would help him. It took only a few seconds to pray these things. Jill glanced at the angel again. Once more it was concentrating. Jill thought its glow seemed brighter, and it appeared to emanate a color, but she wasn't sure. She noticed the glow spread into Joel like the sun coming out from behind a cloud and illuminating a room. The classroom discussion was still going on, she knew, but she couldn't seem to break her attention from the angel and Joel. It felt like her eyes were glued to the angel for hours, but it actually was only minutes.

The angel gazed at her again, briefly, then walked away through the classroom wall and was gone.

Jill realized that her classmates were buzzing with talk all around her. One leaned over and commented, "Joel really hit her with good questions, didn't he?"

She merely nodded in agreement, wishing she had heard what he had said, yet knew that her connection with the angel had been well worth it. She also knew that she had to talk with Joel soon!

The teacher finally succeeded in calming the class down and said, "Well, Joel, you certainly have brought up some very fine points. You're right—if the school is teaching tolerance, then this material should be as wrong to embrace as something that embellishes slavery. You may be able to bring about some change if you," and she paused, looking at the class, then continued, "and your classmates can submit a well-thought-out comment to the principal." She raised her eyebrows at them as the bell rang. "Great discussion, class! You are dismissed!"

The class erupted in mayhem as many worked their way over to Joel and clapped him on the back. Jill watched in amazement. She had never thought of Joel as a religious rebel, but her classmates were certainly impressed, maybe because he was able to bring their teacher to a point of compromise or even surrender. Jill wasn't sure since she hadn't heard the discussion. She gathered her things and headed for the door, only to come face to face with Joel!

"Hey, Jill! Did you recover from me bowling you over this morning?" Joel asked innocently, walking away from his new fan club.

"Oh . . . yeah . . . uh . . ." Jill responded, stuttering as she often did when needing to talk to others. She had never really gotten over her shyness from when she was a little girl. The same fear seemed to grip her, making it impossible for her to say anything to Joel.

Then, suddenly, she saw the angel! It wasn't the angel-girl—rather, it was the one who had stood behind Joel, but this time it appeared like a teenage boy, fitting in with the students on either side. It was leaning up against the wall opposite the door leaving the classroom. It smiled at Jill and then motioned for her to come over.

Jill gulped, not knowing what to do, when Joel spoke up, "Uh . . . I need to catch up with someone, so . . . see ya later!"

Joel moved off, bracing himself as he crossed perpendicular to the wave of people weaving up and down the hall.

Jill mentally corrected herself for thinking the angel had motioned to her; she dropped her head and moved into the stream of student traffic when she heard her name.

"Jill, Jill—over here!"

The teenage boy-angel caught her eye and again motioned for her. Jill nodded and then noticed that Joel looked surprised, not at the angel next to him, but at the angel calling for Jill, and Jill acknowledging it.

The angel waited until Jill wove through the throng and reached the other side.

"Hello, Jill," the mellow voice of the angel said. "Thank you for listening to the Spirit and praying for Joel during class. I know you are new to this, but I am glad that you were ready."

Joel was still staring at Jill, but broke the stare to look at the angel. "What do you mean, 'during class?'" he asked.

Jill spoke now, feeling confident in the angel's presence, "He was in there," she motioned toward the classroom with her head, "helping you stand for Christ."

Joel's eyes went wide. "I didn't see him . . ." he mumbled and then directed his questions to the angel, "Were you there? . . .Where were you?"

"She's right. I was behind you, with my hands on your shoulders, giving you the Father's power to speak wisely and truthfully. She obeyed the Spirit and prayed for you when she saw me," the angel finished.

"I didn't see you or feel you," Joel said with a sigh. He had enjoyed the positive attention the teacher and classmates had given him, but now he realized that he had been bold because of the angel's help, not on his own. "It wasn't really me, then, was it?" he asked, somewhat rhetorically.

Jill sensed the struggle Joel was experiencing and offered, "But you were willing to be used—it wouldn't have happened if you weren't willing. The Father's power went right into you and helped you say what God wanted to be said."

Joel pondered her words and then smiled. "Thanks," he said.

The angel spoke, "It is time for you both to get to class. Jill, will you make arrangements with your father to bring you to Joel's house this evening to, uh," he paused, and then proceeded to say, "study?"

Smiling, Jill replied, "Sure! I know my dad won't mind." She wrote something on a piece of paper sticking out from a book and then tore it off. "Here's my phone number. Call me when you get home, OK, Joel?" And with that, she winked at the angel, noticing its twinkling eyes, and hurried off. A few steps away she thought to herself, *And I talked to them without stuttering! Yes!* She shook her head in an affirmative motion as she fisted her hand in triumph.

Joel turned to the angel before he headed the opposite direction, and said, "I'm a little confused . . . So there are others?"

"Oh, yes, Joel," Twinkle-Eyes replied. "You are not expected to do this alone. You need more than my help. You need the help of other Christians. They are being prepared to use their gifts and talents to serve the Lord, just like you are." He paused, seeing that Joel wanted to hear more. "Not now, though, Joel. You need to get to class. I will talk to you and Jill this evening, OK?" With that the angel faded into the lockers.

Joel raced to his next class, squeezing in through the door as the teacher was closing it.

"Running a little late, Mr. Stevens?" the teacher said, raising his eyebrows.

"Ah . . . yeah . . . sorry" Joel stammered with a lilt, hoping to avoid a problem.

"I do not tolerate tardiness in this class," the teacher paused and then continued, "but since this is your first time, I will overlook it. Do not let it happen again!"

Joel responded, "Thank you. . . . I won't!" He quickly found his desk, sat down, and breathed a sigh a relief.

The rest of the school day was so busy that Joel had no time to think about what Twinkle-Eyes had said until he got on the bus at the end of the day. He had just settled in to his seat and was starting to ponder the fact that there were other Christians that God was going to use, when someone plopped down in the seat with him. Joel turned, expecting to see Twinkle-Eyes as he had before, but someone else had sat down.

Chris Anders clapped Joel on the back and exclaimed, "Wow, Joel. That was some discussion you threw out in English Lit! I was thinking the same thing, but I didn't have the nerve to speak up. Miss C said we could write a letter to the principal to stop the Christianity bashing . . . and I was thinking that maybe you and I could come up with something. . . . What do you think?"

Joel was taken aback by Chris' offer and was surprised the popular guy had even agreed with him. Chris was one of the school's male cheerleaders, and, although he was not one of Joel's best friends, the two had conversed occasionally. Joel respected

Chris because he never said anything bad about anybody, was rather agreeable, and always seemed to be smiling.

"Ah . . . yeah . . . sure . . ." Joel stuttered.

"You know," Chris continued, "my pastor has been talking about how Christians are being persecuted now, and we've let this tolerance thing go against us. It's time to turn it back onto the people who started it."

Joel nodded in agreement, "God can turn even the devil's schemes into something He uses for good."

"Right! That's what I'm talking about!" Chris exclaimed. "So, how about you and me getting together this evening and coming up with a letter to send to the principal?"

Joel quickly recalled the angel's plan for Jill to come over.

"I'm studying with Jill tonight, maybe . . ." Joel was cut off by Chris.

"Great! The three of us working together can come up with a good letter for sure!" Chris enthused. "I'll be over at seven! Here's my stop—see you tonight!"

Before Joel could say anything more, Chris had hopped up and hurried off the bus.

Now what do I do? Joel thought with a sigh. He looked around the bus, hoping Twinkle-Eyes would appear, but only the regular riders were seated throughout the bus. A Bible verse popped into his head: *"Trust in the Lord with all your heart, and lean not on your own understanding; in all your ways acknowledge Him, and He shall direct your paths."* Joel felt a wave of peace flow over him, and somehow he knew that this would be OK. He got off the bus and thoughtfully made his way inside his home.

Joel had been used to weeks of time spent alone with the angel. He had grown accustomed to the private lessons, and now he began to realize that others would be part of his secret. In times past, he would have been upset, but he had learned more than one lesson about being a servant of God in his study time with Twinkle-Eyes. He was just one part of the body of Christ. He had known, deep inside, that the day would come when others would share in the tasks ahead—it was not all about him. It was about Jesus, plain and simple. Anything that he was a part of was about bringing glory to God through obeying the Lamb, as the angels called Jesus.

Absentmindedly, Joel went to his bedroom. He pulled out his notes from swing time, and leafed through the pages until he found one in particular. THE BODY OF CHRIST was written in the top margin. He read over the notes and smiled. He felt better. It was clear to him that Twinkle-Eyes had prepared him for this day, and he was ready! He pulled out Jill's phone number from his pocket and headed out to the phone.

"Hello . . . is Jill there? Oh, hi. Uh . . . this is Joel. Would seven be OK for you to come over? . . . Good." Joel then gave her directions to his house. He kept it short, not knowing exactly what he was to tell her about the angels and figuring that Twinkle-Eyes would have that covered.

Joel nonchalantly told his parents that two classmates were coming over at seven that night to study. Kathy and Doug showed no surprise at the plan and simply remarked, "Sure."

Chris arrived first. He only lived a few blocks away and knew where Joel lived from the bus pick up in the mornings. Joel was introducing his parents to Chris when Jill arrived.

"I think we'll head outside to study, OK guys?" Joel stated more as direction than really asking them. He grabbed his swing time notebooks that he had ready on the kitchen table and then led them out the back door. The swing set was silent and still. Joel quickly decided to sit at the picnic table on the patio. He looked at his classmates with anticipation, yet hesitating to speak. Jill seemed confused that Chris was there. Chris excitedly unfolded a laptop, and, after getting to the right field, gazed at Joel.

"So, how should we begin?" Chris asked with enthusiasm.

Jill cleared her throat nervously.

Joel scouted around his backyard one more time. When the angel had not appeared, he took a big breath and decided to take charge. He knew that this was what God wanted. He had not realized previous to this that some of his training was for this very moment, but now that the time was here, he was ready to go!

"Chris, I know you came here tonight thinking that we were going to work on a letter to the principal about how the story we read in English Lit is just an example of persecution of Christians, but . . ." here Joel paused briefly before continuing, "you are here because God means to use you in an even greater way."

Chris, for his part, was not unnerved by Joel's pronouncement. "I sort of figured that there would be more to this because of how you talked in class. That was so incredible to hear you say exactly what my pastor had said last Sunday in church. So much of Scripture has fit together lately that I just *knew* God was at work. I've been sort of ready for something to happen, and you're saying that you think that, too?" Chris finished with an excited smile.

Joel grinned, seeing right away how God had been preparing Chris. He glanced over at Jill, who smiled in relief but then seemed to be staring past him. Looking back to Chris, Joel noticed that his classmate was no longer smiling but rather appeared shocked and was turning pale. Joel then perceived a warmth flowing through him, and suddenly he knew that an angel had touched him. He turned to see Twinkle-Eyes and two other angels standing behind him. Their hands had been touching his shoulders, resulting in the energy Joel had felt. Joel jumped up from the picnic table, overjoyed to see the heavenly beings.

"You *are* here! I knew you'd come, but I also knew Chris was to be here, and I was to tell him about you, and . . ." Joel's words came out in a torrent of thoughts which ended abruptly as he took in the sight of three angels more fully.

The Beings stood majestically, their wings shimmering and their robed bodies glowing with heavenly energy. Their faces were serene and kind, yet almost regal. Joel had forgotten how incredible they appeared, but he, too, was awed with their splendor.

No one spoke for a minute.

Finally, Twinkle-Eyes directed his gaze to Chris and said, "Hello, Chris. We are messengers of the Most Holy God and servants of the Lamb That Was Slain. You have found favor with Him and have been chosen to be a part of the work bringing His kingdom to the world."

Chris lost his shocked look after hearing the angel's announcement. He stared at Twinkle-Eyes in contemplation and then looked at the other angels, his eyes finally resting on one.

"I've seen you before, haven't I?" Chris asked. When the angel did not respond immediately, he added, "I've seen you in my dreams. There were others, too, but you were the one I mainly saw."

The angel nodded serenely with the hint of a smile.

Chris tilted his head thoughtfully and then said, "It always seemed that whatever you talked about in my dream, my pastor would preach on or the youth leader would discuss or a devotion would cover. I thought that was really weird and coincidental, but it wasn't, was it? Those were things I really needed to grasp and understand, and the repetition nailed it for me."

The angel again nodded.

Chris was still pondering this revelation when Jill spoke quietly, "You are the angel I saw this morning."

Both boys followed her gaze to the remaining angel. The angel smiled and the resultant glow seemed to envelope the three angels and the teens.

Joel recognized this last angel. It had been one of the three that he had seen at church the night he had felt such fear, and then the three angels appeared around him. He studied the face more closely. There was something that made him think that this angel had endured much in its life. Its stature was the same as the other two angels, yet it almost seemed frail. He wondered how that could be. Maybe he'd ask Twinkle-Eyes sometime.

Twinkle-Eyes spoke, "We have been sent by the Most High God to guide you in His work. You three have been given abilities that will be useful in these end times. We are to help you learn how to use your gifts and to work together as a team. There will be others who are needed, but the Most High God has chosen you to be the core to lead them."

At this the three teens looked at each with questioning, furrowed eyebrows.

The angel continued, "You must trust God! The enemy is very powerful and dangerous. You must understand that he does not value you or anyone's lives. You need to learn how to access God's great power for yourselves and others so that the enemy will not succeed in destroying you!"

This pronouncement should have made Joel, Chris, and Jill tremble with fear, yet the nearness of the angels blanketed them in peace. Jill noticed a particular hue to the light that surrounded them and was further soothed by its gentleness. Chris was reminded of the story of Jesus' baptism by John the Baptist when the voice came out of heaven instructing the crowd to listen to His Son, and he half-expected to hear God speak!

Joel stared at the three angels, feeling the awesomeness of the mission they had just described. He sank to his knees and gazed ahead without seeing his surroundings.

In his mind, he saw a huge gathering of people in a large outdoor arena. A man was at a podium on a stage. In one hand he held a book, and the other arm was outstretched toward the throng of people. An enormous screen behind him showed printing—it was a Bible verse! *"But as many as received Him, to them He gave the right to become children of God, to those who believe in His name."*

The man and the crowd were excited and joyful! Many seemed to be making their way to the front, and once there, some were kneeling, others standing with arms raised to the sky. There were all ages involved and all types of people. It was a great response to the gospel message! Within minutes, everyone in the arena appeared to be worshipping God and praising Him for salvation! The man at the podium knelt on the platform before the crowd and raised his hands to the Lord, leading the thousands in a prayer of repentance.

Joel gasped at the enormity of what he saw. The sight faded and he breathed deeply as the angels and his friends peered into his face.

"Are you alright?" Chris cried anxiously, with a hand on Joel's shoulder.

Jill had also put a hand on Joel's other shoulder. She saw something around him—another faint color, different from what she had noticed with the angels. She *knew* Joel was OK.

Joel's eyes cleared, and he looked up at Twinkle-Eyes. Chris and Jill helped him up, and the three teens sat again at the picnic table.

"What did you see?" Jill asked.

"How do you know he saw something?" Chris questioned.

Jill bit her lip in thought and replied, "I'm not sure, but I know he saw something." She again looked at Joel and added, "Didn't you?"

"Yeah," Joel answered, looking at Twinkle-Eyes who nodded slightly to encourage him to continue. Joel took a big breath and began sharing the vision he had seen. He finished and then gazed at the angels as if he had something more to say.

Twinkle-Eyes spoke, "What do you think that was, Joel? The Lamb That Was Slain has given you that knowledge as well."

"Really?" Joel asked, but then knew immediately that the angel was correct. He moved his eyes around as he searched for the right words.

He looked quickly at Twinkle-Eyes for confirmation that he should tell the others, and, receiving a barely perceptible nod, proceeded.

"That gathering of people is what will happen if we," he paused, "meaning those of us involved in this, ah, mission . . . if we are able to complete the task God has for us." He continued solemnly, "All of those people will be saved."

Chris leaned forward and exclaimed, "You said there were thousands!"

Joel nodded, and admitted, "Yeah."

"Whoa!" both Chris and Jill blurted in low tones.

There was a moment of silence as the teens contemplated what that meant.

Chris spoke first, "How are *we* going to do that? I mean, we're just a bunch of teenagers, and . . ." His voice dropped away as he contemplated his words.

Joel and Jill stayed silent as Chris searched for what he wanted to say. He had taken the words out of their mouths. They, too, wondered how *they* could do anything to result in that many people getting saved.

Chris cocked his head to one side and chewed on a knuckle. "Oh, yeah," he mumbled.

"What?" Jill asked.

Grinning, Chris faced his friends. "You guys! Come on! Don't you know your Bible?" Without waiting for them to respond, he continued, "How old was David when he killed Goliath?"

Joel shook his head and looked over at Jill for help.

"Uh. . . we don't know," Joel answered sheepishly.

Chris threw his arms up in mock disbelief and cried, "He was a kid! Probably like us! Don't you see? It doesn't matter, because God can use anybody! With His power, David tossed a little stone, and it knocked out a giant! He wants to use us as His Hands to get things done *by His power*! We just have to believe, and let Him use us!"

"Yeah . . . I get it!" Joel exclaimed. "Pastor George talked about it when all this started happening to me. It was . . ." He scattered his notebooks apart until he found one he had kept from church sermons and youth group. He thumbed through the pages until he spotted what he wanted. "Here. *1 Timothy 4:12–16 Let no one despise your youth, but be an example to the believers in word, in conduct, in love, in spirit, in faith, in purity.*" And he finished the Scripture portion.

"So . . ." Chris explained, "God is showing us clearly that He *can* use us if we let Him!"

Jill sat back, amazed. "So, how are we to do this?" She looked first at the guys and then at the angels.

Twinkle-Eyes smiled at them and said, "You will be instrumental as being laborers in His harvest, along with us. There are many others involved, but your jobs will be to lay the foundation for the preachers and evangelists to work. We must prepare the fields for harvesting—in other words, prepare the souls so that the work of others will succeed. You will not be in places of visibility, but in the trenches of life, using your gifts. It is too soon for you to see how it will work, but you must trust God at all times. You may not see the result of your work, and that is why it is so important for you to have the support of each other. But, I must also warn you that your work, although not quite so visible to man, will be visible, at some point, to the enemy. He knows the damage you can do to his cause, and you need to be alert to his demons. Chris, I believe you know some Scripture that tells us how the Lamb That Was Slain instructed his disciples regarding that."

Chris looked surprised at the pointed suggestion, but quickly rose to the task, and responded, "In the Gospels, Jesus sent His disciples out into the communities with a caution to *'be wise as serpents and harmless as doves.'*"

Twinkle-Eyes nodded in agreement. "You will need to be alert, but we, and others, will be teaching you and training you so that the work gets done; we are also here to protect you, and," he gazed for a moment at Jill, "*you* will learn how to help *us*."

The three angels moved around the teens, encircling them with one angel standing behind and between each. Laying a hand on the shoulder of the youth on either side, the angels completed the circle.

Twinkle-Eyes lifted his eyes toward the heavens and spoke out a prayer, "Most High God, prepare these youth for the task ahead. Anoint them with Your power and help them to use the talents You have given them. Bind them together as friends because *'a threefold cord is not quickly broken.'* Protect them from the evil one and those who would do them harm. We praise You and the Lamb That Was Slain, for You are worthy of all our praise."

The teens were enveloped in a blanket of warmth. They grasped each other around the wrist instead of actually holding hands. The result was a feeling of power and hope unlike anything the three had ever experienced.

The backyard and picnic table vanished! The three stood before a great throne with another large one at its right and other, smaller thrones circling around. The heavens themselves seemed to be the vast throne room. The light penetrated everywhere such that there were no shadows. Standing before them was One . . . *clothed with a garment down to the feet and girded about the chest with a golden band. His head and hair were white like wool, as white as snow, and His eyes like a flame of fire.*

Joel, Chris, and Jill could no longer stand. They sunk to their knees in awe. They realized that they were seeing the One who had saved them. Hearts pounding, they bowed their heads low to the ground. This was no earthly king—here was the King of Kings!

"Rise, my children. I send you out with My strength to accomplish what needs to be done before I come again to rid the world of Satan. Any time you need Me, I will be here to help you. I have given you my trusted servants to be with you until My Father determines the time for Me to come Myself. This bond with each other is a powerful means to resist Satan and his demons. Use it in times of trouble and fear. Trust Me, for I love you!"

CHAPTER 12

The next thing they knew, Joel, Jill, and Chris were back sitting at the picnic table on the patio at Joel's house. The angels were gone. No one spoke for a few minutes.

Finally, Joel breathed heavily and then spoke. "Chris, I see that you have a gift of knowing Scripture."

Chris looked at Joel and nodded. "It would seem that way," he shrugged his shoulders and grinned.

"Do you remember the verses the angels used?" Joel asked.

"Yeah," Chris pondered, "I think I do."

"Could you keep a journal of anything scriptural that comes up? Even how . . ." here Joel searched for the right words, ". . . how the Lamb appeared to us? I think I remember something in Revelation about that, but I'm not sure."

Chris' eyes lit up. "That's right! I'll find it—I'm pretty sure I know where it is!" He reached inside his backpack and pulled out a Bible.

While Chris searched for the Scripture, Joel turned to Jill.

"You seem to see things or sense things more than Chris or I," Joel said.

Jill initially shrank into herself, then bolstered her confidence and answered, "I think that may be the gift the angel talked about for me. Sometimes I see sparkles and colors. I'm not sure what they mean just yet all the time, but the sparkles do seem to be around the angels."

Joel smiled encouragingly, and nodded at her, "Yep, I think you're right! Could you write down what you saw and anything you sensed that now seems to be related to our mission? I believe it's important for us to keep track of it all now. I've been keeping journals since I first saw the angel."

Jill shook her head in agreement, "That's a great idea! I just happened to bring a composition book along to write stuff in."

As Jill pulled her notebook out, Chris exclaimed, "Here it is!"

Joel and Jill both looked with interest over to their new friend.

Chris excitedly read, "*Revelation 1:13–14: And in the midst of the seven lampstands One like the Son of Man, clothed with a garment down to the feet and girded about the chest with a golden band. His head and hair were white like wool, as white as snow, and His eyes like a flame of fire.*"

He looked up and said, "That's what I saw; how about you guys?"

Both Joel and Jill nodded in affirmation, and Joel spoke, "Good job, Chris! Get that marked down so that we can remember it. Why don't we all write down what happened tonight, in our own words, sort of like the Gospels told different aspects of Christ's life, depending on how each person perceived what was going on. What made an impression on me may not have impressed you and vice versa. I think it will help us stay together in our mission and appreciate how each other is feeling."

Chris and Jill's eyes opened wide in amazement at Joel's instructions, contemplating on how much sense he made. It seemed that he was a different kid than they had known him to be—now decisive and authoritative (in a good way), rather than a go-along-with-the-crowd follower. They felt a huge amount of respect for him and could see the gift of leadership had been given to him. It was a crowning moment for all of them, recognizing the worth of their threefold bond, yet placing the role of leader on Joel.

Smiling at each other, they all began writing, Joel and Jill in notebooks, and Chris on his laptop. They were each busy recording their thoughts when the door from the house opened and Kathy Stevens emerged with a pitcher of lemonade and a plate of cookies while juggling some plastic cups under her arm.

Joel jumped up and grabbed the cups just as they popped out from his mom's arm, heading for the ground.

"Whew! Good save, Joel!" Kathy breathed as she placed the items on the table. "I thought you all could use a snack, even though you just came out." With that, she smiled and returned to the house.

Chris looked down at his watch, and exclaimed, "Hey, guys, it's still only 7:15! That's the time we started! Were we in a time warp or something?"

Joel just stared ahead for a moment and then said, "I think we were on heaven time. You know, in the Bible it says that a thousand years is as a day to God. It seems that when we're in God's presence or with the angels, sometimes, not always, but sometimes, time stands still."

"You're right," Jill agreed. She grinned and said, "Let's call it HT for heaven-time!"

Joel and Chris laughed and shook their heads in agreement. Everyone grabbed a drink and a cookie.

"Well, anyhow, I'm done writing my journal entry," Jill announced. "Do you think we should work on that letter to the principal now?"

Joel and Chris raised their eyebrows as they remembered the original reason for the study group that night. Both laughed.

"You're right, Jill," Joel agreed. "You never know. That letter could be part of the foundation the angel was talking about. We need to get kids and teachers to see the discrimination against Christians. It may allow for rules to change and for it to be easier to share the gospel with others."

They spent the next half hour throwing out ideas and coming up with thoughtful, yet provoking points to bring to their principal's attention. It was getting dark as Chris put the final touches on the letter, leaving room for signatures. They had decided to get others to sign, like a petition. Chris was put in charge of this because of his broader association of friends and acquaintances.

A car horn sounded as the teens entered the house. Jill peeked out the window and said, "Oh, there's my dad. Chris, do you need a ride? We could go that way."

"Sure, that'd be great!" Chris responded.

The three stood awkwardly for a second, looking at each other. So much had happened that night. It was hard to let go of the moment.

Joel finally spoke as the horn sounded a second time, "I'll see you both tomorrow. Be open to the Spirit for when we should meet next. I . . ." He stopped short as he pulled his hand from his pants pocket.

Slowly opening his hand, they all saw a pure white stone. Jill and Chris both opened their hands to reveal the same thing.

Staring at the stones, Jill whispered, "I got a blue stone this morning when I first met the angel."

"I never saw a stone like this," Chris said reverently.

"I've gotten two other stones," Joel offered. "Let's all make a note in our journals about them. I'm not sure of their significance."

The other two nodded.

Joel spoke again, "Thanks, you guys. It was fun and special to have the angel all to myself, but I really like having you both know about it, since we can't tell our parents, at least, not yet. See you tomorrow."

Jill opened the door and said, "Bye!"

Chris clapped Joel on the shoulder and grinned, then headed outside with Jill.

Jill opened the front car door and said, "Sorry, Dad. We had some things to finish up. Can we drop off Chris on our way home?"

"Sure, but I want to get over to the hardware store before it closes. I need some things to fix the kitchen sink. Hop in, Chris!" Mr. Baker called.

"Thanks! I just live over two streets," Chris replied.

The two kids got in the car, and Mr. Baker backed out of the driveway. In a minute, they were at Chris' house and then on their way to the store.

Pulling out onto a main road, Mr. Baker sped up to the speed limit but soon was forced to slow down for a car that was going half that speed. Mr. Baker sighed deeply.

"We're not going to make it in time at this rate," he said anxiously. "Maybe I can get around that car in the passing zone."

But, just as he went to pass, another car appeared in the approaching lane, and he had to back off.

Jill had not been paying attention to her dad's plight. The day had been incredible, and she replayed the visit with the angels over and over again in her mind. It wasn't until her dad heaved another deep sigh that she looked ahead at the slow vehicle in front of them.

Her eyes widened in surprise as she noticed the angel from the morning lying serenely across the trunk of the car. The angel seemed much larger than earlier, with its one arm touching the pavement on one side, and one foot dragging on the other side. The end effect was to keep the car from moving quickly!

Mr. Baker, although usually mild-mannered and laid back, was obviously irritated at the slow-going. He looked at the car clock and shook his head.

"We'll never make it with that slowpoke in front of us!" he commented aloud.

Jill kept her mouth shut as she continued to gaze at the angel. She found it hard not to laugh as she watched the angel turn on its stomach and then back on its side, much like someone relaxing on an air mattress in a pool. Finally, as they neared the shopping plaza where the hardware store was, the angel alertly looked ahead and motioned to the side of the road. The car immediately braked as Mr. Baker and Jill noticed a squirrel run across the road. The cars had to almost stop to allow the safe passage of the squirrel. Just as they thought the squirrel was safely across the road, it turned and headed back and then stopped in front of the cars! Mr. Baker couldn't help but laugh as the squirrel continued its confused antics, sitting up on its haunches as if to scold the cars for interrupting some kind of daily trek! At this point, all traffic was stopped for about thirty seconds while the squirrel finally decided to cross the road and disappear from view in the headlights and streetlights.

All the while, Jill was focused on the angel. The minute the cars were stopped, it stood up beside the road and seemed to glow. It was a different hue than before, and Jill realized the angel had actually been this hue the whole time on the car, but it was just lighter or less intense. Jill had the strangest inclination to pray, but she thought, *For what?*

The angel turned ever so slightly to look at Jill, its eyes encouraging her, so Jill quickly prayed, *Lord, help this situation, whatever is happening that you want me to pray for, please give strength and Your power to those who need it right now!*

Jill watched the angel intently and immediately noticed the hue deepen. The angel seemed to be concentrating, staring ahead with its arms outstretched.

Suddenly, Jill and her dad heard a loud horn blowing and then a terrible crashing sound! They both jumped and looked at each other.

"What was that?" Mr. Baker exclaimed.

"I don't know, but it came from up ahead by the plaza!" Jill said with concern.

The traffic now seemed to be moving normally, and the car in front of them even sped up to the speed limit. The Bakers reached the plaza in a moment and turned into the parking lot. Their eyes met with a horrible sight!

A tractor trailer had plowed through the parking lot and crashed into the very hardware store at which the Bakers had intended to shop! Mr. Baker parked their car quickly and jumped out.

"Jill, stay here! I'm going to see if anyone is hurt. Call 911 just in case no one has yet!" Mr. Baker yelled as he ran from the car.

Trembling, Jill grabbed the cell phone from the dashboard caddy and pressed the numbers for help. The 911 center operator answered and thanked her for calling—they had already dispatched emergency vehicles.

Jill sat in the car and needed no encouragement to pray. Only a few minutes had passed when her father jogged back to their car. She got out of the car and hugged him. She heard the sound of approaching sirens and watched as fire trucks, police, and ambulances descended upon the small shopping area.

"What happened, Dad?" she questioned.

"Well, it seems that the tractor trailer lost its brakes coming off the highway exit; you know that one is fairly steep. Luckily, there was no traffic when it came through the intersection and came straight through the parking lot without really hitting anything until it ran into the front of the hardware store. The store happened to be empty because they were closing in five minutes, and the clerks were able to get out of the way because the driver hit the horn. But, the front of the store is a mess!" Mr. Baker described.

"What about the driver? It doesn't look like he could have survived that impact!" Jill blurted out.

Mr. Baker shook his head in disbelief, "I thought the same, but he had a new cab that had an airbag in it. It deployed and protected him from all the broken glass as well. He was climbing out of the cab as I got there. He's shaken up, bruised, and with some little cuts, but amazingly, seemed OK. It's incredible!"

They watched the emergency crews for a short time and then got back into their car to head home. Mr. Baker put the key in the ignition to start the car but stopped and sat back.

"What's wrong, Dad? Are you OK?" Jill asked.

Her dad stared ahead at nothing in particular and then looked at her. "I was so upset about not getting to the hardware store in time, but if we had been there, we could have been killed, either when we pulled in to park, or walking into the store, or getting the things I needed because they were right at that front window," he admitted and then continued, "That slowpoke driver saved our lives, Jill." He looked at her with tears in his eyes. "I will be a lot more patient with slowpokes in the future!"

She hugged her dad and carefully ventured a response, "Dad, maybe God sent angels to slow us down so that we wouldn't be there when the accident happened."

He stared at her with the lights from the parking lot shining on her face. She looked to be an angel to him at that time.

"You are so right, Jill! God says He will take care of us and could send ten thousand angels to help His own," he responded. "Why don't we take time to thank Him right now?"

Jill nodded and then bowed her head while taking her dad's hand.

Mr. Baker began, "Dear Father, Thank you for slowing me down tonight and keeping us out of the way of this terrible accident . . ."

Something made Jill raise her head and peek in front of the car. There stood a number of angels, including the one that had slowed the car in front of them. Apparently God *had* sent some angels to help lessen the effect of the accident. Jill saw a brightness around them that seemed to intensify as her father prayed. There was something to this, she just knew it! The hues and brightness of the light surrounding the angels seemed to mean something. She determined to pay attention to that and ask the angel the next opportunity she had. Joel and Chris had not indicated that they saw it at all. *I'll ask them tomorrow*, she thought, although the angel had said this morning that seeing the sparkles was *her* gift!

CHAPTER 13

Joel slept well that night, after staying up to write in his journal. He didn't remember any specific dreams, but he felt a sense of peace, which continued all the way to school, as his dad dropped him off on the way to a meeting with a client near the school. Excitedly, he looked for Chris and Jill as he entered the main door. The two were already together nearby, obviously watching for Joel to come. They both waved him over to join them.

"Hey, Joel!" Chris began. "Weird 'coincidence,' if you know what I mean," he said in mysterious tones and then smiled. "Out of the blue, I was switched to second lunch," he informed Joel. "And now, Jill tells me that's when you two eat!"

Joel grinned as the three made arrangements to eat together and then hurried off to first period. He could see Chris showing friends along the way the letter to the principal, and many were signing it.

The morning went quickly, and soon it was lunchtime. Chris waved to some friends as he headed to where Joel and Jill were seated.

Jill noticed and quickly asked, "Won't your friends get mad if you eat with us?"

Chris shrugged his shoulders and said, "If they are good friends, it shouldn't matter. We spend lots of other time together. Anyhow, they know we're working on this letter to the principal, and I needed to show you how we've done!" He excitedly pulled some papers from his backpack and placed them on the table.

Joel and Jill each picked up a paper, looked on both sides, and then up to Chris in amazement.

"You mean you got all these signatures just this morning?" Joel asked eagerly.

"Yep!" Chris exclaimed as he sat down and pulled out a packed lunch. "I don't know what's happening, but everyone I talked to has gotten so fed up with all the rules against religion in the schools that they want it to stop. One guy got in trouble for doing a research project that explored how Christianity was the basis for a lot of our laws that actually give people the freedom to worship as they please or to believe or not believe in any god! And he doesn't even really believe in Christ—he just saw that there was a correlation and did the research to support his claim. His Social Studies teacher gave him a D because it was 'too biased!'"

"Wow!" Joel and Jill exclaimed together.

"Tell me about it!" Chris agreed. "Like they want us to forget that our country was started because Christians in Europe wanted the freedom to worship God differently than their leaders allowed. Do they want to rewrite the history books?" he scoffed.

"Don't laugh, Chris; that's exactly what some anti-Christian groups are doing, and they're succeeding!" Joel offered. "They are forcing textbook authors to skim over the truths of how our nation came to be so that our generation doesn't really learn that Christians came here for religious freedom and made laws that followed Christian morals and instructions from the Bible. The importance of that is being watered down so much that soon kids won't even know about it!"

Jill spoke up, "And even worse, Christians are shown in a bad light because we *do* stick to those biblical principles. Unfortunately, too many Christians use their Christianity to bash those who don't agree, instead of showing love for the person and disagreeing with the sin they do or support."

The three thoughtfully ate their lunches while digesting the conversation.

Jill shyly interrupted their thoughts, "Um . . . something really neat happened to me last night after my dad and I dropped Chris off." She paused as Joel and Chris looked up in anticipation then proceeded in telling them about the accident and how the angel kept the car in front of them slowed down to prevent them from being involved in the mishap.

"That's really cool!" Chris exclaimed as Jill finished her story. "I wonder how often that's happened to us without us knowing it!"

Jill and Joel looked curiously at him.

Chris continued, "Don't you get it? We just haven't *seen* the angels before, but I bet they've prevented a lot of accidents by holding up traffic, slowing us down, etcetera. From now on, I'm going to think again before I complain about someone going slow in front of me! I'll just tell myself that it's 'angel traffic!'"

Joel and Jill laughed in agreement.

"Well . . . back to the letter to the principal. Chris, how many signatures do you have now?" Joel asked.

"Hmm . . . let's see, I had counted forty-five, but then a few more signed, so that brings the total to fifty-one! I'm going to keep working on it until English Lit class and then show our teacher, if that sounds OK with you guys," Chris suggested.

The other two nodded, and they all began to gather their things as lunch ended.

Joel asked, "When would you like to meet again? I have church tonight."

Chris frowned, "I have to cheer at a game tonight and won't be home until around nine. My church normally has our youth meeting tonight. I hate when I have to miss it."

"I go to a small church, and we don't really have any youth group. There's an adult prayer meeting tonight that I usually go to," Jill said.

"Well," Joel spoke as he thought quickly, "why don't we try to meet again tomorrow at lunch and in the meantime, pray about how, when, and where we're to get together."

Chris and Jill nodded affirmatively, and then the three departed in opposite directions to their afternoon classes, anticipating seeing each other in English Lit.

Jill got to the English Lit class early and decided to spend a minute praying while the rest of the students filed in. She noticed a ruckus as Chris came in waving the letter to the principal. Kids who hadn't had a chance to sign it gathered around him as he explained the letter's content. Joel was one of the last ones to enter the class. He clapped Chris on the back and gave him a thumbs-up sign.

"OK, class!" the teacher called. "Everyone to your seats! What's all the excitement about here?"

As the students sat down, Joel remained standing and replied, "A few of us went ahead and formulated a letter to the principal about the discrimination against Christians, and now we're getting signatures from those in agreement."

He motioned for Chris to take the letter copies up to the teacher, and then he sat down.

"Hmm . . ." she murmured as she took the papers from Chris. "Let me see . . ." She sat on the edge of her desk and read the letter while the class remained amazingly quiet. After a moment, she looked out at the class and said, "Joel, Chris and . . ." Here she looked down at the letter again, and then continued, "and Jill—please stand."

Jill's heart raced. She hated getting called on. The blood drained from her face and her whole body trembled as she stood. Suddenly, however, she felt a peace come over her. She looked over at Chris and Joel, and saw their angels standing behind them with hands placed lightly on their backs. In that moment, she knew her angel was behind her as well!

The teacher looked at the three students and then looked back down at the letter, sighing deeply.

"I am utterly . . ." here she paused as if unable to find the words.

Jill, Chris and Joel braced for the inevitable criticism.

The teacher shook her head and continued, ". . . utterly *amazed* at your well-thought-out approach to this subject!"

Immediately, the teens released the breaths they all had been holding. The class buzzed with excitement!

She went on, "You have brought up some very good points, and I believe the principal and school board will have their hands full in answering your assertions! Well done!"

The class erupted in clapping, and Jill, Chris, and Joel grinned broadly at each other as they sat down.

The teacher waited for the class to settle down and then added, "You have reminded me of my own decision long ago to not be ashamed of my faith. For too long I have let the squeaky wheel of minority voices—and I'm not talking of race—tell me what I can and can't do." She paused again and then, with a hint of emotion, asked, "Would you allow me to sign this as well?"

Joel's eyes widened in disbelief! The class became silent as the same shocked look appeared on each student's face.

"Um . . ." Joel hesitated. He turned to look at Chris and then Jill. He stood, and the whole class waited expectantly for him to speak.

Jill and Chris both gasped almost imperceptibly as three angels appeared behind Joel. They touched his shoulders and began to glow. Jill and Chris both prayed and stared at Joel. The angels' glow spread throughout the classroom, and the two teens had to squint their eyes slightly to endure it.

It was only a matter of seconds before Joel spoke again. He stood tall and resolute as he said, "We would be honored if you would sign along with us!"

The teacher smiled and nodded at Joel, "Thank you." With that, she chose a pen and signed her name on the letter. She handed the papers back to Chris and holding her head high, she directed, "Class, in light of this letter, let us return to the short story you read and catalog the instances where discrimination occurs against *any* group. Perhaps I will add my own voice to remove this book from our curriculum, just as many wonderful works of literature have been removed because they emulate Christians."

She then led the class in a spirited discussion of freedom of speech, separation of church and state, and where some things have crossed the line and gone too far.

When the bell rang, she thanked the class for the lively, intelligent dialogue and then asked if Joel, Chris, and Jill could remain afterward for a moment.

The three students gathered around her desk. Her face and eyes seemed to glow with excitement as she breathed a huge sigh.

"You three have reminded me of myself many years ago. I vowed that I would not let popular opinion and the complaining words of a few to keep me from living out my faith," she explained. "But I did. Over time, I just got tired of fighting the administration and other teachers in the department about allowing Christian literature. It really has gotten out of hand, and I'm so thankful that God has shown you how to pick up the fight and use their own strategies against them. You must realize that my participation in this movement could endanger my job as a teacher here."

Joel's heart pounded as he listened to the teacher's confession. He reached out and touched her arm. Jill and Chris did likewise.

"We will pray for you," Joel stated.

Her eyes glistened with tears and showed her consent.

"Father, You know the needs of Your servant, Miss Clawson; give her courage to continue to do Your will and protect her job according to Your will. We thank you. In the name of the Lamb That Was Slain, amen."

Miss Clawson smiled her thanks and then quickly rose, ushering the students out into the hall. "Hurry now, so you're not late for your next classes! Thank you!"

Four angels surrounded the teacher. She had a prep period, so she could think about what she needed to do. She was excited, but feared she would lose her job over her support of the students. Peace flooded her spirit, and she made a new commitment to the Lord she had loved but had forgotten. She knew that a call to her old pastor would be necessary, along with a call to her family, who had never ceased to pray for her return to the Lord.

The angels remained with her the whole time, imparting the strength she needed for her new tasks. As students began to arrive for her next class, three angels departed, returning to the teens the Lord had charged them with to protect and train. The fourth angel stayed, knowing it had an enormous, wonderful responsibility to this first fruit of the Joel prophecy harvest!

CHAPTER 14

Joel, Chris, and Jill found that lunch at school was the best time to get together and update each other due to Chris' many activities after school. The weekend brought some free time for him, so the teens made plans to meet at Joel's house Saturday afternoon. The angels had appeared a number of times throughout the week to each of them, providing reassurance about the tasks ahead of them by means of Scripture verses and short discussions. They all, however, were looking forward to being able to meet together for an extended time.

Saturday dawned rainy and cool. Joel realized that the gathering of his friends would have to be inside, so he prepared the living room for them, arranging some chairs closer together to help them to talk quietly.

The phone rang, and Joel heard his dad speaking. *It must be one of his clients,* he thought.

"Who was that, Doug?" Kathy Steven asked.

Doug sighed, "That was one of my clients. He needs to get some information to me, so he asked if he could drop it off this afternoon since he was coming close by this way. I told him OK—it would save him a trip to my office on Monday. I hope he doesn't need to tell me too much about it. I had planned on working in the basement this afternoon."

Jill and Chris arrived together. Mr. Baker had offered to pick Chris up since it was raining. The group quickly got settled in the living room. Kathy Stevens brought in some drinks and snacks, and then excused herself to work on some items for a school board meeting the next week.

Once the kids were settled, Joel asked, "How about we pray before we get started? Jill, could you lead us?"

Jill paused ever so slightly before saying, "Sure." She was not accustomed to praying in front of others and felt nervous.

Chris sensed her hesitation and added, "Pretend we're not here, and you are just talking to the Lord."

She nodded and then closed her eyes. Immediately, she felt a calm, and then she began, "Father, we thank You for choosing us to help You further Your kingdom. Be with us as we study and try to do Your will. Help our spirits to be open to what You want us to do as we choose to follow You. In Your name, amen."

As the teens opened their eyes, they saw the three angels standing around them. Excitement filled them as the angels guided them through some key Scriptures, and they discussed what next step to take regarding the letter to the principal.

Joel spoke up, "My mom is getting ready for a school board meeting now. Maybe she'd have some advice for us as to how to proceed."

Jill and Chris nodded in agreement.

Looking at the angels, Chris asked, "Is that a good idea with you being here, or should we wait until later to ask her?"

Twinkle-Eyes responded, "It is always good to obtain reliable counsel. We will not be apparent to her while you speak with her."

Joel smiled and rose to get his mom, "Aw . . . She's pretty cool. She'd probably just ask if you wanted something to drink or eat!"

The angels laughed along with the kids while Joel went to get his mom.

"Well," Kathy Stevens began as Joel brought her into the living room. The angels stood back, and at first, Joel was sure his mom really did see them, but she focused her eyes on Jill and then Chris before continuing. "Joel tells me you have a question about some letter to the principal at your school."

Chris then explained what they had done and why, finishing with their letter and the list of those who had signed in agreement.

"Hmm . . ." Kathy murmured as she read the letter and looked at all the names. "OK. Wow . . . this is a great letter and really says nicely what you want to say. I would suggest that you give it to your principal and ask that he bring it up to the school board. You may even want to offer to come before the school board directly, so that you can answer any questions or make further comments in support of your supposition here. This certainly brings up some very good points. I have to be careful not to coach you in any particular way, but I believe you may actually be able to make a difference regarding this. Let me know what your principal says—I think I'd really like to be at the board meeting if he lets you address the Board!"

With that, she hugged Joel around the shoulders and went back to her work.

Joel thought for a moment and then said, "I think it would be good for the three of us to take this to the principal on Monday. If we're going to take a stand, we need to be there for each other."

Jill and Chris nodded, and then Chris asked, "Should we get to school early and see him then or wait until lunchtime?"

Just then, the doorbell rang.

Joel jumped up, and blurted, "Oh . . . that must be my dad's client." He looked at the angels with concern. "Are you going to disappear or just not be seen?"

Twinkle-Eyes smiled and said, "We do what the Lamb That Was Slain directs us to do, Joel. It is fine to answer the door."

With relief, Joel moved to the front door as the doorbell rang again. He pulled open the door and said, "Come in! Are you here for my dad?"

A pleasant voice answered, "I'm here to give Mr. Stevens some papers that I missed giving him." The man pulled a rain slicker hood down from his head and continued, "This is one of my students. I hope you don't mind that I brought her in with me; it sure is raining out there, and I needed to explain some things to Mr. Stevens and didn't know how long it would take."

"Here I am," Doug Stevens called out as he emerged from the basement steps and came to shake the man's hand. "Come on into the study where I have your file. Joel, can you take his coat and hang it up?" With that he ushered the man out of the entryway to the back corner of the house where the study was.

Joel carefully placed the rain slicker on a coat tree, allowing the rain pellets to drip on a rug underneath. He looked over at the student the man had brought with him so he could take the raincoat. A girl with long black hair tied back in a ponytail was standing in the entryway with her rain slicker partially off.

"Um . . . I can take that for you," he prompted.

The girl seemed to be frozen. Joel followed her gaze into the living room, and his stomach went into a ball. She was staring directly at the angels!

Jill and Chris had noticed the same thing and were also at a loss as to what to do.

Joel gulped, frantically wondering why Twinkle-Eyes had indicated the visitors wouldn't see the angels. *Did something go wrong?* he thought.

Twinkle-Eyes spoke, "Elizabeth, come in; you are welcome here!"

Joel gasped and looked at Chris and Jill, who were astonished as well.

Again, Twinkle-Eyes addressed the girl, "Liz, please come in!"

The girl finally seemed to come out of her reverie and looked over at Joel who was attempting to help her off with her coat. Joel guided her into the room, and all four teens focused on Twinkle-Eyes for an explanation.

"Joel, Chris, and Jill," Twinkle-Eyes began, "I'd like you to meet Elizabeth, or Liz, as most people call her. She has been tasked, just as you have been, with helping the Lamb That Was Slain and His messengers prepare the world for His coming. Liz, these fine young people will be your friends and teammates in the mission ahead."

140

Liz still had not spoken. She stared around at the group of teens and angels, finally resting her eyes on a fourth angel who had appeared during the introductions.

"You . . ." Liz mumbled, "you're the one I saw at the back of the auditorium, aren't you? Father John told me to believe, but I don't know that I really did until right now." She paused and then directed a question at the other teens, "You see angels, too, right? I'm not just seeing things, am I?"

Chris stood and answered, "We not only see them, but we talk with them, and they help us learn about Jesus and the Father."

Joel noticed that Liz was trembling. He reached out, touched her arm, and asked, "Are you OK? Do you want to sit down?"

She stared at him and then cocked her head. A curious expression came over her face. "Your name is Joel?" she questioned.

"Uh-huh," Joel replied.

"You're the one the angel told me I'd be working with," she said incredulously and then almost gasped. "I can hardly believe this is all true!" She made the sign of the cross, looked up, and began mouthing something.

Chris started to talk, but Jill quickly touched his arm to restrain him. "She's praying," Jill whispered. "My grandparents are Catholic, and I sometimes go to Mass with them, so I've learned a little about the traditions. Shh . . ."

Jill, Chris, and Joel waited patiently while Liz prayed. The rhetoric had long been lost on many worshippers who said the prayers without really knowing what they said, but Liz had embraced the many truths such that the words rang true in her spirit and pleased the Lord.

Liz finished and hesitantly looked around her, feeling conspicuously different than the other teens.

"We're glad to meet you, Liz," Joel exclaimed, putting the newcomer at ease. "Won't you sit down and join us?"

Liz nodded and smiled warmly, letting out a breath of relief.

"Tell us about yourself," Chris invited. "When did you meet the angel?"

"Well . . ." Liz began and quickly summed up what had happened at her school.

Joel and the others shook their heads in amazement as Liz described the movement for the Lord that had started at St. Luke's.

"Oh, Father John will be so excited to meet you and see the angels again!" Liz exclaimed to the heavenly beings.

The angels had been respectfully silent while the teens talked, but now Twinkle-Eyes spoke. "He will not see us again until the Lord's coming."

Liz turned to the angel. "What? Why not? He saw you before!" she stammered.

"It is no longer his time," the fourth angel said gently. "He has a work to do at the school, and he will always have the Lord's help, but it is now time for you, and we are here to help you and *this* group."

Liz solemnly acknowledged the pronouncement.

"Father John will continue to be your friend and mentor," the fourth angel reassured Liz. "He already knows that your mission is different, and he has accepted that. He also knows that you are not to speak of this to anyone else, and he will not press you for information. You are given wisdom and discretion regarding this."

The other teens had listened with rapt attention to the interchange between Liz and the fourth angel. Joel heard some noises and timidly spoke, "Here comes my dad!"

The angels nodded and backed away ever so slightly.

Doug Stevens' voice got louder as the two men entered the living room.

"Oh, guys, this is Father John from St. Luke's Catholic Academy," Doug introduced.

Liz gazed at Father John as he entered the room. She sighed sadly when she knew that he had not seen the angels standing behind the teens, but then she seemed to brighten as she said, "Father John, this is Chris and Jill," pointing at each as she named them. She paused and then said with a certain emphasis, "And this is Joel."

Father John had nodded politely as Liz introduced Chris and Jill, but his head jerked up as she got to Joel. His eyes widened, and he furrowed his eyebrows in an unspoken question as he looked over to Liz.

Liz just smiled and gave a little nod.

Father John shook his head and grinned with a slight up-look of his eyes toward the ceiling before grabbing Joel's hand and pumping it. "So you're Joel, are you?"

Doug Stevens hadn't caught any of the furtive glances going on between those in the living room. He just glibly answered, "Yep, that's my son, Joel!"

Nodding more, Father John perceptibly commented, "What a nice group of young people, Liz! Perhaps you'll want to grab their phone numbers or e-mails to keep in touch!" He turned to her and winked, although nobody else could see it. "You can never have too many good friends, can you?" he added, raising his eyebrows with a knowing look.

Liz immediately picked up on the hint and exclaimed, "Oh, that's a great idea, Father John! Do you have some paper I can put your phone numbers and e-mails on?"

Chris responded quickly, "Uh, sure—here's a pen and paper. Give us yours while you're at it, OK?"

Liz nodded silently as she first wrote her name, phone number, and e-mail address, then ripped it off the paper and handed it to Joel. The other teens rapidly wrote the same things for Liz and handed the paper back to her.

Father John placed his hand on Liz's shoulder and said, "I'm afraid we have to leave now—I promised your parents I'd have you back by two o'clock. It's very nice to meet you—Chris, Jill, and *Joel*," he emphasized. "May God bless you," he added sincerely. "Thanks, Doug! Call me if you need any other information," he finished.

Liz smiled as she waved to her new friends, casting a quick glance at the angels, who childishly waved back to her. She giggled as she put on her raincoat, almost skipping out the door to the priest's car.

Doug waved at the two as they backed out of the driveway, and then he closed the front door. "Well, I'm getting back to my project. Sorry to have disturbed your study group!" With that, he hurried off to the basement again.

Twinkle-Eyes came forward. "Liz is the first of the group the Lamb That Was Slain has prepared for you. The others will be gathered to you shortly. Be mindful of your gifts now. Do not take pride in them—you are nothing without the power of Him who abolished death. I must warn you that difficult days are ahead. Build and strengthen yourselves so that you are ready for the days to come." The angels then vanished.

CHAPTER 15

The young man sat up, straightened his back, and raised both arms above his head in a stretch. It was very late, and the art project was finally done! He knew he'd get a good grade on it, even though he had procrastinated in finishing it. It had been due today, but the art teacher had given him until tomorrow before first period to turn it in. He rolled into his bed and for a moment thought, *At least I'll have an A in something this term!* Then he heaved a big sigh and was fast asleep.

The dream was almost immediate: He was in a group of kids walking up to the small church on the edge of his family's farm. He quickly unlocked the door and ushered the others inside and closed the door. Light filtered in through old windows. The one-roomed chapel was not ornate in any way, and the simple, straight-backed pews looked uninviting. The ten rows were interrupted in the center by a walkway which linked the two aisles heading from the doors to the front platform and pulpit. An old organ sat on the left. Kerosene lanterns hung from the ceiling, but regular electric lights had been added as well. Small side pews ran to the front until choir-row pews faced perpendicular.

The teens looked around, intrigued. It was perfect! They sat down, utilizing the ends of the pews so that they were more or less in a circle. One boy led them in prayer. As he finished, there were suddenly others in the church. *Angels!*

The young man awoke, his heart pounding, not in fear but in excitement! The dream had come nightly for a week, but the figures had always been somewhat indistinct. However, tonight, he had seen faces, and he recognized one!

He had been called to the principal's office at school, *again*, because of his don't-care-attitude and the possibility of failing if he didn't get the art project in. While talking with the principal, he noticed a framed picture of her family on her desk, showing her with a man and a teen similar in age to himself. Now, tonight, that same boy was in his dream—he had led the others in prayer! The teen smiled to himself and went back to sleep.

He got to school a little early and immediately went to turn in his art project. His teacher took one look at it, shook his head in relief, and then patted the boy on his back.

"You know, Garrett, if you would apply yourself and do things sooner, you could probably have a scholarship for art school. But, turning things in at the last possible second won't get you any recommendations," the art teacher said admonishingly.

Garrett just grinned and tossed his head to throw some hair out of his eyes. He turned, without a word and ran up the hall to the office. He looked at the clock on the wall—he had ten minutes before first period. Sauntering in to the anteroom of the principal's office, he nodded at the secretary.

"Is the principal in yet?" he asked.

The secretary gave him a critical look and didn't answer, but raised her eyebrows like a parent waiting for a child to be polite.

Garrett was used to the put down. Usually he didn't mind, but today he really needed to talk to the principal and was irritated at the implication that he was a no-good kid.

"May I *please* see the principal, if she is in?" he forced out politely.

The secretary, pleased at gaining the upper hand, responded, "She just arrived—I'll ask if she can see you."

She hit the intercom, "Excuse me, but Garrett Waterford is asking to see you."

"Send him in, Monica," Garrett heard the principal say.

Garrett then walked behind the counter and headed back to the principal's office.

"Hello Garrett," a cheery voice called as he entered the room. "Did you get that art project turned in this morning?"

"Already done," he chirped back.

"Then, how can I help you," the principal asked sincerely with none of the prejudice that was so evident in the secretary's voice.

"I wondered if that is your family," Garrett said, pointing to the framed picture on the principal's desk.

She hesitated just for a moment, reflecting that attacks on principals' families were not uncommon these days. She sensed that the question was not because of any vengeance and went ahead with answering, "That is my husband and son. Why do you ask?"

Garrett was unusually excited when he asked, "I think I know him—your son, I mean. What's his name?"

"Joel," Kathy Steven answered and then waited for Garrett patiently.

Garrett chewed his lip nervously. "Would I be able to meet him sometime soon?" he asked with trepidation.

Kathy looked at Garrett with interest. Praying silently that she was doing the right thing, she said, "My husband and Joel are meeting me here at the end of school to go and do some shopping. You are welcome to come by when school's over."

Flexing his arm and fisting, Garrett cried, "Yes!" Noticing Principal Stevens watching him, he awkwardly mumbled, "Um . . . that would be great . . . um . . . thanks."

Nodding her dismissal, she commented, "You'd better be off to class now, Garrett. I'll see you after school, here."

He smiled and then swaggered off in his usual way.

Kathy Stevens sat back at her desk, thinking, *Lord, what is this about? Protect us and help me to be sensitive to your Spirit.*

The angel standing behind her smiled. All had gone as the Almighty had planned.

In some ways, the day was more interesting since Garrett was excited about meeting Joel at the end of the day, yet it also seemed to drag because he couldn't wait until the school day was done for the same reason. The excitement, though, appeared to have a general, good effect on Garrett, and he decided early on that the best way to make it to the end of the day was to participate in what he usually considered to be boring requirements of education. His Civics teacher was amazed that Garrett actually had some very good thoughts on the upcoming primary elections. The English Lit teacher thought Garrett had probably skimmed one of the readily available guides to the short story they had read, thus cheating on the graded class discussion of the story. Even the gym teacher was shocked to see Garrett do more than just stand around in passive objection to the physical fitness requirement. He was so used to putting a zero next to Garrett's name for class participation that he had to stop and erase the zero and put in 100 percent! The subject even came up in the teacher's lounge at lunchtime, as the morning teachers prepared the afternoon ones for the changed attitude. The art teacher mused that maybe his admonition to Garrett that morning actually had sunk in.

Thus primed, the afternoon instructors wondered how Garrett might surprise them. He did not disappoint them—in math (a subject he usually scorned and his grades concurred) he had the class cheering him on with working a problem on the smart board successfully. The girls in his grade gathered together in the hall afterwards, eager to pass along the amazing feat to many of Garrett's admirers. Although he would not be considered handsome, he was liked by many girls because of his ability to be friendly and cool. He would have fit right in with some 1960s hippies, complete with some artistic tattoos and long hair.

By the time Garrett made it to band, his last class of the day, his classmates were buzzing with anticipation of more atypical behavior. He sauntered in, and the students all became quiet. The silence was embarrassingly apparent, but Garrett merely smiled his usual smile and waved his drumstick at the band director, while he took his place by a snare drum.

"Alright, alright, everybody," the band director called as he tapped his baton on the music stand. "Take your seats and get ready. And, Mr. Waterford, if you have any unconventional behavior to display, could you please do it immediately so that we can get down to practice?"

Mr. Wagner, having actually lived through the sixties, openly accepted Garrett for his romantic flare, so he could readily acknowledge the boy without any partiality. However, he did have a class to teach, so theatrics would have to wait!

Garrett spread his arms out and shrugged his shoulders in a nothing-out-of-the-ordinary gesture and silently waited on Mr. Wagner to begin.

The disappointed band members slumped in their chairs and obediently prepared to play.

Mr. Wagner tapped the stand to set the beat and then pointed to the percussion section in time to begin the syncopated piece. The lead-in was perfect, and the trumpets led the number as the director brought in other instruments at the appropriate times. They were practicing for a special marching band performance and competition the following week and had been having trouble with the syncopation. The drums were key, so Mr. Wagner nearly cringed as they came to the difficult portion, hoping the drums could carry the unusual beat for the rest of the band to follow. He looked out to the percussion section and poised his baton to direct them, but Garrett wasn't looking at the music! He was serenely staring at Mr. Wagner with a grin. Mr. Wagner almost stopped the band, but decided to continue conducting. Garrett hit the syncopated beat perfectly, and the rest of the band followed suit, the result being a wonderful rendition of their competition piece! Mr. Wagner excitedly directed them to the end, listening happily as each instrument halted exactly on his mark.

The room held silent for just a moment and then roared into boisterous cheers at the accomplishment! Everyone was pleased with the performance, and Mr. Wagner congratulated them all. They rehearsed a few more times before the end of the class. Many students left, boasting about how they'd annihilate the competition if they did that well again.

Mr. Wagner patted a few students on the backs as they left, but he eyed Garrett curiously as he grabbed his backpack to leave.

"I didn't think you knew that syncopated part before, but you sure nailed it today, Garrett," Mr. Wagner stated approvingly.

Garrett nodded but said nothing as he stuck his drumsticks into his back pocket.

Mr. Wagner surveyed the smiling teen, hoping for some response but knowing none was forthcoming. He smiled back and gave a slight lift of his head in dismissal.

Garrett strolled out of the band room and went to his locker to gather his things. *Cool day!* he thought to himself.

The Being with him grinned broadly. It *had* been a cool day. There was quite a bit of enjoyment in helping this one, who took nothing for granted and saw it all as a gift from God. The change recently had been enormous, although it had been a matter of the heart and not externally seen. Garrett had retained his self while acquiring selflessness. It was a unique quality, and few could handle the gift. The Creator had done something very special with this one.

Garrett watched the halls clear of students as buses loaded outside of the main door by the office. He went in to the anteroom and looked for Monica. No one was there, so he cautiously knocked on the gate.

Principal Stevens peeked out from her office and called, "Hello, Garrett! Just have a seat out there. It may be ten minutes or so before my husband and son get here, and I have some work to do, OK?"

Garrett nodded his reply but then added, "Sure."

Kathy Stevens returned to her desk and pondered the events of the day. The unusual behavior of Garrett had not gone without her notice, especially with teachers and students calling it to her attention, and she wondered if the anticipated meeting with her son had sparked some kind of strange transformation in the boy. She sighed, said a quick prayer for guidance, and then started on some paperwork.

It wasn't long before the office door opened, and Doug Stevens peered into her room.

Kathy greeted her husband, and asked, "Where's Joel?"

"Oh, he was working on something, and I said I'd just come in and get you. Do you know a boy is waiting out there for something?" Doug commented.

"That boy," Kathy offered, "thinks he knows Joel somehow and asked to meet him when you two came today after school."

"Really?" Doug exclaimed quietly. "He doesn't look familiar to me. Does he go to school here?"

Kathy nodded. "Would you mind asking Joel to come in for a moment?"

Doug shrugged, "Sure. I'll go and get him."

Doug left and Kathy gathered up her things. She pulled her door closed, locked it, and then came out to where Garrett was waiting.

"Joel didn't come in, so my husband went out to get him," Kathy informed Garrett. "Do you need a ride home?"

"Ah, no . . . thanks . . . I drove today," Garrett said.

At that moment, Joel entered the office.

"Hey, Mom, what's up?" Joel greeted.

"Joel—Hi! How was your day?" Kathy asked.

Joel shrugged and said, "It was fine."

"Good. Uh, Joel, this student recognized you in the picture on my desk and asked to meet you. This is Garrett Waterford. Garrett, this is my son, Joel."

Garrett had stood up when Kathy began explaining why she wanted Joel to come in. He gazed at Joel thoughtfully.

Joel looked at Garrett. "Hi! I'm afraid you don't look familiar to me. Where do you think you know me from?"

Garrett continued to stare at Joel for a few moments and then asked, "Could I talk to you alone, Joel?"

Joel seemed to look past Garrett for a second and then nonchalantly responded, "Sure. Let's go out in the hall. We'll just be a sec, Mom, OK?"

Not waiting for his mom to answer, Joel escorted Garrett out into the hall, pulling the office door closed behind him.

Kathy looked over at Doug and exclaimed, "Well, I guess he's got things under control. We may as well sit down and wait for them."

Doug nodded in agreement, sighed, and slouched down in a chair.

Out in the hall, Joel smiled at Garrett, "How do you know me, 'cause I know I haven't met you?"

For a split second Garrett questioned whether he should reveal about his dreams or not, but he suddenly knew he had to.

"I've seen you and a bunch of other kids in my dreams lately," Garrett told Joel.

Joel laughed, "I'm in your dreams? That's a new one! Tell me about them!"

Joel then listened quietly as Garrett told him about the dreams, and how just last night he had finally seen Joel's face, matching it with Principal Stevens' family picture.

Garrett finished and queried, "Now, can you tell me what's going on?"

Stroking his chin and still with a smile on his face, Joel pretended to be deep in thought, then he laughed again, and said, "Turn around, Garrett, and you'll see what this is about!"

Although Garrett was not one to be easily surprised, his face did show some shock as he turned around and beheld two angels standing behind him.

Twinkle-Eyes smiled and said, "Hello, Garrett!"

Garrett stared at the Beings silently. The angels and Joel did not speak as the teen took it all in. It wasn't long before Garrett visibly relaxed and cocked his head to one side, as if to say, "Bring it on!" Yet, he simply nodded and blew a low whistle.

The other angel spoke up, "You have been given a gift that will assist our Lord in the harvesting of souls in the end times. It is now time for you to join with others who also have been given gifts for this purpose. Each of you is needed to complete the task ahead. You have already seen some of what will take place. The Spirit will guide you in the use of your gift as you yield yourself to His leading."

Again, Garrett gazed at the angels, but finally, he spoke. "OK. I'm in. What's next?" he asked nonchalantly.

Twinkle-Eyes chuckled with raised eyebrows and spoke to the other angel, "You were right! He does take things rather easily!"

Turning back to Garrett, Twinkle-Eyes continued, "You will need to meet with the others. Give your phone number to Joel, and he will contact you when he sets up the meeting for everyone. It will be soon."

Garrett complied, writing in a notebook he pulled out of his backpack, and then ripping it off for Joel. Joel then wrote his phone number down in the notebook for Garrett to have.

"Cool!" Joel exclaimed. "I'll call you soon!"

With that, the angels disappeared.

Garrett nodded and gazed at the place where the angels had been. Their disappearance had seemed to have no effect on him until he murmured, "Now *that* was sturdy!"

Joel looked at him questioningly, not having heard that expression before.

Noticing Joel's inquiring look, Garrett explained, "It reminds me of a sturdy tree—it's there . . . it's connected . . . but you don't see the roots. . . . You just have to believe that there's some awesome stuff happening when all of a sudden in the spring, the leaves just appear. Those angels—they're connected somehow so that they can go places we can't see, and they know stuff we don't know—it's strong, like that sturdy tree." He finished, letting the comparison sink in, while he nodded his head thoughtfully.

Joel wasn't sure what to think. It was clear that this guy dealt with life very differently than most.

"Well," Joel began, "I'll call you about meeting with everyone."

Garrett responded, "Yeah . . ." but there was a hint of question in his voice.

Joel asked, "You OK? Seeing angels is not the norm, you know."

Laughing easily, Garrett spoke with clarity now. "Yeah, I realize that. It'll be good to finally do something about the dreams and act on them. I was getting kind of impatient for something to happen."

He grabbed his backpack and went out the front door of the school, leaving Joel wondering how the Lord was going to use such a motley crew!

CHAPTER 16

Joel didn't have to wait long before he knew the group was to meet all together. He had told Jill and Chris about meeting Garrett, calling each of them when he got home that evening. Both of them had felt a strange inclination to meet the following night and were about to call Joel when he called them. Then Liz phoned to tell Joel that she just couldn't get it out of her head about the group and could they meet?

Asking each other to pray, Joel told them he'd call them back in an hour. As he clicked the phone off, it rang immediately. He was surprised to hear Garrett's distinguished drawl.

"Hey . . . uh . . . is this Joel?"

Joel responded quickly, "Yeah. This is Garrett, isn't it?"

"Whoa . . . yeah. It's me," Garrett said. "Weird thing, you know . . ."

"What's that?" Joel asked.

"Well . . . I was thinkin' about the dreams I've had, and I remember that I did see angels, and, like, right away, I was with a bunch of other kids. That made me think we need to meet, like, tomorrow," Garrett explained.

Joel paused and silently prayed, *Is that want You want, Lord?*

Immediately, he knew.

"Garrett, I think you're right. Did you see in your dream where we should go?" Joel decided to ask.

"Yeah . . . I did . . . and I also saw where I picked everyone up at," Garrett offered.

The two exchanged the necessary information, got each other's e-mail address, and hung up. Joel called the other three and filled them in. The pick-up place was easily accessible to all. Joel finished the arrangements, sat back in his chair, and thought, *Wow, that was easy!*

Instantly, he felt a sense of foreboding.

Joel tried to shake the feeling that something was wrong, but he couldn't. He fell into an uneasy sleep. When he woke up in the morning, the apprehension was still present. He spent some time in prayer and devotions, willing for Twinkle-Eyes to appear, but the sensation of mild anxiety persisted. He sought out Jill and Chris as soon as he got to school. Neither of them had experienced anything unusual and both were quite excited about the evening meeting. Joel decided to keep his strange feeling to himself.

Heading to his first class, Joel heard his name called out. He turned to see Kyle jostling through the crowd to get to him.

"Hey, Joel! You are hard to find anymore!" Kyle exclaimed.

Joel smiled at his friend, and said, "Yeah . . . I guess we've both been busy! How's karate?"

"That's what I want to talk to you about," Kyle hurriedly said. "I'm in a tournament tomorrow, and I really need to practice, but the gym is closed tonight for some special event. I thought you could come over later and spar with me like we used to do in my basement. There's a form I'm having trouble with. I know you haven't been doing it for a couple of months, but you're the only one I know who could help."

Kyle looked at Joel expectantly.

Joel's face fell and his stomach went into a knot. He wanted to help his friend, but the meeting introducing Garrett to the gang was already set.

Kyle right away read Joel's face and knew his plan was in jeopardy.

"What—it's not a church night; I know you've gotten into that, and I haven't bugged you about it. I really need you, Joel. You haven't been around, and we haven't talked for ages," Kyle stormed, his characteristic anger taking hold.

"It's just . . ." Joel began.

At that moment the bell rang, warning students to get to their first class.

Kyle glared at Joel and muttered, "Thanks for nothing. I thought you were my friend!" And he turned and rushed away.

Joel felt terrible. He grabbed his books, slammed his locker shut, and nearly ran to his first class. He had trouble paying attention as he thought how quickly the day had twisted into problems. The past month or two had been incredible as he spent time with Twinkle-Eyes, Chris, and Jill. Joel had actually forgotten about his friendship with Kyle. Kyle and his parents hadn't been at church a lot, which normally happened during this hectic karate time. The two boys had rapidly drifted apart.

Maybe I could help him right after school, Joel thought.

He looked for Kyle after each class and finally caught up to him.

"Kyle . . . *Kyle,*" Joel almost yelled, as he attempted to talk to his old friend. "I could come after school for a while, if that would help."

Kyle heaved a sigh as he turned to face Joel. "Oh, so you think you can spare a few minutes with me?"

Joel noticed a sinister look on Kyle's face. The energy he had felt from days with God's servants seemed to drain out of him, and he realized that this was the look Kyle had always used to control him in the past. He now wished he hadn't offered to go to Kyle's house after school. Kyle had played him, and Joel had fallen for it. The worst thing was that Joel also realized he had not prayed about the situation. It had happened so fast and had left him just wanting to please his friend, that he had missed asking God to help him and show him the right thing to do.

Kyle's face relaxed into a sly grin, and he walked away saying, "See you at my house after school!"

Joel sighed and rubbed his forehead and then headed off to his last class before lunch. He was distracted and unable to participate in class as had become the norm lately. His stomach continued in a knot while he maneuvered into the cafeteria and found Jill and Chris at a table they had sat at routinely.

"Hey Joel!" Jill greeted and then added, "What's wrong with you?"

Joel sat down and looked at his friends in the Lord. "I just messed up, and I don't know what to do about it." He summed up what had happened and then asked, "Any suggestions?"

Chris raised his eyebrows and shrugged his shoulders, "You can't let Kyle control you, Joel! God should be controlling you."

"I know," Joel sighed again.

Jill spoke up, having gained more boldness in the past days with the angels, "Why don't we pray? You admit that you should have done that before dealing with Kyle, but it's not too late to ask God for guidance now!"

Joel and Chris looked at each other and then at Jill. Both realized they had missed the simplest answer.

Jill led the prayer, "Dear Father, we come to You to ask that You will help Joel know what to do regarding Kyle. Remind Joel of who he is and who he belongs to. Help him to treat Kyle with respect and kindness so that Kyle may see Your greatness, yet don't let Joel allow Kyle to use and control him. Thanks for helping Joel, Lord. Amen."

Joel looked at his friends. "I think I need to spend some time alone with the Lord. I'm going to go out by the flag pole—nobody is usually there, and there's a bench to sit on."

Chris nodded and said, "We'll be praying for you."

Joel gave a wan smile of thanks, and then headed out of the cafeteria.

The flag area was deserted, as Joel had hoped. He sat on a bench that was shielded from the school by some bushes.

"Lord, I'm sorry for not coming to You when Kyle did his thing. I never saw before how he treated me and would trick me into going along with anything he wanted. I'm different now, but

I acted just like I did before, and now he got me to do what he wanted. It's not that I mind helping him—it's just that I see him differently now, too. He doesn't bring me up like Chris and Jill do. He brings me down, and I don't like that anymore. Should I still go to his house and help him? Or should I tell him I can't?" Joel prayed quietly out loud.

"Got a problem, son?" a kind voice said from behind Joel.

Joel jumped up to see a man in gardener's overalls with bush clippers hanging on a loop of the pants. He had never seen the man before, but something seemed familiar about him. An old fishing hat covered his head and protected him from the sun's rays. His hands looked gnarled and his skin was leathery, but his eyes were kind and beckoning.

"Uh . . ." Joel stammered with his eyes downcast.

"I couldn't help but overhear what you said . . . I wasn't eavesdropping. I happened to be trimming the bushes here and didn't want you to go on thinking you were alone," the old man explained.

Joel sighed, "That's OK. I was just trying to figure something out."

"It sounded like you were praying," the gardener prompted.

Swallowing hard, Joel responded, "Yeah . . . I was."

"Hmm . . ." the man contemplated, "I always found praying to be very helpful when I had a problem." He stopped and then added, "But sometimes I needed to talk it out to someone, too."

Joel looked over at the man, noticing his raised eyebrows which seemed to summon Joel to talk.

Nodding his head, Joel spoke, "Yeah . . . I think I would like to talk about it, if you don't mind?"

"Not at all, son," the man answered as he sat down on the bench. "I sometimes talk to the bushes and plants, but they don't talk back to me, and sometimes I just need to hear a voice to see my way outa a problem." The man's voice had slipped into some colloquialisms, making the atmosphere seem very comfortable.

"Well," Joel began and then quickly summarized his relationship with Kyle, the development of his new friends, and the day's encounter with Kyle, leaving out any mention of angels or the underlying reason Joel had for making some new friends.

The gardener sat quietly, nodding every once in a while to encourage Joel until he was finished.

"So," he said, finally, "you told Kyle you would come after school."

"Yeah," Joel admitted.

"It seems you should do as you said you would," the gardener said, getting up and starting to leave.

"What!" Joel nearly shouted, shaking his head. "I thought you'd tell me God would provide somehow so I wouldn't have to go!"

"Ah . . ." the man spoke as he stopped but still had his back turned away from Joel. "It seems you already had decided what to do, so why did you want my opinion?"

Joel sighed, "I don't know. I do know that I don't like how Kyle can control me, and I want to stop it. I just thought that if I didn't show up, it would prove to him that I don't have to listen to him."

"But it was you who suggested coming after school, not Kyle; so if you don't show up, he will say you lied, and any witness you would have had to him would be lost," the gardener voiced.

Suddenly, Joel realized that he recognized that voice, and he gazed at the old man as he once again turned to face Joel.

The face was definitely known to him, but why hadn't he seen it?

It was Twinkle-Eyes.

As quickly as Joel realized it was the angel, it disappeared from before his eyes.

Joel made his way slowly back into the cafeteria against the stream of students heading back to class after lunch. He spotted Chris and Jill and worked toward them.

"Hey, Joel!" Chris greeted. "Any breakthrough?"

Nodding, Joel told them, "I'm going to Kyle's after school. I have to do what I said I would do. Could you guys pray that I say and do the right things?"

"Sure," both Jill and Chris replied, and soon they each were off to their classes.

Sensing something, Joel looked out the cafeteria windows and saw Twinkle-Eyes, dressed as a gardener, smiling at him. Joel paused and then smiled back.

Joel changed clothes as soon as he got home, left a note for his parents, and headed over to Kyle's house on his bike. Kyle only lived two miles away, and Joel had probably ridden this route a hundred times over the years. This time, he prayed the whole way, asking God to help him to be a witness to Kyle.

Kyle answered the door, and the boys hurried down to the finished basement. The workout area was small, but complete, with mats and large enough for most of the forms that Kyle now used. They stretched and did a quick warm-up before Kyle explained to Joel what he needed for the new move. Soon they were sparring, just like they used to. Kyle worked on the form he was having trouble with, finally getting to the point that he felt he had mastered it. It took only an hour, but the guys were sweaty and hot by the time they finished. They grabbed towels and water before heading outside to cool down on the front porch.

"Thanks for your help, Joel," Kyle exclaimed, throwing himself down on a porch swing. "I think I'll be ready now."

Joel smiled at his friend, "No problem! That was fun! I may not be into it as much as you, but I do still enjoy it! I think you'll do great at the tournament. Where is it?"

Kyle sighed, "It's over in Smithfield—you know, where the Tornados are. They are really good. I don't know that I have a chance, but I'll just try my best!"

Joel looked thoughtfully at his friend, noting the sincerity.

"Would you like me to pray for you, Kyle?" the words came out before Joel even realized what he was saying.

Kyle looked over at him, his eyebrows half-furrowed and half-raised, as if to say, *you've got to be crazy!* But, the look passed, and he shrugged his shoulders and said, "Sure—I need all the help I can get!"

Joel nervously started, "Lord, please be with Kyle and help him to do his best tomorrow in the tournament. Protect him from injury. Help him to do the forms correctly. Give him strength and energy. Amen."

Sitting up, Kyle grinned, "Thanks! I appreciate you coming over, and thanks for the prayer. . . ." He stuttered slightly, "Uh . . . that was nice."

"Sure," Joel replied. "Uh . . . I gotta go now. See ya tomorrow in school!"

Jumping off the porch, Joel waved at Kyle and pedaled away.

"Thank you, Lord!" Joel breathed as he sped home.

CHAPTER 17

Garrett met the other teens as planned and after some quick introductions, they loaded into his car and headed out of town. They soon were passing through a heavily forested area that was posted as game lands. Garrett slowed the car a few times as deer trotted across the road.

Chris exclaimed from the back seat, "Where *do* you live, dude?"

Laughing, Garrett responded, "Out in the boonies, *dude*!"

The group all laughed and continued chatting until Garrett called, "There's my house, and here's our farm!"

The car emerged from the woods as the road twisted down from the mountaintop. A few houses dotted the picturesque landscape that had morphed into farmland. A barn with some sheds housing farm equipment was on their right and immediately past it was a small farm pond. A couple of ducks paddled around at the far edge. Fields stretched back to woods on their left and again on the right past the pond.

Garrett slowed down and drove into the grass as the land leveled out.

Before them stood a small church. It was painted white, with a steeple reaching into the sky. Two large maple trees seemed to guard the sacred ground in front, and woods secured the back. A small stream passed on the left, and a pasture bordered the right.

Garrett pulled in front of a gate in the pasture fence and stopped the car.

"Here we are—come on inside!" he urged them as they emptied out of the car.

The teens gazed around them, silently coming to the consensus that this was the *perfect* spot to meet.

Garrett unlocked a door at the front of the building and pleasantly invited them to step through the threshold.

It was like stepping backwards in time.

The straight-back wooden pews were simple, dating back to a time when ornate and comfortable seats were not affordable. In fact, the whole structure was quite plain, with the exception of oil lamps hanging from the ceiling with red oil filling the glass bases. A small, old, pot-bellied stove stood in the center. An organ was to the left of the platform, which held a little pulpit. There were ten rows of pews and then several pews in the front on each side which were turned perpendicular to the rest. A board hung on the front wall, indicating the attendance from some service of 47. The air was stuffy and musty.

"I . . . uh . . . saw this in a dream," Garrett offered. "Kids that I didn't know came in here and were talking, and then," he thumbed to Joel, "he prayed, and I saw his face. . . . It was the face of my principal's son." Noticing some questioning looks, he added, "I . . . uh . . . sorta got to know the principal really well." He shrugged his shoulders and unashamedly grinned.

The others chuckled, and the group sat down in some of the pews.

"Wow . . . these are *not* the most comfortable seats!" Chris good-naturedly complained.

"Nope," Garrett agreed. "You sure don't want the preacher talkin' long when you're sitting here on a hot summer day!"

"Do people still come to church here?" Jill asked.

"Not really—there are services a few times a year—folks come out from the town church, but most of the time it just sits here, unused. The one time in the fall is a cool service, though—Lamplight. They hold an evening service and light the kerosene lamps. It's really neat!" Garrett informed them.

"Are you sure it's OK for us to come in here and meet?" Joel asked.

"Yeah . . ." Garrett replied, "my parents said it was OK as long as we turn off the lights and don't make a mess."

Joel nodded, "Cool. Alright, everybody! Let's get started! How about we take turns telling about our recent experiences? I want to encourage everyone to feel free to say *anything*, even if it seems impossible. We are a unique group, and we need to trust each other. I'll start."

Joel told his story, including how he first saw Twinkle-Eyes, to the latest encounter with the angel at the flag pole. Jill went next, then Chris, and Garrett. Finally, it was Liz's turn.

"You all are different from me. Um . . . I'm Catholic," Liz started, her eyes downcast.

The others looked at Joel, not knowing what to say.

Joel cleared his throat and peered at Liz until she raised her eyes.

"It doesn't matter how you've been raised to worship, Liz; some of us are pretty different in that even though we're Protestants. It's apparent to us that the Lamb That Was Slain has chosen you. You are an integral part of this group and don't ever forget that! Please tell us what happened to you," Joel implored.

Liz looked around the group and seemed to gain strength.

"It all started one day with Mass, that's our church service at school," she began. Gaining momentum, she soon had the others mesmerized with her story.

"Wow!" the rest all murmured together as she finished.

"It sure would be great if that happened at our school," Jill voiced.

Liz smiled with appreciation at the comment, feeling acceptance by the group immediately.

Chatter broke out amongst the teens as they shared more with each other, discovering commonalities and differences.

After about fifteen minutes, Joel sought their attention.

"Hey . . . everyone! There are some things we'd better do before leaving tonight," he called.

The noise died down as the group focused on Joel.

Joel checked some notes he had pulled out from a backpack.

"I jotted down some things while I prayed and had devotions this morning," he started. "The first thing is to encourage everyone to keep a journal of things that happen. That way we will more accurately have a record, like Acts in the Bible. I'm not sure why that's important, but it was really a strong thought that kept coming back to me. I think we each will have different perspectives and memories, and that will come together to form a complete story, rather than just one person writing down how they see it. The Gospels show that concept, and if it was vital for the disciples to do it, then we should!"

The others nodded in agreement.

"Second," he went on, "is to name ourselves. That way we can refer to the group and know exactly who we are talking about. Does anyone have any suggestions?"

Garrett offered, with a grin, "How about the Crusaders? That was a noble time!"

Joel nodded, and pondered the name.

"What about the Harvesters? The angels have talked about the harvesting of souls," Jill suggested.

Chris countered, "But, remember, we probably will set the stage for others to harvest and not actually do the harvesting. Isn't that what the angel said?"

"Oh," Jill considered, "that's right. I do remember that."

The group sat silently for a moment, contemplating a good name.

A voice quietly spoke up.

"What about the Joel Prophecy, or JP for short?" Liz asked. "It's the Scripture that started things for Joel and me."

The group sat up and looked at each other. It made sense!

Garrett was the first to speak, "I like it! It does describe what has happened to us—visions, prophecies and dreams."

Jill grinned and said, "It goes right along with HT, heaven time; now we'll be the JP group!"

Chris, Jill, Garrett and Liz chatted about their positive impression of the name until they noticed Joel wasn't participating. In fact, he looked uncomfortable.

"What's the matter, Joel," Chris asked. "Don't you like the name?"

"I don't know, guys," Joel admitted. "It just seems sort of weird to have the group name begin with my name . . . like it's my group. This is something God has done, not me, and I don't want people thinking that I'm some sort of guru or something, you know!"

The others immediately understood, yet the name had seemed perfect to them. They all sat silently again, pondering the dilemma.

Finally, Garrett spoke up. "Joel, you are our leader, and that's the position God placed you in. It seems to me that you are named Joel for a reason—because God planned to use you to fulfill the last days' prophecy written in the book of Joel. It doesn't really matter, you know, because we can use the JP abbreviation, and anyone outside of the group won't know what it means. It could stand for Jesus People, like in the 1960s and '70s." Garrett paused before continuing, "Does anyone know what my middle name is?"

They all shrugged their shoulders and shook their heads.

Garrett nodded, "OK. Well, we talked that the dreams part of the prophecy may apply to me, because that's what led me to you guys and to using this little church." He smiled and raised his eyebrows up and down. "Well, guess what my middle name is . . ." he paused for emphasis, "Daniel, the interpreter of dreams and a prophet!"

The others gasped in surprise and then laughed.

"Now," Garrett continued, "when I started having the dreams, it didn't hit me right away, but now it just makes sense that God would give me a name to live up to and represent. So, Joel, I think it makes perfect sense that your name is Joel and that we are to be the Joel Prophecy group. That's what God has planned from before any of us were born!"

Chris chimed in, "Yeah . . . uh . . . Psalm 139, verses 13–16 talks about that!" He pulled out his Bible and read: *"For You formed my inward parts; You covered me in my mother's womb. I will praise You, for I am fearfully and wonderfully made; marvelous are Your works, and that my soul knows very well. My frame was not hidden from You, when I was made in secret, and skillfully wrought in the lowest parts of the earth. Your eyes saw my substance, being yet unformed. And in*

Your book they all were written, the days fashioned for me, when as yet there were none of them."

Chris looked up and exclaimed, "So you see, Joel, your name and what all of us are doing was planned and set up even before any of us were born! The Joel Prophecy group isn't here because of you . . ." He paused and then continued excitedly, "We are here because of the Joel Prophecy!"

Garrett, Jill, and Liz all chorused, "Wow!"

Joel stared at Chris and then at the others. He exhaled with a chuckle and nodded, "You're all right!"

"Yes!" Garrett called exuberantly.

Joel continued to laugh softly and then he shook his head in astonishment. "You know, guys . . . God does seem to tie everything together."

The others nodded, waiting for Joel to finish.

Joel glanced at Chris and said, "That Scripture you just read . . . Psalm 139, right?"

Chris gave him a thumbs-up sign.

"Well, I didn't remember this until just now, but the song the youth group was singing when I first saw the angel was from those same verses in Psalm 139! It made me feel special in a way I had never felt before. For me, the fact that you brought up those verses, Chris, is the confirmation that what we are doing and what we want to call ourselves are both the Lord's will. It seems that when the Lord wants us to really understand what He is doing, He repeats the point He is trying to make over and over again until we get it!" Joel concluded.

"Cool!" Garrett exclaimed with a slow nod.

"So . . . I would like to call the first meeting of the Joel Prophecy group, or JP for short, to order," Joel pronounced.

Chris grinned and nearly shouted, "All right!"

The newly formed group of teens quickly made arrangements for meeting weekly at Garrett's one-roomed church and promised to call one another frequently as well as e-mailing or texting any important information.

They completed everything on Joel's list for the night and ended with a short prayer—just as Garrett had seen in his dream.

The Beings stood around the little church. One surveyed the area carefully, while two others left with the group of teens.

"The area continues to be secure," Samek spoke solemnly as he returned to the rest of the Beings.

"Good," Twinkle-Eyes said. "The key ones of the group are now in place. We must let them learn to work with each other without us for only a little while. They all have allowed their gifts and talents to begin to grow. They need to gain confidence in themselves and in each other. We must protect them and guide them in the coming days. The time draws near when the Most High God will use them!

CHAPTER 18

Joel sighed as he lay back in bed. The past few weeks had been incredible, with frequent meetings of the JP group. The teens were learning so much each time. Twinkle-Eyes had appeared to Joel shortly after the first JP meeting and told him that the angels would not immediately be obvious to the group.

It almost seemed as if each of the JP group had been programmed to do things that impacted each individually, but it all worked together cohesively at the end so that they were all amazed! One example was shortly after they had their first meeting at the church.

Joel was doing his devotions involving how the body of Christ works together. Suddenly, he had a vision where he saw a body, but it was no ordinary body, because it was disfigured. There appeared to be two or three heads, and each of the heads had different numbers of eyes, ears, and mouths. There was no left arm, but two right arms and two hands on each arm. There were three legs, and the feet were proportioned all wrong, with a tiny foot on the largest leg, and the other feet too large for the particular leg they belonged to.

The image was distasteful at best, and Joel tried to shut his eyes to rid himself of the sight, but it didn't change anything. He stared at the creature and wondered what he was supposed to do. Then, as he watched, the monster seemed to twist on itself. It contorted and writhed, and some other shapes appeared to develop from the one, gross image. Surprised, Joel realized that normal bodies were emerging from the monstrosity! He saw three people—two men and one woman, all with appropriate parts. They smiled and hugged each other and then seemed to gaze at Joel with wistful expressions as the vision faded from his eyes.

Joel was disturbed by the vision, unaccustomed to the graphic, offensive scene that he had seen. His others visions had been glorious and uplifting! This one troubled him, and he felt uneasy all day. Fortunately, a JP meeting had been planned, so he decided not to bother his friends with what he had seen until they were all together, and he could get their input.

It was apparent from the time Garrett picked them up that each was more pensive than usual. They were all outwardly happy as greetings were called out, but something was bothering them all, that was certain.

Joel called the meeting to order once they were settled in the church. He led them in a simple prayer and then asked if anyone wanted to say anything. Chris chewed on his lip, Jill rubbed her ear and looked away, Liz twisted her fingers like she was saying the rosary, and Garrett simply stared at the rustic kerosene lamps.

"Uh . . . it looks to me as if we all are bothered by something tonight. I thought I was the only one who had something weird happen, but it seems that maybe you all did too?" Joel asked.

Startled, the others focused right on Joel and voiced an affirmative in one way or another.

Feeling relieved in a strange way, Joel went on to tell them about his vision. As he finished, he realized that none of them seemed shocked.

Chris was the first to speak. "That pretty much is what I dreamed last night."

"Mine was the same, but in cartoon form," Jill offered.

Garrett snorted and drawled, "My clay art project came alive and did the same thing!"

Liz voiced, "I was watching a movie, and it somehow had the characters do that, too! I knew it wasn't part of the film—it was so creepy!"

"Does anyone have an idea of what it means and why we all saw the same thing in different ways?" Joel asked.

The four other teens sat thoughtfully, with none willing to immediately offer an opinion.

Joel reached for his Bible. "Do you all have your Bibles?" he questioned.

In response, all but Garrett rummaged in bags or backpacks. Garrett simply reached into a pew and grabbed a worn book from a stack of hymnals. The others looked curiously at him.

Sheepishly, he quipped, "Uh . . . I knew there'd be a Bible here!"

They all chuckled, breaking the tension from the seriousness they had been feeling.

Joel spoke up, "Go to 1 Corinthians, chapter 12, verses 12–26. This is what I had read for my devotions right before I had the vision.

"For as the body is one and has many members, but all the members of that one body, being many, are one body, so also is Christ. For by one Spirit we were all baptized into one body—whether Jews or Greeks, whether slaves or free—and have all been made to drink into one Spirit. For in fact the body is not one member but many.

"If the foot should say, 'Because I am not a hand, I am not of the body,' is it therefore not of the body? And if the ear should say, 'Because I am not an eye, I am not of the body,' is it therefore not of the body? If the whole body were an eye, where would be the hearing? If the whole were hearing, where would be the smelling? But now God has set the members, each one of them, in the body just as He pleased. And if they were all one member, where would the body be?

"But now indeed there are many members, yet one body. And the eye cannot say to the hand, 'I have no need of you'; nor again the head to the feet, 'I have no need of you.' No, much rather, those members of the body which seem to be weaker are necessary. And those members of the body which we think to be less honorable, on these we bestow greater honor; and our unpresentable parts have greater modesty, but our presentable parts have no need. But God composed the body, having given greater honor to that part which lacks it, that there should be no schism in the body, but that the members should have the same care

for one another. And if one member suffers, all the members suffer with it; or if one member is honored, all the members rejoice with it."

Joel breathed heavily as he finished the reading. "I think that God was reminding each of us that we must work together. That grotesque monster was us—if we forget that we are part of a greater whole—the body of Christ. It may seem that something may not be as important or showy as another thing, but that's just like there not being a left arm or hand, to those of us who are right-handed, like on that creature. We still need our left hand to balance, to hold things steady, even if our right hand is doing much of the work. So, you see, we have to value each other fully for what God has chosen us to do. At one time, Jill's sense of the angels may be totally important, and Chris' Scripture talent may not be needed; but then it will turn around, and Chris is able to help us through the Word, and Jill's sense has no place."

He paused, peering into each one's face, and then continued, "I used to think that what was happening to me was really cool, and, not that it isn't, but that made me think a little more of myself than I should have. And then Jill saw the angel, too, and it wasn't my little secret anymore. A part of me was upset about that until the friendship with Jill and Chris made me feel better than that. I was part of something; I wasn't alone . . . and it is so much greater to be an integral part of the body of Christ! Now, I can't imagine myself alone in this! I need each of you to be who God has made you to be. . . . Chris can't try to be Garrett or Liz forget that she's a Catholic. That would be all wrong! That would make us into a monster that God can't use!"

"The Scripture pointed out that we are part of *one* body. Perhaps we could substitute Protestant and Catholic for the Jews and Greeks. We have . . ." he paused and checked his Bible, *"been made to drink into one Spirit. One Spirit."*

Garrett sat up and said, "Yeah . . . it's like one power or energy helping us all."

"Like electricity," Liz said, smiling, "one current makes the TV run, a computer, a microwave, a light—very different apparatuses that do different things, but it's the electricity that makes them all run. They are nothing without it—just a bunch of junk!"

"So . . . what does this mean for us?" Chris pondered rhetorically. "I think what we saw was a warning. If ever any of us starts to consider him- or herself more important than another, the image of that thing will be enough to bring us back down to size!"

"Warning . . . Yes . . . a warning!" Jill exclaimed, and her excitement made them all look quickly at her.

"I . . . uh . . . saw a bit more than what Joel described, but I didn't realize it at the time," Jill continued. "There was a lot of color in what I saw. There was no sparkle, no power. . . . It was dull in that sense, but bright like . . . like . . ." she stuttered as she struggled for the right description. Her eyes wondered to something outside the church's window. She stood up and pressed her face to the glass. "Yes, like the triangular warning sign on the back of that tractor." She turned to the others and pointed to a field beyond the church.

They each got to a place where they could see out a window. A tractor was parked in the field. On one of the rear supports of the cab, an orange triangle was attached to alert those coming up behind it that it was a slow-moving vehicle.

"Chris is right. It's a warning for us to behave like the body of Christ or we will be ineffective in what we're supposed to do. That thing we saw couldn't function at all. I don't want to be like that . . . ever!" Jill concluded.

The round of me-neither's and yeahs echoed in the small church.

Joel looked at his friends with a new confidence. "Are we the body of Christ?" he asked.

"Yes!" the rest called.

"Louder!" he encouraged.

"Yes!" they yelled.

"All right!" Joel exclaimed and started clapping.

The others joined him, and soon they were dancing around inside the little church.

Outside, if the teens had been privileged to see, a ring of angels circled the church, glowing as they had not done since starting their mission with the JP group. The brightness was almost unbearable, as God's power filled them and heaven seemed to come down to earth!

The JP group met again on the weekend. The remembrance of the monster they could become helped each of them be humble, yet supportive of each other. They filed into the little church, bubbling with excitement about what they were learning.

"OK," Joel began. "Does anyone have anything for prayer?"

"Uh . . ." Garrett began, "could we pray for my dad? He hurt himself yesterday, plus, the hay bine broke, and he has to either fix it or call a guy to fix it."

Chris asked, "What's a hay bine?"

"Oh . . . it cuts the hay so we can bail it; it's also called a mower," Garrett explained.

"Um . . ." a voice started.

Everyone looked at Liz.

"Your dad should rest today instead of working, and the hay bine will start OK on Monday," Liz said with an unusual authority.

The others looked curiously at her, not knowing what to say.

Liz suddenly shook her head, like she was clearing cobwebs. She looked around at the JP group and chewed on her lower lip.

Swallowing hard, she said, "I don't know why I said that; I don't know anything about farm equipment or Garrett's father."

"Don't be embarrassed, Liz," Joel admonished. "I think God gave you that to say!"

The others murmured their agreement, and Liz smiled with their encouragement.

"Let's pray!" Joel urged. "Lord, be with us as we meet today. Help us to do what You need us to do. Teach us to be Your servants. Be with Garrett's dad. Help him to rest today and . . ." Joel paused, searching for the right words, "and . . . heal the hay machine so that he can use it! Amen!"

The JP group laughed, while Joel shrugged his shoulders good-naturedly.

"Can everyone open their Bibles to Joel 2:28–29? I think we should study this passage since we named ourselves after it!" Joel instructed.

He waited while the kids helped each other find the obscure little book in the Old Testament.

"I'll go ahead and read it," Joel said. "*And it shall come to pass afterward that I will pour out My Spirit on all flesh; your sons and your daughters shall prophesy . . .*"

Joel stopped, and the group waited for him to continue, but when he didn't, they all looked up at him. He seemed to be mumbling something, intensely looking at his Bible.

"Are you OK, Joel?" Chris asked.

Joel jerked his head up, as if he had been deep in thought.

"Oh . . . yeah . . . um . . ." he seemed to stammer. "I was just thinking. . . . It says, '*your daughters shall prophesy,*' and I think that's just what Liz did." He looked at her directly to continue, "What you said about Garrett's dad and the hay thing—I think that was a prophecy. Then this talks about people prophesying, so I wonder if that's your gift!" he finished excitedly.

Jill added, "I bet that's it, Liz! I wasn't sure, but I thought I detected something a little different while you were saying that, but I wasn't paying close enough attention to be sure; I bet there *was* something! You have the gift of prophecy!"

Liz stared at them, unsure of what to think initially, but then she smiled and said, "I think you're right! I know I'm saying something, but it seems that I'm not really in control of it—it just comes out! But I also am totally convinced of the truth of it. It's weird!" she exclaimed.

"Alright!" Garrett pondered while nodding his head. "I guess I'd better encourage Dad to take off today and not to call the repair guy just yet. Cool!"

"How about I start over reading?" Joel questioned.

The group collectively agreed.

Joel started again, "*And it shall come to pass afterward that I will pour out My Spirit on all flesh; your sons and your daughters shall prophesy, your old men shall dream dreams, your young men shall see visions. And also on My menservants and on My maidservants I will pour out My Spirit in those days."*

All of a sudden, the interior of the church began to glow, and it wasn't just Jill who saw it this time. All the teens gazed about them, not realizing that they had grabbed onto each other as the phenomenon started. Hearts pounding, they anxiously watched figures appear before them.

Joel was the first to relax, yet he breathlessly anticipated the reaction from the JP group as he took in the sight. Even he was mesmerized!

Garrett breathed softly, "Whoa!"

Jill could barely take in all the sparkles and hues as she eagerly looked around.

Liz felt tingles all over, and Chris dug his fingers into her arm.

Twinkle-Eyes appeared in grandeur. Other angels stood around the inside of the tiny church, nearly filling it with a translucent light. The sight was magnificent! The angels' wings were evident, and they fluttered slightly, just enough to cause a shimmering effect. The result was to make the room radiant without shadows.

"Favored ones: You have been chosen, even before birth, while you were still in your mother's womb, to participate in this latter fulfilling of the Joel Prophecy! Our God Most High has given you gifts and talents to be used in this last harvesting of souls. Although each of you already knows the gift you've been given, you must hone your skills to help the harvesters reap what the Lord has sown," Twinkle-Eyes announced. "You will each have at least one of us to instruct you in the use of your gift, and there are others, sometimes unseen, who are watching and protecting you. We will proceed quietly in spirit, so as to not alert the legions of the evil one, but at some time, it will become known to him, and your very lives may be in danger. Satan has seen what gifted Children of God can do, and he will want to destroy you! You must remain true to the One God, recognizing that your every breath is by His power. His Word says:

"The everlasting God, the Lord, the Creator of the ends of the earth, neither faints nor is weary. His understanding is unsearchable. He gives power to the weak, and to those who have no might He increases strength. Even the youths shall faint and be weary, and the young men shall utterly fall, but those who wait on the Lord shall renew their strength; they shall mount up with wings like eagles, they shall run and not be weary, they shall walk and not faint."

Twinkle-Eyes had raised his arms over the young people as he spoke the Word. The other angels had their arms lifted as well. Arcs of light emerged from near the angels but not from them. The rays touched each teen and gently enveloped them. The effect was individual and personal, such that each knew they had received power directly from God! A sound like a whispering wind could be heard, as God communicated His will to them. His purpose was written in their minds and hearts. It was to be shared with no one, not even each other. The energy lingered on them, in them, and around them, filling them with His love, untainted by the curse of the world. Such Love had sent His only Son to die. Such Love was perfect goodness! Such Love asked them to surrender to His will. The choice was there. Any of them could have refused. But that Love fulfilled every desire within, so that each youth submitted and yielded to Love's plan.

A defining moment, each would admit later, but none would speak otherwise of what happened.

CHAPTER 19

Jill looked around at the cars going past them while Garrett drove the JP teens to the farm church. She had gotten used to seeing angels at various places, but the sight never bored her. One time she even saw an angel sitting in the driver's seat, essentially doing the driving for a little old lady who could hardly see over the dashboard. Jill got the sense that the angel was protecting the senior and those around her until the family saw fit to not allow her to drive anymore. It was a bittersweet realization, because Jill could also see a hue that she had discovered meant the older citizen would be passing on to Glory soon.

There was so much they all had learned in the past weeks since their "Pentecost." They spent a lot of time sharing with each other and working with the angels. The small church had become like a special club house, with each teen honing their skills in the corners. Garrett liked the back left area. He had drawn representations of his dreams and tacked them up on the walls. Chris had the front right choir pews where he had various Bible versions spread out so that he could easily look up verses that the group talked about and those God brought to him. Liz was in the back right with a study Bible, learning to discern when to speak and when to listen. Joel had taken the platform, at the urging of his friends, so he could lead them while continuing to study with Twinkle-Eyes.

Jill was in the front left area, where an ancient organ sat. She had a view of the fields outside as well as of the other JP teens. Her angel worked with her to see the auras and sparkles. There were times she could tell something was special, but was unable to differentiate the shades and tints. She also was amazed at the numbers of angels that she could now see, although sometimes they were so faint that she struggled until her eyes hurt. It was at those times that her angel comforted her with Bible verses and songs. Occasionally, two other angels came, and the three would teach Jill praise songs and prayer songs.

It was one of these times that Jill grasped an important truth that would carry the JP group into the season of harvesting.

Jill and the three angels were singing a praise song when Jill discerned a slight increase in the angels' sparkles. It was as if the proverbial light bulb came on.

"Everyone!" she cried, "Everyone, sing along with us!"

All the other JPs had been busy with their angels, but they quickly joined in the upbeat tune, having learned it during one of the earlier meetings with the angels. It actually could be a round, so a few waited and came in a little later, allowing the harmony to peak.

Jill's face could barely hold her excitement as her gaze went from one angel to the other.

"Louder!" she called.

The JPs shrugged with grins and chuckles while they belted out the simple praise.

Jill lifted her hands and directed the choir of voices, sometimes softening their tones and other times raising them nearly to shouts. Finally, she calmed first one group and then the other, bringing the song to a close. Her face was frozen in astonishment and wonder. The JPs gathered around her as the angels stepped back.

"Jill," Joel quipped, "what's up? You look like you've had an amazing discovery!"

"Yes! Oh, yes!" Jill exclaimed, her eyes moving from one angel to another. "Let's sing a different one."

Before anyone could object or ask another question, Jill got them started in another praise chorus, conducting them like a professional choral director, urging them up in a spectacular crescendo and then bringing them down in a finale. All the while, her eyes were glued on the angels, who smiled with understanding of her discovery.

"Come on, Jill," Chris insisted, "Let us in on it. What goes?"

Jill sighed with elation, "We help the angels!" She looked excitedly to her companions. She continued, "They have more power when we praise!"

Garrett queried, "So . . . our praise gives them power to do things?"

Jill shook her head, "No, no, it's not like that; they already have the power from God to do anything He wants, but we . . ." She paused, struggling to find the right words. "We . . . we . . ." then her face lit up, "we can turn up the volume of the power when we praise. It gives them more strength. like when someone is running a race, how they feel more energy when a friend yells out encouragement for them to continue. The angels are strengthened and helped when we praise!" She looked to her angel before continuing, "And I think they are empowered when we pray, too."

The angel smiled and gave a little nod.

"So . . ." Joel offered, "some of what we're learning is so that we can be conduits of God's power to those who are harvesting: we can pray more specifically, we can recite Scripture for encouragement, we can act on our dreams and prophecies—do all these things for God to work through man or angel?"

The angels looked at each other, astounded.

Twinkle-Eyes stepped forward and said, "Our God has truly blessed you with understanding far beyond your years, Joel. Yes, you are correct. The Most Holy God needs those who understand the connection between His power and His servants more fully during these last days. All of you are needed to bridge the gap that has developed through misunderstanding and misuse of the gifts. The saints of old knew the connection, but, over time, it has been lost. The Lord needs you to rouse the soldiers of His army on earth through the gifts He has given you. You can stimulate the children of God by your faith in what you have seen and what you will see."

The teens stood around, amazed at what they had heard. They hadn't really thought much about how their gifts would help, although a few of them secretly had wondered about it.

Garrett was the first to speak up. "So, when I have a dream, how does that help you?" he asked, pointedly.

The angel working with Garrett moved forward, while Twinkle-Eyes stepped back slightly.

"Up until now," he began, "your dreams have mainly guided *you*. But, soon, you will also have dreams involving others who are needed in the harvesting. In fact, you just had a dream about someone who needs you to encourage him to take a step that will make a big change in his life, isn't that right?"

Garrett's eyes widened in acknowledgement of the angel's truthful words. He gulped and heaved a big sigh. The others waited for him to explain, but Garrett merely leaned against a pew and looked at the floor.

Joel gazed at Garrett's angel for a moment and then at Twinkle-Eyes. Something inside him said, *Wait*.

The little chapel seemed heavy with silence.

"Don't be afraid, Garrett," a soft voice spoke, interrupting the quietness.

Liz took a step towards the young man and laid her hand on his arm.

She looked up into his eyes and straightened with resolve as she continued, "It is the right thing to do. It won't ruin things, like you think it will. He needs *you* to tell him to do it, because he's holding back. He won't do it without you saying something."

Garrett's face looked pained, but he nodded his head.

The JP meeting had ended on a solemn note as the group recognized that Garrett had something difficult to do. No one had asked him who the dream was about, but they had all promised to pray for him as he took them home that night. He drove home, barely paying attention on the winding, mountain road, as he contemplated what he should do.

Suddenly, a deer ran out onto the road from the woods on the right. Garrett gasped as he tried to react to the encounter, but his mind was not ready to respond with the haste he needed to avoid either hitting the deer or running off the road.

Abruptly, he seemed to be in slow motion, and the images he saw held him in amazement.

No less than five angels were in view with one on each side of the car, keeping it from going off the road, even though he had turned the steering wheel hard to try to avoid the collision. Another angel had absorbed the forward motion of the car and was slowing it down. Two other angels picked up the startled deer, barely raising it above the ground and in an instant had moved it to the left side of the road, out of harm's way. Garrett thought he may have seen some more angels behind the car from peripheral vision in the side mirror, but he wasn't sure, and he had felt the warmth and peace of an angel's touch in those brief, terrible moments when he thought his life was going to end.

Just as quickly, time regained its normal march, and Garrett found himself slowing the car as the deer ran off into the thick brush on the left side of the road. His heart was pounding and his hands shaking as he pulled off to the side and stopped. He realized that he was holding his breath, so he exhaled and fell back into the seat from the straightened position he had instinctively gone to when he first saw the deer. He closed his eyes and let his head drop forward with a sigh.

Thank you, Lord! he thought, as he tried to settle down. It was then he felt the warmth again, so he opened his eyes and turned his head to the right.

His angel friend was behind him, laying a hand on his shoulder! "Now you have seen what few people see these days, Garrett," the angel said with a smile. "When God the Almighty says that He even cares about a sparrow, you know that His children are so much more valuable to Him than a small bird. He sends us regularly to protect His children from the harms of this world. You need to understand this so that you will trust God with the future. You fear that all will be lost, but, don't you see that God has everything under control? He could have kept that deer from walking into the road at the very moment you went past, but you needed to see His power to save you right now! It is our pleasure to do the Almighty's will, whether He needs one thousand angels or just one."

Garrett slowly nodded his head in understanding, and in an instant, knew what he needed to do regarding his dream. He gazed at the angel, who smiled and nodded, and then disappeared.

While Garrett drove the rest of the way home, he prayed, asking God for strength.

Garrett's dad was sitting in the dining room when Garrett arrived home. Stacks of papers and notebooks were spread out on the table, and Garrett recognized the set-up as his dad's bill-paying routine. Mr. Waterford would start paying bills and then break to do some Bible reading or study. He had told Garrett that it helped him not to be anxious about their finances, which were always tight.

"Hi, Dad!" Garrett greeted as he entered the room.

"Oh, hi, Garrett. Your meeting over?" Mr. Waterford asked.

"Yeah," Garrett replied. "Where's Mom?"

His dad straightened up in his chair, stretching his back, and answered, "She has her herb club meeting tonight. Hey, could you turn on the outside light for her?"

"Sure," Garrett responded as he strode to the front door and flicked a switch. Their front yard lit up with a welcoming glow.

As Garrett returned to the dining room, his dad heaved a sigh and ran his fingers threw his thinning hair.

Garrett hazarded a question, "Not enough to pay our bills again?"

Mr. Waterford glanced at his son. "You don't need to worry about that, Garrett. God will provide," he said, but his face still showed signs of concern.

"Dad," Garrett began, "did I ever tell you how I got to know those kids who come to our little church?"

His dad shook his head and answered, "No." He eyed his son and added, "What does that have to do with me paying bills?" Then he grinned, and asked, "Are they gonna pay rent or something?"

Garrett acknowledged his dad's joke with a smile, "No, I don't think so . . . but it has to do with our farm."

Mr. Waterford tilted his head and gave his son a questioning look, "What do you mean?"

"Well," Garrett began, "I started having dreams . . ." He let that sink in a bit and was a little surprised that his dad didn't seem shaken by the news.

"Uh-huh," was all that his dad voiced.

Garrett continued, "Well, I actually dreamt that those kids were in the church. I didn't know any of them until I recognized the one boy as being my principal's son."

Mr. Waterford raised his eyebrows at the mention of the principal but said nothing. He had been required to talk to Mrs. Stevens on more than one occasion!

"I asked Mrs. Stevens about her son and ended up meeting him after school one day. He and some other kids were the ones in my dream . . ." Garrett paused. "Dad, my dream came true," he confessed slowly.

Mr. Waterford gazed at his son. A wistful look came and passed so quickly that Garrett didn't notice.

"What are you trying to tell me, Garrett?" he asked.

Garrett swallowed hard, and then took a big breath.

"I had a dream that you sold the farm." There. He had said it. He looked at his dad, attempting to read his face.

Mr. Waterford stared at Garrett for a moment, and then turned back to the table, flipping a pencil up and down between his fingers. After a few seconds, he reached toward one of the piles and withdrew an envelope. He handed it to Garrett without saying a word.

Garrett took the envelope and looked at the return address: Miles Grady, Residential Developer. Garrett's stomach went into a ball. His trembling hands removed the paper from the envelope, unfolded it, and began to read it.

Dear Mr. Waterford,

Our community has recently experienced an incredible economic expansion of industry and business, with the end result being a housing shortage of higher-end homes to accommodate the influx of upwardly mobile executives and professionals. In a study done by my firm, these upper class individuals are looking for homes away from the city, yet easily accessible to the city. The mountain area where your farm is situated would be considered a prime location for one of the developments we are proposing to the city council. I am prepared to offer you a very lucrative amount for your property.

Please contact me at the number below to discuss this possibility.

Sincerely,

Miles Grady

Garrett gasped as he read the letter. He looked at his dad and then, feeling his legs weakening under him, pulled a chair out to sit down.

"I received this a few days ago," his dad said.

"Have you decided to do it?" Garrett asked. "Did you call this guy?"

Mr. Waterford shook his head, "I haven't even shown it to your mom. I was going to throw it away, but something made me keep it. This is my family's farm! How could I sell it? But, then, I sit down to pay bills, and I can't keep going like this! Small, family farms can't make it anymore. We basically live on what your mom earns. What I do here doesn't even pay for itself . . . and I need to get new equipment. Where's the money to come from?"

A strange feeling came over Garrett as he listened to his dad's lament.

Peace.

Garrett sat up in his chair.

"Dad, you need to call that man," he urged. "I can't exactly tell you why or what may happen, but I *know* you need to talk to him."

Mr. Waterford stared at his son and then said, "You're right. I know you're right, Garrett. I just tried to ignore it, because I don't want to sell the farm. But, what if that's what God wants us to do? He told his disciples that some would have to sell all they had and come and follow Him. It may be that we are being asked to do that

188

now." He sighed heavily and continued, "I wonder what your mom will say. She loves it here."

Garrett reached toward his dad and touched his arm, "I bet she'll be fine. We're being asked to trust God, Dad. If we stick together as a family, He will provide more than we ever thought possible!"

Just then, the garage door opened as Mrs. Waterford arrived home. Garrett squeezed his dad's arm in encouragement, and his dad reached for his son's shoulders.

"I am so proud of you, Garrett! You have really matured and grown in the Lord lately," his dad exclaimed. "How about staying here while I tell your mom, and we pray about what to do?"

Garrett was tired at school the next day. He and his parents had stayed up quite late, discussing what they should do regarding the offer for the farm. They prayed, and in the end decided that his dad should make the phone call to the developer the following day. Even though Garrett had dreamed about his dad telling him that he was selling the farm, he was still somewhat anxious about going home and living out his dream.

Halfway through the day at school, he was surprised to see Mrs. Stevens walking toward him.

"Hi, Garrett!" she called, motioning for him to come to her. "Joel asked me to give this to you." She placed a note in his hand, smiled, and walked away.

"Thanks," Garrett murmured.

Opening the paper, he read: *Trust in the Lord with all your heart, and lean not on your own understanding; in all your ways acknowledge Him, and He shall direct your paths. Do not be wise in your own eyes; fear the Lord and depart from evil. It will be health to your flesh and strength to your bones. Proverbs 3:5–8.*

Peace.

There it was again! Garrett knew that everything would be fine, although he had no clue how it could be. Losing the farm was something Garrett had never imagined. It had been in his family for over a century. Even when his ancestors had struggled to survive, they held onto the property, and somehow, things had always worked out. This time would be different, however. Garrett had seen it in his dream. He knew that it would come to pass.

Peace.

The worry had been uncharacteristic for Garrett. With a quick and definitive decision, he shrugged his shoulders as if to cast off an unwanted coat and strode off, light in heart and unconcerned about the future. He knew God would handle it.

The struggle with the demon had been brief, but significant. The angel had drawn power from the Scripture passage and used it to loosen the demon's hold long enough for Garrett to feel relief. Then, with Garrett's spirit discarding the blanket of worry by choice, the angel could tear the demon away from the boy and send it screaming into the air. The angel watched the demon sneer in disgust at having lost its prey. Then the demon shot out its tentacle-like fingers to grab another human passing by, but was hit by a bolt of energy coming from another direction. A different angel had appeared and rose up in defiance of the beastly creature. The demon cowardly shrank in submission.

"Leave this place!" the angel commanded.

The demon whimpered, but obeyed, darting quickly out of the building.

Twinkle-Eyes moved over to the other angel, and asked, "Is Garrett OK?"

"Yes," the angel replied. "He and I were both helped by the Word of the Lord. It gave us the strength to defeat that demon."

"Good," Twinkle-Eyes responded. "That demon will not return here again."

"Garrett's family's farm . . .?" the angel hesitatingly inquired.

"It is as the letter to the Ephesians states," Twinkle-Eyes smiled.

The other angel nodded in understanding.

"The others' prayers are helping to bring this to pass?" the angel asked.

"Yes," Twinkle-Eyes said, as they both disappeared through a wall.

Garrett pulled the slip of paper from his pocket and eyed the verses Joel had written down for him one more time before entering his house after school. A strange combination of excitement and concern filled him as he walked into the kitchen, but he sighed as he realized that nobody was home yet. He went to his room and pulled out his homework. Deciding to get it done quickly was still unusual for him, but the last weeks with the JP group and the angels had made him somewhat more conscientious, even though it was for ulterior motives. Getting his homework done right away meant he could spend the rest of the evening documenting his dreams and studying the journal for guidance. He had bought a special sketch pad and often enjoyed drawing depictions of the dreams and the experiences with the JP kids. Although he had quite a number of the pictures hung up in the farm chapel, there were many more he had kept to himself at the urging of his angel.

It wasn't long before Garrett heard the garage door opening and the sounds of both his parents' cars coming in. The arrival of his parents together was atypical, and Garrett immediately jumped up to go and meet them, curious as to the events of the day.

Mary and Daniel Waterford appeared to be bustling with excited chatter as they entered the door from the attached garage.

"Garrett!" his dad exclaimed. "We're so glad you're here! Wait 'til you hear what God is doing!"

Garrett's mom chimed in, "You won't believe it!" Then she caught herself, and added, "Well, *you'll* probably believe it, but you may still be surprised *how* God answered our prayers!"

Garrett grinned as his dad clapped him on a shoulder, and then they all proceeded to sit down in the living room. Daniel Waterford pulled a bunch of files out from a shoulder bag and sifted through one until he found a particular pack of papers stapled together. This he handed to Garrett with a smile.

"Read what Mr. Grady has in mind, son," Mr. Waterford instructed, his eyes shining with excitement.

Garrett's hands shook as he took the bundle of papers and began to read. His eyes opened wide in amazement while he read the first page. He momentarily looked up at his parents with his mouth agape then resumed reading the rest, albeit skimming the pages rather than reading word for word.

His parents waited quietly while he finished, with Mr. Waterford reaching for Garrett's mom's hand and holding it in anticipation.

Speechless, Garrett gasped as he read the last paragraph and then fell back in the chair, chills coursing through his body.

"That's pretty much how I responded, Garrett!" his mom admitted, beaming. "Your dad called me at work and asked if I could meet him at Mr. Grady's office as soon as possible. He told me I wouldn't believe it, and he sounded so excited, but I still was pretty apprehensive until Mr. Grady presented the offer, as you see there."

Daniel Waterford sat joyfully looking at his son's face, recognizing the same emotions of relief and knowing gratitude that he himself had experienced a few hours before.

"Thank you, Garrett, for listening to God and encouraging me to call Mr. Grady. If you hadn't . . ." Mr. Waterford paused and then continued, "If you hadn't, I probably would have thrown that letter away, and we would have missed the blessing of the Lord. I want you to always feel free to talk to your mom and me about your dreams as they apply to our family. We promise to listen!"

Garrett smiled and replied, "Thanks, Dad!" Then he hesitated a moment before adding, "You know . . . there was one more thing in my dream that I didn't tell you."

At this, his parents' eyebrows furrowed a bit, and his dad said, "Garrett—it's OK. Is there more we're to do?"

"Oh . . . no. I didn't mean that!" Garrett exclaimed.

His parents sighed with relief.

"Well, what, then?" his mom asked.

"There was some Scripture that kept coming to mind during the dream. I alluded to it when Dad and I first talked, but I didn't specifically tell you. It was Ephesians . . ."

His dad interrupted him, "3:20. Ephesians 3:20–21, right?"

Garrett nodded with surprise.

His dad quoted, *"Now to Him who is able to do exceedingly abundantly above all that we ask or think, according to the power that works in us, to Him be glory in the church by Christ Jesus to all generations, forever and ever. Amen."*

The Waterfords started laughing with joy at the realization that they were recipients of the abundance promised in the verse from Ephesians. Garrett jumped up and pulled his mom and dad off the sofa. Together, they danced around the room, whooping and shouting praises to God!

The group of angels stationed around the house glowed intensely. The three angels gathered in the corner of the living room beamed with a heavenly light as the family offered their gifts of thanksgiving to the Lord.

Nearby, a few demons sensed a slight change in the atmosphere around them, but they haughtily assumed that the Believers on the mountain were no threat to their master. Garrett's angel had placed a shield around the farm in order that the local demons would not suspect the building of the Lord's army that was happening in this remote, forgotten area. The protection was further strengthened by the praise of the Waterford family. It would soon be time for the Believers to come together as one for the great harvest.

CHAPTER 20

Unfortunately, the master of the fallen world was also quietly building his own army. Many of the world's populace had succumbed to apathy regarding spiritual things. Technology brought filth and temptation into unsuspecting homes. As more people learned to tolerate sin, the self-proclaimed lord planned his final takeover. He dispatched his most trusted and loyal demons throughout the world to take up watch for any sign of growing power on the Lamb's side. Other strong demons he sent out to wreak havoc in those who had weakness. Although he used prophecy and Scripture out of context to lure the ignorant of society into his realm, he inwardly knew that what was predicted for the end times was accurate. He would use his knowledge of these things to thwart the petty efforts of Believers before they could do any harm. He loved to see them fall and flail, and then, when they were at their lowest, he would accuse them regarding their failure. This tactic had worked quite well with public figures in the Christian church, and he knew it would continue to boost the numbers of souls who would turn away from the Lamb.

The school day had flown by while Garrett basked in the glory of God's abundant grace. A few had noticed the happy demeanor, but Garrett was so prone to joy over minor things that they hadn't questioned him at all. He entered the boy's locker room to deposit his things before heading out for gym class.

The bully demon lurked inside the boy's locker room. This was always a good place to work his nastiness, as athletic guys bullied those less gifted in sports. The demon watched all the boys entering the locker room and almost missed noticing Garrett, but the glow around the teen caught its attention. The demon slid into a locker to more closely observe the Believer. It was then it saw not one, but two angels guarding the young man!

This is unusual, the demon thought.

It knew better than to confront two angels, so it melded into the back of the locker, hoping to avoid detection. It peered through the locker vents the best it could, trying to ascertain what kind of angels this human child had protecting him, all the while wondering, *Why?*

Samek felt it immediately and fell back against Garrett to better shield him from any attack. He had honed his skills over the millennia so that even a puny, relatively insignificant demon would alert his senses.

In less than a second, he had sent his warning thought to the other angel who quickly assumed a protective posture on the opposite side of Samek. Both angels scanned the area, and soon the demon saw the burning eyes of an angel penetrating its hiding place.

It reacted hastily and scrambled out the top of the locker, gaining momentum as it sped out through the room's ceiling, continuing out of the school into the atmosphere.

The other angel followed only long enough to confirm the demon's departure, and then returned to Samek.

"Do you think that demon will warn the prince of the air?" he asked.

"It may," Samek replied. "We know the time of secrecy is soon to end so that the main harvesting may begin. We must be careful to do the work assigned to us, and not let Garrett unprotected. He must gain the confidence to act on his dreams, as Joseph of old."

The two angels continued their watch, but saw no sign of any other demonic activity.

Meanwhile, the demon hastened to a gloomy, run-down section of the city. Decrepit bars lined the streets, and drug dealers sold their wares in back rooms, while gambling and pornography drew those in who knew no hope.

The cellar of the business was crowded with demons. From time to time, one would rush in and boast of its successful attack on an empty soul, but most of them preyed upon those already inhabited. The city was filled with people who had rejected God, many of whom were unaware that seemingly trivial bad choices had opened the door to their soul, allowing demons of greed, hate and pride to find residence. The scores of little demons were still used to prepare the unsuspecting, uncommitted people for stronger demon possession.

This enclave of demons had been flourishing until a recent revival had surprised them and stole hundreds of souls from the prince's clutches. The prince of the air had punished the demon in charge severely, and the group left was awaiting the arrival of a new leader with trepidation.

Hurrying in to the large room, the bully demon searched for others of his type. Protocol demanded that it report any irregularity to the chief of bully demons. Finding a corner where the others loitered, it spotted the demon pushing others aside in order to sit on a makeshift crate-chair.

"Sir," it whimpered, "I must report an unusual confrontation with angels."

"Oh, really," the leader sneered, "And who are *you* to dare tell *me* about our enemy? I can see by your size that you don't earn your keep!"

The demon shriveled in fear but decided to explain.

"It's just there were *two* guarding one human boy!"

The demon leader moved its head forward until it was inches from the other's face.

"You think *two* of the enemy is unusual?" it asked.

The little demon stuttered, "I . . . I . . . just thought it was strange, and . . . and . . . that you should know."

The larger demon sat back for a moment, and the small demon bowed in deference, thinking it had somehow avoided embarrassment.

"Yes . . . yes . . . you're right to tell me," the leader began in a soft, low tone. Then it screamed, "But it's not worth the telling, is it?" With a swoop of its arm, the chief of the bully demons threw the little demon against the cement wall, causing dust to fly.

The situation had resulted in hardly a change in the commotion within the room. Demon leaders constantly dealt with underlings in this way, so only the other bully demons had noticed.

Quietly, a weathered demon went over to the crumpled creature.

"Here, let me assist you," a kind voice offered.

The small demon looked up to see a cloaked figure reaching out and pulling it to its feet.

Since thanks was something demons knew nothing of, the action received no response.

"I couldn't help but overhear you trying to report something unusual?" the figure prompted.

"Yes . . . yes . . . sir," the creature replied.

"Can you tell me about it?"

The little demon hesitated, checking over its shoulder to where the bully leader sat pompously.

"I assure you," the voice lulled, "your report will not result in any further punishment."

"I guess it wasn't much," the creature offered carefully.

"Let me be the judge of that," the voice almost purred.

Nodding, the small demon went ahead, "I was in a school locker room where I've been very successful, and I saw two angels guarding a boy."

"Hmm . . ." the voice acknowledged. "Have you noticed this boy before?"

The creature thought for a while and then replied, "I think I have tried to entice him to bully others, but was unsuccessful. He didn't appear to be a Believer before, but . . ."

"But what?" the cloaked figure encouraged.

"Now I remember," the demon exclaimed quietly, looking around again to make sure the bully leader had not taken notice of the conversation.

"Yes?" the purring voice enticed.

"I saw a glow around the boy!" the demon reported. "I was trying to get a better look when the two angels came into view. They seemed to be guarding him! I hadn't seen that before around the school. There are Believers, but the glow is what set him apart."

The figure contemplated the demon's words before speaking back to it, "You have done well and will be rewarded."

The little demon was about to ask who the stranger was when the figure stood upright and threw off its cloak!

The cacophony of shrieks from the nearby demons made all turn to view the menacing stature of a demon lord in their midst!

"I am the lord of guile disguise, and I have been sent from the supreme master to monitor for a stirring of the enemy," it spoke resolutely, its voice now loud and sinister. "You have already failed our master once, and you will not fail him again!"

With this, the lord gazed purposely around the room, and each set of demons it looked upon shriveled with fear, trying to escape the ominous glare from the lord's eyes. Finally, its stare fell on the chief of bully demons. The chief noticed a softening of the gaze, and instead of cowering as the others had done, it rose off of the crate-chair and arrogantly faced the lord towering before it. The chief clearly expected a reward from the lord, and puffed out its chest in a boastful posture.

The lord spoke quietly, "You are a chief of demons?"

"Yes," it replied confidently, "yes . . . I am chief of the bully demons. We are proud to report great advances in this area. I am personally responsible for many workplaces and schools where Believers are persecuted and intimidated by those who proclaim tolerance!"

"Ah," the lord said, positioning its fingertips together before its chest in a thoughtful pose.

The chief stood haughtily, waiting for the lord's reward.

The energy bolt that emanated from the lord's fingertips was unexpected and terrible. It cracked into the chief like lightning striking a tree and rammed the demon into the concrete wall as if the demon was a rag doll. Each demon in the large room jumped and then cowered with the swift attack, none wanting to be the next victim.

The lord held the demon in the energy beam for a few moments and then released it, letting the form disintegrate into a handful of worthless dust. Moving its head slowly around, the lord peered once again at the creature it had helped while cloaked. The little demon bowed its head low in expectation of a similar punishment for daring to speak to the lord in its ignorance earlier.

However, this time the lord opened its fingertips, allowing a cold red fire to emerge from its palms. The beam focused on the small creature's head. All the demons watched fearfully as the flow of the energy seemed to fill the little demon as air fills a balloon. Just as they all thought the creature would burst in another display of punishment, the beam stopped coming from the lord's hands. They gazed frightfully at the dreadful sight.

Where once had cowered a simple little demon, now stood a menacing beast that even the demons backed away from. Its eyes blazed an unearthly green, and its body was covered in scales of a serpent. Wings protruded from its shoulders, and great claws took the place of fingers and nails.

The lord then spoke to it, "You were once the smallest of demons, but now you will be my servant! I have given you the power I took from the other and added more. Go now and search for the Believer boy you saw with the angels, and only come back to me when you have found him!"

The beast growled ferociously, and then, with a great movement of its wings, it was gone in a second, using its new powers to penetrate the surroundings and soar into the air back to the school.

The lord stood tall and with a slight twitch of its finger, the crate-chair transformed into a hideous throne. The demons nearby fell back hurriedly to avoid the approach of the lord as it moved to sit down.

"Now, let us get to the business at hand!" the lord spoke. "Our master declares that the time is at hand for the annihilation of Believers from this world and the overthrow of God and His Son. There are signs that God's army is being prepared, and we are to disrupt every attempt to strengthen the enemy's forces. You are being sent out to watch for any possible hint of treachery from those known as Believers. Observe them and report to your chiefs regarding more sightings of angels than typical or odd light around the Believers. Our master must know where the enemy is planning to attack so that we can ambush them and squash their feeble efforts to destroy him! All chiefs must be diligent to inform me of anything unusual."

Here, the lord paused, peering into every demon's eyes. They all shrank back in terror.

"All loyalty will be rewarded," the lord pronounced, and the memory of the beast lingered in all their minds. Continuing, it roared, "And all failures will be punished! Now, go!"

The demons screeched as the lord dispersed them with small bolts of red light which seemed to empower and enrage them. They scattered to all directions as a smoggy mist enveloped the building, and the environs plummeted to the depths of sin and wickedness fueled by the mere presence of the demon lord.

CHAPTER 21

Twinkle-Eyes acknowledged the approach of the new angel. He had not expected this one to be included in the harvest preparations, but he would humbly yield to the angel's authority.

"I bring word from the commander of the army of the Lamb," the angel said without introduction or greeting, its very presence commanding respect.

Twinkle-Eyes bowed his head slightly in submission, but didn't speak.

"The false prince has sent powerful demons out. Your work will no longer be secret," the angel declared. "Those you have prepared must stand ready."

Again, Twinkle-Eyes nodded without speaking.

The other angel stared intently at Twinkle-Eyes and then added, "I am sent to assist you."

Twinkle-Eyes jerked his head up slightly, the quick movement barely perceptible but still noted by the other angel.

Once more, Twinkle-Eyes lowered his head in submission and then quietly, but distinctly spoke, "I will gladly carry out your orders."

The other angel's eyes softened as he replied, "I am not here to take charge, Tsadde. The Lamb That Was Slain is very pleased with the work you have done."

Twinkle-Eyes lifted his head and curiously eyed the other angel.

"I am sent to assist you," the angel repeated.

At this, Twinkle-Eyes addressed the other angel respectfully, "Your assistance is greatly appreciated, Gimel. I am honored to have your help and the trust of the Lamb!"

Then Twinkle-Eyes beckoned toward the little farm chapel.

"Would you like to address the others?" he asked.

Tilting his head to one side, Gimel considered the offer and then responded, "No. You have gained their trust and are their leader. A change would adversely affect the relationships you have built."

Twinkle-Eyes reflected on his words. "I would appreciate any advice you would have to offer, and I welcome your presence. Would you like to hear Garrett share with the others how the Almighty has blessed his family?"

Gimel answered, "I prefer the company of angels and saints, but perhaps the praise of these children could be refreshing."

Twinkle-Eyes nodded politely and then turned to guide Gimel inside the church. He sighed silently, offering another prayer for healing of the wounded leader of angels.

Garrett had waited excitedly for the arrival of the JP group. Joel's mom had offered to bring the teens out to the farm while Garrett's car was getting serviced. Garrett had eaten a quick dinner with his parents, who were going to meet with Mr. Grady again. After they left, he ran down the road to the chapel, clutching a folder of drawings from his dreams that he wanted to show the others. Now, he peered out the front door, anticipating the sound of the car echoing down the hill.

He was surprised to see the forms of two angels walking toward the chapel. Although the angels were always present at the JP meetings, they seemed to appear sometime after the teens had arrived, not before.

Twinkle-Eyes greeted Garrett with a smile. Other angels joined the two, and they all filed in to the little chapel, arranging themselves around the perimeter inside just as a horn tooted and the rest of the JP group arrived. The teens were amazed to see all the angels already there and hesitated at the door before Twinkle-Eyes motioned for them to come in. Garrett closed the door and joined his friends, who still stood together instead of gathering in the front to pray as they typically did.

Joel was the first to notice the new angel and although he looked quite stern compared to the angels they had come to know, Joel sensed a deep awareness of the Lord's Word within the newcomer. The angel gazed at him with a penetrating look that could have caused fear, but Joel held the gaze without trepidation as only one can who has been cleansed from sin by the blood of the Lamb and pulls strength from the miracle of forgiveness.

Gimel halted the depth of his gaze and allowed a look of acquiescence for a brief moment before Twinkle-Eyes spoke.

"Welcome, friends! We have come to praise with you tonight! Please continue on, and let us participate with you," Twinkle-Eyes encouraged.

Joel stared curiously at the stern angel for only a second and then responded to Twinkle-Eyes, "Let's pray for the Lord to bless our gathering."

The teens moved into a circle and Chris volunteered to pray, remembering that Garrett had needed strength to do something difficult and praising God for answering their prayers.

Jill led the group in a few choruses but finally stopped and exclaimed, "Garrett, will you *please* tell us how God took care of your problem? You are beaming so bright that I can barely look at you!"

The others laughed with delight and joined Jill in good-naturedly egging him on to speak.

Garrett grinned widely, unable to hold in his joy any longer. His head bobbed in thought as the others sat in the pews.

Twinkle-Eyes gave a slight tilt of his head to Gimel as the new angel folded his arms once again in a stern posture.

"Well," Garrett said with a deep breath, "the dream that had bothered me . . ." Here, he paused, formulating his thoughts into a coherent presentation. Closing his eyes for a moment, he then opened them and continued, "The dream was that my dad sold our farm." He stopped, noting the looks of shock on the faces of his friends.

Chris jumped up and put his hand on Garrett's shoulder and remarked, "Oh, man . . . no wonder you were so upset! What are you gonna do?"

Garrett shook his head, and said, "No . . . you don't understand!" He struggled to find the words to explain. "Ephesians 3: 20–21," Garrett blurted, looking at Joel.

Joel cocked his head to the side and furrowed his eyebrows, not comprehending how that Scripture fit with the Waterfords having to sell their farm, but he shrugged his shoulders and recited: "*Now to Him who is able to do exceedingly abundantly above all that we ask or think, according to the power that works in us, to Him be glory in the church by Christ Jesus to all generations, forever and ever. Amen.*"

Chris sat back down with the others, and they all waited for Garrett to explain.

"That's what God did for us . . . I mean He did more than we could ever expect!" Garrett exclaimed.

"So . . . your dad selling the farm is a good thing?" Liz questioned with disbelief.

"Um . . . well . . . yeah!" Garrett replied.

Gimel rolled his eyes minutely at the cumbersome attempt of the boy to share what the Almighty had done. For a brief moment, he longed for the holy and perfect praise of the saints in heaven, but then he remembered his duty to the Lamb and pushed his own discomfort aside, wanting nothing more than to obey the Lamb That Was Slain.

Samek quietly moved alongside Garrett and touched his shoulder. The teen felt the power immediately and breathed deeply. Acknowledging the help with a quick look at the angel, Garrett calmed down and proceeded.

"I was worried about telling my dad about my dream, but the encouragement of all of you helped me, and God showed me how He takes care of me, so I told my dad. First I had to tell him that my dreams were coming true, and that's how I met all of you. He took that rather well . . . better than I expected. Then, when

I told him about the dream where he sold the farm, he showed me a letter from a developer who was interested in this property. He was sitting there, trying to pay our bills, and didn't have the money to pay them." Garrett's voice softened, "We knew the dream was confirming what Dad didn't want to do. . . . Anyhow, Mom, Dad and I all talked and felt peace about going ahead and calling the developer. The next day Dad went to see him," Garrett's eyes glistened as his voice cracked with emotion.

Taking another deep breath, Garrett continued. "God did something so incredible and so much bigger than what we ever could imagine! We thought all was lost, but we still knew that God would take care of us, even without the farm."

Twinkle-Eyes glanced over at Gimel. The stern face had softened, and his arms now had fallen forward with his fingers clasped prayerfully!

Chris was sitting on the edge of the pew and exclaimed, "Then what? What did God do? Did the developer, like, uh, give you money to pay your bills, or what?"

Garrett shook his head. "No. We are selling the farm," he said calmly.

"Then how is this good?" Chris said, somewhat desperately.

The JP group stared at Garrett whose smile widened in contrast to his friends' downcast expressions.

"We don't have to sell *all* of it," he stated.

The other teens breathed sighs of relief together.

"How's that work?" Joel asked. "And how does Ephesians 3:20–21 fit in?"

"That's the best part," Garrett replied. "It turns out that the developer was looking for a place where a CSA and an upscale housing development could exist together."

Noticing the blank looks on their faces when he said CSA, he explained further. "A CSA is Community Supported Agriculture, so what is grown on the farm is bought or used by the people right there in the community. What happens is that part of our farm is sold in order to put in a bunch of nice houses on a little bit of acreage, and then the rest of the farm is used to grow organic food for the people in the development. Since they would live right here, there wouldn't be shipping of produce anywhere, which saves tons of money. We'll get enough money from selling part of the farm to update the machinery, buy livestock, and even hire some help!"

The JP group listened in amazement as Garrett went into a little more detail, and then they all stood up.

Liz went over to Garrett, placed one hand on his arm and raised her other arm up to heaven. Chris did the same on the other side. Joel and Jill joined them to form a small circle.

"God, we praise you!" Joel began. "You have done *'exceedingly abundantly'* beyond anything we could have imagined in how you have not only saved the Waterford's farm, but also provided for their welfare in a way that helps others!"

The teens interlocked fingers with each other as their hands were lifted up in praise. The chapel seemed to fade away, and the bright light of a heavenly place replaced the shadows. The group took turns giving praise as tears of joy and thankfulness ran down their faces.

Gimel stared in wonder. He was back where he belonged! How had these young, inexperienced Believers returned him to heaven?

Twinkle-Eyes came to his side. "We are not actually in the heavenly places, Gimel."

Perplexed, Gimel looked around but said nothing.

"Their innocent, pure praise has brought the glory of the Almighty here to earth. You were sent for a reason, my leader . . . my friend," Twinkle-Eyes whispered. "He could have given the message to any number of lower angels, but *He* knew you needed to see this again. You have forgotten."

Gimel nodded. The scars of the battle had left him hardened. He had thrown himself into service and not allowed healing, and it had made him spurn the race for which the Lamb had been slain. He scorned Adam's seed after the sacrifice of the Son. Their stupidity at not recognizing the Son of God had made most humans unbearable to him. Believers were tolerated at best. He had only felt safe among the saints and other angels in heaven. There, his failings seemed invisible.

208

But, God had known all along. His love for His people had been hard for Gimel to understand. Indeed, the apostle Peter had written how angels desired to understand the salvation given to man.

Gimel gazed at the aura surrounding the praising children of God and felt his spirit lifted. He had been a leader of angels for millennia, but it took a rag-tag group of kids to energize him again with power from their salvation. He could not experience salvation, but they could, and through them he gained a little understanding.

Twinkle-Eyes was right. The Almighty could have sent a messenger from lesser ranks of angels. But he was chosen to leave heaven's protection, and only by leaving, could he finally be healed.

Garrett's angel sensed it first. A disturbance. It was probably nothing, but Samek quickly broke his gaze away from the praising teens and quietly slipped outside.

He whispered to Qoph, who was standing near a fence, "Did you feel it?"

The other angel barely nodded and stayed quiet but alert.

Samek spoke in hushed tones, "Let's check the perimeter again. We must be sure that this place is shielded from the eyes of the enemy!"

Before either had taken a step, a roar pierced the night air! The beast of the demon lord was flying over the top of the mountain and would soon be above the little chapel!

Quickly, the contingent of angels keeping watch scattered around the church. The glow from the praise going on inside had to be hidden from the enemy! Samek and the others went to various spots around the perimeter, and, facing outward, turned their faces toward heaven, and spread their wings such that each tip touched the wing of the angel next to them. Although the shield previously placed had screened the heavenly energy much like sunglasses block some of the sun's rays, the glow could possibly be seen by a stronger demon, especially if it looked directly at the little church.

As soon as the angels' wing tips had touched, something like a veil seemed to rise from the earth and close above the church. Any glow that had been faintly visible was now erased. The angels stood silent and still, awaiting the arrival of the demon.

The beast thought it had seen something from the top of the mountain, and it had roared foolishly with its first possible lead. In a blink, the light was gone, and the beast flew around the narrow valley for a few minutes before determining there was no sign of the heavenly enemy. With another roar, it looked ahead at another possible glow, and, with renewed energy, sped off, away from the secret gathering.

Samek waited a full five minutes before relaxing his wings. His reaction resulted in a domino effect of the angel wings retreating, and the veil rolling back down to the earth. Samek and the others huddled quietly to discuss the encounter.

"What was that?" one of the angels inquired.

Samek and Qoph glanced at each other before Samek answered. "That was the servant of a demon lord."

The reality of such an identification was not lost on even the least of the angels.

"You'd better tell Tsadde and Gimel," Qoph warned.

"Yes," Samek replied. "Stay vigilant!"

Samek returned to the inside of the chapel. The teens were just finishing their praise, and the heavenly glow had subsided to a large extent.

Jill glanced curiously at Samek as he went over to Twinkle-Eyes.

Joel noticed immediately, and asked, "What do you see, Jill?"

"I'm not sure, but Garrett's one angel looks different right now," she replied.

Shaking his head, Joel responded, "I can sometimes see a glow or some sparkles, but nothing like what you can see."

Jill smiled and said, "Well, I started with just seeing the sparkles, so, maybe with practice you'll be able to see more."

The two of them then turned around to talk more with the other teens.

Samek approached Gimel and Twinkle-Eyes and softly reported, "We just had an incident."

Twinkle-Eyes nodded in response and said, "Yes, I sensed evil near, but it did not seem typical."

"It was the servant of a demon lord," Samek stated with alarm.

Gimel and Twinkle-Eyes turned to look at each other with concern before returning their gaze to Samek.

"How close was it?" Gimel asked.

"It flew right overhead," Samek answered.

Twinkle-Eyes sighed and breathed aloud, "It has begun, then." The other two angels nodded.

"I had hoped for more training," Twinkle-Eyes murmured and then added, "but we must prepare them now for battle."

"How can I help?" Gimel offered.

Twinkle-Eyes thought for a moment and then said, "We need to reveal to them more of what their obedience does. They are ready. We must teach them to be bold like Paul, strong like Peter, steadfast as Steven, and loving as John."

Gimel said, "Yes, the witness of the new covenant apostles and saints are excellent, but the lessons of the faithful old covenant saints can also be helpful, for *they* had to believe before the promise became salvation. These children of the Lamb . . ." he paused, thankful for the healing he had just experienced, "will need to stand and believe when they have yet to see the final victory of the Lamb."

Twinkle-Eyes tilted his head in reflection of this idea.

"You are absolutely right, Gimel," he pronounced. "Would you be able to teach them about the faithful saints? You were close to and assisted many of them."

For the first time in ages, Gimel smiled. At that moment, he saw the wisdom of the Father in sending him, not only to allow healing, but also to use him as He had used him in another time and place.

"Yes," Gimel said with joy. "Yes, I will tell them about all of the saints!"

"Good!" Twinkle-Eyes nodded. "Now we must discuss the present situation with them."

The five teens had noticed the apprehension that had followed Samek's reappearance within the little church and the discussion that had commenced. They had questioned Jill with their eyes as she peered at the angels, trying to decipher the change in the auras around them.

Kaph quietly came to her side, having recognized the same change in her fellow angels.

"It is the sign of war, or," Kaph paused, "a preparation for war."

Jill looked at her angel with fear.

"Do not be afraid," Kaph admonished. "It is the beginning of the final battle for which we have been preparing. Fear can be seen by the enemy and quickly be fueled. You must learn to be able to be alarmed without giving in to fear."

Jill nodded and relaxed her spirit by remembering Jesus' promise to give peace.

The others had been listening to the conversation, and all had also felt some amount of dread. Each responded to the angel's admonition by focusing on some aspect of what they had learned. By the time Twinkle-Eyes, Samek and Gimel had turned their attention to the teens, each one had calmed their spirit and waited for the angels to speak.

The purposeful relaxation was not lost on Twinkle-Eyes. He looked at each youth individually before he spoke.

"You all have learned well to trust in the Almighty and His Son when fear threatens to take the peace that has been given to those who believe," Twinkle-Eyes reflected. "We have learned that the final battle has begun." With this pronouncement, he nodded at Gimel to proceed.

Gimel stood tall and walked to the front in order to address the group. His face had lost the sternness which it had when he had first arrived. Now, a gentle look of authority had taken over as he started to talk.

"I bring word from the commander of the army of the Lamb," he announced.

Joel and the others looked at each other in surprise, then gazed back at the new angel.

"The false prince has sent powerful demons out. Your work will no longer be secret," the angel declared. "You must stand ready."

Having given his appointed message, Gimel added, "I hope to be able to assist you in your part in this battle." With that, he bowed slightly and retreated.

Twinkle-Eyes took over. "Tonight, while you praised, a servant of a demon lord came near. The other angels outside provided appropriate protection so that we were not detected, but the time has come for you to apply your gifts and talents to the work of the Lamb. You *will* be troubled by the enemy. Do you know how to resist the attacks of Satan and his demons?"

Chris spoke up immediately, "Well, Jesus used Scripture to counter Satan's temptations in the wilderness."

"Yes," Twinkle-Eyes nodded. "What else?"

Liz cleared her throat before responding, "It's sorta the same, but maybe a little different from what Chris said," she began, "uh . . . knowing prophecy can help reassure us that Jesus wins."

"Right," Twinkle-Eyes asserted.

"I've been able to see various hues, auras and sparkles," Jill offered. "That helps me to prepare slightly faster than those around me and to start praying."

Twinkle-Eyes grinned broadly, "Exactly, Jill!"

The teens were now getting warmed up to the exercise.

Garrett drawled, "So . . . I may dream about something, and I need to act on that, if I can, and prepare for whatever battle or demon may be lurking around."

"Yes, Garrett," Twinkle-Eyes responded.

Joel peered at the new angel in thought and then said, "Learning about how the saints of the Old and New Testaments handled their battles could help us have ideas on what to do here and now."

Gimel stared curiously at the boy and then smiled.

"You are much like the boy David who slew Goliath," Gimel pronounced loudly. "He had ultimate faith in the God of Israel, and with that faith, he became King."

The booming voice of the angel was unexpected and startled the teens, but they quickly were engrossed in the story of the shepherd boy, David. Gimel told the tale as none had ever told it, and the youth sensed that it was an eyewitness account.

The angel continued for an hour, telling the JP group about Moses, Joshua, Joseph, Esther, and Daniel.

"Now," Twinkle-Eyes said when Gimel had ended his stories, "can you tell me how your obedience in these matters will help?"

Garrett piped up, "Well, obviously God can't have an army if the soldiers all do their own thing!"

Twinkle-Eyes and the other teens smiled at the illustration, while Garrett shrugged his shoulders in return.

"More specifically?" Twinkle-Eyes encouraged.

Jill scrunched up her face in thought and then asked, "Does it have something to do with what we talked about the other night—how our praise and prayer affect the angels?"

Gimel and Twinkle-Eyes both nodded.

"You all must be sensitive to the needs of God's army as a whole, along with individual skirmishes with demons that soon will be commonplace," Twinkle-Eyes informed them. "Joel, do you remember that one night at the church?"

Joel's face paled a bit at the memory of the chill. The other teens noticed, but as quickly as it had come, another look took its place. Jill noticed the glow, but the others could only tell that he seemed to have a vivid rosiness come into his cheeks.

Now nodding, Joel answered, "Yes, I remember, but I also remember the warmth from your touch and how I could see you and two other angels, and you told me it was the Lord's power that I felt—the very power that raised Him from the dead. And I was to always remember that moment." He looked directly at Twinkle-Eyes before stating, "I do remember, and I will honor that memory by obeying."

Joel then looked at Chris and Jill. "Remember on my patio? We have to keep that alive in our hearts."

They nodded solemnly, each contemplating the heavenly vision.

Garrett then asked the question no one had voiced yet, "So . . . how *are* we to deal with demons?"

Gimel turned to face Garrett and responded, "You must keep the Lamb's power in you at all times, resisting temptations of your human body and practicing the commandment to love others."

Liz listened carefully and then offered, "A few years ago, there was a fad going on—WWJD—What Would Jesus Do. Everyone seemed to have wristbands or necklaces with it on. I think we need to really take that to heart and always consider what Jesus would do in each situation we face." She pulled her lower lip in, chewed on it in thought, and then continued. "So, if we come up against real demons . . . we are to do what Jesus did?"

Twinkle-Eyes nodded, "Yes. He used Scripture against Satan. He commanded demons to come out of people—all with the power the Father gave Him." He turned back to Joel, and spoke, "You were attacked by a demon that night in the church. You did not know at the time that it was a demon."

Joel shook his head, "No, I just felt a chill and an intense fear."

"All of you must be prepared for demon attacks by remembering the power within you given by the Holy Spirit," Twinkle-Eyes encouraged.

"Ephesians," Chris muttered softly, and then, looking around at his friends, he spoke with emphasis. "Ephesians—the whole armor of God. Everybody, that's the key—we must put on the whole armor of God," he said excitedly.

The teens all grabbed their Bibles while Chris instructed them to turn to the sixth chapter.

"Verses 10 through . . . uh, around 18, I think," Chris added as they all got to the right page. He then read: *"Finally, my brethren, be strong in the Lord and in the power of his might. Put on the whole armor of God, that you may be able to stand against the wiles of the devil. For we do not wrestle against flesh and blood, but against principalities, against powers, against the rulers of the darkness of this age, against spiritual hosts of wickedness in the heavenly places. Therefore take up the whole armor of God, that you may be able to withstand in the evil day and having done all, to stand.*

"Stand therefore, having girded your waist with truth, having put on the breastplate of righteousness, and having shod your feet with the preparation of the gospel of peace; above all, taking the shield of faith with which you will be able to quench all the fiery darts of the wicked one. And take the helmet of salvation, and the sword of the Spirit, which is the word of God; praying always with all prayer and supplication in the Spirit, being watchful to this end with all perseverance and supplication for all the saints."

Chris looked around at the others and said emphatically, "This is what we need to do!"

Garrett jumped up and pulled out a stand-up easel that he had placed in the corner. Grabbing some markers, he quickly drew the figure of a basic person, and then nodding to Chris, he asked, "OK, the first piece was truth, wasn't it?"

Chris, who knew the passage by heart, responded, "Yes, around the waist."

Garrett drew a belt, and labeled it *TRUTH*.

"Alright, next?" Garrett inquired.

"The breastplate of righteousness," offered Liz.

Drawing swiftly, Garrett outlined a type of vest and printed *RIGHTEOUSNESS* diagonally like a sash going from the right hip up across the chest to the left shoulder.

"Feet!" Joel called out. "The feet have 'the preparation of the gospel of peace' on them!"

Pondering this for a moment, Garrett then designed something like running shoes with mythical wings at the heels. On one wing he printed *GOSPEL*, and on the other one was *PEACE*.

Jill was ready with the next piece. "The shield of faith," she said eagerly.

Garrett smiled with enthusiasm as he fashioned a strong shield for the left hand, detailing a lamb standing on a background of red. "This is the Lamb That Was Slain," he explained, as he added a title of *FAITH* to the shield.

"Next is 'the helmet of salvation,'" Chris volunteered.

"Hmm . . ." Garrett muttered. He chose a purple marker, commenting as he drew, "I always think of Easter when I think of salvation, and purple often represents the resurrection." Across the forehead of the helmet he wrote, *SALVATION*.

Before anyone could say another word, Garrett had already started on the last piece of the armor, rapidly sketching a formidable sword in the right hand and labeling it, *SCRIPTURE*.

Murmurs of "Wow!" and "Cool!" echoed throughout the little church as each one reflected on the final product.

"There's one more item," Gimel stated as a challenge to the teens.

Each one scrambled to look at the verses again.

"I know!" Jill exclaimed even before examining her open Bible. "It's prayer, isn't it? We always need to be praying!"

Smiling, Gimel and Twinkle-Eyes both displayed their affirmation.

Garrett went to grab a yellow marker, but Jill interrupted his decision.

"It's blue," she pronounced. "Praying Believers give off a blue hue—it gets deeper blue with more concentration."

The others stared at her with admiration and wonder. Garrett picked up a blue marker and created the background of the spiritual warrior.

"Well done," Samek stated.

The group huddled around the depiction and spent some time discussing each element. In the end, Garrett promised to make copies for each of them by the next meeting.

During this time, Gimel had gone outside. He found a spot against the church's back wall and stood, looking up into the heavens. The sentry angels continued to walk around the chapel, but, with deference, did not disturb the respected leader. As the teens finished their discussion, Gimel simultaneously lowered his head and closed his eyes for a moment and then retraced his steps inside the building.

He made no noise as he entered, yet the teens and angels present all stopped to look at him. His magnificence was unparalleled by any angelic presence the JP group had yet seen! It was powerful and mesmerizing. Only the heavenly visions were greater than this spectacular event.

"I am restored," Gimel quietly stated. Pausing for a moment as his eyes met Twinkle-Eyes, he then turned to the teens and pronounced, "The Almighty and the Lamb desire to send you forth with Their blessing." He approached the five youths and opened his outstretched hands over-top of them. "By the power of the Lamb That Was Slain and with the power that raised Him from the dead, you are sent out with His power to do the will of the triune God, to prepare others for the final battle against Satan. You are given authority over demons and their beasts to resist them and order their retreat. But, take care not to let this authority seem to become your own, lest you fall and become prey of the very ones you think you command!"

The warning was not lost on the group of teens, as each felt a sickening sensation throughout their body.

"However," Gimel continued loudly, "DO NOT FEAR! As the Lord said to Joshua, *'Be strong and of good courage; do not be afraid, nor be dismayed, for the LORD your God is with you wherever you go.'* And, remember what the Lamb That Was Slain said to His disciples: *'Peace I leave with you, My peace I give to you; not as the world gives do I give to you. Let not your heart be troubled, neither let it be afraid,'* and *'These things I have spoken to you, that in Me you may have peace. In the world you will have tribulation; but be of good cheer, I have overcome the world.'"*

The youths immediately sensed peace envelope them and permeate every part of their being.

Gimel gazed at each one with penetrating looks, and then smiled as he withdrew his arms and let them drop to his side.

"It is late," Twinkle-Eyes said softly, breaking the stillness, "and you must all head home now."

The teens remained silent as they gathered their things and headed out. Mrs. Stevens rounded the curve above the chapel just as Garrett closed the chapel door and locked it. Their good-byes were warm yet simple, exhibiting the unity of an athletic team while still having the connection of family. The new disciples of the Lamb were ready.

CHAPTER 22

Although the demons existed in the same spirit world as the angels, their sense of spiritual things were fairly limited to proximity, so the event at the little church was not picked up by any evil creature, the beast having left the area that night. Their abilities were also restricted to more of a black and white picture, not having a real judgment of degree, so that they wouldn't necessarily be able to tell if a person was weak in spirit until they touched them. The grounded Believers' very skin seemed to repel most demons' attempts at entering their bodies and controlling them. However, over millennia, the demons had learned they could affect even strong Believers by "planting" small seeds of temptation on the surface of their spirits. In time, weakness would allow the seed to enter into the spirit and sprout, giving the demon opportunity to get through the defenses. The rooted temptation became actual sin, and only cleansing and covering by the blood of the Lamb could rid the person of the iniquity.

The demons had become quite capable of inflicting damage to the spirits of Believers. Some demons were especially talented at using those already under their control to hurt those who belonged to the Son. The humanness of the wicked could more easily penetrate the spirit of Believers and hasten the choice of sin. Each sin created a hole in the spirit, and each hole widened as the person continued to allow the temptation seed to grow until the soul was exposed, and the protection of the spirit was compromised.

Certain temptations could escalate into sin within seconds in those who had been prepared and weakened by unwise choices. Such had been the case with Joel when the woman's demon found him in the church service. Years of being afraid to stand up against Kyle had made him susceptible to fear, and the demon had no trouble finding the hole that had been made in his spirit.

The angels were able to see the holes created by seeds of temptation that had found root in Believers. At times they could provide extra protection in that area because of the prayers of others, but they knew that only full commitment to the Lamb could destroy the seeds that led to iniquity. Weeks spent with the angels had allowed each teen to come to terms with actual sin in their lives. Close communion with the Lord and the choice to follow Him had cleansed them of the seeds of temptation for the time being, even repelling any lure of sin, but the world around them still was evil, so they had to stay vigilant!

Garrett's school was a virtual hotbed of demons the next day, the demon lord sending more out to assist his beast in tracking down the Believer with the glow, but warning them not to touch him or alert him to their presence. A small demon of tardiness happened to be the one to spot Garrett. It usually lurked around the parking lot early in the morning, trying to keep students from entering the building in time for the first bell. It loved to cause parking problems and irritation that led to lateness. Garrett had previously been fairly susceptible to its general ploys in the past.

Today, however, the demon had decided to search for victims at the bus drop-off, making students bump into each other, causing others to trip, and knocking book bags and purses off shoulders. It was having a splendid time when Garrett got off the bus. The glow around the teen was unmistakable.

The curious demon had itself been late to the early morning gathering held by the demon lord, so it had missed the particular instructions to not approach Garrett. It snuck up behind Garrett and touched the glow. Garrett spun around just as electricity seemed to hit the demon and cause it to lurch backward.

Barely above a whisper, the demon heard Garrett say, "I am *not* going to be late! *Get behind me, Satan!*"

The demon scampered off, rubbing its numbed palms. It had not gone very far when it ran right into the demon beast! With a roar, the beast grabbed the demon around its neck and flung it to the ground!

"The Believer was *not to be touched!*" the beast screamed. The energy bolt was swift, and the little demon was no more.

Garrett heard the noise. Even a day ago, the sound would have sent chills up his spine. But, the dream during the night had been clear—the war had begun, and the demons would seek to destroy the band of Believers who now called themselves the JP Knights. The term had come up as the group had pondered Garrett's drawing of the armor of God. It had stuck, and Garrett had solemnly titled the sketch, "A JP Knight."

The dream had solidified Garrett's resolve. In it, he saw the attack by the little demon on those before his arrival and he knew the demon had frequently been successful in his own life. He saw the beast as well, and knew that it looked for him. The scream in his dream was terrifying and almost woke him, but he clung to the sight in his mind and willed the dream to continue. He now knew what lay ahead.

The beast was dreadful indeed, but Garrett saw more than the beast, more than the scores of lower demons that flanked it. Garrett's eyes were opened, and he observed hundreds of angels surrounding the school, lining its halls and guarding its classrooms! The text he had sent early that morning to the other JP Knights had resulted in many prayers, and those many prayers had brought the angel army to stand guard against the demons at Garrett's school.

Garrett had seen in his dream what he was to do.

He looked at the demon beast and slowly walked toward it. Their eyes met and the beast roared again with the knowledge that the Believer actually saw it.

Garrett raised his arm, and the demons saw the boy transform before them into an armored soldier. Most of the demons immediately backed away from their adversary, but the beast held its ground.

In Garrett's right hand now gleamed a sword. On his head was a helmet that shone with the deepest hue of purple. A chain-mail tunic dropped to his hips and was held in place by a belt studded with two or three gems. He grasped a shield with his left fist; the unmistakable Lamb on a red background was evident. He had sleek, light-weight ankle boots that had protective leather curving up and around his shins.

The demon beast's eyes narrowed in contempt as it viewed its enemy. Pulling a sword from under a wing, it poised to strike.

Calmly, Garrett moved his sword in what initially looked like a salute. Speaking quietly, but firmly, he said, "In the name of the Lamb That Was Slain, I order you, and all these demons, to leave this place!"

The demon beast sneered, "I do the will of my master! I do not heed any 'orders' from you!"

With that, it lunged at Garrett!

Garrett stood coolly, bracing himself ever so slightly and spoke, "By the blood of the Lamb!"

The sword tip glowed. An envelope of energy flowed out from it, quickly forming a cover around Garrett. The demon beast collided with the force field with such strength that it almost bounced off and then crumpled in a heap! Enraged, it flung itself again at Garrett but was similarly repelled.

Garrett repeated his earlier command, "In the name of the Lamb That Was Slain, I order you to leave this place!" And then he added, "or I will wound you!"

The beast roared with anger, brandishing its sword in a wide arc, the blade of which would certainly kill Garrett!

The angels in view of the battle stood alert, but none moved to engage the beast. However, a noticeable change in them began to take place. It seemed as if tongues of flame erupted from their upheld swords and soon enveloped the angels. This incredible sight had also become visible to the demons, who huddled together in fear.

Garrett steadied himself and positioned his sword, while exclaiming, "By the blood of the Lamb!"

The beast's sword hit Garrett's shield as Garrett plunged his sword toward the beast. Sparks flew and smoke billowed from the collision of the two entities. Terrible screams erupted from the beast, but one could not tell if they were sounds of triumph or pain.

Nearby, Samek and Gimel waited, their swords at the ready, flames still shooting from the tips. They seemed to absorb the fire as the seconds passed, boosted by the unseen prayers of the JP teens.

A breeze lightly arose from the increased beating of the angels' wings, clearing the smoke from the battle site.

Static noises were heard first. Then, the helmeted head of Garrett became visible, and the angels could see him standing over what had been the demon beast! Garrett's sword was still in the flesh of the creature, which now writhed in agony on the ground, having lost its power with the piercing of Garrett's sword into its substance. It was once again a small, fearful demon.

Samek approached Garrett and spoke, "It is not ours to destroy at this time."

Garrett nodded in understanding, and pulled his sword out of the disgraced demon.

Looking out at the scores of demons who now cowered before him, Garrett pronounced, "In the name of the Lamb That Was Slain, I order all of you to leave this place!"

The surrounding angels now moved toward the demons. A few demons dared to attack, but were quickly held in check by the angels. The noise of static could be heard as these demons failed. Soon, numbers of demons were scampering away in defeat, many whimpering with wounds inflicted by the angels.

The former demon beast now sat on the ground in front of Garrett.

Gimel spoke softly to Garrett, "I believe you have a message for this creature to take back to its master?"

Garrett blinked in thought, and then gazed at the demon servant with his sword leveled at the demon's chest. "The day of the Lord is at hand!" he said simply.

The scrawny demon shuddered with understanding and then, with an urging from Garrett's sword, scurried away.

Letting a big breath out as if he had been holding it, Garrett felt a surge of relief. Dropping down on his knees and letting his shield move back onto his forearm, he held his sword flat in both hands and raised it up while bowing his head.

"Thank you, Lord, for Your strength and power! Your Word has defeated the enemy, and I offer it back to You in praise!" Garrett prayed.

The sword glistened and sparkled and then disappeared. In a moment, the armor of God had also vanished. A magnificent gem of orange appeared on the ground in front of Garrett. As he picked it up, an electric sensation coursed through his fingers. He then stood to face Samek and Gimel.

"Be on the alert, Garrett," Samek told him. "The demon lord, no doubt, will be enraged over this loss. You will be a target for his wrath. Stay vigilant, *'bringing every thought into captivity to the obedience of Christ.'*"

Garrett nodded. The angelic beings all around him vanished. He became aware of the shouts and calls of teens heading into the school building. He found himself near the main entrance to the school, bustled by students hurrying in from the buses. Picking up his backpack, which lay at his feet, he joined the crowd, and headed into the building. It was strange to have gone through a spiritual battle that no one else seemed to have been aware of in time and place. He shrugged his shoulders and stretched his neck, arousing himself to the reality before him, and went to his locker.

Garrett had not been alone in his trip into the spiritual world, where flesh and blood time had seemed to stand still. Two others had been drawn into the unearthly pause.

Kathy Stevens had stood at her office window, which was a routine of late, watching the students offload from buses. She had started to pray for them, first collectively, then by bus arrival, and finally by groups or individuals that her gaze led her to. She had noticed much more peaceful beginnings to the school day, and her own heart held more compassion for the students under her charge.

Today, she had been surprised to see Garrett step off the bus again. She had quietly thought, *His car must not be available*, and she prayed that everything was OK—with him, his car, and his family.

Suddenly, she saw him step quickly away, dropping his backpack. She was almost inclined to run out of the office and head outside to see what was the problem, but something held her back. It seemed like one of those weird commercials or TV programs where everyone stops moving except one person. He seemed to pose in some sort of stance. She saw his lips moving, but heard no words, even though her windows were open, and she should hear the noise of many students. She thought she had heard a strange sound—something that made her stomach go into a ball. But, then she felt a peace. It looked as if Garrett was pretending to be in a sword fight with someone, but Kathy saw nothing else, then, quite rapidly, she saw Garrett go to his knees, bow his head and hold his hands up as if offering something. Before she knew it, he was in front of the building, picking up his backpack as if nothing had happened. Everything was back in motion and the typical noises filtered in through the window.

Kathy sat down. *What just happened?*

Across from the bus drop-off, the girl watched in disbelief as the scene unfolded before her. The scream from the monster made her jump. Her terror was quickly replaced by a tremendous peace, and she was aware of a warmth spreading through her body. She looked on in amazement as Garrett fought the creature. The angels and demons were merely wisps of vapor, but she was still able to discern them all around. As Garrett offered up the sword, she was more conscious of a presence immediately by her. She turned and saw an angel. It had just removed its palms from her shoulders.

"It is time, Emily," it said as it took her hand. "By the end of this day, you must speak to the boy, and join with others the Almighty has chosen for this task."

Emily stared wide-eyed at the angel, but nodded her understanding.

The angel smiled and disappeared with the rest of the spirits.

In Emily's hand lay a polished yellow stone.

CHAPTER 23

The group at the little chapel now held twelve teens. Each of the five original members had, over the course of several days, met one or two others who also had seen angels, had visions or dreams, or simply been led to talk about spiritual things. In the end, it had been apparent that the JP Knights were strengthening their forces for battle.

Garrett had humbly told the others of his particular encounter with demons. Emily confirmed the conflict, adding in graphic details that Garrett had purposely left out, not wanting to appear heroic.

Brent and Nathan, twin brothers from Liz's neighborhood, were studious and exact, taking notes as the skirmish was described.

Chris had brought a fellow softball player from his church league by the name of Shane. Although athletic like Chris, he was mischievous and optimistic, grinning with enthusiasm as the new teens heard how the JP group had come together.

The group's angels stood around quietly as Joel led them in a short Bible study.

"That one is like a wild horse!" whispered an angel to Twinkle-Eyes, nodding toward Shane.

"Hmm . . ." Twinkle-Eyes pretended to brood in response, and then added, "He is your charge, He."

He's grin momentarily left his face, but then he smiled broadly, and chuckled, "We are a good fit, I think!"

Twinkle-Eyes laughed as well and said, "That's what I thought! I may need two more angels here just to keep you and Shane from getting into trouble!"

Joel was now finishing with the study and led the group in a short prayer. As soon as he was done, he looked at Twinkle-Eyes for guidance.

Twinkle-Eyes then nodded at the other angels. They dispersed amongst the teens, pairing themselves with their chosen wards. Quickly they went to work, discussing each one's talent and providing direction for its use.

Gimel now stood with Twinkle-Eyes.

"There is only one angel with the brothers," Gimel stated. "Would you want me to assist so that each boy has a helper?"

Twinkle-Eyes responded, "No. The brothers are as one and think much alike. They would be distracted with another angel." He paused, and then offered, "Joel would appreciate your experience."

Gimel's eyes narrowed slightly in thought.

"Yes," he nodded, "he has uncommon perception. But . . . isn't he your responsibility?"

"Oh, yes," Twinkle-Eyes stated matter-of-factly. "But he is a mature individual and recognizes valuable advice from those who have it to give."

Gimel smiled at the diplomatic answer, reading between the lines. "You are a good friend, Tsadde. Now I understand why the Lamb chose you for this duty. It is refreshing to serve at your side."

Bowing slightly to Twinkle-Eyes, Gimel went to Joel and engaged him in a thoughtful discussion.

The chapel was fairly crowded with angel and teen pairs throughout the building. The angel Yod was talking quietly to Marissa, a young lady whose family had been torn apart by a nasty divorce. The comfort Marissa was receiving brought healing to her hurt soul and revived a spirit of gladness in her. Pastor Eric had brought her to church after meeting her in a separate outreach program he did for the homeless. Marissa had stayed with her mom when her dad kicked them out of the house, keeping her two brothers with him and bringing home his girlfriend. Marissa had become a Christian during a summer camp, so she had clung to the hope of Christ when she and her mom had to stay in a homeless shelter. Pastor Eric and Jenny had then taken her in to live with them while her mom stayed with a friend. It had only taken a few days for Marissa to flourish spiritually under the evident love in Pastor Eric's home, and she had felt particularly drawn to Joel at the last youth meeting. He had encouraged her to pray for the Lord to open her eyes regarding her work for His kingdom. She had then confided in him about a dream she had recurrently for weeks about meeting a bunch of other teens who loved the Lord. Joel's doubts about the story vanished when Marissa described their little chapel to a T.

Abby and Chloe, sisters who went to Jill's church, had approached her after youth group about strange things that had been happening to them. Jill had clearly discerned a certain sparkle and hue around them and had cautiously asked them about angels. The girls had excitedly told her about how they both had thought they had seen angels as they worked on some music and lyrics for a fine arts competition. The sisters were quite talented in singing and playing instruments. Now, the angels Beth and Shin were eagerly sharing praises with them. Chloe and Abby's eyes shone with adoration of the Lamb as they joined the angelic duo in song.

Joel asked them all to finish up, and Garrett passed out more JP Knights drawings to the new members of the group.

"Everyone!" Joel called out, then, "Hey, everyone!" to get their attention once again.

The excited teens and angels turned to face the young leader.

"I am really encouraged to see each of you getting deeper and deeper into fellowship with the Lord through the help of His angels!" Joel spoke heartily. "But, I think we all have to remember what happened with Garrett. This is not a game! The Lord needs us to stand up for Him. Look at the drawing of the soldier of the Lord, or knight, as we sort of started saying."

The newer JP Knights looked closely at the details of the picture.

Joel continued, "Jill, Chris and I have put together a little notebook that describes each part of the armor with Scripture verses to help you with understanding how each piece should help you. Also, we made this notebook so that you can put more pages in and even use it as a journal. What we have learned so far is that I may see things differently than Garrett, and he could perceive stuff differently than I and so on. If we can keep track of our impressions and thoughts, we will help others, including ourselves."

He paused to grab his own notebook.

"Tonight, we heard how Garrett faced that demon beast. I wrote down some things he told us. But then I also jotted down what Emily saw. Garrett describes the monster, while Emily tells us about the hundred angels that were there!"

The others sat in rapt attention, waiting for Joel to pull it all together.

"You see," Joel continued, "if I focused on what Garrett told us, I'd be scared of what I might face tomorrow. But then, when I pair it with what Emily saw, I'm reassured that His angels will be right there with us in the battle!"

The teens all murmured with understanding.

Joel finalized his thoughts, "Garrett showed us how to fight, and Emily reminded us that we're already the winners!"

The glow of the angels was intense, increasing as Joel spoke.

Outside, one of the sentries called quietly for reinforcements. A cloud was coming rapidly out from the city in their direction. One angel tapped on the chapel door to alert Twinkle-Eyes, while the rest formed a circle around the building. The envelope went up quickly as before.

Twinkle-Eyes motioned to Joel.

"Quick, JP Knights, we must pray for protection! The enemy is close! Be sure you are covered completely in the blood of the Lamb!" Joel barked out and then fell to his knees in prayer.

Jill closed her eyes to pray, but still she saw them. They were hideous creatures! She shrank back as if to hide from them. Their shrieks made her cover her ears. One turned, and Jill gasped as it started to see her as through a lifting fog!

"Remove the fear in Jill, Lord," a small voice prayed. "Help her to let You cast it out for *'perfect love casts out all fear.'*"

Jill forced her eyes to see the vision of the throne room. She could still hear the demons approaching, but the noise was less. The sight of thousands of angelic beings filled her mind, and the Love which purchased her life by the sacrifice of His Son filled her heart and spirit. She collapsed on the floor of the chapel as the demons streaked past the secret place.

The others rushed to Jill as soon as the demon scouts were gone.

Marissa held Jill's head in her lap and slowly removed her right hand from Jill's back.

The JP group and the angels could see a dark spot on Jill's shoulder blade that was fading and soon disappeared.

"You had a hidden fear that the demons could see, even through the angels' defenses," Marissa explained. "I didn't see it until the demons got closer."

"What did you do?" Joel asked, staring at Marissa's hand.

Marissa shrugged her shoulders and said, "I don't know . . . I just prayed."

"What did you do with your hand?" Joel persisted.

"What?" Marissa looked quizzically at Joel. "I just put my hand on her back as I prayed for her." She smiled apologetically, "I think I thought I could keep the demons from seeing her, and us, by covering the spot." She shook her head, "That was silly."

"But something *did* happen when you touched the spot," Joel insisted, looking over to Twinkle-Eyes.

The angel leader stood still and silent for a moment. He finally said, "There are mysteries that are not for you to understand yet."

All eyes were on Joel. The angel's statement wasn't a rebuke, but it did seem like one, or maybe a challenge.

Joel digested the declaration thoughtfully and then said, "That's fine. I look forward to the time it can be known." Turning to the group as if nothing had happened, he announced, "It's time to go. We all need to be in prayer for each other. And, I think we all could do some self-examination to make sure we offer every part of us for cleansing. Any of us could have drawn the demons right here. We must bring every thought into captivity. . . . What is that verse?"

He looked to Chris, but was surprised to hear Garrett speak, *"Bringing every thought into captivity to the obedience of Christ,* from 2 Corinthians 10:5."

Smiling with his characteristic face, Garrett shrugged, "Uh . . . my angel impressed upon me that verse recently, so I made sure I learned it!"

The group laughed while they gathered their things. Soon the little church was quiet as the teens dispersed to their homes.

"How long can we protect this place?" one of the sentries asked.

The chief guard looked up and sighed, "Not much longer. They can't battle if they stay concealed."

The other nodded with understanding and then continued around the perimeter watch.

CHAPTER 24

"Hey, Joel!" A voice called across the school hallway. Joel turned to see a familiar face looking for his attention.

"How are ya, Kyle?" Joel answered, making his way to meet his friend. They rarely talked anymore, as Kyle was busy with karate. He and his parents had not been in church for weeks. Joel had spent much time in prayer for his friend, recognizing his spiritual need.

Joel spoke again, no longer feeling any deference toward Kyle, "How are you doing in competitions?"

Kyle nodded, "I'm doin' OK, in fact, really OK!"

Smiling, Joel clapped Kyle on the shoulder, "I knew you'd go far—you really have a talent in karate!"

Kyle took the compliment with ease, "Yeah . . . it's been hard, but fun. Say, would you be free to come to States to cheer me on?"

"States!" Joel nearly shouted.

Kyle grinned from ear to ear.

"You bet! When are they?" Joel asked.

"This weekend, and they're actually holding them here!" Kyle informed him.

"Sure! Do you know when?" Joel inquired.

"My match is around eleven on Saturday," Kyle said.

Nodding, Joel punched his friend, "I'll be there!"

The JP Knights met briefly Thursday evening. No one had battled any demons, but they all felt a sense of foreboding and spent the whole time in prayer for each other. Joel mentioned Kyle's competition, and they prayed for him to use his skills to the best of his ability. Silently, Joel also prayed for his friend to be committed to the Lord.

Saturday dawned cloudy and raining. Joel's parents had decided to go along and cheer. They found Kyle's parents in the stands and sat down next to them. They hurriedly caught up on family things before the announcer called for Kyle and his opponent.

Sparring started quickly, and the two on the mats seemed well-matched. Joel yelled excitedly as he saw Kyle make some aggressive moves that caught his rival off-guard and gave Kyle an advantage. The other teen, however, stayed calm and regained his composure, doing some complicated forms that surprised Kyle. Seeing that he had lost some ground, Kyle made his move.

Joel's stomach went into a ball as he saw his friend do an illegal move and bring his opponent down. Kyle's parents were cheering, as were his parents. It seemed that no one else had noticed what Kyle had done. After a long pause, the referee awarded the match to Kyle. The home crowd erupted into applause, and Kyle jumped up and down with excitement.

"Joel, why aren't you clapping?" his mom said into his ear to be heard during the mayhem.

"Oh . . . nothing, Mom," Joel said quickly and clapped lightly.

"Come on, Joel, I know you better than that," she insisted.

The arena was settling down, preparing for the next match.

Joel paused and then whispered into his mom's ear, "That was an illegal move—that one that he won by . . . it's illegal."

"How do you know? You didn't get as far as Kyle has," his mom whispered back as they sat down.

He looked her in the eye. "I *know*, Mom. He and I had talked about it before, and he figured he'd keep doing it until he was caught," Joel confided.

Kathy Steven bowed her head in thought and then said, "I guess there's nothing we can do. I understand why you couldn't cheer when he won. Do his parent's know?"

Joel shook his head, "I don't think so. They didn't before."

Kathy looked back out to the judge's table. "Uh oh . . . I think someone else may have seen it."

Joel watched as the opponent's sensei spoke to the referee. They moved around to a monitor and seemed to be engrossed in something. The coach pointed at the screen, and the referee's eyebrows went up in surprise. He conferred with an official and then showed him the monitor. The two whispered, and then the referee nodded to the instructor.

Grabbing a microphone, the announcer spoke, "There has been an appeal regarding the last match. It is the opinion of the officials that Kyle Thompson performed an illegal move to win. He is therefore eliminated from the tournament and his win forfeited."

The Thompsons stood angrily and yelled, along with most of the crowd.

"That's ridiculous!" Mr. Thompson called.

They could see Kyle running along the edge of the mats, punching the air in fury. His face was red with rage as his sensei held him back from rushing at the referee.

Someone else came to restrain Kyle while his sensei approached the officials. They took him to the monitor and showed him the clip. The instructor sighed and shook his head in disbelief. He bowed to the officials and then returned to Kyle.

The Stevenses could see that Kyle was furious, sneering some comment to his teacher and coach. The sensei stood calmly and spoke to him. Joel couldn't hear him but read his lips, "You're off the team."

The sensei turned to go back to the rest of his students. Kyle's anger boiled inside him.

Joel saw immediately what his friend was about to do. Time seemed to slow. Joel leaped from his seat and jumped into the tournament area, making it to Kyle and grabbing his arms as he lifted a wooden chair to hit the sensei. Joel held the chair with strength, knocking Kyle off balance enough to stop the forward motion and twist the boys to face each other.

Time resumed its normal march as Kyle looked in the face of his friend and made a choice.

Others had not seen where Joel came from. They only saw him and Kyle with the chair. Someone yelled. The sensei turned.

Officials ran over and restrained the two youths while the chair was taken from them.

Joel looked with love and concern at his friend. What he saw in Kyle's face was defiance and guile.

"Explain yourselves," one of the officials demanded.

For a moment, Kyle's eyes softened, but then the demon within him squeezed tighter, and Kyle blurted, "*He* was going to hit my sensei with the chair, but I stopped him!"

Sensei Jerry looked astounded and then asked Joel, "Is that true, son?"

The instructor had known Joel when both boys took karate lessons. He was a strict sensei, but he had been a fair man who had seen his share of sorrow in the world. Joel was not someone he remembered as revengeful.

Joel looked at his friend then at the officials, "No."

"What were you doing with this chair, then," one official questioned.

Joel looked again at Kyle, but said nothing.

"I'm telling you, he was going to hit my sensei!" Kyle shouted angrily.

By this time a crowd had gathered, including security men for the arena.

"Break it up! Let us through!" they called.

The officials quickly explained what they thought had happened.

Sensei Jerry peered at Joel. There was something about that boy. He had noticed it when he taught him his forms. Kyle was another matter. He was like a volcano ready to explode, which made him quite successful in karate, but dangerous.

"Jerry," an official called to him. The sensei talked quietly with the officials and the security men.

"OK," the head security guard spoke. "You both are to leave the premises now and are not permitted to return."

"Aren't you going to do anything?" Kyle yelled.

Jerry eyed his student, "You are out of the competition. Do you wish for more discipline? Fine. You are no longer welcome at my dojo unless you apologize for your indiscretion. We hold to our honor. You did not learn to cheat from me, and I will not condone it."

Kyle's face screwed into a malevolent contortion. Before he could retort, his father pulled him away saying, "Let's go, Kyle. We'll leave these pansies and find you someone who appreciates your talents!"

The Thompson family pushed their way through the crowd as the officials tried to settle the onlookers.

Kathy and Doug Stevens had rushed to join Joel as the situation unfolded. The sensei regarded them with a slight bow.

"You did not assert your innocence, Joel," Jerry stated.

Joel shook his head, "I was hoping I wouldn't need to. He is . . . was my friend."

His parents placed their hands on Joel's shoulders as they flanked him.

"Thank you for trying to help him *and* protecting me," Jerry said. "I blame myself for what happened today. He has such talent, but I saw evil in him. I just ignored it because I wanted to have a winning team."

Jerry stood dejectedly for a moment. Joel reached out and took his hands.

"Sensei, in the end, you did the right thing," Joel encouraged.

The man looked with gratitude toward Joel. "Thank you, but perhaps I could have done something to stop the growing anger in him, using karate to redirect his energies instead of using them for wrong. I must live with that."

"God still needs you to train your other students properly," Joel admonished.

The sensei looked curiously at Joel, and then responded, "You are right, my young friend—*that* I can do!" He bowed to Joel and returned to his students.

The security guard still had Joel by the elbow.

"I'm sorry, but you need to leave," he said.

Joel nodded. He and his parents made their way out of the arena and then headed home.

The three Stevens were quiet, all deep in their own thoughts. Joel could feel God's peace flooding through him and with a grateful look, thanked the angels who brought comfort to him and his parents.

When they got home, Kathy and Doug quickly made sandwiches while Joel got drinks. They went to the dining room and sat, while the rained poured down outside.

"Thank you, Lord, for this food. We acknowledge Your sovereign will, but we are distressed with today's happenings. Please show us Your way and help us to trust You. Amen," Kathy prayed.

They each played with their food for a few moments before Doug spoke.

"Your mom and I are very proud of what you did today, Joel. You stayed true to your friend without jeopardizing your morals. We're sorry for what has happened to Kyle. You apparently saw that coming?" he finished in a question.

Joel nodded with a sigh. "Yeah . . . I had tried to talk him out of doing that move before, but he believed winning was more important. You know," he paused briefly, "I used to really be a follower of Kyle's. He never made me do anything wrong, but there were times that I thought he would. I used to go along with whatever he'd suggest, and sometimes things would be a little questionable, and I'd feel like I shouldn't go along with it. A few months ago I knew I couldn't be like that anymore, but we really weren't spending any time together for me to show that I wasn't his follower any longer."

Kathy nodded, "I know there were times I was concerned that he was leading you away from God, but then he and his parents would be at church, and I convinced myself that things were OK, but my heart knew they weren't. I never felt like Kyle or his parents had a true relationship with the Lord. I should have been praying for them or trying to encourage them in the Lord's things."

The three were silent once again.

"Well . . ." Doug finally ventured, "there's nothing to stop us from praying for them now and daily, is there?"

Joel and Kathy grinned and both replied, "No!"

As Doug led his family in a prayer, Twinkle-Eyes and three other angels circled them. The angels glowed as the Stevenses poured out their hearts to the Lord and interceded for the Thompsons. When the prayer was over, the three other angels gathered around Twinkle-Eyes.

"Is there enough to plant the seeds?" he asked.

Each of the other angels nodded in affirmation.

"Then, carry the seeds of hope to the Thompson home. May the Lamb's work on the cross protect you, and may you find a way to plant the seeds without the enemy knowing," Twinkle-Eyes admonished.

In a moment, the angels were gone.

The following week at school, Kyle spread a rumor that Joel had lied and told the officials that he had done an illegal move, kicking him out of the state finals. The few who had been at the event had not been close enough to see what had happened, so there was no one to refute Kyle's assertion.

Joel noticed some sour looks soon after he got to school, and he was saddened to finally hear what Kyle had said about him. Jill and Chris decided to cheer him up at lunchtime, but found that Joel was not really swayed by the rumor.

"We knew that the enemy would be after us. It's just sad that we had been friends for so long. Now, I'm concentrating on praying for him—I know he's not really a bad guy; he's just made some bad choices, and I want to be ready to help him when he's ready to choose the right way," Joel said with confidence.

Joel's reaction, or lack of one, proved to lessen the impact of Kyle's lie. Within a day or two, the student body was tired of hearing Kyle talk about losing because of Joel, and they moved on to different concerns. This made Kyle even more furious. His parents had quickly found another dojo that wasn't as morally strict, so

Kyle put his energy and anger into sparring and practicing more with the new sensei. This instructor prided himself on teaching revenge techniques and unleashing his students' frustrations on those who could not defend themselves. Kyle liked the feeling of power. Sensei Jerry had always cautioned against the use of karate as a means of threatening others—it was for self-defense and self-control. Now, Kyle excelled, using raw emotions, performing even lethal moves, as he learned the so-called rewards of revenge. The demons he had allowed to enter his spirit grew in strength with each bad choice Kyle made.

CHAPTER 25

The demon lord grinned hideously. He had ordered his hordes to back off after his beast had been destroyed. The message the scrawny demon brought back had enraged him. This kid had shown incredible spiritual power against his beast, such as he had not heard of for centuries. He had quickly sent a messenger to his master and had just received his instructions back. The order was exactly what he had hoped for!

The JP Knights met solemnly at the chapel. They had heard of what had happened with Kyle, but each wondered how Joel was doing and had been praying for his comfort and wisdom in the situation.

As they began with a prayer, Jill and Marissa sensed something and looked up. The air was suddenly filled with unearthly screams. Flashes of light and sounds of clashing swords emanated from the surroundings.

"We are under attack!" Twinkle-Eyes whispered urgently. "Garrett, are the front doors the only way out of here?"

Garrett started to nod, but then shook his head and pushed around some of the group to the front of the chapel. Prying with his fingers, he swiftly lifted a piece of the floor, revealing a crawl space underneath.

Motioning for the others to follow him, Garrett quickly disappeared into the hole. Twinkle-Eyes held the lid while the others slipped in, then he replaced the flooring. Pulling a sword from his robe, he strode to the front door and pushed it open.

A ghastly demon met him with a swing of a sword. The angels were outnumbered, but each one was fighting two or three demons with the strength of ten angels! Twinkle-Eyes rapidly dispensed with the demon before him with a quick jab, but then found himself face to face with the demon lord!

Below the floor of the chapel, the teens interlocked fingers and prayed silently.

"Strength for the angels, Father! Help us! May Your power from on high come and defeat the enemy!" They all prayed quietly in unison.

Twinkle-Eyes parried and struck at the demon lord. Out of the corner of his eye he saw one angel go down. He turned his full attention to the battle at hand, striking with a volley of jabs and cuts. The demon lord seemed immovable, and his hordes were winning!

Two demons hiding behind a nearby tree knew their mission: get into the little church while the angels were occupied outside and destroy the small group of Believers who were gathering inside!

They crept in through the door Twinkle-Eyes had opened, while the demon lord distracted the angel leader with another set of moves. The lit chapel showed no humans visible, but there were many pews to hide behind or under. The demons searched the tiny building quickly and found no one.

Coming out the front door, the demons slunk toward the lord, who now had his back to the chapel.

"Master, there was no one in the building!" one demon hissed.

"Ah!" the demon lord screamed, "Look again!"

The demon lord fought with a frenzy, his rage feeding each move, until he had knocked the sword from Twinkle-Eyes' hand and poised to strike for the kill.

His sword pierced the air where the angel had been, missing its deadly mark as Twinkle-Eyes whirled in a karate-style move, kicking the demon in the arm. The demon leaped at the angel, and the two grappled and punched in hand-to-hand combat.

In the meantime, the two little demons went through the church again. Finding no one, they turned to go. With the noise of the battle outside, neither one noticed a miniscule scraping sound behind them.

The force hit them so hard that it sent them sprawling in the grass ten feet in front of the church's door! Light like a canopy of lightening emanated from the chapel. Demons and angels alike paused in their fray, wondering what this new power might be and whose side it was on.

Joel led the group out through the front door, the force field from his shield enveloping each one as they exited the church. In fact, each of the JP Knights held their own shields and the force field arced between them creating a continuous defensive line. The demons shuddered with fright. None but their leader had ever seen such a display of any Believer's power. The demon lord hesitated in battle, recalling, with a chill, a day two thousand years previous when another rag-tag group of Christ-followers had used similar power to turn Jerusalem upside down. He had nearly been run out of town that day, but had found curious refuge in a Jewish zealot, who rose up and persecuted the Believers for a time. He had grown strong within the man, glorying in the evil that was accomplished. That is, until one day when that canopy of light erupted around the man from an unknown source, and the demon was cast a league from the site! It had taken centuries of menial possession of men before the demon had been able to rise up to its former level of power.

The brief hesitation was all Twinkle-Eyes needed. He lunged at the demon lord, picking up his sword and plunging it into the lord's belly. The demon seemed to evaporate before his eyes!

With renewed strength, Twinkle-Eyes rushed at another demon while each of the JP Knights set off for others. The lesser demons were no match for the band of Believers and angels. The loss of their leader had weakened them immensely, and the demons were destroyed within another ten minutes.

The JP Knights gathered behind the chapel and offered their swords up to the Lord. The armor that had been visible as the

Knights stormed from the church disappeared along with the offering. They knelt for a while, each thanking and praising the Almighty and the Lamb for the victory.

Returning inside the chapel, each JP Knight cleaned up their area. This place was no longer safe for meeting. Quietly, they stood in a circle and prayed for guidance.

CHAPTER 26

The youth group found seats as Pastor Eric announced the start of the meeting. There were some special services at another church that Sunday night that the adults were attending, but the youth had decided to keep their own service. Marissa and Joel sat together, discussing some spiritual things. They quickly stopped and joined in singing a chorus that Pastor Eric typically used. The praise and prayer time was shortened tonight because of a special guest.

"Kids," Pastor Eric began, "this is Zech Douds. He and I were roommates in seminary. I think he has a word from the Lord tonight that we all need to hear."

"Thanks, Eric," a compelling voice spoke from the back of the room.

Joel turned to look at a young man making his way to the front. He stared with surprise at a figure he had seen before.

Zech looked in earnest at the group before him. He prayed first, asking the Spirit to open their hearts to the word of the Lord and then quickly got their rapt attention as he described the second coming of the Lord and how all people needed to hear the message of salvation.

Joel could tell that Zech had a burden for souls, but there was also a strange fear that seemed to hold him back. The other teens must have sensed it, too, because no one responded to the invitation at the end.

Pastor Eric put a hand on Zech's shoulder as he took over the closing of the meeting. Soon, the youth were busy talking in the back of the room, enjoying refreshments and playing some games. Marissa smiled at Joel and made her way to some of the girls she had recently gotten to know.

Joel watched as Pastor Eric whispered to his friend and then retreated to the back, where he started to organize the fellowship time. Zech bowed his head and sat down in the front row, shaking his head in a kind of self-rebuttal.

"You know you have a gift," Zech heard a voice say in front of him.

He looked up to see Joel initially standing before him and then taking a seat next to him.

Zech sighed and shook his head, "I used to think that, but somehow I don't think it's really there."

"Oh, it's still there, believe me," Joel insisted.

"How do you know?" Zech asked dejectedly.

Joel looked at Zech with a smile that emitted hope and said, "Because I have seen you ministering to thousands, bringing the message of salvation to a broken world, and I have seen them responding to the Word. You are not to fear—your ministry is waiting for you!"

In a moment, angels surrounded the two, although Zech could not see them.

Joel placed his hand on Zech's arm and urged, "Release the fear that has held you captive since the accident."

Zech's eyes grew wide as he stammered, "How . . . how'd you know?"

"It doesn't matter," Joel assured him, "but the Almighty needs you now! Let it go!"

The dark spot that Joel had perceived on Zech's back grew like a bubble coming to the surface. Zech stared into Joel's eyes as he willed the demon of fear to leave his spirit.

Suddenly, the demon hissed and screamed, shooting out of Zech like a bullet!

Zech seemed to gasp in pain as the last vestiges of the demon left him. The angels were quick to come to his aid, laying their hands on him, releasing the comfort, peace, and love of the Lamb.

Marissa had been listening to her friends talking about a summer camp when she heard the demon. She turned to see the demon leaving Zech. She hurried to the front and squeezed between two angels at Zech's back. Placing her hand where the demon had exited, she prayed for the man to be healed.

This time, Joel kept quiet, silently acknowledging Marissa's gift.

The glow on Zech's face was unmistakable. He breathed deeply and sat up straight.

"Thank you," he said sincerely.

Joel smiled in response, and said, "You have a great work to do, and today is a good time to start!"

Marissa now came around to face Zech. As his eyes met hers, a look of shock came over his face.

"B-b-bonnie?" he stammered.

Marissa smiled sweetly, "No, I'm Marissa."

Zech shook his head as if to clear cobwebs, rubbed his temples, and then looked back at Marissa.

"Sorry," he offered, "you just look like someone I used to know."

He turned to speak to Joel, when Marissa spoke up again, "My mom is Bonnie. Perhaps you met her somewhere."

Zech looked as if he had seen a ghost. "What?" he barely whispered.

Marissa smiled again and said, "My mom is Bonnie. People say I look just like her."

Reaching for her hands, Zech trembled and asked, "Where is your mother now?"

"Oh, she's meeting me here in a few minutes," Marissa said, and then paused, looking over at the entrance to the room. "There she is now."

Zech looked at the doorway and slowly stood up. As he stared at the woman entering, his face paled, and he nearly collapsed.

Marissa's mom appeared to have the same reaction, grabbing a chair to prevent her from falling.

Joel reached for Zech and steadied him, while Marissa rushed over to her mom.

Zech was shaking badly, yet he pushed Joel aside and stumbled over to the mother and daughter.

"Bonnie?" he asked with trepidation.

Marissa's mom blinked hard, and then she started to cry, "Zech . . . Zech . . . Is it really you?"

The two grabbed each other in a tearful hug. Marissa and Joel looked at each other, and Marissa shrugged her shoulders in confusion.

By this time, Pastor Eric had noticed the small commotion and had approached to see what was going on. Joel and Marissa both indicated that they had no clue.

Finally, Zech held Bonnie out from him and shook his head, saying, "You're alive!" With tears streaming down his face, he then shouted, "You're alive!"

Bonnie tenderly touched his cheek, and they hugged again.

The whole youth group had now gathered around the two emotional adults. Many were shaking their heads in bewilderment.

"Tell me, tell me," Zech insisted, "where have you been? How did you survive?"

Bonnie shook her head, "I don't know."

Zech inquired, "How can you not know?"

Bonnie wet her lips before answering. "Until this moment, I had no memory of my life before seventeen years ago. But, as soon as I saw you, I remembered you, Zech. Please tell *me* what happened!"

Zech closed his eyes and bowed his head, swallowed hard, and then spoke, "You were on a train trip with Mom and Dad. They had left me at Grandma's because I had school. The train derailed and many were killed . . ." His voice trailed off. He hesitated before continuing, ". . . including Mom and Dad, and we thought you, too, although your body was never found."

Bonnie stared in disbelief and then nodded, "Well, that makes a little sense of things, even though I still don't remember the train accident. They told me I just showed up in Connersburg, and all I could tell them was my first name."

"Connersburg!" Zech exclaimed. "That's like one hundred miles from the train wreck! No wonder nobody even thought to relate your appearance to that!"

As everyone realized the enormity of the reunion they had just witnessed, Pastor Eric called for quiet.

"I think this deserves a prayer of thanksgiving, don't you think?" he asked while raising his arms. "Lord, You have done a great thing tonight. One who was thought to be dead, is alive and reunited with her family. And one who had suffered great loss has received a loved one back from the dead. *We praise you!*" he shouted.

With the youth group dismissed, Zech and Bonnie were invited back to Pastor Eric's house to reacquaint themselves. Before leaving the church, however, Zech caught up with Joel.

"Young man!" Zech called as Joel headed for his dad's car parked at the curb.

Joel turned and took a few steps toward the man running in his direction.

Zech grabbed Joel's hand, "Thank you for what you did tonight! I know what happened with my sister sort of overshadowed what you had done, but I wanted to tell you that I *will* use the gift the Lord has given me. I feel . . ." Here, he grappled for the right words. "I feel free, if that makes any sense."

Smiling, Joel nodded, "Yeah, it does."

"Thank you," Zech repeated.

Joel moved to get in the car.

"Oh, hey, what's your name?" Zech asked.

"I'm Joel," Joel responded.

Zech looked at him with a penetrating gaze and then questioned, "You said thousands, right . . . that I would minister to thousands?"

Joel grinned, "That's right!"

Straightening up, Zech got a faraway look in his eye, "Yep, that's what I thought you said." Then he waved to Joel and walked back into the church.

Staring at the evangelist he had seen in his vision, Joel thanked the Lord for the events of the evening. The two angels flanking

Zech glowed with the power of the prayer as they escorted him into his new life.

Marissa could barely contain her excitement at the Wednesday night prayer meeting. "Joel! Joel!" she called, running over to him as he and his mom got out of the car.

"How are you, Marissa?" he blurted.

She looked as if she would burst with excitement. "We have a home with Uncle Zech!" she exclaimed.

Joel regarded her with hesitation, "Oh, so you'll be leaving town?"

"No, no, no!" she shouted with joy.

Many people entering the church looked at her and smiled.

Joel laughed, "OK, fill me in!"

Marissa took a big breath to calm herself and then proceeded, "It turns out that my great-grandparents had lived right here in town! When they died, Uncle Zech got their house. That was why he was in town to speak to the youth group—he had just moved in!" She paused thoughtfully, "To think that we really had family here all this time and didn't know it!"

She went on to explain that her mom and dad had met in Connersburg, where a family had taken her mom in after her strange arrival. Her parents had gotten married relatively quickly.

"We called my brothers, and they don't want to stay with Dad, so we're moving them in this weekend! I can hardly believe all this is happening, Joel! My mom and I went from having no home, no family, to a new home and family restored! Isn't the Lord incredible!" she bubbled.

Joel nodded happily, "It sounds like we've got some praising to do tonight!"

Marissa stopped, "The demon . . . the one that came out of Uncle Zech?"

"Yeah?" Joel asked.

"It had been in him since the accident when he lost my grandparents and thought he lost my mom," she confided.

"I know," Joel said.

Marissa grabbed his arm and whispered, "Thank you, Joel! You saved his life, and in saving his life, you saved my mom's life, too. She accepted the Lord last night!" Tears rolled from her eyes. "I know that my brothers will come to know Him, too, *and* that Uncle Zech will be starting his evangelistic meetings right here in town."

Joel smiled and hugged his friend, "I'm so glad for you, Marissa!"

"Joel?" Marissa asked.

"Yeah?" he replied as they walked into the sanctuary.

"My new house has a large, finished basement," Marissa began, "and I wondered if the JP Knights would want to meet there, now that the chapel at Garrett's farm is no longer safe."

"Hmm . . ." Joel mused thoughtfully. "Are you sure your family wouldn't mind? I mean, you're just getting to know your uncle Zech and your brothers moving in. . . . That's a lot happening."

"I know," Marissa admitted, "but I really feel that it's the right thing to do. My mom and Uncle Zech were fine with it. There's a separate outside entrance so my family wouldn't be bothered when we meet."

Joel nodded, "Well, let's pray about it and text the others after the prayer meeting, OK?"

Marissa smiled, "I know that spiritually, a lot is going on, but I have to tell you that this is the happiest I've ever been!"

Joel gave a little laugh, "You know . . . I feel the same way! Even though we're battling demons, I have a joy that I didn't have before. I think it's because we are trying to live in the center of God's will for our lives."

"I think that's right. . . . Well, I'm going to sit with my mom. See you later!" Marissa whispered as the music started, announcing the beginning of the service.

Joel turned to go to a seat when his mom caught his arm. Looking at her, his stomach went into a ball. Her face was pale, and he immediately knew that something was wrong.

"Joel," his mom's voice trembled, "there's been an accident . . ."

"What . . . Mom . . . who?" he said cautiously, as he grabbed her hand.

She gazed at him with tears welling up in her eyes, "Your dad . . ."

CHAPTER 27

The church was filled to capacity for the service. Although Doug Stevens had been a quiet man, there were many who had benefitted from his honest work. The community had been shocked by the accident and had come out to support Kathy and Joel.

Pastor Art and Pastor George stayed with them in an anteroom, while Pastor Eric played his guitar in the front of the church until the service started. The youth group sat together at the one side. The JP Knights met in the foyer before entering, and then followed Marissa in to seats she had saved for them behind the Stevens family.

Kathy and Joel came in last, being escorted to seats by the pastors, joining some other family members. The mother and son clung to each other with heads bowed.

Pastor Art made his way to the pulpit, but then, seemingly as an afterthought, moved to a side podium and began to speak.

The host of angels encircled the church outside, standing guard, as it were, but also in honor of the child of God who had been faithful in his service to the Almighty. These had come from many areas and had not known the one now in the Lord's presence. On the inside, however, stood angels who had come to know the man and his family intimately. Many of them had not left the side of their charges since the tragedy, giving comfort and strength from the Lamb, who had Himself cried with grief at the death of His friend, Lazarus.

The message was poignant with memories. Pastor Art was careful to present the gospel and then offered for any who desired to comment on the life of Doug Stevens to stand and speak.

Kathy and Joel heard many tell of Doug's integrity and commitment to excellence. It comforted them greatly to hear how quite a few had come to know the Lord because of Doug's life. Since he was a quiet person, it was not surprising that most focused on his actions . . . going out of his way to help people . . . his willingness to do that extra step that made a difference. All of it was somehow credited to the Lord's goodness, with Doug merely being His hands.

Finally, the time of sharing came to an end, and Pastor George got up to finish the service. Before he could begin, however, Joel rose and came forward. Pastor George grabbed his hand and then hugged him. A few in the front could hear the retired pastor whispering to Joel and then stepping aside.

Joel moved to the podium. The sanctuary was quiet as they waited for him to speak. A long minute went by.

Looking up, Joel saw the crowded church. The sight warmed his heart, knowing that his father's life had been one of value for the kingdom of God. The angels' presence had helped him and his mom tremendously through the past days, bearing them up during their great sorrow and feelings of loss.

Joel sighed deeply, and then spoke, "Thank you all for coming to commemorate the life of my dad. It means a lot to my mom and me." He paused.

The JP Knights could see that Twinkle-Eyes and Gimel were on either side of Joel, each with a hand on his shoulder. Joel looked at Twinkle-Eyes and closed his eyes briefly. Then, with tears, Joel continued.

"My father is gone from us now, and we are going to miss him so much . . ." again Joel paused. "But, he would want all of you to know that he is alive in heaven this very moment, and Mom and I hold to that hope of seeing him again when Christ comes back for us very soon! You see, my dad believed that Jesus had died long ago to pay the penalty for the badness in each one of us. But, it didn't stop there—Christ was made alive again by God's power so that we can go to heaven when our time on earth is over. Dad knew that. He believed that. So . . . this separation from him is just for a time. We want to celebrate his life! It would honor him, and us, for any of you who don't have a relationship with Jesus to make that commitment to Christ today. Don't wait. We never know when our time on this earth will be over. Thank you."

Joel breathed deeply and made his way back to the pew to sit with his mom. The angels hugged him and embraced his mom as well.

Pastor George said a few words and then invited any who wanted to know more about how to have a relationship with Jesus to come see him after the service. The angels moved throughout the sanctuary, glowing with power.

One person stood. The JP Knights turned at the sound of a demon screaming, just in time to see it streaking upward through the ceiling. The man whose body it had inhabited nearly passed out, but the angels were already there to strengthen him and soon helped him to the side of the sanctuary where Pastor George rushed to meet him. The two grasped hands and tearfully began to pray.

In a moment, another demon screeched. The JP Knights joined hands in prayer as the angels went to numerous individuals and harvested souls for the kingdom. The response was so great that Pastor Art asked all those in the service to pray for the work of the Spirit to be accomplished and for everyone to wait quietly as the staff ministered to those seeking the Lord.

Sunday afternoon was quiet. Family and friends had left after lunch, and Kathy Stevens had gone to lie down. Many had assisted them lately, boxing up Doug's files for his clients and distributing them to other accountants in the area. One close friend had checked Doug's computer and worked on his accounts receivable, calling those who owed money and making sure bills were sent out. An uncle had gone through clothes and bagged up things for a charity store.

Joel sat on the swing in the back yard. Twinkle-Eyes sat next to him. The angel had hardly said a word to Joel since the accident, but had stayed with him night and day.

"Why?" Joel murmured. He then looked at the angel.

Twinkle-Eyes shook his head, "I do not know, Joel."

Joel nodded distractedly.

"Did he have an angel with him?" Joel asked.

"Yes," Twinkle-Eyes replied. "He was surrounded by the messengers of the Lamb."

Joel looked quizzically at him, "Were you there?"

Twinkle-Eyes did not respond immediately, but then queried, "Why do you wish to know?"

"You could have saved him, couldn't you?" Joel inquired.

"No," Twinkle-Eyes answered.

"Don't you have God's power to do those things?" Joel pushed.

Twinkle-Eyes peered with concern at Joel, "I can only do the will of the Lamb or of the Almighty."

Joel nodded, "So They wanted this to happen?"

"It is not a question of want, Joel," the angel explained.

"Is this because I did something wrong?" Joel persisted.

"No," Twinkle-Eyes replied without elaborating.

Joel pushed the swing while lost in thought. Then, he suddenly stopped.

"I don't understand," he said emphatically and then ran into the house.

Throwing himself on his bed, he sobbed. Feeling a hand on his back, he yelled, "Go away!"

"Joel," his mom said softly.

He rolled over and cried, "Oh, Mom, I didn't know it was you!"

Furrowing her eyebrows, she thought, *Who else could it be?* But she kept that thought to herself and instead asked, "Would you like to talk?"

Sitting up, Joel swallowed hard, "I don't know. Mom, why did this happen?"

Kathy took a big breath and shook her head, "I don't know, Joel. Sometimes, we don't have answers. We may never know. But . . ."

She paused, releasing a huge sigh. "The Bible tells us that *'all things work together for good for those who love God.'* I have to believe that, somehow, good will come out of this. Not that this was good—it certainly wasn't . . . but somehow, something very good will come out of this. We just have to believe . . . and we can't lose hope. Your dad would want us to be strong, but when we aren't strong, God will help us. Jesus was comforted by angels, you know. Perhaps, we will be helped by angels, even if we can't see them."

Joel grabbed his mom in a hug, and cried, "You're right, Mom. I *know* you're right."

They held onto each other for a long time. The angels gathered around them tightly, glowing with a rainbow of colors.

At the home of one of the prayer warriors that very moment, a large group prayed for the Stevens family, spending over an hour entreating the Lord to send comfort.

In the meantime, Pastor George sat in his kitchen. A picture of Mabel looked down on him from the wall as he laid his head on his arms, praying for Joel and Kathy.

The JP Knights were meeting in Marissa's basement room. Holding hands, they prayed for Joel and his mom. Their angels circled behind them, raising their arms in offerings of love and praise.

The youth group filed into Pastor Eric's home solemnly. Sitting on the chairs or the floor, they all sang a few songs about God's love and then prayed for Joel, asking the Lord to comfort him and help him not to give in to despair.

The throne room was silent as the Lamb reflected on the time He felt great loss when Lazarus died, and the Father remembered the terrible day when He allowed His Son to die for the sake of those He had created.

The prayers offered up from Joel, Kathy and their friends came before the Almighty and the Lamb. The sacrifice was as a sweet fragrance rising from a flower. The Almighty gathered it in His Hands and nodded. The sacrifice was pleasing to Him.

He summoned some holy messengers. The doves carried His gifts to Joel and Kathy swiftly, as they sat together in their home, now looking at a photo album.

"To console those who mourn . . . to give them beauty for ashes, the oil of joy for mourning, the garment of praise for the spirit of heaviness; that they may be called trees of righteousness, the planting of the LORD, that He may be glorified."

The oil sprinkled on Joel and Kathy was like a spring shower, washing over them. Two doves held a cloak in their beaks, and then draped it over the shoulders of Kathy and Joel. It seemed to adhere to their very flesh.

Joel and Kathy felt something, but neither said anything. Kathy pointed out a particular photo to Joel and the two smiled. Joel remarked more about it, and they both burst out laughing. This went on for a time as the healing balm from the Almighty restored them and comforted them.

Kathy went to get some drinks. When she returned, Joel noticed the difference in her appearance. He could tell that it was spiritual and not physical. He'd have to ask Jill what it could mean.

"Do you know that quite a few people came to know the Lord at the funeral service?" Kathy asked Joel.

"No . . . I guess I really hadn't noticed much that went on," Joel answered.

"Pastor Art told me that thirty people either accepted the Lord or returned to Him!" Kathy remarked.

Joel stared at her in surprise. "Thirty? Wow!" Joel shook his head and let out a breath of amazement. "That's part of the good, Mom," he said with a wan smile.

Kathy sat down and nodded, "You're right, Joel. It certainly seems to be some of the good referred to in Romans." She paused and then continued, "Would you be OK if we praised the Lord right now for that good?"

Joel breathed heavily and then said, "Yeah, Mom. You know, Dad would be really happy to know that others came to the Lord through his death. He wasn't the type of person who was in the spotlight. He was more of a backstage guy . . . yet his witness was still important for the harvesting of souls."

"You're right, Joel," his mom agreed. She reached for his hand, and then bowed her head. "Dear Father, You know we mourn the passing of Doug, but we want to praise You that others came to know You through his life and death. That knowledge lifts our spirits and comforts us. Be with those who have chosen Your Way through this situation and help them to be mighty for You in the coming days. We praise You! Amen."

The doves which had been lingering nearby caught the praises and carried them to an angel waiting outside.

"Thank you, my friends," Daleth said as he received the gift. "These praises will give power to the new children of God so they may complete the work He has for them. The death of this righteous one will indeed bring many to accept salvation from the Lamb That Was Slain. One day this family will know how important their praises have been."

CHAPTER 28

Joel's first day back at school was busy as he talked to many students and teachers, thanking them for their support during the past week. He looked forward to seeing Chris and Jill at lunchtime. The JP Knights had been constant friends, stopping by his house and sending texts or e-mails to remind him of God's love, but Joel hoped for something familiar to help him through the day.

He wasn't disappointed. As he entered the cafeteria, one look brought a grin to his face as he saw his friends at the same ol' table, waiting for him to join them.

"Hey, guys!" Joel exclaimed, greeting Chris and Jill.

Both looked at him closely with questioning eyebrows.

Joel jutted his head forward and widened his eyes, while he asked, "OK, what's up?"

"Something's different, Joel," Chris offered. "You have a sort of glow?" he finished as an inquiry.

Joel shrugged his shoulders as he sat down. "What do you mean?"

Jill peered at him intently, and then spoke, "You look like you have tanning oil on, but . . . yet it's different."

Joel got excited, "You mean I have it, too?"

Chris and Jill both looked startled.

"It's just that," Joel began, "I noticed that my mom looked different yesterday after we had been going through some photo albums. We both felt real peaceful and comforted somehow. She went to get drinks, and when she came back, I saw it. Like you said, Jill, sort of . . . like we had put oil on to tan."

Chris snapped his fingers and exclaimed, "I know what it is . . . at least I think I do." He then pulled a Bible out of his pocket. Fingering through it, he finally nodded his head, "Here it is: '*To console those who mourn in Zion, to give them beauty for ashes, the oil of joy for mourning, the garment of praise for the spirit of heaviness; that they may be called trees of righteousness, the planting of the LORD, that He may be glorified.*' That's from Isaiah 61:3. I think you received the *oil of joy!*"

Jill and Joel nodded excitedly.

"That's it!" Joel agreed. "It makes sense! We started laughing with good memories the pictures brought back, and I honestly felt joyful and thankful for the great times I had with my dad." He paused in thought and then asked, "What came after the *oil of joy?*"

Chris looked down at his Bible again and read, "Uh . . . *the garment of praise for the spirit of heaviness.*'"

Nodding, Joel laughed, "Yeah! Right after that Mom told me that thirty people came to know the Lord or returned to Him at the funeral service, and we prayed, praising God for the harvesting of those souls! That's really cool!"

The teens continued talking while they ate lunch. As they finished, Joel asked if the JP Knights meeting was still on for the next night. Chris confirmed the gathering, and they ended with a short prayer. Joel left the cafeteria with his spirit lifted.

In the hall, Kyle kept his distance from Joel. The demon within him squeezed tightly, but Kyle resisted the temptation to hurl some hurtful comment. The demon rechecked his hold and finding its tentacles still deep within Kyle's spirit, it turned its attention away from Joel and urged the teen to trip another student going past. Kyle merely shrugged and went to his next class, leaving the demon somewhat distressed and confused over the temporary loss of control over Kyle.

Nearby, an angel looked on with hope.

Joel found much comfort in meeting with the JP Knights. Although he questioned his dad's death, he discovered that offering up his confusion to the Lord helped him to let go of it. He was able to accept what had happened, acknowledge that he may never understand why, and begin to move on. At first, it was just the JP Knights who knew about the comfort and healing that was taking place. They witnessed the *oil of joy* in his appearance and a few even caught sight of the garment of praise that was now embedded in his spirit. It wasn't long, however, before others came to him at school and at church, asking him how he could go on so well after his dad's death. He now understood the Scriptures that spoke of comfort: *2 Corinthians 1:3–4: Blessed be the God and Father of our Lord Jesus Christ, the Father of mercies and God of all comfort, who comforts us in all our tribulation, that we may be able to comfort those who are in any trouble, with the comfort with which we ourselves are comforted by God.*

Kathy Stevens found the same thing to be true as she returned to her work and sweetly dealt with the challenges a widow faced. A number of staff came to her to personally offer their condolences, but most came away feeling uplifted and encouraged. Many of those then went on to renew a relationship with the Lord. Some staff had seeds of faith planted that began to grow and were "watered" by other servants of the Lord.

Joel and Kathy knew of some of the changes that their witness had brought about, but most of the good that came from Doug's death would not be known by them in this life.

CHAPTER 29

Satan listened to the reports from his demons. He was pleased that the world was increasingly under his control. The erosion of any morals was essential to his victory, and the watering down of Christianity fit right into his plan. He was puffed up with pride at his accomplishments when a scrawny demon told of its escape from a small group of Believers. He scorned the small demon for inadequacies and dismissed it from his presence with a wave of his hand. It would be some time before that error would become evident.

The evangelistic meetings drew more than expected. Zech's passion for sharing the gospel had blossomed with the miraculous reunion with his sister. He spoke with conviction and love, the result being the salvation of souls. Listeners accepted salvation through Jesus Christ, and they brought their friends and families to hear Zech's words. His recent experiences resulted in an uplifting and positive message that the people of the town desperately needed to hear.

The JP Knights studied with the angels in Marissa's basement. Twinkle-Eyes had warned them that the current boom of harvesting would be short-lived. Very soon, the work of the Lamb's brethren would become evident. The earlier battles may have escaped Satan's notice, but the group needed to be ready for the coming war.

Twinkle-Eyes and Joel sat together quietly. The angel sensed that Joel was still dealing with some deep emotions regarding his dad's death, and had questions that were difficult to ask. He patiently waited for the young man to speak.

Joel sighed and then asked, "Was my dad's death because of what I'm doing?" He peered at Twinkle-Eyes with an almost tangible seriousness.

The angel looked upon Joel with such compassion that Joel teared up.

"Would that make a difference?" Twinkle-Eyes queried.

"It seems to," Joel began, "I mean, I keep thinking that maybe Satan caused the accident to happen to try to stop what the JP Knights are doing."

"Does that make you feel bad?" the angel asked.

Joel thought for a moment, and then responded, "Sort of . . . because it makes me feel responsible for his death."

Twinkle-Eyes nodded and then said, "That's a big burden to carry."

Scripture verses seemed to flow into Joel's mind: *Take My yoke upon you and learn of me for My yoke is easy and My burden is light.*

Joel pondered these thoughts for a moment and then asked, "Was it that God allowed it to happen?"

Again, the angel queried, "Would that make a difference? Would that make you feel bad?"

"It makes God seem mean," Joel answered.

"What do you remember about God's character?" Twinkle-Eyes asked.

"He is holy and just," Joel said. Then a light bulb seemed to come on and he said, "God is love. . . . He sent His only Son to die so that we could live eternally with Him. . . . He didn't just allow Jesus to die." Tears flowed now. "He actually sent Him. That was the whole reason for Jesus to be here. It wasn't an accident. It was purposeful."

Twinkle-Eyes hugged Joel as the young man came to grips with the love of God in a different way. Joel had already seen some good that had come from his dad's death.

But, Joel wondered if he, himself, could have purposely let the accident happen, knowing that more people would come to know Jesus by Doug's death than by his life at this particular moment in time? He knew he wouldn't have. That realization brought him face to face with the immense depth of God's love.

Joel gazed through his tears at Twinkle-Eyes and said, "So . . . it really doesn't make a difference why my dad died. If Satan did it because of the JP Knights, then God turned it around for good and brought souls to salvation. If God allowed it," he paused, "or . . . or if He purposed it to happen for some reason, it was only because of His great love for all of mankind, so that somehow good would come of it."

The angel nodded. He hugged Joel as the boy cried. Tears of loss, tears of grief, tears of incredible, unfathomable love flowed.

Held in the angel's arms, Joel suddenly felt strange. He opened his eyes and found Jesus before him. The Son took him in His arms and held him securely. Joel cried again. He hugged the Lamb for what seemed a long time.

"My Father loves you, Joel. Trust Him, even as I trusted Him in the Garden of Gethsemane. *His understanding is unsearchable. He gives power to the weak, and to those who have no might He increases strength. Even the youths shall faint and be weary, and the young men shall utterly fall, but those who wait on the LORD shall renew their strength; they shall mount up with wings like eagles, they shall run and not be weary, they shall walk and not faint,*" the Lamb spoke gently, but firmly, and with almost tangible compassion.

Joel nodded. The vision began to fade. Joel breathed in quickly and spoke for the first time to the Lamb, "Jesus!"

The Son became more visible again. He smiled and replied, "Yes, Joel?"

Tears ran again as Joel looked into the eyes of the One who had sacrificed His life for all of mankind. "Thank you," he said quietly.

The Lamb placed one hand along Joel's head. "Blessed are you, Joel, son of Doug and Kathy, for My Father has given you an increased measure of His Spirit to do His work among men. Go forth in the strength of the Father! Your faith has given you the peace you seek! Remember, '*I am with you always, even to the end of the age.*'"

Joel felt the power of Jesus' touch course through his body. An intense peace rested upon him. He closed his eyes, bowed his head, and gave glory to God.

Becoming aware of his earthly surroundings once more, Joel sighed deeply, hanging on to the presence of the Lamb for as long as possible. Opening his eyes after a time, he gazed at Twinkle-Eyes, and then smiled. The angel hugged him. Joel opened his hand as the two moved apart and saw a brilliant purple stone!

CHAPTER 30

The JP Knights were glad to have Joel back with them in their meetings. They met often now as the school year drew to a close, and those involved in activities had more free time. Sometimes they gathered at Marissa's home, and other times they sat together at one of Zech's meetings. "Salvation Is Mine Because Of Christ," a phrase that Zech had the people repeat frequently, made one of the attendees coin the term, SIMBOC. Soon, signs were seen inviting area residents to SIMBOC meetings!

The victory over the demons at the chapel had proven to scatter many of the local demons, such that there seemed to be less involvement of Satan's hordes for a number of weeks. The result was that many did come to know salvation through Jesus, and the Believers were becoming strong. More angels had quietly amassed and were ministering to the new Christians. Some helped backslidden ones return to a real relationship with the Lord. Christians throughout the city responded with excitement and began volunteering to disciple those making decisions for Christ. They came from various churches and Christian walks. A spirit of unity had infiltrated nearly every Christian church as Zech continued his ministry.

The last day of school seemed to rush upon Joel. So much had happened in the last few weeks that he could hardly believe it when the day arrived. They only had a short assembly, would receive their report cards, and then be dismissed. Other of the JP Knights had already finished school for the summer, and a few had another day or two to go. Joel was looking forward to spending more time with his friends and preparing themselves for more battles with evil demons, which he knew were soon to come.

When the assembly was over, Joel went to his locker to clean out the last items. Filling his backpack, he closed the locker door and was surprised to find Kyle behind it, waiting for him.

"Oh, hi, Kyle. Sorry, I didn't see you. Were you waiting there long?" Joel asked, his tone as if nothing had happened between the two of them.

Kyle shook his head, "Nah . . . I just wanted to tell you sorry about your dad." He shuffled his feet nervously, not able to keep eye contact.

Joel sighed with a nod, "Thanks. Mom and I are doing OK now, especially knowing that we'll be seeing Dad soon when the Lord returns."

"Uh . . . yeah," Kyle mumbled.

"Kyle, I know things have changed between you and me," Joel began, "and we're not the *good* friends we use to be. That doesn't mean we can't still be friends."

Kyle gave a small smile, "Really? We could still hang out sometime?"

Joel grinned, "Sure! In fact, would you want to come to the SIMBOC meeting tonight with me?"

Shrinking back a bit, Kyle looked at the floor and whispered, "I don't know . . ."

"Ah, come on! Mom and I will pick you up at 6:30, OK?" Joel prompted.

The demon inside Kyle screamed as it tried to gain control. This was *not* supposed to happen! The teenager belonged to Satan and used to be easy to sway to do evil, even when everyone thought he was a good church-going Christian. Now, going to this Believer meeting was trouble! The demon had already known of other demons who had been cast out of long-time possessions at these meetings.

Wrapping its icy fingers around Kyle's heart, the demon squeezed. Normally, this would result in an immediate outburst of anger from the youth. Nothing. Not even a hint of irritation was produced. The demon reached for the brain and attempted to cause confusion. Nothing. Now the demon was anxiously trying anything to get back control of Kyle. Its years of being within the boy had allowed for some easy ploys or short cuts to command him, but nothing was working.

"OK," Kyle said cautiously as the demon screamed again.

Joel tilted his head, aware of some unearthly noise. Making note of it, he smiled at Kyle and said, "See ya at 6:30!"

Kyle turned and hurried to his bus. Joel watched him go. A strange mist hung around him that Joel sensed was very evil.

"Lord, please help Kyle!" Joel prayed silently and then ran to catch his bus.

The angel grew brighter the moment the prayer was said. It held out its hand with the palm upward and a tiny beam of light emanated from its index finger. The light went straight to Kyle and entered his heart, where the angel had carefully planted the seed deep within a few weeks back. The demon had been distracted at the time, so the angel was able to cover the seed with a spiritual cloak, allowing the seed to grow without the demon's knowledge or awareness. If the angel continued to send the power of prayers to the seed, it would soon grow enough to drive the unsuspecting demon out!

"Mom! Mom!" Joel called as he entered his house. His mom's school district had finished up the day before, and she had promised to be home from in-service when he arrived.

"I'm on the patio, Joel!" Kathy Stevens yelled.

"Mom! I think our prayers are being answered!" he exclaimed breathlessly as he ran outside.

His mom sat up from the lounge chair she was on and looked excitedly at him. "What do you mean?"

Joel jumped and touched a bird feeder hanging from a tree branch. "It's Kyle! He came to me at the end of school and said he was sorry about Dad, then I asked him to come to SIMBOC tonight with us, and he said yes, and I can tell he's different. I know it's from our prayers!" Joel finished and took a big breath.

Kathy smiled and stood up to hug her son. She knew the breaking apart of Joel and Kyle's friendship had really bothered Joel, even though she was glad that Joel no longer was such a follower of his friend.

"That's great, Joel! I know this means so much to you!" Kathy replied with enthusiasm.

Joel nodded, "Yeah, but it's more than that, Mom." He looked into her eyes and said soberly, "It means that he may truly come to know the Lord and really accept salvation."

Kathy looked at Joel tenderly and shook her head. "Oh, Joel . . . the Lord has blessed you incredibly the past number of months . . . ever since Pastor George spoke that one time. . . . I am so proud of you for obeying the voice of the Lord!"

"Mom, can we pray for Kyle right now? I just know that our prayers make a difference!" Joel said with determination.

"Absolutely!" Kathy answered. She reached for his hands and began, "Dear Lord, we lift up Kyle right now and ask that You will continue to work in his life to bring him to a real relationship with You. May he understand his need for salvation and choose to commit his life to you. Be with Joel as he relies on You to help him as he talks to Kyle. Help us tonight to say what You want us to say to him, not what we think we need to say. Be with his parents. May they somehow be brought to the place where they can confess their need for Your salvation."

The purposeful pause signaled to Joel to continue, "Holy Father and Lamb That Was Slain, I thank You for answering our prayers to help Kyle come to know You. Thank you. Please help him to believe in You *tonight*. Work on his parents so that they will believe in Your salvation, too. You are great! Amen!"

Mother and son hugged and then went inside to grab a bite to eat before getting ready for SIMBOC.

The angel glowed with the power of the prayers. The Spirit had multiplied the energy, because *if two of you agree on earth concerning anything that they ask, it will be done for them by My Father in heaven. For where two are gathered together in My Name, there I am in the midst of them.*

Quickly, the angel headed to Kyle's home. He was in his room, sitting at his desk, holding his hands to his ears, and trying to drown out the arguing of his parents. Everything had seemed to go downhill after the state karate championships where Kyle had been disqualified. The new karate place was very intense, and Kyle had improved, but the attitude of the sensei was terribly mean. Kyle initially was impressed, but somewhere deep inside he had started to feel very empty and very alone.

His parents had seemed to change after the championships, too. Mr. Thompson blamed Joel and his parents for interfering and had begun to speak badly of them, cursing them often. His mom now suffered from his dad's anger and negative attitude. The fights were frequent and had worsened, for some reason after Doug Stevens's death. Kyle sometimes caught his mom crying, but she would just dab her eyes and comment something about her allergies being bad.

The angel arrived in time to watch Kyle's demon extend away from Kyle, adding its daggers to the argument between his parents, since it was having temporary trouble affecting Kyle at all. Smiling, the angel aimed the prayer energy stream at Kyle. *This should do it,* the angel thought.

The demon was distracted enough that it did not notice anything happening behind it. The prayer energy quickly melted into Kyle's heart and seemed to disappear. The angel nodded and moved away to conceal itself while it guarded its charge.

Kyle slowly put his hands down as his eyes came to rest on a framed picture that had been pushed back into the corner behind his light. He reached for the small frame and held it, fingering the edges of the handmade border. Foam pieces had been glued on to a main cutout and the photo inserted. A flimsy metal strip had been bent to become a stand. Pre-cut foam phrases like "Best Friend" and "Kool Kid" had also been glued on in-between various athletic equipment items. The picture showed a younger Kyle and Joel, arms draped over each other's shoulders, grinning from ear to ear. Kyle stared at the print, his features softening as he remembered the day the picture had been taken. They had made the frames at a Christian summer camp. A counselor had snapped their picture together and printed it out for them. Kyle recalled that very evening he and Joel had talked to the counselor and gave their hearts to Jesus.

He had never felt such peace before. It lasted for a few more days until camp was over. When he went home, he told his parents that he had accepted Jesus, and his dad had called him wimpy-boy, saying that you had to do things for yourself, not rely on some god out there somewhere. Kyle's mom had tried to turn the conversation around, but she was put down as well. In the end, Kyle decided to forget his decision, and do what his dad did—go along with things as long as he got something out of it for himself. Going to church looked good and helped the Thompsons make some useful friends, like the Stevens.

Jim Thompson had received some great advice from Doug Stevens about taxes, but he used it to make fraudulent reports, escaping detection. Doug would have been appalled, but Jim was good at hiding his schemes. Kyle had seen others used by his dad and had paid attention to the process. His dad never called him wimpy-boy again.

God did not forget the choice Kyle had made at camp.

Mrs. Stevens pulled into the Thompson's driveway and saw Kyle jump off of the porch almost immediately. Kyle got into the back seat and closed the door before Joel could get out and welcome him.

"Hi, Mrs. Stevens," Kyle said cautiously.

"Hello, Kyle!" she responded pleasantly, noticing Kyle let out a breath of relief. "Everything OK? Your parents alright with you going with us?"

"Oh . . . yeah," Kyle said with a hint of evasion.

Kathy Stevens and Joel eyed each other with a look of concern. Joel then gave a little shake of his head to signal his mom not to ask any more questions.

She swallowed, disguising a nod, and backed out of the driveway.

Changing the subject slightly, she asked, "Are you glad school's out for the summer?"

Kyle murmured, "Hmm . . . yeah, I guess so. It gets sort of boring, though."

Joel piped up, "The meeting tonight should be good. Zech asked Pastor Eric to lead the singing!"

Kyle visibly brightened, "Oh, really? That's great!" He then sighed a bit, "I've sort of missed him and the youth group . . ." Catching himself, he added, "ah, because of karate and stuff."

"Of course!" Kathy said agreeably. "So you haven't been to a SIMBOC yet?"

"No," Kyle answered, "but I've heard loads of people talk about them. My mom wants to go sometime." He stopped abruptly.

Joel and Kathy knew the rest of the sentence was, *but my dad won't let her.* They wisely let it go.

"Here we are!" Kathy announced a few minutes later after continuing some small talk with Kyle.

The three made their way inside the little arena and found seats behind the other JP Knights. Joel did some quick introductions before Pastor Eric came to the microphone. The JP Knights warmly welcomed Kyle and then turned around to face front, all of them whispering a prayer for Joel's friend.

The angel guarding Kyle had stayed close by, making sure no other demons interfered. Twinkle-Eyes approached inconspicuously.

"How is the Spirit's work?" he asked quietly.

Daleth merely nodded.

Twinkle-Eyes moved away and returned to Gimel.

"It is prepared," was all he said.

With a look, both angels sent a message around the seating, and soon prayer warriors were releasing their prayers to God—some very specific, others quite general, but all asking for sinners to find salvation and for those backslidden to return to the Lord.

Pastor Eric joyously led the hundreds attending in songs of praise and worship, finishing with a word of prayer, which he said by means of a tune, much like song leaders had done for years. It was moving and uplifting.

Zech moved to the podium and spoke, "Thank you, God for hearing our prayers. May our worship be incense rising up before You, and may our words be acceptable in Your Sight! Amen!"

"Please remain standing for the reading of God's Word from Isaiah 25:6–9 then chapter 26:16–18 and finally chapter 40:1–5, 10–11:

'And in this mountain the LORD of hosts will make for all people a feast of choice pieces, a feast of wines on the lees. And He will destroy on this mountain the surface of the covering cast over all people, and the veil that is spread over all nations. He will swallow up death forever, and the Lord GOD will wipe away tears from all faces; the rebuke of His people He will take away from all the earth; for the LORD has spoken. And it will be said in that day: "Behold, this is our God; we have waited for Him, and He will save us. This is the LORD; we have waited for Him; we will be glad and rejoice in His salvation.

"LORD, in trouble they have visited You, they poured out a prayer when Your chastening was upon them. As a woman with child is in pain and cries out in her pangs, when she draws near the time of her delivery, so have we been in Your sight, O LORD. We have been with child, we have been in pain; we have, as it were, brought forth wind; we have not accomplished any deliverance in the earth, nor have the inhabitants of the world fallen.

'Comfort, yes, comfort My people!' says your God. 'Speak comfort to Jerusalem, and cry out to her, that her warfare is ended, that her iniquity is pardoned; for she has received from the LORD's hand double for all her sins.' The voice of one crying in the wilderness: 'Prepare the way of the LORD; make straight in the desert a highway for our God. Every valley shall be exalted and every mountain and hill brought low; the crooked places shall be made straight and the rough places smooth; the glory of the LORD shall be revealed, and all flesh shall see it together; for the mouth of the LORD has spoken.

'Behold, the Lord GOD shall come with a strong hand, and His arm shall rule for Him; behold, His reward is with Him, and His work

276

before Him. He will feed His flock like a shepherd; He will gather the lambs with His arm, and carry them in His bosom, and gently lead those who are with young.'"

"You may be seated," Zech instructed. "I know this was a lot to read, but hopefully you will see the grace and salvation our God has provided for us through these Scripture passages."

Zech went on to explain how God had planned for our salvation many centuries before Christ came. He showed how our attempt at deliverance was like giving birth to wind—futile. Then God showed the prophet Isaiah how salvation would come through the shepherd God was sending and that the birthing process would finally yield lambs that stayed with the shepherd who delivered them. The people of the earth had tried to do it their own way, but only God's salvation would work.

Jill watched in wonder. Her spiritual gift had been increasing, and her awareness of the hidden spiritual world had broadened. At first, she hadn't noticed anything during Zech's meetings, but as more of the unsaved had started attending, it had become more and more obvious. Words and phrases that Zech spoke seemed to become glittering symbols in the air. As they hovered, it seemed they would multiply and then rush toward the attendees. Then, a group would enter simultaneously through a person's eyes and ears. Sometimes their presence would pause and then trickle down to the heart or be so weakened that it appeared as a mere dusting like powdered sugar. Other times the symbols would race as a torrent around inside the head and then collect as one before funneling into the heart!

Fascinated by this image, Jill paid attention to the individuals more closely. She discovered that the ones who received the words into their hearts were those who responded to the invitation to accept Christ! The others, the ones where the symbols barely touched the heart, stayed at their seats and left the arena quickly.

Jill had remembered that Chris had told them how God's Word never returned void, but it would accomplish what He pleased (Isaiah 55:11). The apostle James had written of the *implanted* word, which was able to save souls. Finally, the Word of God in Hebrews was described as *living*, and *powerful, a discerner of the thoughts and intents of the heart.*

She believed she was seeing some of this happen. As she watched sinners accept salvation through Christ, the spiritual heart glowed celestially. The effect was immediate as the warmth of God's love spread through the person. Sometimes a covering, like one described by Isaiah in Zech's Scripture reading, would fall off, revealing a heart shrunken and lifeless. The words would come to it and, as a dried sponge receiving water, would fill it with life, wonderful and new!

There were others who were possessed by demons, who seemed to almost shake off the tendrils of the evil things, leaving the demons shrieking and rushing out of the arena as if chased by wolves. The heart, now without the demon mist, looked different, but Jill was still trying to decide what she saw.

Tonight was no different. The words that Zech spoke were almost like race horses, scrambling out into the crowd, nosing their way into receptive spirits. Jill praised God for His Word, as she witnessed its effect.

Jill had been late, so she had sat farther in the back, away from the other JP Knights. From this vantage, she was also able to see that the angels were busy. Many of them glowed brightly, receiving God's power. Often, however, she began to see something unusual happen. The glowing angel would turn its palm over, and a tiny thread of light, barely perceptible, would shoot out. Jill had to squint to try to see where it went, and when she did, the proverbial light bulb came on.

Excitedly, she looked around and quickly found someone who was receiving the Word eagerly. Sure enough, soon an energy strand was directed at the woman's heart, and the Word seemed to erupt into a blossom, much like a poppy flower pops open! The angels were busy, focusing on the harvest. All over the arena, people were accepting the message of salvation through Jesus.

"It's incredible to witness, isn't it?" a gentle voice whispered.

Jill turned to see her angel sitting next to her.

"Yes!" Jill answered quietly. "I see how the power of our prayers gives strength to the angels, then they disperse its power to help those who receive the Word, accept it, and believe in Jesus!"

Her angel nodded with joy.

Something caught Jill's eye. "There, that boy—what's happening there?"

The angel followed her gaze. "Ah . . . you have noticed! He has had a demon for many years."

Jill furrowed her eyebrows and commented, "But, he's so young! He's my age!"

"Yes. He chose to serve evil, like his father," the angel responded.

Peering closely, Jill continued, "His heart looks . . . looks, well, different."

"Yes. He has received the seed of prayers said specifically for him. His angel was able to plant it and then carefully guarded him while the growing seed of faith got stronger. The demon no longer has control of him and will soon realize it has lost its prey," the angel explained.

Jill watched intently, and within moments, the demon left the boy, screeching as it exited the arena. In its wake, the demonic mist evaporated, and Jill could clearly see a heart drinking in every word that Zech spoke. It seemed like the words themselves sensed the boy's thirst for the Lord and rushed to fill his heart and soul with truth.

The nearness of the demon had been evident to Joel as it struggled in a last attempt to regain control of Kyle. Joel prayed for God to deliver his friend from the evil within. He furtively reached for his mom's hand and grasped it, willing her to understand his intent. She did and silently prayed for Kyle. The power of their prayers was instantly gathered by the angel and directed to Kyle's heart. Joel prayed that his friend would accept the forgiveness offered by the Lamb's sacrifice.

Zech finished speaking with his cry, "Salvation is mine!"

Erupting in response, the attendees shouted, "Because of Christ!"

"Salvation is mine!" Zech exclaimed.

"Because of Christ!" the arena echoed.

Then, Zech quieted the crowd and entreated any who wanted to know Christ to come forward. Pastor Eric strummed his guitar in the background as Zech fell to his knees in prayer for the lost and backslidden.

Joel's heart pounded as he prayed for Kyle. A tap on his arm from his friend made him look over at Kyle.

"I need to go," Kyle whispered.

Joel's heart sank, but he knew that the Lord would save his friend at some point. He nodded to Kyle and then leaned toward his mom to let her know.

Kyle tugged on his arm just before Joel got to say anything to his mom.

"I mean go up there," Kyle said quietly. "I need Christ!"

Chills went through Joel's body as he followed Kyle out of the row and headed to the front. They both knelt before the platform with perhaps a hundred others.

"Joel, what should I do?" Kyle asked.

Joel walked his friend through a few questions and then led him in a simple prayer of confession, accepting Christ's offer of salvation.

Jill witnessed the new birth with excitement. Kyle's heart was changed, and the glow of his salvation spread throughout his body. The prism of colors was close to what she had seen in the heavenly visions, but contained some different hues. She rejoiced that Joel's friend had finally found the truth.

The singing began quietly, but then crescendoed to a magnificent chorus of angels rejoicing over the salvation of so many souls. The JP Knights listened with awe at first and then added their own voices in praise.

The arena was full of joyful people—the many who now had a rebirth and a new relationship with the Lord and those who already knew the Lamb and were helping with the harvest. However, there were still a few who had hardened their hearts and refused the tugs of the Spirit. Jill watched them leave the arena hurriedly, almost hunched over in an attempt to prevent truth from getting into their hearts. Some were followed by angels who watched for any way a seed could be planted. Jill happened to see an angel accomplish this when the man was distracted briefly by the voice of Zech beginning to wrap things up. The angel quickly saw an opening in the covering sin had formed over the man's heart. Deftly, it directed a thread of prayer energy through the aperture, which formed a protective ring. With a slightly different flick from its hand, the angel inserted a tiny bead of light through the portal. Within a second, the sin covering sealed itself. The angel stepped away and with a small nod to a fellow-angel, straightened and followed the man outside.

"Not many are fortunate enough to see the seed implanted," Jill's angel whispered.

"That was incredible!" Jill exclaimed in a low voice. "What happens now?"

"The angel will stay close to that man," the angel explained, "looking for opportunities to feed that seed with the power of prayers, or redirecting the man toward those who have been prepared by the Lamb to assist in the watering of the man's spirit, until the seed grows enough to break through the covering of sin. Once that happens, his angel will be ready to minister to him in whatever way God needs to bring him to salvation.

"How can anyone resist or refuse, then?" Jill asked.

"Oh, all too easily," the angel sighed. "Sin is a very hard surface to begin with. Remember it was sin that separated the human race from God in the first place! There is a lot of preparation done to try to soften the hardness of someone's heart from sin, but people still have a choice, and they all too often choose to resist any attempt by God to save them. They allow layer after layer of sin to build, and only the power of God released from dedicated prayers of His followers will change that. God continues to let earth's people choose whether they want Him to be in charge or not. They will have that choice until Satan is defeated."

Jill acknowledged the angel's words solemnly, understanding that the work of the JP Knights was more important than ever.

Zech walked down the steps of the platform to try to meet as many of the new Believers as possible. There were numerous counselors engaged in discussions or prayer with those who had come forward. A man near the edge of these walked toward Zech with purpose.

"Pastor Douds?" the man spoke with an air of authority.

"Yes?" Zech replied as he met the man.

Angels surrounded the two men as they quickly moved off to the side and continued an intense conversation.

Joel welcomed the counselor and introduced Kyle and then kept quiet as the counselor talked with his friend. He felt as if his heart would burst, he was so excited for Kyle's salvation! The singing of the angels had lifted his spirit even more.

Kyle and Joel chatted continuously on the way to take Kyle home. The years of friendship had built a good foundation so that the months they were estranged seemed to melt away and be forgotten.

As they pulled into Kyle's driveway, however, the reality of facing his parents set in. Kathy and Joel prayed for him, knowing this could be the first trial of his new life in Christ.

Kyle looked sincerely at Joel, "Please keep praying for me!"

Kathy offered, "We certainly will, Kyle. Call us if you need anything, OK? I'd be happy to have lunch with your mom sometime soon—I've missed her!"

"Thanks, Mrs. Stevens. I'll let her know," Kyle responded.

"God will help you, Kyle. Remember that! Trust Him. Pray—He *does* hear you," Joel said earnestly.

Kyle nodded and got out of the car. He waved and then went inside his house. Joel watched the angel follow and felt a sense of peace.

Back at home, Joel was pleased to find Twinkle-Eyes waiting for him out at the swings.

"You are glad about Kyle, Joel?" the angel asked.

"Oh, yes!" Joel replied. "But . . ."

"Yes?" Twinkle-Eyes prompted.

Joel breathed a deep breath and said, "Will he be part of the JP Knights?"

"Hmm . . ." Twinkle-Eyes mused. "I do not know at this time."

Joel nodded. "I suppose I should not say anything about seeing angels then?"

"There are many gifts of the Spirit, Joel. What God has in mind for Kyle may be for something very special, yet not the same as you," Twinkle-Eyes offered.

Joel pondered this while swinging and then smiled and exclaimed, "He could end up like Zech—you know . . . preaching or something like that! He's really a natural leader!" Pausing, he added, "I just don't want to feel like I'm excluding him when I'm with the JP Knights."

"God would want you to pray about this, Joel; your motives are honest," Twinkle-Eyes encouraged.

"I will pray . . . pray that God would give Kyle a work to do of his own for the Lord right now!" Joel exclaimed with determination. "He's still part of the body of Christ, so there is an important function for him."

The angel and young man talked while the stars came out. At the end, the angel alerted Joel that the brief time of peace was nearly over, and the JP Knights had work to do. In fact, there was very little time and much work.

CHAPTER 31

Kyle woke early. He got his Bible and studied some passages before kneeling beside his bed to pray. He had anticipated a very difficult time with his parents, but, in fact, he had experienced little, if any, opposition to his decision to live for Christ. His dad was just happy that they weren't arguing. He seemed rather glum and distracted most of the time and didn't even put up a fuss when Kyle told him that he didn't want to go to the other karate dojo anymore.

Ellen Thompson responded in a positive way, encouraging Kyle to attend the SIMBOC meetings and quietly affirming Kyle's decision to rest from karate over the summer. Kathy Stevens' call to go to lunch was met with enthusiasm, and Kyle noticed his mom reading her Bible while she waited for laundry to dry on the outside clothesline.

Pastor Eric had e-mailed Kyle after seeing him go forward at the arena. The two had met at the youth leader's home a few times, with the sessions really helping Kyle to grow rapidly in his faith. Pastor Eric was quick to see the leadership qualities that flourished in Kyle as he submitted to the Spirit. The youth group had grown in numbers of teens attending since the SIMBOC meetings had started and assistance was needed. Kyle had a lot of knowledge of biblical things from his years of going to youth group, but he had never really applied them to his own life. Now, the seed sown was growing quickly, much like it had in Saul-turned-Paul when confronted with Christ.

Kyle prayed in earnest about the request from Pastor Eric. He had asked Kyle to serve as president of the youth group. It seemed like a hasty move for one so new to a true relationship with Christ, but Pastor Eric had assured Kyle that God uses the willing, not necessarily the highly trained or prepared. He reminded Kyle of the disciples—ordinary people called to do a higher work, rather than the educated scribes and Pharisees who thought they knew it all already. As Kyle finished praying, he had an answer for Pastor Eric.

The youth room was crowded that night. Pastor Eric's traditional strumming on his guitar no longer was loud enough to get everyone's attention to start the meeting. He grinned tonight, however, as he plugged in an amplifier and hit a chord.

"NYRR," the guitar strings played thunderously, and the teens jumped.

"Alright, everyone!" Pastor Eric called. "Time to get started! Isn't this a great way for you all to hear the music now?"

A few kids yelled out, "Yeah!" as they all found places to stand. There was no sense in sitting because the initial praise portion of the meeting was so exciting that they all stood and clapped along.

Pastor Eric led them in a praise song before opening the meeting in prayer. They sang boisterously but sincerely over the next minutes until ending in a thoughtful hymn. The group was somewhat surprised when Pastor Eric announced that they would be nominating leaders of the youth group that night to help in organizing and shepherding the many who came for fellowship. He asked for nominations for senior leader, assistant leader, secretary, treasurer, and member at large. After each nomination for a position, Pastor Eric asked the individual if they would consent to being in the leadership group. A few declined, including Joel (his involvement in the JP Knights precluded more participation in the youth group), but in the end, there were some fine choices. Kyle had been nominated for senior leader! Each nominee was asked to prepare a statement for the next meeting to read to the group. All were encouraged to pray about the election, that God would bring the right people into leadership positions.

The next week seemed to pass quickly, and soon the youth were gathering again to hear the nominees and then to vote.

Kyle felt at peace. His suggestion to Pastor Eric to have an election had been received enthusiastically, and the condition to keep Kyle's name out of any credit for the idea had been followed. The statements made by each nominee were sincere, as those willing to serve had realized the great impact they could have. Some individuals included jokes or fun memories from youth group, and one person reminded them that God had a sense of humor, with the result that everyone took the event seriously but realistically.

An area had been set up with three private voting desks. Ballots were filled out and then counted by Zech, who had been asked to come and pray for those taking the leadership positions.

Joel waited with excitement as he sat next to Kyle. The change in his friend had been noticed by everyone, but no one more than Joel!

Pastor Eric silenced the group with a wave of his hand after Zech finished counting the results of the election. Starting with the senior leader position, Pastor Eric called out, "Devon Carson—you are our new senior leader!"

The popular, handsome young man stood and gave a thumbs-up sign as the room erupted into applause.

The other positions were then named, and Pastor Eric asked all of them to come forward to be anointed by Zech.

Joel was disappointed. He felt sure that Kyle would be elected to the senior leader position. His friend looked unaffected by his loss in the election as they both reached out with their hands, joining in the prayer of anointing.

Afterwards, the group had snacks and played games, enjoying the fellowship of Believers.

Joel grabbed Kyle before heading to the refreshments.

"Hey, I'm sorry you didn't get the senior leader," he lamented.

Kyle shook his head and shrugged his shoulders, "It's OK. It's not what God wants me to do right now. I think Devon will do a great job, don't you? He's really humble but knows how to get things done."

Joel nodded in agreement, "Yeah, he's been a fantastic quarterback for the football team. I can't believe he said he's giving that up to focus on what the Lord wants him to do! I guess . . ." Joel paused. "I guess I really thought you were made for that job."

"Well," Kyle said thoughtfully, "I think I could have done a good job, but there are people who still don't believe I could have changed after what happened at the karate competition when I blamed you. You've become a good friend of a lot of the kids here, and they show their loyalty to you by not voting for me."

Joel's eyes grew wide in surprise, "But I never held that against you, Kyle! I just prayed for you, and so did the youth group!"

Kyle smiled, "Exactly. That's why I'm here now, Joel. Don't worry—I know God has a plan for me, like Jeremiah said: *'For I know the thoughts that I think toward you...thoughts of peace and not of evil, to give you a future and a hope.'*"

He continued, "He's given you something to do with that group of friends you developed while I was going the wrong way. I know that's important, Joel—God's told me that. I also know that I'm not part of that. But I *do* know that God is ready for me to do something for Him. I just have to be patient, pray, and study so that I'm prepared when He calls me!"

Joel shook his head, "Man, Kyle, I wish we both had loved the Lord this much before—it would have been great!"

Wisely, Kyle responded, "All in God's timing, Joel!"

They smiled at each other and headed for the games.

"Kyle," Zech called as he approached the two. "Could I talk to you for a moment?"

"Sure," Kyle answered. "Go ahead, Joel. I'll see you over at the ping-pong table."

Joel watched his friend move to a quiet area with Zech. Instead of joining the others, he silently prayed for Kyle to find his place in the harvesting of souls.

Twinkle-Eyes and Gimel came aside him and directed the power of his prayer to Kyle's angel, who hadn't left his side in weeks. The growth of the seed into a tree with deep spiritual roots was still at a fragile period and must be guarded. Kyle's own work at securing his foundation in the Lord had already taken root, so the angel was pleased to see strong tendrils reaching deep within Kyle's soul as Joel prayed.

Hearing his name called, Joel ended his prayer and joined some teens playing his favorite: ping-pong.

It was a while before Kyle and Zech finished talking. Then they both spent some time speaking with Pastor Eric. Joel watched curiously, wondering what was going on. He lost his concentration in the game at hand, missing an easy play and ending the game. As he turned over his paddle to the next player, Kyle tapped on his shoulder.

His friend was noticeably excited as he pulled Joel to a place where they were alone. "Guess what, Joel!" he blurted, but continued without waiting for an answer. "God did it—He has a plan for me. I told you He'd do it!"

Joel grinned with anticipation, "What'd He do, Kyle? What does He want you to do?"

"It's with Zech," Kyle began. "He's been asked to hold some SIMBOCs in other, bigger cities, and he needs someone to help him! He prayed about it and God showed him my face—I can help him over the summer, and then he will know what kind of person he will need in the fall if the meetings continue. Isn't it cool?"

"Wow!" Joel exclaimed. "Absolutely! I guess that's why you didn't get senior leader for the youth group. God wanted you to be somewhere else!"

Kyle nodded and then asked, "Would you pray with me that I will be open to whatever this work needs me to do and be?"

Joel shook his head and immediately prayed, grabbing his friend's hands. "Thank you, Lord, for leading Zech to Kyle. Thank you for having a plan for him in these end days. Give him courage and wisdom to do what You need him to do, and bless him and Zech in their ministries. Amen!"

Twinkle-Eyes and Gimel gazed at the friends happily talking about Kyle's opportunity and then looked around them at the young people enjoying the fellowship of Believers.

"All is in place now," Gimel commented.

"Yes, It is time for the Blessing," Twinkle-Eyes replied.

As if on cue, all the angels that were dispersed around the room positioned themselves in a circle, raised their arms, and began to glow.

The young people didn't notice at first. Joel and Marissa saw the angels and both stopped what they were doing. Pastor Eric and Zech heard a hum. Kyle, Devon and the other newly elected youth group leaders thought they saw a brightness develop in the room. Everyone then moved toward the center of the room, trying to figure out what was going on.

The Spirit of the Lord filled the room. Some teens began praising the Lord with singing, others fell on their faces in humbled obedience, and the rest stood silently in prayer. All received a confirmation of the work God needed for them to do. A few had specific jobs, but many were merely encouraged to purify themselves and remain true to the Lord, dedicating their lives to living for Him and being witnesses of His salvation through Jesus.

Joel and Marissa watched excitedly as arcs of light touched each one in the room. The memory of a similar event reminded Joel that the individuals were all being given a choice. Marissa trembled slightly as she faced Love in her spirit and willingly accepted what her choice would bring. All the others in the room responded in a comparable way, choosing to give their lives to the One who loved them so much that He sacrificed Himself.

The Blessing was completed.

The angels lowered their arms and stepped back. Quietness hung over the place as each person hung on to the last tingles of the experience. No one spoke or moved for a couple of minutes.

Finally, a voice was heard and all turned to pay attention.

"We have received a Blessing from the Lord to complete His work in these end times. As Mary treasured her experiences when the shepherds came to worship Jesus, we are to keep what has happened here privately in our hearts. We each need to do what we were told to do without hesitation so that the harvesting of souls may continue even as Satan begins his final battle," the speaker finished.

Joel looked with amazement at the speaker. It was Kyle! His gift was evident to all as he calmly instructed them with regards to what had just happened. All the adults and leaders nodded in agreement. As soon as he was done, it seemed that everyone split into several groups: the newly elected leaders with Pastor Eric, Kyle and some others with Zech, kids known for musical abilities together by the keyboard, and various teens dispersed throughout the room in small groups.

Marissa and Joel were left alone, taking in the remarkable scene.

"The army of the Lord is now ready here," a voice said behind them.

Turning, they saw Twinkle-Eyes and another angel that Joel recognized as one who worked with Marissa.

Twinkle-Eyes continued, "This same Blessing will be given to many Believers throughout the world soon."

"Does that mean that Christ returns now?" Marissa asked.

"We do not know the day or hour of the Lamb's return," Twinkle-Eyes explained, "but we expect that the final war with Satan will begin very soon. There still are many souls to harvest before the second coming of the Lamb."

The four talked quietly. Outside the church, angel watchmen continued their protective shield, receiving additional power from the Believers inside to shore up the defenses.

One angel whispered, "It's so peaceful now; surely the demons and their master have been fooled."

A wiser angel noted, "This is the calm before the storm."

CHAPTER 32
THE WAR BEGINS

The reports poured in to the demon lord. It shook with realization that the Believers had gathered under their very noses and now were united in task. The master would be angry. Very angry.

Screams and shouts echoed from the ghoulish throne room after the demon lord entered and gave the report. Its existence came to an end.

Orders were given to a new demon lord. The attacks were to start immediately.

Across the fallen land, demon messengers raced to various destinations. Angels were ready to delay them. The heavenly forces had quietly gathered and waited for this very event. The skirmishes would further anger the ruler of darkness, but he had not been idle either, and the demon army was still formidable. The little battles would upset some plans, but the primary targets would not be protected for long. He had spent eons working up to this moment, planting deceit and wickedness. A few minor attempts by some angels to thwart attacks would be met and conquered. Now, nothing would stand in his way!

The JP Knights met in Marissa's basement with their angels. A messenger had come to Twinkle-Eyes just before the meeting started. Joel watched their short conversation, seeing the concern on the angels' faces. The messenger left quickly and Twinkle-Eyes conferred with Gimel.

Motioning to Joel, Twinkle-Eyes included him in the discussion.

"We have just received word that the prince of darkness has begun his siege," Twinkle-Eyes whispered to Joel. "We have our orders concerning some important events soon that the JP Knights must be prepared for."

Joel nodded. He knew this day was coming. His heart beat excitedly, and he gulped with anticipation.

"Everyone! It's time to start!" Joel called out in low tones.

The room quieted immediately, and the teens gathered around, some sitting, others standing.

Joel looked at Twinkle-Eyes for a moment and then began. "We have learned that Satan has launched his forces of evil into the world. The captain of the army of the Lord needs us to be ready for an onslaught here and in the surrounding areas. Each of us needs to wear the armor of God and be prepared at all times. Use the gifts you have been given to further the kingdom. We need to commit ourselves to Him who is able to keep us from falling! Let us pray!"

Everyone bowed their heads as Joel led them in a prayer. They stayed silent as the Spirit spoke to each one and directed their paths.

Ellen Thompson grasped Kathy Stevens' hands as they sat outside on the patio. Tears streamed down her cheeks as she poured out her heart to the One who died for her on a cross. Kathy cried tears of joy for her friend, knowing that Ellen now had the relationship with Jesus that she had lacked for the many years the two had known each other.

Smiling, Ellen gave Kathy's hands a squeeze and then let go, brushing a strand of hair out of her eyes.

Exhaling deeply, she said, "Thank you, my dear friend, for not giving up on me!"

Kathy responded, "Oh, Ellen, how could I when I wanted you to know Christ like I know Him! Now, we can be even better friends by sharing His love and being able to fellowship together."

Looking away briefly, Ellen then turned back and said, "How I wish Doug was still here to help Jim come to the Lord!" Noticing Kathy tear up, Ellen quickly added, "I'm sorry, Kathy. I'm sure you wish that Doug was here, too!"

Nodding, Kathy replied, "Yes, I really do!" Pausing, she then said, "But . . . I am comforted knowing that God is in charge, and somehow Doug's death will bring more glory to God than his life on this earth would have. I admit that I don't understand."

Both were silent for a time.

"Kathy?" Ellen asked cautiously.

"Hmm?" Kathy prompted.

Licking her lips nervously, Ellen carefully worded a statement, "You know, Kathy . . . um . . . well . . . um . . . Jim has been different since Doug's death."

Kathy shook her head knowingly, "I'm sure he felt bad that they were a little at odds when Doug died, and they didn't have a chance to make up with each other."

"I don't know," Ellen responded, shaking her head. "That's what I thought at first, but I just don't know!"

Feeling the tug of the Spirit at her heart, Kathy asked, "What do you mean?"

Ellen looked into her friend's eyes with concern, "Well . . . after the karate thing, Jim would spout off about you guys in a bit of a rage . . . pretty often, unfortunately. And it didn't lessen over time. He even would say things about getting even." Ellen paused and shook her head, "I'm so sorry, Kathy! We were all far away from the Lord, you know, and we gave into hate and blame. It was much easier to blame you and Joel than to face up to the fact that we almost programmed Kyle to do whatever he needed to do to win, even if it meant doing something illegal."

Kathy looked sympathetically at Ellen, "It's OK, Ellen. We never held any of that against you, or Jim, or Kyle. We just prayed all the more for your family."

"I know," Ellen smiled. "I'm sure that's why I finally gave my life to the Lord—all your prayers helped me!" She paused and then continued, "But something changed the night Doug died."

"What do you mean?" Kathy asked.

Ellen's face muscles tightened as she drew her lips together and sighed, "That's just it . . . I can't really put a finger on it, except even before we knew Doug had passed away, Jim seemed nervous and upset. He had come back from a drive, parked his car in the garage and came into the house like a madman—looking out the window, yelling at me if I dared speak to him, telling me to be quiet. . . . It was very strange. When the phone rang with a neighbor calling to tell us about Doug, Jim nearly jumped to the ceiling! He didn't even want me to answer the phone."

Kathy looked puzzled, "Maybe he drove by the accident and knew it was Doug's car."

"I wondered that and asked Jim, but he got all mad, saying he hadn't been anywhere near Scarlet Mountain Road," Ellen replied.

"Oh . . . well, I guess you'll just have to wait until Jim feels like talking about it," Kathy offered.

"Kathy," Ellen shook her head, "you don't get it. The only thing the neighbor knew was that Doug had died. We didn't find out where the accident was until the newspaper item the next day."

Kathy's heart beat wildly. The police had said there were no known witnesses to the accident. Someone driving along the road had seen the car on its roof in a small gully and had called 911. They thought Doug had died instantly after losing control on the lonely country road, hitting a tree and rolling down an embankment. He had been returning from seeing a client and was going to meet Kathy and Joel at church.

The police had told Kathy that they were still investigating the accident because they thought there may have been another car involved. Just the night before meeting with Ellen, the officer in charge of the investigation had phoned Kathy and let her know that the investigation had indeed identified another car as probably forcing Doug off the road, resulting in the accident that claimed his life. They hypothesized road rage and told her that the driver would be charged with vehicular homicide if they were able to track down the car.

Kathy sat back in her chair, feeling lightheaded.

"So, you see," Ellen continued, "I know that Jim isn't telling me the truth about that night. He missed a few days from work, and he wouldn't let any of us come to the funeral. And now, he insists that something is wrong with his car, so he takes my car to work all the time. I've been driving the car we had gotten for Kyle, because Kyle has been getting rides with Zech Douds to the meetings, and he's been spending a lot of time with Zech anyhow. Kathy, are you alright? You look pale! I'm sorry . . . I shouldn't have brought up all this stuff about Doug and the accident. It hasn't been all that long. Here, have a drink."

Ellen busied herself with attending to her friend.

Kathy could say nothing. Her throat was dry and her stomach cramped into a ball. She took the iced tea from Ellen and tried to gather her thoughts.

"Uh, Ellen, what kind of car does Jim drive?" Kathy managed to say.

"Oh . . . you know . . . I'm so bad at cars . . . um . . . it's some foreign-made, fuel-economy car, not all that expensive He got a good deal on a used one in the fall. Why do you ask?" Ellen queried as she walked back to her chair and sat down. One look at Kathy put the pieces together for her and she brought her hands to her cheeks with a gasp.

Kyle was surprised to see that his dad was home from work early. He had made up his mind to talk to his dad as soon as possible and share with him about a relationship with the Lord. He knew his mom was on the verge of coming to the Lord and he excitedly had prayed for her meeting with Kathy Stevens that day, hoping that this would be the day of her salvation.

His dad was different. Kyle felt a special burden for him and didn't know of anyone who would influence him toward the Lord. His dad's buddies at work were barely more than drunks, and Kyle had always been surprised that his dad preferred not to go drinking with them, but instead had spent time with Kyle, teaching him to fish and taking him to karate. They had a good relationship . . . that is, until the karate tournament when Kyle was kicked out.

Kyle had been angry about what had happened, and he knew that it really hadn't been Joel's fault. His dad had taken it all very personally and had sworn revenge on the Stevens. After a while, Kyle had finally confided to his dad that Joel really hadn't done anything and that the karate move had been illegal. He even told his dad that Joel had kept him from hitting the sensei with the chair.

Jim Thompson had refused to believe Kyle, however. Both Kyle and his mom had tried to reason with him, to no avail. In the meantime, Kyle had thrown off his demon and began praying for his dad. The urge to talk to him had become a fervor in his spirit, and he knew he had to do it *now*.

"Dad," Kyle called as he entered the house. "Dad, I'm home!"

Hearing no answer, he went through the home looking for his father. Puzzled, he became aware of a car motor running, and he opened the door into the garage.

He saw his dad slumped over the steering wheel of his car.

"Dad!" he shouted, hitting the button to open the garage door as he smelled fumes. Coughing, he hurried to the driver's side car door and flung it open, pulling his dad back in the seat and shutting off the motor.

"Dad!" he yelled. With incredible strength, he grabbed his dad and pulled him outside onto the driveway. "Help! Someone—I need help!" he screamed.

Trying to remember CPR, he went through the steps of the ABCs as a neighbor ran up.

"Call 911!" Kyle instructed and then checked for a pulse. Amazingly, he felt a pulse in his dad's neck, but saw no attempt to breathe. Positioning himself, he started mouth-to-mouth, as others from the neighborhood appeared. Seconds seemed like hours, but his dad moved and then coughed, turning on his side to vomit. Sirens raced toward the scene. Kyle began to cry and hug his dad. Before long they were both in the ambulance, heading to the emergency room.

Kyle sat alone in the waiting room, praying. His mom was on her way, but for right now Kyle was left to question why his dad had attempted suicide.

The nurse called for him, assuring him that his dad was alive and alright because of his quick response, and then she led him to the room where his dad was.

"Dad?" Kyle said after closing the door.

Jim Thompson looked away, too ashamed to face his son.

"Dad—what's going on? Why did you want to die?" Kyle asked, crying.

Shaking his head, Jim answered, "I've done something really wrong, Kyle, and I saw no way out. I couldn't live with myself anymore!"

"Dad, there is *nothing* that bad that Jesus can't help you through!" Kyle spoke with conviction. "Talk to me! The thing with Joel and his family is not an issue. They've forgiven me, and I know they'll forgive you."

At this, his dad sobbed uncontrollably.

"Dad, please, tell me!" Kyle urged.

"Oh, Kyle . . ." Jim Thompson began. Gazing through tears, he cried, "I'm the one who killed Doug!" He then wept hysterically.

Kyle stood frozen in place.

Jim Thompson cried more, "I know they're gonna find me. The police called my work today, trying to find me. I can't go on. You shouldn't have saved me. I . . . I . . ."

His weeping overtook him. Hiding his face in his hands, he shook with remorse and regret, crying, "Oh, God, help me!"

The angels in the room had been waiting for such a cry. With a leap, one angel grabbed the demon who was pushed out of Mr. Thompson's spirit ever so slightly with the plea for help. Other angels focused power from on high at the struggle, giving the angel the strength to pull the demon from the tortured soul. From inside, a seed of hope grew. It had been planted at a fragile moment when the demon had been distracted and then nurtured by Kyle's changed behavior when he committed to the Lamb.

Kyle looked at his father. The shock of the confession had rendered him speechless, but his spirit had asked for help. His angel ministered to him, guarding him from human frailty and enabling him to be the catalyst his father needed.

Jim Thompson felt it. Looking up, he gazed into his son's eyes and saw forgiveness and love. Kyle hugged him and held him tight.

"There is forgiveness, Dad. Let go of the hate. Let Christ bring healing," Kyle spoke softly. "I love you, Dad! No matter what you've done . . . I will always love you!"

The battle between the angel and demon abruptly ceased when the demon's hold gave way. The demon screamed with rage as it wildly left the man. The man had chosen forgiveness through Christ. The demon could no longer abide in the man; it could no longer hide. Hissing, it struck out at the boy, but there was no entry point with the boy covered by the blood of the Lamb. The demon pulled a sword and swung at an angel in one swift move, but the angel had been ready and pierced the demon with its sword. The wound removed all power from the demon, and it slithered away.

The angels quickly surrounded the father and son. The seed of hope needed one final choice from the man. It was the same choice given to the first man and woman and the same choice every man and woman has had to make since that time.

Jim looked at his son, "Do you really think God still loves me after I did such a horrible thing?"

Kyle peered into his dad's eyes and said, "Dad, God loves you so much that he gave of Himself, through Jesus, to pay for all we've done bad, way before we were even born. Dad, you have loved me so much that you sacrificed everything when you thought I was wronged. God loves us so much more than that!"

Pondering this for a moment, the man made his choice.

The angels saw the seed erupt into a beautiful bloom that emanated light to every part of the man's spirit. The prayers for the Thompson family watered the precious blossom even as a policeman entered the room.

Kathy Stevens sat in the waiting room. This day had become another blur in time as she and Ellen realized that Jim Thompson was probably responsible for Doug's death. They had rushed to the hospital when Kyle had called, but the place was already crawling with police when they got there. Pastor Eric was bringing Joel, and

Kathy struggled with how to tell her son that his best friend's father had run Doug off the road in a fit of rage, causing Doug's death.

"Father," she prayed, "help us right now. Show us how to react to this news. I know You teach forgiveness, but I feel angry and upset right now. What do You want me to do?"

Joel walked in and hurried to his mom. Pastor Eric followed, but stayed a few steps away.

Kathy gulped and then hugged Joel tightly.

"Mom," Joel then spoke, "Mom, what happened? Is Kyle's dad OK?"

Kathy bit her lower lip, and with her voice trembling, replied, "Joel, Kyle's father was the one who caused the accident that killed your father."

Joel stared with unbelieving eyes at his mom. Slowly, he sat down and cried.

Gimel gazed at the sight. "Can he bear it? This will be too much for him!"

Twinkle-Eyes sighed, "It is the supreme testing of his faith. The Lamb believes in him, but he still has the choice."

Gimel looked around. "Are there no prayers for him right now? Can we not strengthen him?"

Twinkle-Eyes, for once, had no answer.

The JP Knights had been together when Joel got the phone call from his mom to get to the hospital. Pastor Eric had come by Marissa's house to give something to Zech, so it had seemed reasonable that he take Joel, rather than one of the JP Knights giving him a ride.

The moment Joel left, Liz got a strange look on her face and then spoke, "A great trial has come to Joel. The help of his friends is the difference between victory and losing it all!"

Chris and Garrett moved to her side as the strange look faded.

"What do you mean?" Chris asked.

Liz looked slightly confused, "What did I say?"

Garrett repeated it back to her.

"Uh . . . I'm not sure, but it seems like I maybe prophesied about Joel," she offered.

"Does that mean it's going on right now . . . that this trial is happening to him now?" Chris queried.

Emily stared at Liz and seemed to freeze.

"Emily, what's wrong?" Liz cried.

Now the group knew that unusual things were going on.

"Everyone! Pray. Pray. Let the Spirit use you . . . use your gifts to see what we are to do!" Garrett called out.

Some grabbed others hands, while a few knelt down to pray.

Soon, Emily spoke, "Hey, I just saw Joel and his mom crying at the hospital, and the angels were standing there unable to help. We need to pray for him!"

A cacophony of voices filled the basement as the young people prayed for Joel.

But, before long Jill called out, "Our prayers aren't going anywhere! Something's wrong!"

Chris shouted out, "*Where two or three are gathered together in My name, I am there in the midst of them. Matthew 18:20.*"

"Jesus, be in our midst so that we can pray according to Your will!" Jill cried.

Now all of the JP Knights held hands. Beginning with Chris, they prayed in turn for Joel and the situation confronting him. When it was Marissa's turn they all waited for a prayer, but no sound came from her lips.

Everyone looked to see what was wrong. Marissa let go of the hands holding hers. She stared straight ahead for a moment, and then closed her eyes and clutched her hands to her chest. She had not really understood her gift before, but one thing was clear to her now.

"Joel needs to forgive!" she whispered. Her eyes shot open, and she nearly shouted, "He needs to be able to forgive someone!" She then covered her mouth with her hands before gasping, "He needs to forgive the person who caused his father's death!"

Around the room, the others looked shocked.

"Oh, my!" Garrett breathed. "I saw it in a dream, but I didn't know 'cause they said he lost control of the car. I saw Kyle's dad forcing a car off the road!" Tears streamed down his face as he and the others realized what Joel was facing.

"Pray!" yelled Chris.

This time, the mix of voices blended as the Knights united in prayer for Joel. Jill sighed with relief as the prayers sped off to a waiting messenger.

Gimel was worried. Twinkle-Eyes even seemed concerned. Joel's spirit looked crushed within him. The healthy blossom of faith had quickly withered with the troubling news.

Pastor Eric slowly moved toward the mother and son. Placing his hands on their shoulders, he prayed silently, but earnestly for the pain they were feeling, asking God to bring healing to them.

The prayer power was surprisingly strong, and the angels quickly focused the energy toward Joel's withered faith. The next beam went to Kathy's spirit. The angels saw a surge of color within Kathy's faith flower and were encouraged, but then a look at Joel's blossom showed that his spirit was losing the battle.

Twinkle-Eyes held out his hands in desperation, willing any power left in him to go to his ward, but he had given it all.

The bloom began to turn black.

The messenger raced along with the prayers. The air was full of demons, and it had to dodge their evil darts constantly. Just as it thought it had made it through the siege, a weapon pierced it, and it fell, using its last bit of strength to protect the vital package it carried.

Suddenly, the messenger was aloft again! Angels appeared in battle array and fought back the evil forces. One of the angels carried the messenger swiftly to the hospital waiting room.

Twinkle-Eyes was still standing, ready to give his last spirit-breath to Joel to try to help him when the messenger and the angel arrived. The prayer power was quickly dispersed to Joel and Kathy.

The angel left to take the messenger to the Most High God for healing while Twinkle-Eyes and Gimel watched Joel closely. Were the prayers enough? Did they come in time?

Back at the Knight's gathering, the group merged their gifts into a flowing stream of powerful might. The twins, Brent and Nathan, had discerned a spiritual battle in the area, and had directed the group to pray for the Lord's army to assist. Those prayers had mustered the angels to rescue the fallen messenger and hold back the evil siege. Abby and Chloe raised their voices in song, calling for help from God, which released another battalion of angels to come and make a way for more messengers. Jill, Liz, Emily and Marissa kept the group informed as to the progress of their prayers, while Chris and Garrett led with Scripture encouragement. Soon, the messengers were unhindered in their path to Joel and Kathy, but were they too late?

Kathy's spirit was the first to show real response. Her faith blossom began to perk, as if revived by water after a dry spell. Tears flowed freely, taking away her grief, and allowing her to choose.

She hugged Joel tightly again, whispering the words she had resisted within her own spirit, "Forgive . . . we must forgive him, Joel."

"No!" he screamed, jumping up and away from his mother's arms. "I can't! That is too much to ask of me!"

A petal of his faith blossom fell off, dead.

"The throne room! Chris, remember the throne room!" Jill called desperately.

"But we need Joel!" Chris cried out, shaking his head frantically.

"Just do it—remember the throne room!" Jill insisted.

The two grabbed hands and closed their eyes. The image of the majestic throne room and the One they had seen filled their minds. They both sensed a peace coursing through their spirits and relaxed, allowing the One to speak to them.

"What is it, My children?" the Lamb asked.

Bowing before the King, Jill answered boldly, "Our friend, Joel, needs You."

"You are faithful friends to seek Me regarding Joel," the Lamb replied. "How may I help him?"

Jill and Chris looked at each other thoughtfully, and then Chris spoke up, "He needs to see You here with us again. You told us that the bond between us would be strong. Maybe that would help him not to give in to hate."

The Lamb nodded in agreement. In a moment, Joel was beside them.

Chris and Jill grabbed Joel's arms as he teetered and nearly fell down. Then they hugged him.

"What am I doing here?" Joel asked in amazement.

"We asked Him to bring you," Jill responded. "We know what's going on, Joel, and you need your friends and the love of the Lamb to help you right now."

Joel slowly turned and saw the throne room and the one. But this time, he could not look at the Lamb eye to eye.

"Why are you distressed, My child?" the Lamb asked.

Joel gulped. "You know that Kyle's dad . . ."

"Yes."

"How can I forgive him?" Joel asked, his voice trembling.

"Your father has," the Lamb said.

"What? Dad knows he did it?" Joel questioned with surprise.

Jill and Chris stood with their friend, their hearts aching with the sorrow they knew Joel felt.

"Doug saw who forced him off the road and with his last breath, told Jim that he forgave him," the Lamb revealed. "That is why Jim attempted to take his own life in remorse."

Tears sprang like a rain shower from Joel's eyes.

The Lamb took him in His arms. "Three souls are saved from eternal damnation because of your father's death. The Thompsons would not know me now if your father's life had not been forfeited."

Joel squeezed his eyes shut and sobbed while Jesus held him.

After some moments, Joel took a big breath and looked at Jesus. "Can You tell my dad that I love him, and I will see him when this is over?"

"He knows you love him, Joel, and we have a grand celebration planned when this is over," Jesus replied with a smile.

Joel stood and embraced his friends.

The vision faded for all three. Joel saw Twinkle-Eyes and Gimel standing nearby, looking concerned. His mom and Pastor Eric watched him carefully as well.

The choice was made.

Suddenly, the blossom of faith within him sprouted like a tree in springtime! Instead of one bloom, many blossoms erupted in full color.

Joel walked back to his mom and sat down. He took her hands and said, "We will forgive!"

The next week was busy with police involvement. The charge was vehicular homicide against James Thompson in the wrongful death of Douglas Stevens. The local news was full of articles about the near suicide of Mr. Thompson and the subsequent discovery of his connection with Doug Stevens' accident.

The demons had a heyday with the whole situation as numerous people around the area were easy targets for rumors and suppositions. But, those closest to the two families experienced only love and understanding as Kathy and Joel spoke with forgiving hearts to Jim Thompson and his family.

Jim seemed like a new man to his family and friends. The anger that had so consumed his life had left with the demon. Ellen and Kyle were happy to have back the one who had truly been gone from them for a long time.

Consequences, however, still came. Jim stood silent as the judge pronounced the verdict as guilty. He bowed his head in quiet acceptance of the decision. The sentencing of four years in prison was expected and given.

Kathy and Joel hugged their friends in sadness. They had still hoped and prayed for mercy for Jim.

"It's OK," Kyle reassured the Kathy and Joel. "We spent a lot of time in prayer, and Dad was sure that, no matter the outcome, God had a work for him to do . . . maybe even in prison! Who needs the forgiveness Christ has to offer more than those who have done bad enough things to be in prison? In fact, Dad was feeling very much that God needed him to witness to those in prison, so we are not surprised or upset with the sentence, except we will really miss him!"

"We would have missed him so much more if God hadn't brought Kyle home at the right time to save him from suicide!" Ellen added. "Then we would have had eternal separation from him, but we can endure any separation in this world, knowing that Jim knows the Lord and wants to serve Him now! We will be together for eternity, experiencing God's love and forgiveness for the wrongs we did to you, as well as others. Thank you, Kathy and Joel, for not giving up on us!"

The group hugged again and then headed out. The angels surrounding them had been busy guarding them from demons, using the energy from many prayer warriors throughout the area. As people left the courthouse, angels dispersed, giving as much protection as possible to the Believers.

CHAPTER 33

The JP Knights had forged a tight bond through the events of recent days. Each had been given new insights into their spiritual gifts through Joel's trial and testing. They had realistic views of the enemy, understanding his power, but also came away with deeper trust in the Lord, who they knew already had the victory. Their job now was to fully involve themselves in the battle, securing the way for more souls to be saved.

Joel was treated with a respect earned with his godly choices. The JP Knights knew their leader had come through the fire with the Lord's help and had survived, now being even stronger in his faith. Only Jill could see what had happened with Joel's faith seed, but the rest of the group could immediately tell that he had a new, quiet confidence and conviction about their work for the Lord. He constantly reminded them that the battle was the Lord's, and anything the JP Knights did was only through the power of the risen Christ, not through their own strengths.

The meetings were now very intense, with Chris arming the Knights with Scripture and the angels working closely with each charge to fully prepare them for fights with the enemy. They spent much time in prayer for those they were shown needed strength to choose the Lamb.

Liz and Marissa began teaming up as they realized their gifts of prophecy and empathic imaging fit well together. Shane and Garrett hit it off, and Shane found that he could interpret Garrett's dreams. Jill and the twins honed their skills with seeing the spiritual world. Abby and Chloe led the group in singing praises and worshipping at the beginning of each meeting and began to write their own lyrics and music with help from Chris, whose knowledge of Scripture led to some vital songs that the group could remember in times of need. Emily and Joel discussed the meaning of the visions they had. Emily recorded the prophecies, dreams and visions in her computer and then printed them out for each of the JP Knights to have copies in loose-leaf notebooks. Joel routinely discussed these so that the group would be alert regarding their mission and could praise when prayers were answered or a mission completed.

The Thompsons were doing amazingly well, in spite of the negative press and even threats to their lives. Jim was taken to a state prison about an hour away, where Ellen and Kyle could visit him every weekend after a preliminary period. They knew his incarceration was a consequence of his crime, but they were quite unprepared for the conditions Jim experienced in the correctional facility.

"Mom?" Kyle questioned, seeing tears run down her cheeks. "What's wrong?"

Too emotional to respond, she handed Kyle some pieces of paper, and then reached for a tissue.

Kyle recognized the papers as a letter from his dad, and looked at his mom briefly before sitting down to read it. It was the first communication from his dad since the trial.

Dear Ellen and Kyle,

I am finally settled into a cell here. There were many interviews and meetings for days, as they explained rules and regulations, paired me with a counselor, and made sure I had no contagious illness. I was put in a holding area for that time, with no interaction with any inmates. It was like solitary confinement. I was given a physical exam, but really wasn't allowed to speak to the doctor. I got two meals a day and had one shower. No personal items were permitted, as they were being examined to make sure I was not smuggling anything in. They did let me have a copy of a Bible, which I was thankful for. I spent my days reading the Bible and praying. God brought me much comfort.

The guards don't talk to the inmates other than to bark orders. It's a little hard to get used to no one speaking to you.

I was brought to my cell yesterday and given my personal items that were allowed. They will probably contact you about the things that they didn't accept. I thought we had followed the instructions to a T, but apparently some employees make up their own rules. My personal Bible was not allowed—the reason was that there were too many notes written in it. That was discouraging, since I had lots of comments from Pastor Art's sermons that I wanted to study, now that my heart wants to learn it.

My roommate is Muslim. I haven't figured out how to spell his name. Although he said his parents had named him Dante, he rejected that name when he became a Muslim. He goes often to meetings with other Muslims. I asked a guard when the Christians met, and he just shrugged his shoulders, mumbling something about once a month!

It is very noisy here. I have the bottom bunk, which is very hot. The mattress is about four inches thick. There is a toilet and a sink. A small, dirty window with bars lets a little light in. The common room has a TV. I tried to sit out there to relax last evening, but everyone just yelled and shouted to each other so that I couldn't hear the program, so I came back to the cell. I tried to read the Bible I was allowed to keep from the preliminary area, but the noise was so deafening that I couldn't concentrate.

I haven't met anyone yet who would seem to be a Christian. It looks like I have my ministry cut out for me! I really didn't think prison would be like this. TV makes it almost look glamorous, with inmates using computers and the Internet. Let me tell you—it is nothing like that! There have been times that I've been afraid for my life, and I cry to God to have mercy and let the sentencing be rescinded somehow.

But, I am trying to trust God. Please continue to pray for me that I will adjust to this place. I want so much to tell others of God's love, but fears keep haunting me. Here, I am just one more human who messed up and was caught. Pray that I can have a vision for what God wants me to do and be now.

I love you both and am so sorry to have put you through so much!

Kyle didn't know when the tears had begun, but they ran down his face in torrents now. He felt his mother hugging him and immediately reached for her. They held each other for minutes, sobbing.

At first, neither heard the doorbell. After a few times, finally Ellen became aware of the noise, but ignored it, supposing it to be another reporter asking to interview them.

"We have to answer the door, Mom," Kyle spoke up.

Ellen looked at her son curiously.

Kyle shook his head and added, "I don't know why or how, but I just know we need to answer the door this time."

Ellen stared at her son for a moment before answering, "OK; you're right. I don't know how either, but I know you're right."

Kyle held back while his mom went to the door. The past weeks had been grueling, and rude reporters had made it even worse. Some had camped out at the end of the driveway, hoping to catch some human interest story. It didn't take long for the Thompsons to decide not to answer the door or phone unless caller ID showed it was someone they knew. They had needed to get new cell phone numbers because of so-called friends who had turned on the family and had harassed them with texts.

"Oh, come on in!" Ellen said after opening the solid wooden door.

Kyle smiled when he saw Joel come into the living room.

Ellen continued, "I'm so sorry that we didn't get the door sooner, Joel. It's just that we've had some unwelcome callers lately."

"That's OK, Mrs. Thompson. I should have called first, but this happened so quickly that I just hopped on my bike and sped over here to tell you!" Joel blurted out.

She smiled quizzically at Joel, "What do you mean? What happened so quickly?"

Joel paused as he noticed their tear-stained faces, and his excitement abated for a moment.

"You're both upset from something—what happened? Did someone write another rude letter to the paper?" Joel asked, referring to some letters to the editor about Jim Thompson that were quite scathing.

Kyle shook his head, "No, we got a letter from my dad." He picked up the pages and handed them to Joel. "Go ahead . . . read them."

Joel took the letter and questioned, "Are you sure? I mean, this is pretty private."

Ellen nodded, "It's OK, Joel. Of all people, you could have turned on us, but we'd never have made it through this if it weren't for you and Kathy."

Joel sighed slightly and then read the letter.

Kyle and Ellen sat and waited patiently, tears coming easily again.

Finishing the letter, Joel looked at Ellen and Kyle. He tried to blink away the tears, but they still came. He went to his friends and hugged them.

When Joel released them from the embrace, Ellen and Kyle were surprised to see him smiling, though tears still welled up in his eyes.

"*This* is why I'm here!" Joel stated with conviction.

"What do you mean?" Kyle exclaimed.

Joel gazed at both Kyle and his mom a moment before answering. "Your dad, right now, is starting that ministry that the Lord desires for him to have there in prison. It does come in the middle of some fearful time, but God is giving him the discernment to do the right thing and to be His witness in that place."

"Really?" Kyle asked. "How do you know?"

"Well, I was sitting in my backyard studying the Word, and I saw it happen," Joel declared.

"Huh?" both Kyle and Ellen asked together.

Joel tried to think of a way to explain the vision he'd had, without compromising the JP Knights' mission or disclosing the relationship they had with angels.

"Your gift no longer needs to be in secret, Joel," a voice said.

Twinkle-Eyes appeared behind the Thompsons. Joel smiled at the news and immediately understood the angel's message.

"You see," Joel began, "I have visions of different things. It is a gift from the Lord for the end times."

Kyle's eyes widened with amazement. "Really?" he said with a grin.

Ellen looked dumbfounded. A touch from Twinkle-Eyes allowed understanding into her spirit, and she began to cry.

"Joel, please tell us what you saw?" she pleaded.

Joel reached for her hand and grabbed Kyle's with the other. When he was through telling them every detail of what he had seen, they all hugged.

"Thank you, Joel," Ellen said. "That has given me great peace about Jim. Now, Kyle and I will be able to pray effectively for him. And this vision of yours has helped me to see that God is in control every step of the way, even when we can't see it." Then she added, "May God guide you with this incredible gift He has given you."

The three chatted a bit more as Twinkle-Eyes and another angel watched.

"It *is* exciting to see the Believers use the Almighty's gifts, isn't it," the other angel commented.

Twinkle-Eyes chuckled and nodded, "It only gets better."

CHAPTER 34

The demon lord sneered at the messenger, "How long did you think you could fool us?"

The messenger stood silently as demons held its arms firmly at the sides.

Directing a question at another demon, the lord asked, "How many times do you think it got back to the enemy?"

"I think twice it met another to pass classified information," the other demon replied. "I was in a different sector when it started, and when I returned, I immediately detected some unusual activity by this one. It tried to get away, but I had set a trap and caught it."

"Hmm . . ." the demon lord mused. "Fortunate for you that I am a tolerant superior, or you would suffer for this," its voice crescendoed into a roar at the other demon. Turning back to the traitor, it commanded, "Take it away and see what information you can obtain about its contacts; use any means necessary!"

The demon guards roughly pushed the messenger out of the room. The abandoned mine served as a demon lair now. The lower portions were reserved for the highest level of demon, with lesser ones having to bear with the sun and fresh air of the upper areas. The prisoner was nearly dragged to an underground lake, where it was plunged into the icy water repeatedly, while the tormentors laughed and struck it.

The torture went on for hours, but the messenger remained unyielding. Finally, it was thrown into a tower, wounded and weak. A small, barred window far above let in a bit of light. It was shackled to the floor and wall and then left alone, since the daylight had come. The demons retreated back underground to the dark they preferred.

The prince of the air had given the demon lord power to protect the lair from the enemy. The place was considered one of the favorite spots for the master to come to, so the unseen spirit defenses were formidable. The enemy had never found the spot, let alone attempted to get through the barriers.

The messenger struggled to sit upright. The wounds were significant, it knew. It may not survive the night. No matter—the information had been important, much more important than its life. With the demons gone, it could relax a little and try to hold on with selfless strength until the end.

Detecting no nearby evil, it raised its eyes to the heavens and sang, barely above a whisper, *"He hangs the earth on nothing. He binds up the water in His thick clouds."*

What was that? It heard a noise! Cocking its head to one side, it heard more clearly.

"He stirs up the sea with His power."

A raspy voice sounded from a dark corner of the tower. The messenger had frozen, expecting a demon guard to come rushing toward it.

Instead, the hoarse voice got louder, and the messenger's spirit lifted in response.

"By His spirit He adorned the heavens."

Joining in, the messenger completed the song with the other. When they were done, the messenger peered into the darkness, trying to see, but could make out no forms in the dim light of the tower.

"Who joins me to praise the almighty God?" the messenger queried quietly.

"It is your friend from long ago. I have been a prisoner for millennia, since the uprising when Lucifer was cast out of heaven. Long have I waited for rescue, but this place has been an impenetrable fortress. It is unfortunate that you are now here, although your company is appreciated," the voice said.

The messenger probed his memory. *Was it possible? This angel was thought to be lost!*

"Tau, is that you?" Resh, the angel, asked.

"Yes, my friend, it is. I had nearly lost hope, yet I could never forget the Almighty!" Tau answered.

Now it made sense! Resh had frequently asked regarding Tau's whereabouts, until finally the answer was, "*That which was lost is found, but the time of liberation must wait until you meet henceforth, when the harvest is ripe.*"

Resh had thought and thought about that response, finally giving up understanding its mysterious answer.

"Tau, the Almighty had this planned! You have never been forgotten! There must be a reason that you and I bear this together," Resh exclaimed, but the excitement was too much for his wounds, and he sank back in pain and exhaustion.

A stirring from the corner went unnoticed by the injured messenger, as he tilted over onto the cold floor.

The touch was cold, but gentle. Resh opened his eyes to view the wasted body of his fellow angel. With difficulty, Tau helped Resh to sit up again, minimizing the pain of the shackles pulling on his wrists.

"You are not chained?" Resh asked.

Tau smiled wanly, "Long ago, my body wore out, and I could slip through the fetters, in spite of their demon curse."

"How have you survived all this time?" Resh inquired.

"The sun," Tau replied.

"The sun?" Resh questioned as he looked up at the tiny window, "But very little light comes through there; although all God's creation is filled with His power, it seems such a small amount to keep you alive this long."

Snorting, Tau responded, "I said Son, not the sun in the sky. I mean the words of the Son of God kept me alive!"

Resh smiled and shook his head, "I have erred in my weakened state, Tau! Please tell me how this is so!"

Tau nodded and sat down next to Resh. "The Son of God says that He is the *'bread of life.'* When I thirsted, I pondered His words. When I was hungry, I closed my eyes and remembered His humbleness, His willingness to become the Lamb. These things have come to pass, haven't they?"

"Yes," Resh answered. "He became the Lamb That Was Slain two thousand years ago."

"Ah," Tau mused, "I thought so. There came a time of great upheaval in the demon world, and I heard some of the more talkative demons speak of someone's death with hateful pride, but then, shortly thereafter, the same demons seemed to be shaking with terror, and I heard one say that death had been defied. It was then I hoped that the prophecies had been fulfilled. I was moved often, following the conquests of men, until all the world seemed to be inhabited by them. Lucifer began to use these old mines as his strongholds. I have been in this particular place for two hundred years. The demon lord is unaware of my presence and the guards would like to keep it that way. It would seem that they put you here purposely."

"Really? Why?" Resh asked.

"The guards have promised me better treatment for information," Tau replied matter-of-factly.

"Oh?" Resh queried with concern. "What information?"

"When the Lamb is to return," Tau answered.

"Tau, you know that no one but the Almighty knows that," Resh stated.

"Yes, but they think they will be able to have a surprise attack on the Believers if they can present that time to the demon lord," Tau explained.

Resh winced with a spasm of pain.

"You need to rest now. We will speak more later," Tau said as he helped Resh get into a more comfortable position.

Resh closed his eyes for some respite, but the icy cold hands of Tau sent an alarm into his spirit as he fell unconscious.

When Resh awoke, he was no longer in the tower. He recognized the place of torture. The guards grabbed him and began the ritual dunking in the dank, polluted waters of the mine.

This time, after he had swallowed and gagged on the water, the guards began questioning him about his contact within the enemy army.

Remaining silent, he focused his spirit on the grandeur of the heavenly throne room. Before long, the guards lost patience, hitting him and throwing him into the briny waters of the lake and then dragging him out.

His strength was gone. He didn't even know that he was back in the tower until he felt Tau's cold hands prop him up against the wall.

"Tau?" Resh asked.

"Yes?"

"Would you sing some of our songs for me? It would be such a comfort,' Resh asked.

"Of course," Tau responded and then softly sang while holding Resh's head against him.

This same routine happened over and over again until Resh lost track of time, but he had decided today would be the last time that Tau would sing the songs of Job.

"That was nice," Resh sighed when Tau had finished singing. "How about another one before I give up my spirit?"

"No!" Tau nearly shouted and then he quickly recovered, saying, "You, uh, can't do that . . . uh . . . maybe we can escape together."

"No, Tau. My strength is gone. I am content to have served God," Resh said with difficult breaths. "Join me!"

"The Alpha and the Omega! The beginning and the end!"

Resh closed his eyes, drinking in the sight described by the Apostle John as he sang.

"Worthy is the Lamb who was slain to receive power and riches and wisdom, and strength and honor and glory and blessing!

"Blessing and honor and glory and power be to Him who sits on the throne, and to the Lamb, forever and ever!"

The words gave him strength, and he opened his eyes to look at Tau, who had not started to sing.

319

Although the appearance of his friend had been unsettling to Resh at first, the messenger had accepted the reason for the wasted body without question, knowing that the Lamb had survived without food or water during the forty days of temptation by focusing of the words of God. However, the only songs Tau would ever sing involved creation. And, those cold, cold hands . . .

Resh gazed at Tau and prompted, "Sing of the Lamb's victory with me, Tau, before I give up my spirit."

The wasted body of Tau contorted, and the face sneered menacingly. "Tell me when the Son returns, or your friend, Tau, will die!" the demon imposter screamed.

Resh's spirit leaped with the knowledge that the real Tau was alive!

The demon grabbed Resh with its cold hands and ripped at the wings tucked into the messenger's back. The two wrestled vigorously at first, but Resh's injuries soon weakened him and the demon grinned fiendishly as it reached for a concealed dagger to finish Resh off.

The flash was swift and bright. Resh landed in a heap on the stone floor of the tower.

"Resh, Resh," a voice spoke urgently.

Resh opened his eyes to see a vision of an angel before him.

"Come, we must go quickly!" the voice urged again.

Shaking his head and blinking his eyes, Resh soon realized that it wasn't a vision—a real angel was helping him up!

"No," Resh whispered to the rescuer.

The angel tugged at his arm, but Resh pulled back.

"No. Tau is here somewhere. We must find him!" Resh insisted.

The angel straightened with purpose.

"Stay here," he said while dragging the lifeless demon form into the shadows. "If the guards come, pretend to be unconscious. They will think that demon is still working on you. I will look for Tau."

The angel paused, closed his eyes, spread out his hands and whispered, "Show me, almighty God, where Your servant is!"

With a nod, the angel moved carefully out of the tower.

Resh had received some power from the touch of the angel, so he positioned himself such that any guard would have to come around him to fully check his condition. The demon's dagger had fallen at Resh's feet. He tucked it underneath him in a manner that would make it easy to use if needed.

Time passed, and Resh feared that the angel would not find Tau in time. Resh knew the drill—he had practiced it many times before taking this assignment. If an extraction was necessary, the spiritual powers protecting the angels would only be available for fifteen minutes of man's time. Otherwise, the angels risked detection.

Resh had silently been counting down, a feat difficult for most angels. It was time. Resh listened carefully and was about to get up when he heard faint footsteps. They seemed heavy, and Resh's heart sank, thinking the angels had missed their opportunity to escape.

"Quick, we must go *now!*" the angel said in hushed tones.

Resh felt a powerful hand help him up. He looked to see the angel rescuer urge him with a nod. Over the liberator's shoulder, a thin angel was held.

"My wings are injured," Resh whispered.

The angel responded, "Hold onto me!"

Resh wrapped his arms the best he could around the angel's body. With a powerful stroke of wings, they rose.

The key was the tower roof—if they could make it through there, other angel forces could help.

Resh prayed to the Almighty. His head was tucked under the one arm of the angel, so he couldn't see.

Demon shouts ripped through the air. They had been discovered!

Silence was no longer necessary.

With all his strength, Resh shouted, "Glory to the Almighty! All power comes from Him! Oh Holy God hear me! Save us by Your awesome power!"

Fiery arrows flew through the air.

They were close now.

Fire scorched Resh's leg. He shouted again, praising the Creator and King.

Suddenly, the three angels were cushioned as if a large hand was holding them. In a moment, they were through the tower, into the protective hedge of a legion of angels. They sped away to the heavenly realms before being set down. Their wounds were instantly gone once they were in the realm of the almighty God.

They quickly reported to their commander and told all they knew of the demon lair.

Soon they were summoned.

Resh knelt before God.

"Well done, faithful servant! Your loyalty has also enabled Us to receive back the prisoner, Tau! You now have a period of rest."

Resh bowed his head to the ground and then quietly got up, backing out of the way.

"Tau, come before me!"

Turning, Resh saw his friend, fully restored, step forward and kneel.

"Tell Us what happened, Tau."

Tau leaned back on his heels, and began, "Almighty God, I was captured during the battle with Lucifer. At first, I was given sustenance in the hopes that I would turn from worshipping the one true God, but I did not waver in my trust in You. After a time, I was tortured for no apparent reason other than hatred of You. I was moved often as men inhabited the world, until finally reaching the mine where Your servants found me."

"This has been thousands of man years, Tau. How did you survive?"

"Your love and Your Word has sustained me, oh great God!" Tau replied, bowing before God.

"Receive now your reward, faithful servant!"

As Tau bowed his head to the ground, he was enveloped in a glow.

"You shall labor with the harvesters and strengthen believers with the strength you have received of Me!"

The glow receded. Tau stood and with a bow, backed away just as Resh had done. The audience with the King was over. The angels dispersed.

Resh and Tau embraced.

"How did you know I was there, Resh?" Tau asked. "Our rescuer told me that you would not leave until he had searched for me."

"An imposter was sent to trick me. It was a demon who pretended to be you!" Resh explained. "Once I realized it was not you, I resisted interrogation. The imposter became angry and threatened to kill you if I did not tell it what it wanted to know. Then I knew you were alive and in that horrible place. I thought I would be killed, though, and that was when the rescuer appeared and killed the demon imposter. I could not leave without trying to find you!"

"Thank you, my friend!" Tau exclaimed. "Now, please fill me in on the happenings of the last few thousands of years!"

Resh laughed. It was good to have his friend back.

"One thing, Tau?" Resh questioned.

"Yes?" Tau prompted.

"Your reward is to be thrown into the last battle, and you seem happy about it?" Resh queried. "I would think you'd want to come and rest with me for a while."

Tau shook his head, "Almighty God knows me, Resh. I have spent much time doing nothing, and that is not what I desire. He knows that I receive joy from service. To be around Believers is something I have never experienced. Demon companions are fickle, yet predictable. I can't wait to see with my own eyes the Redeemed!"

Resh smiled thoughtfully. "Ah . . . I can rest later. Do you think God would mind if I tagged along with you?"

Tau grinned, "To be honest, Resh. He already knew you'd want to—let's go!"

The two angels pumped their wings, looked to the earth, and took off.

Teth, the rescuer, watched the two leave and then went to the senior officer of the army he commanded.

"The information from both Resh and Tau indicate a buildup of enemy forces. Prepare your battalion. It is time."

CHAPTER 35

The vision was clear. Joel sat in his room and thought. He was glad the JP Knights were meeting in an hour at Marissa's. They would need this for their work.

The group gathered silently in the basement. All seemed lost in thought.

Joel sensed that the others were somehow prepared, just as he had been with the vision. He motioned for everyone to stand.

"I believe that we all have received messages of some kind from our Lord. Before we share those messages, let's pray for guidance: Father, we have been chosen by You for this work. Prepare us. Guide us. Give us wisdom and discretion to understand what we are to do. Keep us in the center of Your will during this time of harvest. Amen."

Murmurs of "Amen" echoed softly through the room. Chloe and Abby, as if on cue, stepped to the front and passed out sheets of paper.

"Hymns," Abby started, "were wonderful ways to praise and worship in the past."

"Yes," Chloe added, "and we believe they hold really special messages for us still. This one seems to reflect Joel's prayer asking for help from the Almighty."

Abby picked up her guitar and started to play. Chloe's sweet voice led the group. The tune was easily picked up by the others. Reading the words Abby and Chloe had handed out, the group finished the verses.

The room stayed hushed as the last tones melted away. Each Knight reflected on the words sung and committed their worshipful notes to great Jehovah, silently willing the presence of His Spirit to be in their midst.

The angels arrived as the Spirit ministered to the individual members of the JP Knights. They quietly took their places with the one or ones they helped.

Garrett spoke up first. "I had a dream that everyone needs to hear about."

The others found seats and sat down as Garrett began.

"The battles with Satan will start within days. Satan knows that Christ's return is very soon, so he is doing a . . ." Here he struggled to find the right words.

"Preemptive strike?" Shane offered.

Nodding, Garrett continued, "Yes, that's it. He thinks that he will catch the Christians unaware and make a significant blow to Believers around the world. We *must* be ready! We must be sure our armor is intact!"

Chris then stood. "He's right!" he exclaimed. "The Bible tells of a great harvest before Christ comes. We know the devil won't stand for that! It's important for us to witness to our friends, and pray for opportunities to speak of Christ's salvation. If we are alert, the Spirit will help us. As Matthew 10:19–20 says, '*But when they deliver you up, do not worry about how or what you should speak. For it will be given to you in that hour what you should speak; for it is not you who speak, but the Spirit of your Father who speaks in you.*'"

"We are His hands and feet to do His will among men," Liz spoke out. "Each of us has an important work to do individually, but we are strongest when together. Be careful not to go out alone now—the enemy is also strong. Just as Jesus sent out the disciples two by two, so are we to go out. Garrett, you and Shane should minister so that your dreams may be accurately interpreted. Brent and Nathan must continue together, for their gifts of discernment will be needed by those that are searching. Abby and Chloe have a music ministry that will reach those some consider unreachable. Emily and Chris, although you have not worked with each other, the Spirit has seen that your hearts have the same desires and has woven your gifts of Scripture knowledge and visions into a worthy combo. Marissa and I are to go to places where comfort is needed most and offer the comfort we have received of Christ. Finally, Jill and Joel are to go out with their abilities to "see," through visions and spiritual sight, into places where the enemy has strongholds, defeating the demons' grip on lives that were thought to be lost. We sometimes will be only in our teams, but other times the Spirit will call us together for battle against the enemy. *'Be strong and of good courage; do not be afraid, nor be dismayed, for the LORD your God is with you wherever you go.'*"

The JP Knights pondered the prophetic words Liz had just said. The Spirit had prepared each one to move forward, fulfilling the prophecies. But, there was still more they needed to do.

Joel stood, and everyone became attentive to him.

"We all understand about putting on the armor of the Lord that we need to fight against the devil and his demons," he started. The teens nodded in agreement.

"Well," he continued, "we need to clothe ourselves with Christ to help the harvesting of souls, too."

The teens looked at each other excitedly.

"Galatians 3:27 says, *'For as many of you as were baptized into Christ have put on Christ,'*" Joel stated. "This means that we must use His attributes and His words as we assist in the harvest. For example, Isaiah 61:3 says, *'To console those who mourn in Zion, to give them beauty for ashes, the oil of joy for mourning, the garment of praise for the spirit of heaviness; that they may be called trees of righteousness, the planting of the Lord, that He may be glorified.'* Did you hear that—*the planting of the Lord?* I may be reading into this a bit, but if something is planted, it is also usually harvested somehow. If that's the case, since we are helping in the harvest, we should wear *'the garment of praise'* so that we can give it to those who are being harvested!" Joel finished.

Jill snapped her fingers in revelation. "Yes! I've seen that! I just didn't understand what was happening!" She stood up beside Joel to explain. "When we've been at the SIMBOC meetings, I noticed this weird exchange of energy or color or something every once in a while . . . not often, but as Joel said that verse and described it, I could see what he meant! When we praise with someone who is just beginning to believe in Christ, we can give them spiritual clothing to help them in their walk with the Lord . . . to glorify Him. We know how praise really does give strength and power to those who need it for the fight against Satan. Maybe this can help to protect the newly harvested souls from Satan as well!"

Joel nodded and then motioned for others to speak, "Does anyone else have 'clothing' to add?"

Brent raised his hand, "Job 29:14 says *'I put on righteousness, and it clothed me; my justice was like a robe and turban.'* We already know about the *'breastplate of righteousness'* of our armor, but this extends the concept of our righteousness in Christ to actually clothing us completely, plus, being fair and just in our behavior toward others is more that can help in harvesting. If we don't care about doing right, we hurt the cause of Christ. And, if we judge others, we could push them away in spiritual nakedness rather than helping them to understand that Christ paid the price and they don't have to be ashamed anymore."

"Alright! How about the Beatitudes?" Emily called out. "Many of those are attributes of Jesus: meekness, gentleness, peacemakers, mercy. We need to embody, or 'wear' these to attract unbelievers to Christ!"

Marissa sat thoughtfully while the others continued to name fruit of the Spirit and other character traits Christians should have. Slowly, she raised her hand.

"I have a different thought about clothing," she offered.

All eyes turned to the quiet young lady.

"Remember what happened when the woman touched Jesus' robe? She was healed. By 'putting on Christ,' we may bring healing to those who are afflicted," she said with conviction, "but we must be willing to be touched. I think that means we should not be afraid to get involved in other's lives. The Bible tells us to give our coat to the one who needs. Simply said, since we put on Christ, we need to give Him to those we meet."

The JP Knights continued to discuss how to put on Christ, and in the end, prayed specifically for Him to work through each one of them. They made arrangements for the teams to meet the next day and for the whole group to get together in one week.

No one could have guessed that they had met in that place for the last time.

CHAPTER 36

Black clouds raced upon the city and its surroundings. People hurried to get inside, but the deluge caught many by surprise. Torrents of water flooded the streets quickly, and motorists pulled off to wait out the storm.

A group of Beings watched the storm approach near the edge of the city.

"It has started," one Being said to another.

"Yes," the other one agreed. "He thinks that these storms will cause people to curse God."

After a moment, a third Being commented, "He is wrong."

The teams had all met, and, led by the Spirit, had planned where their work would begin.

Marissa and Liz had mapped out various homeless shelters and had volunteered to work preparing and serving meals. Marissa's experience in the shelters had given her even more empathy to try to meet the needs of those who were homeless.

Abby and Chloe felt called to detention homes for teens. Their sweet voices could help them break down barriers through music and allow them to share the love of Christ with kids their age who had gotten into trouble.

Nathan and Brent knew some teen Bible studies that had started recently in their area of town. The groups were non-denominational and cross-cultural, drawing a wide range of teenagers through sports leagues or ultra-sport programs, like skateboarding. The youth would practice and compete within their area of choice and then hear of Christ from the ministry youth leader. The groups needed Christian teens to be part of the discipling process. The twin's knowledge of Scripture, along with some natural sports abilities, were just what the ministry needed.

Garrett and Shane felt drawn to a local arts community center, where residents of the area could take classes. There was something for everyone: acting and drama, painting, dance, and various crafting skills. The center served all ages from preschool to retirement. Garrett was asked to teach a painting class, and the center needed someone, like Shane, to do grounds work and keep areas clean. This setting could provide unique opportunities to reach more middle and upper class people who could afford the class tuitions.

Emily and Chris had prayed thoughtfully about the ministry they were to do, and although they both felt led to work with youth, neither had received any specific directions. However, when Chris got home, he had a message to call the director of a nearby Christian camp—two of the counselors had needed to leave, and the camp was in dire straits to have staffing for the rest of the summer. Chris had done the training in the spring, but had not signed up because of everything going on with the JP Knights. He knew that Emily had trained with a different camp but had also not signed up for the summer. Chris excitedly called Emily, and they prayed over the phone. It was clear to them that this was where God wanted them now.

Jill went over to Joel's house in late morning. They sat out on the patio to pray and talk.

"Has God impressed upon you a certain ministry?" Jill asked.

"Well . . ." Joel began, "I keep thinking about Mr. Thompson in prison and wonder if there is some way to help inmates."

A peculiar look came over Jill's face.

Noticing, Joel questioned, "What? Is that crazy or something? I suppose it could be dangerous."

"No . . . no . . ." Jill sputtered. "I guess it still surprises me how the Lord works," she said, while shaking her head. "You see, our mail comes early, and this morning a flyer came from my church announcing a new prison ministry starting this week." She reached for her backpack and pulled out a piece of paper. "See?" she said as she pushed the flyer over to Joel.

A big grin spread across his face as he skimmed the announcement. Looking at Jill, he exclaimed, "You're right! It is pretty cool to see how the Lord brings us to His work when we trust Him!"

Jill offered, "I went ahead and called to find out more about it, and all we need is permission slips from our parents and filling out some kind of clearance form. Pastor Feyock—he's the one in charge—said that is easy if we've never been in trouble with the law at our age. He e-mailed the forms to me, and I brought them along."

Joel smiled as Jill handed him the papers, and the two got busy filling them out.

After a few minutes, Joel became aware of the patio getting dark.

"Wow, do you see those clouds?" Joel asked.

Looking up, Jill stared intently and then gasped.

"Those aren't just clouds," she almost shouted. "It's demon armies!"

Joel glanced at her briefly and then quickly began gathering the papers spread out on the table. Jill did the same, and the two hurried inside as the first lightening lit up the sky. Joel raced around the house and closed windows and then directed Jill into the dining room. The rain and hail pummeled the windows, and thunder roared.

The noise of the garage door opening and closing was barely heard above the sounds of the storm. Kathy Stevens emerged through the door into the kitchen just as lightening cracked and the lights went out. She brushed a wisp of hair out of her face.

"Whew!" she sighed. "That is some storm!"

Dropping her purse and some bags on the kitchen table, she made her way into the dining room just in time to see both Joel and Jill jump with another crack of lightning and thunder.

"Hey, guys! Quite a storm, isn't it?" she called.

Joel went over to his mom and gave her a hug. With a warning glance at Jill, he answered, "Uh . . . yeah, Mom! It sure came up fast!"

Kathy missed the looks between the two teens and responded, "Wow—it sure did! The weather forecast had something about some pop-up thunderstorms, but this thing looks like it was brewing for days and finally had to let go! Let's find some candles and flashlights, Joel. The way this is going, we could be without power for a while. I'm glad your dad had that generator installed last fall. It's all set to go, but we'll still conserve energy and not run it unless we need to, to keep our food from spoiling."

She continued talking and directing them in her typical no-nonsense fashion, and before long they had a warm glow filling the house from many candles and a few kerosene lamps.

"How about I make us some lunch?" she asked when they had completed the task.

"Uh . . . sure, Mom. That would be great!" Joel agreed.

Once Kathy had left the room, Joel moved closer to Jill and whispered, "I don't think we should tell my mom about what you saw in the clouds, OK?"

Jill nodded, but then stated quietly, "OK, but I think we'd better pray for protection."

Joel shook his head affirmatively and then bowed his head. "Almighty God and Lamb That Was Slain, please protect us by Your power. Shield this house from any attacks of the devil and his demons. Show us Your will regarding the ministry You have planned for us to do. Amen."

When Joel lifted his head and opened his eyes, he found Jill staring at him.

"Oh . . . sorry," she said apologetically. "The colors and hues are so beautiful when you pray that I can't help but watch! Do you ever see them?"

Joel cocked his head to one side, thought for a moment, and then said, "Well . . . I . . . think . . . sometimes there's a sparkle or rays of light when a person is praying or singing worship songs, but I don't think it's anything like what you see."

"Hmm . . . that's a start! Maybe you can learn to see what I see," she offered.

"I don't know," Joel replied. "It is your gift. If we all could see like you do, it wouldn't be as special."

Jill sighed, "Maybe you're right, but I still think that you could learn to recognize the colors if you tried. It's just using your spiritual eyes in addition to your physical eyes."

Just then Kathy Stevens entered the room with a tray of sandwiches.

"Joel, could you go get the drinks? I just grabbed some sodas quickly out of the frig and put them on the counter," she explained.

"Sure, Mom," he replied.

Entering the kitchen, he immediately saw Twinkle-Eyes move into the room.

Eager to tell the angel what Jill had seen, Joel moved quickly towards the angel.

"Jill saw demon armies in those storm clouds," he reported.

"Yes, that is why I am here," Twinkle-Eyes responded. "Your help may be needed soon, for I believe Satan has released demons of disaster. Monitor your news networks and be alert. The situation may deteriorate, and all of you may need to fight in this battle! Call for help if you encounter demons, but always remember *the Lord your God is with you wherever you go.*"

With that, the angel was gone.

Joel stood quietly for a moment, digesting what the angel had said, and then he grabbed the sodas and headed into the dining room.

Kathy kept them chatting through lunch while the storm raged outside. They all helped to clean up, and then Kathy excused herself to do some work in her study.

Joel wasted no time in telling Jill what Twinkle-Eyes had said.

Looking concerned, Jill moved to a window and peered out.

"I don't see any demons now," she commented. "Do you think we should call the others and find out if they're OK?"

"Yeah, that's a good idea," Joel responded. "We'll have to use the kitchen phone—it's a land line that doesn't use electricity . . . unless phone lines are down, too."

They went into the kitchen and called Chris. His mom answered and informed them that the camp needed help right away, so Chris and Emily had packed up and left early that morning. No cell phones were permitted during the camp week, but Mrs. Landos said that e-mail messages were possible or they could call the camp directly.

Next, Joel tried Garrett's cell phone, but he had to leave a message. The same was true of the other JP Knights. It was frustrating to not be able to reach their friends.

Until something else happened, Joel decided to pursue the prison ministry project. He and Jill went to the study to talk to his mom. They found her at her desk, head seemingly bowed in prayer, an open Bible on her lap. When they turned to leave, she stirred.

"Hey, kids, do you need something? I just finished some prayer time," Kathy Stevens told them.

"Uh . . . yeah, Mom . . . could I ask you something?" Joel inquired.

"Sure," his mom responded.

Joel and Jill went on to explain about the prison ministry and how they felt led to participate.

Kathy nodded her head, asked a few questions, and then gave her approval. She signed the forms and added, "You know, during my prayer just now, the Spirit seemed to tell me that you and Jill were going to get involved in a ministry, and I needed to support you in it. I know it could be dangerous, but there is no place safer than the middle of God's will! Let me know if there's anything I can do to help."

"Thanks, Mom!" Joel exclaimed. He gave her a peck on the cheek before he and Jill returned to the kitchen.

Jill called Pastor Feyock. He was excited about their commitment to help in the prison ministry and made arrangements with them to meet him the next morning at a nearby prison.

The storms abated slightly the rest of the day and overnight, but the rain continued. Jill and Joel met Pastor Feyock at 8:00 am in the prison parking lot.

"Nice to meet you, Joel," the pastor said, gripping Joel's hand in a powerful handshake.

Joel was taken aback by the pastor's appearance. He was a huge man, easily over six feet tall, with a muscular build. There were scars on his face which had somewhat disfigured his left cheek down to his chin. His eyes were hard, yet kind. Joel could tell that this man had been through a lot in his life.

"OK. This first time in will take the longest," Pastor Feyock began. "Nothing is permitted in your pockets—no change or money, no handkerchief, no watches, no ChapStick . . . *nothing!*"

The teens emptied out their pockets while he continued the briefing.

"We will be put into their computer system for future identification. Then we will go through a metal detector and be searched. After that, we will proceed through a number of guard gates and finally be admitted into a meeting room. There is limited contact permitted between visitors. You must realize that some of these men are hardened criminals. . . some are serving life sentences for the crimes they committed. This is our opportunity to present the gospel to them. Today, you will observe. You will stay by my side. Do not venture away from me! Although troublemakers are usually not given the right to attend this kind of outreach, we could encounter a disgruntled inmate who would think nothing of creating a hostage situation! Are you sure you want to go ahead with this? It's not too late to pull out," the pastor cautiously asked.

Joel and Jill looked at one another and then back at Pastor Feyock.

"My mom says that one is never safer than the center of the Lord's will, so we believe that God will protect us and only allow His will to be accomplished as we do what He wants us to do!" Joel proclaimed.

"Amen!" Pastor Feyock echoed. "Let's pray then: Lord, fill us with Your Spirit as we enter this place. Place a hedge of safety around us. Help us to minister to those who desperately need salvation. Help us to encourage those who have already received the gift of Your salvation but may need strength to face the consequences of their sinful lives. Help us to be a blessing to those we meet. Especially bless all those who work in this place—give them protection, wisdom and compassion as they deal with the incarcerated day in and day out. Thank you for hearing us! Amen!"

They locked up the cars and proceeded to the visitor's entrance. A uniformed woman met them as they entered the secured area. The in-processing took nearly thirty minutes as Joel and Jill's information was entered and checked against a data base to be sure that they had no offenses. Finally, they were cleared and passed through various security stations before getting to the meeting room.

Two men in matching light blue jumpsuits were placing folding chairs in rows while three guards stood around the periphery of the room.

"Hello, Stan and Charles!" boomed the voice of Pastor Feyock.

The two inmates stood up straight and grinned broadly.

"Yo, Reverend Feyock!" one man called.

Pastor Feyock walked over to them, shook hands, and then motioned for Joel and Jill to come.

"I have helpers today—this is Joel and Jill. They feel God leading them to do some prison ministry this summer," Pastor Feyock said as introduction. "This here is Stan-the-man," he continued, pointing to a thin inmate with a mustache. "And this is Charles, more commonly known as Charlie Brown," placing his hand on the other man's shoulder.

"Uh . . . hi!" Joel stuttered.

Jill smiled somewhat nervously.

"Thanks for getting the chairs set up, boys," Pastor Feyock commended.

The guards slowly circled the room as the two inmates and the pastor talked. Finally, a door opened and men started filing into the room. Pastor Feyock immediately withdrew and steered Joel and Jill to the designated front, where he had them sit in chairs placed near the wall.

Some of those entering the room looked neat and trim, but others were unshaven and sloppy. Many were loud, shouting to others. The guards merely looked on, although occasionally they pointed or called instructions to certain inmates.

Once everyone was seated and the door closed, Pastor Feyock motioned for all to stand. He then led them in a simple prayer. Some inmates crossed themselves, others bowed their heads reverently, and some looked around with disinterest.

Next, the pastor encouraged everyone to open hymnbooks, which had been placed beneath each chair by Stan and Charles. Motioning for all to stand, Pastor Feyock began to sing the chosen hymn.

Both Joel and Jill were surprised to hear a beautiful tenor voice spring out of the giant man. Some of the inmates looked up in amazement, while others had apparently heard him sing before and seemed not to notice.

At one point, Pastor Feyock stopped to introduce Joel and Jill and also asked if there was anyone else new at the service. A dozen men stood and dutifully gave their names, with resultant loud clapping from the other attendees. Pastor Feyock welcomed them and then continued on with reading Scripture and sharing a sermon. At the end, he invited those who wanted to have a personal relationship with Christ to come forward, indicating an area opposite Jill and Joel. Five men responded. Pastor Feyock prayed with them while Stan led a final song. After the service, a number of inmates came to talk to Pastor Feyock, but soon a call from a guard signaled the end of the meeting. The prisoners left in an orderly fashion, and then Pastor Feyock, Joel and Jill were escorted from the room through a different door.

The path back outside was now drenched in a downpour. The three ran, but the security gates were slow to open. By the time they reached the cars, they were soaked!

Jill drove, following Pastor Feyock, back to the outskirts of town and to a small coffee shop in a plaza. Grabbing umbrellas, they all ran inside and sat at an empty booth.

"Well," Pastor Feyock began, "what questions do you have? Are you OK with doing this ministry, or are you having second thoughts? And I'd just like to remind you that it's alright to not want to do it again."

Joel glanced at Jill. She was sitting, thoughtfully holding her chin in her hands. He waited for her to talk first.

She sat up, and spoke, "I think it was great! To think that those men now know Jesus! I'm in!"

Joel grinned, "Me, too! I mean, it took some getting used to—all the guards with guns and some fairly unruly people, but it was exciting to see how they responded to your sermon and those guys accepting Christ! Wow!"

Pastor Feyock smiled, the scars on his cheek pulling his mouth to one side.

"I was hoping you'd see it that way! Welcome to WID Ministries!" he laughed.

Jill and Joel shot questioning glances at each other.

Pastor Feyock chuckled, "That stands for Writing in Dirt and references what Jesus did when the scribes and Pharisees wanted to stone the woman caught in adultery. He didn't judge her, but stooped down and wrote in the dirt until all the accusers left. These men have already been judged—that's why they're here—so my job is to lift them up to see Jesus."

The three continued talking while the storm raged outside.

Pastor Feyock glanced out the window with a look of concern. "This is some storm," he remarked.

At that very moment, lightening filled the sky and a crack of thunder shook the coffee shop. The lights went out.

Even though it was afternoon, the area was dark without electricity. After making arrangements for the next prison visit, the three sprinted out to the cars.

Pastor Feyock called out, "Don't drive through any flooded streets, Jill!" He then jumped into his car, made sure that Jill's car started, and slowly drove away.

Jill stared curiously after him and then drove in the same direction.

"Where are you going? We need to go the other way," Joel said.

"No," Jill answered, "we are to follow him. Look, don't you see the angels?"

Joel peered ahead and relaxed his spirit. Soon, he recognized the forms of three angels around Pastor Feyock's car. One turned and motioned for them to follow.

The streets became unfamiliar, and the rain came down in buckets, making Jill keep her windshield wipers on fast.

Pastor Feyock soon turned into a driveway, and the angels took new positions around Jill's car. The one in front motioned for her to continue on. Lightening flashed frequently, and thunder seemed incessant. Water was pooling in some areas at first, but the route took them higher up, such that water flowed through ditches and low sections, and the road remained clear.

"Lord, please protect us with Your power," Joel whispered quietly, not wanting to distract Jill from her driving.

The cell phone ring startled both of them.

"Can you get that, Joel? I want to keep both hands on the wheel," Jill said.

"Sure," he responded and grabbed the cell phone from the pocket on her purse. "Hello?" he greeted. "Oh, hi, Mr. Baker! Yeah, we're OK. Uh. . . well, I'm not sure where we are right now. Oh, wait a minute . . . I know where we're at. What? You want Jill to stay put at my house until this lets up. Sure . . . OK . . . Bye."

Joel closed the phone. "Uh, turn right here, Jill," he said just as the angel turned ahead of her. Within a few minutes, they reached Joel's house and turned into the driveway.

They raced into the house as Kathy Stevens hurriedly opened the door and shut it quickly behind them.

"Whew! I'm glad you made it home safely!" Kathy Stevens sighed. "I dug out a battery-powered radio and heard that the main roads coming from the side of town where the prison is were flooded and they were asking everyone to avoid them. I was hoping you knew the back way through the hills. My cell phone was dead, so I didn't have Jill's number, 'cause it's in my cell. Anyhow, you are safe. Praise God!" She stopped and then added, "Let's thank God for keeping you safe." With that, she prayed a few words of thanks, which they all finished with an amen.

Almost immediately, they heard a loud tone from the radio, indicating a message from the Emergency Broadcast System: "Attention: We have just received word that the Widdenmere Reservoir, an old earthen dam in the mountains above the northeastern part of the city, has begun to fail. Everyone in the downstream sections from the Widdenmere Reservoir need to evacuate immediately!"

Joel turned to Jill with a panicked look, and gasped, "That's where Marissa lives!"

He grabbed the land line phone and tried to dial, but hung up in frustration, "The phone lines must be down, too!"

Jill ran for her purse.

"Here—I have my cell phone!" she called out, as she found Marissa's number and dialed it. "Marissa! It's Jill! Are you at home? OK, good. But is anyone at your house?" Jill shut her eyes with the response. "You *must* reach them and tell them to get out of there— the Widdenmere Dam is breaking! Do you understand. . . . Did you hear me? OK—we'll pray! Call me back! Bye!"

"Her mom and brothers were at home," Jill cried urgently. "She's with Liz at a homeless shelter. People have been showing up there because of the storms, so they had stayed to help. We need to pray!"

Grabbing each other's hands, Joel began, "Father, we ask for You to protect all those down from the Widdenmere Dam. Lord, we know You can keep it from failing, but even if You don't, please help everyone to get out of the way. Our faith is in You, oh almighty God. Send Your angels to help."

While the three prayed, an angel captured the energy and quickly flew to the area below the dam. There were scores of angels in the residential section and more by the dam. Water lapped over the top of the breast while torrents raced down the spillway. The angels intertwined arms, and with wings flapping, they rose to meet the part of the dam that was failing.

The angel was about to dispense the energy when it heard the clashing of swords. Turning, it saw a legion of demons racing to disrupt the band of angels holding back the dam! An angel or two had flown out to meet the multitude of enemy forces, but they were vastly outnumbered. The angel focused its spirit and sent out a message for help and then sped to join the few fighting to protect those holding the dam.

Drawing its sword, it raced into the fray! Demons scattered around the strong angel, yet the legion advanced quickly toward the dam.

A few of the angels at the breast of the dam turned to see the demon army move toward them.

The angel noticed and shouted, "Hold your positions! Do not move!"

Some demons broke rank and flew toward the line of angels, their backs exposed.

Suddenly, two angels appeared and drew their swords. Lightening flashed as the line of angels held while the battle raged.

Within moments, the air was filled with angel wings! Resh and Tau had arrived barely before Teth's battalion. Now the battle was more equal in numbers. The angels fought with vigor and courage. Soon, the one angel could finish its task.

It stationed itself behind the line of angels holding the dam in place and then released the prayer energy it had obtained from Joel, Jill and Kathy Stevens. The beam immediately began to restore the strength of the angels. The light within them brightened. Before long, another messenger arrived and dispersed the energy of other prayers. The army of angels continued to beat back the demons until those left retreated.

Resh, Tau and Teth approached the one angel.

"Now, go assist in the evacuation! Hurry! The damage is great, and we will not be able to hold the flood back much longer!" the one angel directed.

The angels rushed off. As they approached the residential area, they touched down to the ground and became visible as men and women in emergency uniforms and clothing. Meeting other similarly attired angels, they hurried in different directions, guided by an unseen power. Houses were checked in a methodical manner, and people and pets were brought to waiting transportation that appeared out of nowhere. The refugees were all taken to a staging area, safe from the impending doom.

The disguised angels met at the edge of the town before returning to their spiritual form and racing up to the dam.

"All are safe, Gimel! Should we assist those holding back the dam now?" Resh asked urgently.

"No," Gimel said thoughtfully. "More good will happen for our Lord if we now appear to weaken and allow the dam to break. The demons are regrouping beyond that hillside. Inform those at the breast of the dam to dim their power. As soon as the demons attack again, fight with vigor and force the first line back. Continue this with the second siege, but slowly feign lapse of strength, and let the demons break through our ranks. Tell the angels at the dam to drop away intermittently, until it is obvious that there are not enough to hold the dam back. They should escape with a few skirmishes, but then race away. We will then fall back and retreat to the other areas of the city, encouraging good deeds, kindness and helpfulness. The demise of the dam will spearhead a revival in this town! Now, go! Great is our God!"

The angels received their instructions with excitement and hurried to their respective places. The line of angels at the dam sporadically decreased their glow until the flicker became very noticeable.

A demon scout watched with delight as the angel defenses weakened. It flew back to the commander and announced, "The angels are losing strength! It is time to attack!"

The commander sneered, "You worthless snipe! It is a ruse, for sure! Send out our first division, and we will see what happens!"

The demons cheered and clustered in a massive center group, rather than in ranks, meant to confuse and surprise the angels. They rushed ahead with screams.

The angels had spread out, giving as much protection to the line of angels at the dam. The centered mass effort by the demon army was met with great strength, and the division was again pushed back.

The demon commander snorted, "See! I know their tricks! Now, all three divisions—*Attack*!"

The hidden armies hastily assaulted the angels and before long, advances had poked holes in the angels' perimeter. Slowly, the angel army was pushed back. A few demons evaded defenses and headed toward the dam. One by one, the line of angels were displaced from the line, and soon it was so pockmarked that water gushed through.

"Retreat! Get out of there!" yelled Teth to the angel barrier. Then, to his forces, he commanded, "Fall back! Fall Back!"

The angels turned and flew up and out of the battle. A few gave a last attempt to defeat the enemy hordes, but soon the demons had overpowered the forces of the Almighty.

Cheers arose from the demons before the dam. The commander strode proudly to the front, moving his army up so that they could witness the power of their master.

By now, water spewed from breeches in the breast of the dam. With a mighty *roar*, the dam fell away as the engineers and emergency crews watched in horror.

A TV camera crew member was heard to say, "May God help us!"

The demon commander sneered and retorted, although the human heard nothing, "God is powerless against Satan, you human swine!"

The demons cheered and cackled.

The people at the edges of the broken dam felt a chill.

Quickly, that was replaced by a deep sense of peace and hope.

The angel stayed hidden, but repelled the icy blasts of fear and helplessness from the demon host, replacing them with blankets of optimism and encouragement.

"Ah . . . that's better," the angel whispered.

"Good work, Zayin," Gimel commented.

"The angel smiled, but didn't lose her focus. "Any specific instructions for them now?"

Gimel pondered, as if receiving a message in his ear, and then replied, "It would be helpful for them to report to the mayor."

"Alright. That can be arranged," Zayin said softly.

Gimel turned to go.

"Oh, Gimel?" Zayin asked.

Turning back, he nodded, "Yes?"

"I happened to hear the demon commander declare victory," she offered.

Gimel smiled, "Just what I wanted to hear—thanks!"

He left, and Zayin influenced the group of people to leave quickly for the city.

Some angel scouts followed the winding path of destruction left by the forceful water cascading down from the dam in the mountains. They raced to catch up with the front of the deadly wave of water and then zoomed before it, checking for any stray person or pet that had been missed in the evacuation. They flew around the area, darting back and forth, quickly assessing the vicinity doomed for destruction.

Spotting a kitten rummaging in some garbage, one of the angels hurried to snatch it just before the wall of water hit.

The roar was deafening as the water rushed into the deserted neighborhood. For a moment, the leading edge seemed to be suspended thirty feet in the air, but then it reached out, as if with claws, and thrust a terrific force upon the buildings in its way.

Small utility sheds were the first to be moved off their foundations. Soon, trees snapped, and homes caved in. The rain continued to pour down. A few daring spectators watched from safe perches, but no real views were visible, due to the blinding rain. The thunderous sounds were enough to make one's stomach twist into a ball!

It seemed to be an eternity before the noises faded. The water spread out like a fan, becoming less destructive as the force dissipated and then emptied into the river that flowed through the city. A few riverside areas became flooded, but the damage was minimal.

The mayor's office was crowded with people and television cameras. A number of assistants were taking notes and delivering them to the mayor and other elected officials who had gathered. Finally, it was announced that the mayor would be giving an update.

"As you all know," the mayor began, "the Widdenmere Dam broke late this afternoon, following a severe storm that deposited eight inches of rain over this county in a matter of hours. Emergency workers went door-to-door to evacuate the residents as soon as the failure of the dam became imminent. Power to the area had been cut off the minute the electric company had received word about the impending disaster, and other utilities had done what they could to turn off any lines providing services. We cautiously report that there are no known casualties at this time. Persons thought to be possibly trapped have been found at various shelters. Eyewitnesses at the breast of the dam report an incredible amount of time that went by when they were positive the dam would go, but it seemed to be held back by an unseen force until the very time the last person was evacuated from the area. Now . . . I have to tell you that I have not been a very religious man most of my life. But, today, I believe we have witnessed a miracle! We have received so many reports of emergency personnel helping the evacuation from units that were not known to be involved. Buses that were used to transport evacuees away from the area have disappeared. Someone suggested to me that we may have been visited by angels. Today," he paused, and then continued with emphasis, "*I believe it! I* urge everyone listening to this update to thank God for saving our city! From what the engineers have told me, it is nothing short of a miracle that the dam took so long to break, and that no one was hurt! We have quite a clean-up to do, but I think we all can pitch in and help one another. We've been given a second chance, and I, for one, am not going to let that slip by!"

Motioning to a young man standing inconspicuously at the side of the room, the mayor announced, "I have asked a local evangelist, Zech Douds, whose home may have been destroyed by the water, to come and say a prayer of thanks."

Zech made his way to the front, and faced the crowd.

"Thank you, mayor!" he began. "I am blessed to stand before you right now, after witnessing incredible miracles here today. My family is safe! I had received an urgent phone call from my niece to get out of our house right away, which we did. As we went to help our neighbor, a man with emergency insignia on his jacket came out of nowhere and directed us to a bus that had not been there moments before. He entered our neighbor's house and carried our elderly neighbor out, along with her pet cat. After placing her safely in a seat, he told the driver to leave for the shelter. We asked, in alarm, if we should wait for others, but he calmly said another bus had already arrived to take anyone else, and we should get to safety immediately!

"We turned and saw that another bus had indeed pulled up silently behind us! Our bus sped away with the typical noise buses have. We came to the shelter and got off, filing in with other evacuees. I was curious, however, and left the line to see where the bus went, and it was gone! Even though the shelter was on a straight road with no turn-offs, that bus was nowhere to be seen! It was then I recalled the insignia and name on the jackets of the emergency worker and bus driver, and on the side of the bus—I had been too rushed to think about it . . . it was small, so as to not grab attention: the insignia showed two wings raised at angles, and the name was Paradise Angels Emergency Service!"

Zech paused as a hushed murmur spread through the crowd and then said, "I don't know about you, but I'm pretty sure there's no local ambulance or fire company by that name! We had angels helping us!"

A few angels stood invisibly in the back of the room. One noticed something and nudged the angel next to him. They both looked over to the opposite corner and saw a demon squeezing a woman's shoulders.

The lady developed a cynical look, and then called out, "Why should we thank God when he allowed this disaster to happen in the first place?

A number in the room snorted their agreement, while others shook their heads in dismay.

Zech didn't blink an eye at the question and responded, "At this time, Satan is the ruler of the world, and he orchestrates disasters like these. In a very short time, though, God will defeat him and bring us a new heaven and new earth. But in the meantime, God uses His servants to help us and to show us how much He loves us!"

Raising his hands, Zech pronounced, "Let us pray!"

The angels moved quietly behind the demon and seeing it loosen its hold in response to Zech's call to prayer, they grabbed it and sent it flying! A couple of other demons that had been concealed within their prey emerged and joined the clash. More angels appeared. Some hurried to the people the demons had abandoned and hastened to bring healing. Others surrounded the demons and quickly subdued them.

Zech had sensed the battle within the room, and offered up more prayers of thanks, as well as entreating the Lord for His help. Finally feeling peace in his spirit, Zech finished the prayer and then made himself available for any who wished to learn more about the Lord and His gift of salvation.

The room was abuzz with excitement as reporters gave their assessments regarding what the mayor had said as well as what Zech had told them. Some had heard similar stories from the evacuees, thereby validating the miracles even more.

Not a soul left the room that night unchanged. What Satan meant for evil, God turned around for good.

This may have gone unnoticed by the dark realm if the newspaper the next day had not read: "MIRACLES TRUMP DISASTER!"

Satan wasn't happy.

CHAPTER 37

The change over the community was incredible! Hundreds came out to help with clean-up. Many homes were totally destroyed, including Zech's. Rental homes were made available at no charge to those who lost everything. Churches sponsored meals for the displaced, bringing the good news to many by their actions. Businesses donated needed items, and many stores offered free clothing to those who were left with only the clothes on their backs. Monetary aid poured in from around the country after the news went national.

Zech's testimony about the miracles caught the attention of many news shows. He was kept busy with interviews for a week and shared what had happened with such conviction that many people around the country accepted the salvation of Christ. He also was contacted by a large Christian group who wanted to sponsor his SIMBOC meetings and take them on the road!

The angels worked steadily throughout the community, harvesting many souls daily, using the power of prayers gathered from around the world.

Nearby, an enclave of demons grew increasingly large. The angel lookout delivered a hurried report to Gimel and then quickly returned to its secret post. Gimel meditated on the news, knowing his commander in chief was aware of the build-up. He quietly waited for orders. When they came, he called in the angel leaders and discussed the plan.

Twinkle-Eyes was the last to leave.

"You have concerns, Tsadde?" Gimel asked.

"I have become very attached to the JP Knights, Gimel. This plan puts them in great danger. I must somehow prepare them for the possibility of . . . um . . ."

"That they could be wounded in the flesh, perhaps mortally?" Gimel offered.

Tsadde nodded, "Yes."

Gimel agreed, "Hmm. You will be given the right words to say, my friend."

Tsadde nodded again. "Heth may be able to help," he added.

"Yes. He is a good choice," Gimel commented.

The JP Knights had volunteered, along with many youth groups, to help with the clean-up. They first went to Marissa's house, or at least where it used to be. They held hands and stood at the edge of the lot. The rushing water had torn the house loose from its foundation and had flung it down the street, breaking it into pieces. Now, all they could see was a mud-filled hole where they had previously met in the basement.

Taking time to pray, they thanked God that Marissa still had her family. She had learned during her homeless time that material things could not satisfy, so she encouraged the group with an optimistic prayer. Then, they fanned out and helped others.

On the third day after the disaster, they met together early in the morning. It was apparent that their spirits had all been urged to spend their time differently that day. They gathered in a small park near the border of the destroyed neighborhood. It had been left virtually unscathed with a swing and playground still intact. The angels appeared from nearby woods and stood around the JP Knights.

Joel looked at his friends. They were all strangely quiet.

"I guess we all know a bit of what's ahead," he stated. "We must prepare ourselves for battle. The skirmishes we have had before are dwarfed compared to what we face."

He nodded to Twinkle-Eyes to take over.

The angel moved alongside of Joel and placed a hand on his shoulder.

"Yes. The demon army that brought about this disaster," he said, as he swept his other arm around, "is nearly upon us. They are amassing in the hills and are bent on destroying this town in Satan's name. Their leader is very cunning and will only be fooled momentarily into thinking the Lord is unprepared. We must use that to our best ability. We are to leave from here and join the Lord's army, attacking in daylight, when demons are less comfortable."

The JP Knights listened closely to the instructions.

"Finally," Twinkle-Eyes added, "it is important for you to understand that there is a real possibility that any one of you could be mortally wounded in this encounter."

Garrett swallowed hard. His dream had shown him this, although the identity of the fallen was not clear.

He stood. "I'm in!" he declared. "Because, *'To be absent in the body and to be present with the Lord!'*"

Chris jumped up from a swing and exclaimed, "Like Job said, *'For I know that my Redeemer lives, and He shall stand at last on the earth; and after my skin is destroyed, this I know, that in my flesh I shall see God.'*"

"*'For to me, to live is Christ, and to die is gain'*" Emily stated as she walked over between Garrett and Chris, hooking her arms in theirs.

Abby and Chloe began singing a chorus about battling against Satan. They led the group, who had now gathered arm-in-arm.

Joel then completed the circle and began to pray. The angels surrounded the teens, placing hands on their shoulders as blessings and power channeled from the Lord God were given to them.

Another angel, one called Heth, came into the center and blessed each JP Knight, saying, "The Lord says, *'I am with you always,'* remember this!"

After the prayer, the JP Knights prepared themselves, mentally picturing their spiritual armor. Each spent a few moments rededicating themselves to the Lord's work and examining their spirits for sin or anything that might compromise them in battle.

The procession was quiet, each JP Knight focusing on what the Lamb had accomplished at Calvary, knowing that the power used to raise Him from the dead was available to them right now, through prayer. Each had fasted that morning, understanding that spiritual strength is not dependent on physical nourishment, but on time spent with the God of all power.

They walked through woods that were strangely quiet.

Jill noticed the sparkles immediately as the group came out of the woods and into a meadow. The sun shone brightly, illuminating every inch of the glade. The JP Knights all had the sense that they were in a hallowed spot.

The angel sentries who had let them past now became visible, as did the dome of spiritual protection that had been placed around the area. Suddenly, the teens saw the army.

Chariots that seemed to be ablaze with fire circled the encampment. The steeds pulling them were immense and noble. Archers checked their bows, while swordsmen wiped their swords until they gleamed. The meadow seemed magically enlarged to hold the vast numbers of angels that were present.

The JP Knights stood in awe, fear and wonder gripping their spirits.

The voice, although clear and distinct, was not loud, yet commanded everyone's attention.

"Greetings to those highly favored of the Lord—those fulfilling the prophecy of Joel—those of Adam's race who have chosen wisely to serve the Most High God!"

All the angels turned to face the JP Knights.

As one, the angelic host cried, "Greetings to you who are redeemed by the Lamb!"

Tingles seemed to run from their fingers to toes as the teens witnessed the immense gathering focused on them.

Joel had seen this in the vision, and he knew what he was to do. Stepping forward, he reached for his sword and placed it on the ground in front of him.

"We offer our lives to battle the enemy alongside you, the messengers and army of the Lord!" Joel exclaimed with boldness and respect.

The other JP Knights followed suit, laying their swords by Joel's.

An angel of great stature walked toward them.

"The Lamb That Was Slain has called you forth! He has commanded us to battle the enemy together, and we will proceed with His power!" the commander stated.

Joel's eyes met those of the commander. "We are ready, and will do as you command us," he said with authority.

The commander nodded, "Prepare to move out!"

The JP Knights retrieved their swords and checked their armor. Twinkle-Eyes gave them instructions and the army soon began to advance.

The angels split into two large groups with the chariots leading. The sentries flew into the air and continued to provide some limited shielding. Twinkle-Eyes looked ahead and motioned to a dirt road leading farther into the mountains.

"This is the route we are to take," he said.

The group of twelve JP Knights followed him, walking two or three abreast. Their angels flanked them with the new angel, Heth bringing up the rear.

Joel watched the army of angels disappear into the ridges around them, and suddenly, he understood the tactic that was being used.

Twinkle-Eyes slowed and moved alongside Joel.

"You understand now, Joel?" he asked.

Joel nodded slowly as he gulped. His heart raced, but his resolve grew. He then responded, "Yes."

Twinkle-Eyes stayed by his side for a while. They were now in a narrow valley up in the mountains above the city. He slowed and then turned to the small group.

"Our shield will now be removed. We face the enemy just beyond that turn in the road. Strengthen yourselves with words from the Lamb that His Spirit has given you. Prepare for battle!"

Each JP Knight momentarily focused on Scripture that was instantly brought to mind. Then they drew their swords and steadied their shields.

Cautiously, they advanced, moving off the road and into the brush at the sides of the path as they followed Twinkle-Eyes' lead. They carefully looked ahead.

The sight would have made any mortal's blood turn cold.

Before them, stretching as far as they could see, were demons. The valley had broadened out considerably past the curve in the road and now accommodated legions of the enemy army. An old mine entrance spewed steam and gas, evidence of a demonic lair. More demons poured out of the opening in the side of the hill, many carrying weapons. These were handed out to those lurking around nearby. It appeared that about half of the hordes were armed at the moment, with the number increasing by the minute.

Suddenly, a shriek was heard—the small band of angels and humans had been spotted!

"Prepare yourselves!" Twinkle-Eyes called softly, and then shouted, "*For the Lamb!*"

The JP Knights took up the cry as they ran forward, "*For the Lamb!*"

Those nearest the approaching force jumped to their feet. Unfortunately, they had received weapons already.

Twinkle-Eyes led the group with the other angels fanned out behind him. Before long, the clashes of swords could be heard.

It was only moments until Joel encountered a demon, and soon all of the JP Knights were fighting. The element of surprise had helped, since the demon commander had been far below, supervising the release of weapons and getting reports from his scouts. The demons on the surface were unprepared and although armed, were quickly routed. The JP Knights and angels regrouped as the beaten demons retreated back into the crowd of the enemy, who were scrambling to get into ranks for a counter charge.

Twinkle-Eyes shouted, "Stand firm in the Lord!"

But, as his voice trailed off, a terrible roar sounded from the lair!

A beastly demon nearly flew out of the opening and headed straight for the small band of angels and teens.

The JP Knights were paralyzed with fear!

Behind them, however, they heard the calm voice of Heth saying, "Be gone, oh demon of fear!"

Turning, they all saw a terrifying demon fizzle into steam, with Heth's sword piercing its chest.

Feeling relief immediately, the teens turned to face the rest of the demon army, which had materialized in ranks before them.

"*For the Lamb!*" Joel shouted, saluting the air with his sword.

"*For the Lamb!*" the others yelled in response, raising their swords as well.

The demon commander rushed at Twinkle-Eyes, his own eyes squinted with rage at the surprise attack which had suggested weakness on his part as commander. His fury at the insult made his assault powerful, but unbalanced.

Twinkle-Eyes easily side-stepped the careening monster, bringing his sword down with force on its back. Sparks flew as a hideous scream erupted from its mouth. Realizing its mistake, it turned quickly enough to cause the sword to scrape down its scales rather than pierce its flesh. Now, it parried opposite Twinkle-Eyes, assessing its prey.

Other demons ran at the angels and JP Knights, and the battle commenced.

Joel swung his sword as he had never done before, shielding himself from the blows of the demons. Not all of the demons had swords. Some had clubs, others had knives and daggers, while many had no weapon but just ran at the group to engage them in hand-to-hand combat.

Jill, at first, was distracted by the dark colors and hues that seemed to blur around her, but, focusing more, she was able to use her visual senses to her advantage. Quickly, she realized that a certain color preempted a particular type of attack, and she could prepare herself, meeting the move with precision.

Chris found that he excelled when he recited Scripture in his head, *"Be strong in the Lord and in the power of His might."*

Songs and choruses reminded Chloe and Abby of God's power and helped them to stay on top of the battle. It even seemed like their helmets had music coming through the ear coverings like an MP3 player!

Nathan and Brent had practiced swordsmanship at home the past few weeks, increasing their skills with excellence, and it showed! They were light on their feet and very technical, hitting the mark nearly every time.

Shane's natural energy worked great, but in the opposite way. His form was haphazard at best, but the force in his moves made up for his lack in technique.

Before him, Garrett saw his dream come to life. The demon attackers tried to upset him, but he was ready, reliving the part he had seen while asleep the night before.

The remaining three girls stuck together, forming a central circle from where they fought. Liz, Emily and Marissa protected each other while executing brave strikes.

The demon commander barked out orders while he looped around Twinkle-Eyes. Assessing the situation, the demon laughed at the angel, "You come at me with children and a few others. You think I'm dumb enough to fall for this? Your mistake! Captains, set your ranks opposite, facing the hills, and, you others, block their retreat!"

Continuing the derision, the commander exclaimed, "Tsadde, you are no match for me! Where is your commander? Hiding behind some little human children?" And then, shouting to the hills, he added, "Teth, reveal yourself, you coward!" Seeing no response, the demon commander sneered at Tsadde. "You will die now!"

The demon raced at Tsadde, this time controlling his steps and movement. He swung his great sword at Tsadde.

The angel met the attack with vigor, calling out, *"For the Lamb!"*

With renewed strength, the angels and JP Knights fought their assailants, but the demons had been energized by their commander's taunts and struck with even more power.

It happened so quickly. The JP Knights saw the fatal blow as if in slow-motion. One of their own went down with one stroke. At the same moment, the army of the Lord attacked from the ridges and from the far end. The battle raged, while Heth stayed with the fallen, moving the body away from the combat.

Tears stung as the others fought with tightened throats and deep resolve. Although the army of angels engaged a fierce conflict, it soon became evident that they were vastly outnumbered.

CHAPTER 38

Demons seemed to appear endlessly from the lair's entrance and join the fight. Wounded demons limped back inside the cave.

The combat continued for probably an hour. The demon commander circled Tsadde and engaged him viciously. The angels and JP Knights were tiring out, especially with the loss of one of their own weighing heavily on their hearts. It seemed that soon, they would have to try to escape or retreat.

Jill noticed the change in lighting first. The smoke that hung over the valley and battlefield appeared to dissipate. Then the sparkles came that preceded the hue she knew so well. Strength immediately came to her, and she shouted, "*For the Lamb!*"

The others were energized by her call, and responded alike, "*For the Lamb!*"

For just a moment, the demons paused, whether distracted by the rallying cry or as a premonition, it was not known.

The air cleared as if a light breeze had begun, blowing the smoke towards the other end of the valley. Simultaneously, a disturbance started back where the JP Knights had first entered the demon staging area.

A trumpet blew. The thundering of horses precluded their actual appearance.

Two chariots appeared with majestic angels reining the magnificent steeds pulling them. Gleaming swords arced through the air and claimed demons on either side.

The demon commander hissed as his hordes turned and ran from the formidable attack. He positioned himself to face the approaching chariot.

Teth and Gimel separated as they entered the valley, steering their chariots into crowds of demons. Teth spotted the demon commander instantly and headed straight towards his foe.

Demons continued to scream and run away. The distraction had allowed the angel armies to quickly regroup and focus on preventing escape of the enemy. One band had even blocked the entrance to the demon lair, tactfully keeping those inside from leaving and warding off any trying to retreat into the deep caves of the mine.

The lull in the battle also gave the JP Knights a brief rest, and they watched breathlessly as Teth advanced toward the demon commander.

Just before the two met, however, the mighty demon seemed to falter, and as Teth raised his sword for the blow, the demon's eyes went into a blank stare, and it keeled over with a hiss of released steam.

Surprised, Teth lowered his sword and pulled the chariot to a stop.

As the air cleared, a JP Knight stood next to the fallen demon commander, his sword buried up to its hilt in the flank of the monster.

The demons close by screamed with terror. Others, looking past the chariot, saw an endless sea of angels ready to enter the valley battlefield. The angel army readily took advantage of the diversion and quickly overcame the demons who had scattered after their leader's demise.

Jill watched with interest and commented to Emily who had come alongside her, "It's a trick. Those aren't more angels coming to help."

"What do you mean?" Emily asked.

Jill gazed intently at scene around her, finally resting her eyes on the angels blocking the far exit from the valley.

Shaking her head in amazement, she remarked, "Those aren't more angels—they are a reflection of the angels over there at the other end. The colors were all wrong! I guess the demons can't tell the difference!"

Returning attention to the destroyed demon commander, they ran over to their comrade who had delivered the fatal strike.

Garrett stood, dazed at the sight before him.

"Garrett!" Emily called, shaking him out of his reverie.

He shook his head, as if he had been caught napping during class.

"What happened? How did you do that? Are you alright?" Jill and Emily asked in torrents.

Nodding, Garrett replied, "Yeah, I'm OK. I don't know . . . I had dreamed about the battle and knew the demon commander would turn his back when the angel in the chariot entered. I had killed it in my dream at that point, so I knew exactly what I was to do here."

The girls clapped him on the back in congratulations. Then, as if a blocked memory had returned to each of them at once, they all turned toward their fallen friend and raced over, praying that the demon's strike had somehow missed.

Heth cradled the lifeless body as the JP Knights gathered solemnly around. One look told them that no one could have survived the piercing. The Knight must have raised the left arm, holding the shield, to fend off one attack, but was struck under the other arm from a different attacker, as the right arm prepared to strike. The sword had entered the chest on the right and gone through to the left.

The JP Knights' angels came around the teens, leaving the remainder of the demons to the angel armies. Tsadde, Teth and Gimel stood behind Heth, respectfully bowing their heads. The wings of all the angels seemed to sag in sadness at the loss. For the first time, Tsadde's eyes did not twinkle.

The hue around Heth and the fallen JP Knight was beautiful, yet sorrowful. Jill felt tears start to flow. Her angel enveloped her in a hug.

Humans and angels mourned together. The tears were gathered by the dove and delivered to the sovereign Lord.

EPILOGUE

The JP Knight stood in a beautiful place. The angel had stayed through the passage from death into life, giving comfort. The pain from the mortal wound was brief, and was already forgotten as the Knight was escorted to the throne room.

The dove arrived, delivering the tears and placing them in a golden bowl at the side of the throne.

Bowing before the creator, the JP Knight knelt in reverence.

"You have been faithful, My child! Your departure from the earth is only for a time, so that you may know that I have the power to deliver from death. Your witness is required for the good of those you serve with, that they may be strengthened in their spirits, until the time I will send My Son to get His bride, the church. In yet a little while, My Son will return. Encourage My People with these words! You have served Me well!"

The JP Knight rose and backed away. An angel attendant guided the teen from the presence of the Most High. Without speaking, the angel nudged the youth toward a small group gathered. Amazed, the Knight came face to face with the saints of old. Coming together, they hugged and talked.

Before long, however, the visit was over.

The Knight stood again before the Almighty God.

"Go now! Return to the battle against the enemy. Hold fast until the Lamb returns!"

Meanwhile, the JP Knights had slipped to the ground, weeping in unbelief that their friend was dead.

The noise of the demons being defeated had retreated away from their senses. All was silent and solemn.

Heth noticed it first.

"Gimel," Heth whispered. Locking eyes with the other angel, Heth then looked away, moving his head up toward the sky.

Gimel followed his gaze and then quietly moved away from the group.

The dove alighted on his shoulder for a moment and then flew away. Gimel pondered the message. He smiled. *It was so like the Almighty to surprise His people with blessings!*

Stepping back into the small gathering, Gimel whispered something to Tsadde, who then looked up with a curious glance. Gimel caught his eye and nodded.

With a twinkle in his eyes again, Tsadde spoke softly, "Marissa?"

Marissa raised her head. Her angel peered insightfully at Tsadde and then helped Marissa up. "Your gift is needed," she whispered.

Cocking her head to one side, Marissa furrowed her eyebrows with a questioning look.

The angel merely nodded.

Moving over to the lifeless JP Knight, Marissa gently opened the breastplate. The tunic beneath was wet with blood. She placed her hands on the chest and closed her eyes in prayer.

The others had gradually become aware of Marissa's actions. Quietly, they sat up. Jill saw the glow begin in Marissa's hands.

"Pray!" she whispered to the teens on either side. The message was passed to all of them.

Although Marissa's eyes were closed, the eyes of the other JP Knights were glued to the dead body of their friend. They prayed, thanking the Lord for victory. They prayed, entreating the Lord to do His will, now hoping for a miracle.

Slowly, the glow in Marissa's fingers seemed to jump like sparks onto the bloodied tunic. The prayers of the friends intensified. They held out their hands as if reaching toward Marissa, and arcs of energy flowed from them to Marissa. The glow burned like a fire, scattering embers all over the body. The light became so bright that they all had to close their eyes, and in that instant, the light was gone!

Marissa opened her eyes, sensing that her part was over.

The tunic appeared restored. The body beneath it was warm, and she felt a heart beating again!

Jumping back, she nearly fell, and was caught by her angel. The others had stood, and they all reflexively grabbed each other's hands.

Before them, the JP Knight's eyes opened, and the teen took a deep breath.

"Welcome back, my friend!" Twinkle-Eyes greeted.

And the harvesting continues . . .

Across the Atlantic Ocean, a young woman was being prepared.

Wonderful Are Your Works

Beth Lambert

Wonderful are Your works and my soul knows it very well.

Wonderful are Your works and my soul knows it very well. Your

eyes have seen my unformed substance and in Your book they were all written. The

days that were ordained for me when as yet, there was not one of them

Wonderful are Your works and my soul knows it very well.

Wonderful are Your works and my soul knows it very well. My

frame was not hidden from you when I was made in secret. And

skillfully wrought in the depths of the earth.

Wonderful are Your works and my soul knows it very well.

Wonderful are Your works and my soul knows it very well. For

You did form my inward parts and did weave me in my mother's womb.

I will give thanks to You for I am fearfully and wonderfully made.

Wonderful are Your works   and my   soul knows it very well

Wonderful are Your works   and my   soul knows it very well

Contact Information

To order additional copies of this book, please visit
www.redemption-press.com.
Also available on Amazon.com and BarnesandNoble.com
Or by calling toll free 1-844-2REDEEM.

CPSIA information can be obtained at www.ICGtesting.com
Printed in the USA
BVOW02s1751300116

434823BV00002B/3/P